LIGHT FROM HEAVEN DAILY DEVOTIONAL

INCLUDING

TEACHING & LEARNING CHRIST'S CHARACTER

GRACE DOLA BALOGUN

Grace Dola Balogun

Grace Religious Books Publishing & Distributors, Inc. New York

Presented To:

____

From:

- -

On The Occasion:

____

Contact Author at:

www.Gracereligiousbookspublishers.com

1-203-891-7122

Grace Religious Books Publishing & Distributors books may be ordered through booksellers or by contacting the publisher:

Grace Religious Books Publishing & Distributors, Inc. New York 248 Lombard Street 2nd New Haven, CT 06513

Also available in
Soft Cover ISBN: 978-1-939415-72-1
Hard Cover ISBN: 978-1-939415-73-8

Library of Congress Control Number: 2015910716

Editing, Interior Book Design & Layout:

CBM Christian Book Editing

www.christian-book-editing.com

Cover Design by: The Unique Book Cover

www.uniquebookcover.com

United States of America
Grace Religious Books Publishing & Distributor, Inc. New York

*"Just as Moses lifted up the snake in the desert,
so the Son of Man Must be lifted up that everyone
who believes in him may have Eternal life."*

(John 3:4-5) NIV

*"Yet a time is coming and has now come when the true
worshipers will worship the Father in spirit and truth, for
they are the kind of worshipers the Father seeks."*

(John 4:23-24) NIV

DEDICATION

I DEDICATE this Book – *Light from Heaven Daily Devotional*, which is fully the Word of God to the One and Only, the true Son of God, Jesus Christ, our Lord and Savior. He wants all people on this earth to seek him, and find him, and give their life to him, faithfully and truthfully.

Jesus Christ is the Word that became flesh and dwelt among us. Christ is the Word of God, and he is the wisdom of God. He is the power of God, and he is the light of God from heaven that came down to earth. In him all things consist, those things in heaven, and those things on earth. He is the light that shines from heaven into our hearts and minds, and no darkness can comprehend it.

The Scripture revealed: "For from him and through him and to him are all things. To him is the glory forever! Amen," (Romans 11:36).

The power of God profoundly expresses the awesome power of God. God's wisdom and the judgment of God are unattainable in the redemptive history. The depth of the knowledge of God is also incomprehensible – we just have to say in a loud voice: "To him is the glory forever! Amen."

CONTENTS

ALL DENOMINATIONAL APOSTLE CREED FOR ALL PEOPLE

"I believe in God the Father the Almighty, the maker of heaven and the earth, of all that is seen and unseen. I believe in our Lord Jesus Christ, the true Son of God, the one and only eternally begotten not created of the Father, the God from God, the light from light the true light that shines forever and no darkness can comprehend it. The true God the very God, one with the Father, Through the Son all things were created of things in heaven and things on earth. He came down from heaven for our salvation by the power of the Holy Spirit, he became incarnate from the virgin Mary and was conceived by the Holy Spirit, born of Virgin Mary, and was made man. He suffered from Pontius Pilate; he was crucified, he suffered death and was buried. The third day, he rose from the dead according to the power of God the Father, who called him out of the grave. He ascended into heaven and seated at the right hand of God the Father. He is coming back in glory to judge the dead and the living and all the eyes shall see him; his kingdom on earth will have no end. I believe in the Holy Spirit, the giver of life, who proceeds from the Father and the Son; the Holy Trinity with the Father and the Son he is worshiped and glorified. The Holy Spirit has spoken from the beginning of creation through the prophets and Moses. I believe in the communion of Saints, I acknowledge one baptism for the remission of sins, the resurrection of the body and life everlasting. Amen, Amen, Amen."

The Apostolic Creed is very essential for the worshiping Saints of the Lord to read weekly, especially during the Sunday worship, as well as every time that the mind wonders in sadness, sorrow, affliction, rejection, and oppression and in all the earthly troubles. It is a great source of strength, and a support through the affirmation of truthful words, and is a source of reflection that will help believing Christians to be able to stand firmly on the Rock of Jesus Christ, our Savior. This Apostolic Creed has been handed down from the early Christian era, but many churches think that it is no longer necessary to read anymore.

SEVEN WORDS OF JESUS CHRIST ON THE CROSS

For
Reflection During The Holy Week & Holy Thursday

First Word:

"Jesus said, Father Forgive them,
for they do not know what they are doing"
(Luke 23:34) NIV

Second Word:

Jesus said, "I tell you the truth, today
you will be with me in paradise"
(Luke 23:43) NIV

Third Word:

Jesus said, "Dear woman, here is your son,'
and to the disciple, John, 'Here is your mother.' "
(John 19:26-27) NIV

Fourth Word:

Jesus Cried out in a loud voice;
"Eloi, Eloi, lama sabachthani?
Which means: "My God, my God,
why have you forsaken me?"

(Mark 15:34)

Fifth Word:
Jesus said, "I am thirsty."
(John 19:28) NIV

Sixth Word:

Jesus said, "It is finished."
(John 19:30) NIV

Seventh Word:

Jesus called out with a loud voice;
"Father, into your hands I commit my spirit."
(Luke 23: 46) NIV

ALL DENOMINATIONAL CONFESSION OF SIN

ALMIGHTY GOD, FATHER OF OUR LORD JESUS CHRIST, HOLY SPIRIT ever one God. Merciful God, Maker of all things, and the judge of all people: We acknowledge and expressed great regret of our manifold sins and wickedness, which we from time-to-time most grievously have committed, by thought, word and deed, by what we have done, and by what we have left undone. We have not love for you as we should; we have no love for our neighbor as we love ourselves; we do all these against your divine Majesty, provoking most justly your wrath and indignation against us. We do earnestly repent, and are heartily sorry for all our misdoing; the remembrance of them is grievous unto us, the burden of them is intolerable. Have mercy upon us, have mercy upon us, most Merciful, most Holy Father, for the sake of your Son Our Lord Jesus Christ; in your mercy forgive all what we have done wrong, and help us to straighten out our lives, correct us, protect us through the daily reading of your Word; amend, and direct , and control our thought, hearts and mind. Forgive us all that is in the past, and grant that we may ever hereafter serve you and please you in newness of life, to the honor and glory of your Holy Name through Jesus Christ our Lord and Savior, Who reigns and is to come again. Help us to delight in your will, to walk in Your ways everyday of our life to the glory of your mighty Holy Name. Amen.

THE LORD'S PRAYER

This, then, is how you should pray:

"Our Father in heaven, hallowed be your Name,

your kingdom come, your will be done on

earth as it is in heaven Give us today our daily

bread. Forgive us our debts, as we also have

forgiven our debtors. And lead us not into

temptation, but deliver us from the evil one.

For thine is the kingdom, and the power, and

the glory for ever and ever,". Amen.

(Matthew 6: 9-13) NIV

17

PREFACE

Light From Heaven Daily Devotional (alongside the Prayer written after each devotional), compliment this dynamic devotional. Designed as a yearly devotion, this daily devotional is different from all other daily devotionals because it will feed the reader with the Word of God each and every day. This devotional analyzes the daily Word of God and comes with a simple explanation of the Scriptures that teach the reader in depth what the verse of the day really means, the value, as well as the effect of the daily Word of that day to the reader. *Light From Heaven Daily Devotional* will expand the reader's heart and mind, so that they can fully understand the Scripture. It intends to open up the Scripture to believers and non-believers in a way that the reader will see clearly what that particular Scripture means to them.

Light From Heaven Daily Devotional will help the reader to pray, not just read the daily word. It opens up the reader's heart and mind (believer or non-believer) to build and maintain an intimate relationship with God. It helps them to seek the presence of God every day as they wake up in the morning, or when they are going to sleep at night. They will see that prayer is one of the important keys to opening the gate of heaven and to live a godly life. This daily devotional and inclusive Prayer opens the path for prayer immediately after reading the daily Word of God. By the Power of the Holy Spirit, the reader's spirit will be energized throughout the day and every day because they have a complete spiritual food each day as they read the *Light From Heaven Daily Devotional.*

This daily devotional for each day of the year will open up the Scripture for all the people of all ages as it has never been before. Moreover, it gives the solid meat of the Word of God to the reader without measure with the manifestation of the Holy Spirit. *Light From Heaven Daily Devotional* with the prayer will be a comfort to the reader. It will be an encouragement to the reader and a protection throughout the day. This powerful daily devotional will be a problem solver for the reader in the office and at home within the family. It is a well-structured, well prepared, and a well-organized devotional created to help you handle all that is happening in our world today. It will strengthen the individual reader so that they can be able to cope with all the earthly problems, afflictions, trials, and disappointments. Readers will even convert unbelievers and people of all other religions to Christ.

Readers of *Light From Heaven Daily Devotional* while reading every morning, or at night before sleep, will be in a good emotional state throughout the day with the mercy, love, and truth of Jesus Christ. It will help readers to know God more and more, and to go to him with every earthly circumstance they might be going through, or about to go through. Most importantly it will let readers to know that Jesus Christ is able to meet all their needs at the right time and at the correct time if they seek him every day with his Word in prayer.

Reading the *Light From Heaven Daily Devotional* every day will also bring light of Jesus Christ that will shine in the reader's heart and mind every day. The light of Jesus will flourish, spread like a wildfire, and flow into all the areas of the reader's lives. Readers will come to the realization of how merciful, how gracious, and how powerful the Lord is, and they will continue to live in his Word and pray to him. They will experience the power of the three God Head

Father, Son, and the Holy Spirit – the Holy Trinity ever one God. Jesus Christ will be the reader's daily immortal food and by eating and living in his Word, the reader will follow his commandment from this earth to heaven.

JANUARY

JANUARY 1ST

THE WORD OF GOD CLEANSES US –
LET HIS WORD CLEANSE YOU TODAY

Today's Scripture Reading:

"In the beginning God created the heavens and the earth.
Now the earth was formless and empty,
Darkness was over the surface of the deep, and
the Spirit of God was hovering over the waters."
(Genesis 1:1-2) NIV

This shows the process that God Almighty used in creation and the activities of the Holy Spirit in creation. Even today God the Father, Son, and God the Holy Spirit renew the face of the earth every year, every month, every day, every minute and every second. This also emphasizes how loving our God is and how he always cares for his children. The earth would have been perishing if there were no activities of the three Godheads. The sovereignty of God, the Lord of all by his incontestable right, renewed, purified this universe with his fresh air from heaven pouring to the earth every minute when he opened the gates of heaven. Also his glorious light which he has shined upon us from heaven. We, his people, must rejoice in his providence. We must be happy that he is our God and with whose help and hope, we stand in his Holy Name. The God we serve is worthy of all our praises and thankfulness.

Let Us Pray:

God the Father Almighty you are the maker of heaven and earth sea and everything that dwells in it. We give you glory Jesus Christ the Son of God, full of truth and righteousness; we give you praise our Lord and Savior you are worthy to be praised. Lord Jesus Christ you are the way the truth and the life, the Alpha and Omega, the beginning and the end, the first and the last, you're the great shepherd of the sheep, the chief shepherd and the good shepherd, all life dwells in you. We pray for your mercy and protection every day of life: keep us safe from violence, hatred, wars and rumors of wars, and bless us with your unending protection every day of our lives from all the violence and persecutions that is going on in all the nations of earth. Have great mercy upon us, let this new year be a year of restoration to good health; let it be a year of prosperity and great wealth. In your great mercy make this year a of great wisdom, knowledge and understanding to all the people and students across the nations of the world. Make this a year of peace and tranquility and a year of immeasurable, blessings, abundant blessings. Let this be a year that you provide children to the barren women all over the world, a year that your mercies will be flowing upon us from heaven, a year that souls of all mankind will be rushing unto you in order to have a new life in you and live with you forever in heaven. Lord Jesus Christ make this year a year of joy, happiness, love, and most importantly make it a year of peace on all the earth. In your great mighty Holy Name, we pray, amen.

JANUARY 2ND

THE WORD OF GOD CLEANSES US –
LET HIS WORD CLEANSE YOU TODAY

Today's Scripture Reading:

"O give thanks to the Lord, for he is good,
for his steadfast love endure forever."
(Psalm 136:1) NIV

All the believing Christians must learn how to praise the Lord for his everlasting love for his children. Moreover, let us meditate on what might have been in Christ's mind when he sang it for the last time. Christians are called again and again to make their primary duty to gives thanks to God the Father Almighty, God the Son, and God the Holy Spirit, as well as to offer the sacrifice of praise continually, so that the fruits of our lips, are giving thanks to his Holy Name. The one and only Savior of the Universe, the God who angels adore, from whom all the heaven and earth adored. The Lords of lords, the King of kings, the Sovereign of all sovereigns, let us give thanks to God, our maker, for his goodness and mercy, which is now bestowed upon us on the earth, which shall endure forever. We must give thanks to the Lord, not only because he does good for us, but because he is good. People may ask this question: How many times is God good? The answer is : God is good all the time.

Prayer:

Lord God Almighty, Father, Son, and Holy Spirit, one God forever: We pray for all the people that have a New Year resolution for the Lord Jesus Christ, the one and only who listens to prayers and answers prayers, to help them to fulfill the promise that they promised themselves - some of them they may have prayed that they may be able to throw out some type of bad behavior, a bad habit, or bad words out of their mouths. Some people want to lose weight in order that they may maintain good health, to be able to care for their children. Keep them safe and bless them with strength, courage, determination, endurance, and self-control so that they may be able to meet their New Year Resolutions. God of Mercy and Love, have mercy on all those who believe in you, straighten out their lives, and help them to live on this earth with peace and joy in the Holy Spirit. Be their provider and continuously provide for those who are in need. Help the college students to study with your power and mercy, bless them with your great wisdom, knowledge and understanding of all their subjects. Protect them, guide them, and keep them safe all the time; provide for their parents, so that they may be able to meet all their needs. Lord Jesus Christ let the peace of God that surpasses all understanding rule the hearts, minds, and spirits of all those who call unto you faithfully and sincerely from their hearts. In your Mighty Holy Name, a Name above all names, we pray, amen and amen.

JANUARY 3RD

THE WORD OF GOD CLEANSES US –
LET THE WORD OF GOD CLEANSE YOU TODAY

Today's Scripture reading:

"For this reason a man will leave his father and mother and be united to her Husband, and they will become one flesh."
(Genesis 2:24) NIV

God Almighty, the Creator of heaven and earth, Father of all mercies, sustainer of all things; from the beginning of creation you ordained marriage and the family unit as the first and most important institution on the earth. God's plan for marriage consists of one male and one female who become one flesh; they are to be united physically and spiritually. God Almighty created both men and women in your own image, so that they can work together for your great good and for your great glory. God, you created women to be a helper, supporter, and comforter. From the very beginning of history of the human race has been bound to God through belief in and obedience to His Word as absolute truth. Life through faith and obedience is presented as the governing principle in Adam's relationship to God of Eden. Man and woman were charged with being fruitful and ruling over the earth, and animal kingdom. They were created to form family relationships; this stated purpose of God in creation indicates that he considers a godly family and the raising of children of utmost priority in the world. God's plan and standard for marriage is one man and one woman, joined together for life, and dissolved only by death. Our Lord Jesus Christ gave an exception, namely, only marital unfaithfulness, which includes adultery or any kind of sexual immorality; therefore, when any of this happens divorce is to be permitted when sexual immorality is involved. Our Lord Jesus Christ stated clearly that: Anyone who divorces for other than Scriptural reasons, and then remarries, sins against God by committing adultery. In other words, a divorce is not necessarily recognized a right, or legitimate by God merely because the state, or any human institution legalizes it.

Prayer:

May our Lord and Savior have mercy upon you. May he deliver you from pride against each other. May Christ Jesus shed his light on all the blindness of your heart, vainglory, hypocrisy, envy, jealousy, hatred, and malice. May our Lord and Savior shed his great light unto the darkest part of your heart, deliver us from any work of the enemy; may his glory and mercies be upon us and make us his own forever. Lord God Almighty Father, Son, and Holy Spirit, you are the one that blessed the first marriage in the Garden of Eden. Christ Jesus help us to continue to be present at every true Holy Matrimony between the people of this world; if you know that it is good for them to be together, and it is according to your Will, let your Will be done in their lives, and let your purpose be achieved in their lives. Let your full presence be known in their lives. In your Holy Name, we pray. Amen.

JANUARY 4ᵀᴴ

THE WORD OF GOD CLEANSES US –
LET THE WORD OF GOD CLEANSE YOU TODAY

Today's Scripture Reading:

"So the man gave names to all the live-stock,
the birds of the air and all the beasts of the field. But for Adam no
suitable helper was found."
(Genesis 2:20) NIV

Good women on this earth, the Lord created them as a helper, a companion for men, so that she will always be there on her husband's side in good communication. The woman was created to be a loving companion for a man and to be a helper for him. The wife was to share her husband's responsibility and to cooperate with him in fulfilling God's purpose for her husband's life and the life of their children and the entire family. God gave the wife an appointed task of helping the husband and submitting to him, her most important duty is to love her husband, respect him, and assist him in whatever he is doing. Most importantly a wife must develop a gentle and quiet spirit, as well as be a loving mother to her children. God acknowledges a wife's submission to her husband as an actual part of her obedience to Christ Jesus, as the

Lord and Savior, and as the husband of the Church, marriage of the Lamb from the Calvary tree.

Prayer

God the Father Almighty, Father of our Lord Jesus Christ, Holy Spirit, forever one God, let your blessings be upon all the married couples. Help them to live in Holy matrimony, be the governor of their home, make their home a happy home. Baptize them with the power of the Holy Spirit, put your Word in their spirit, soul, and body. Let them worship you in Spirit and in truth. Bless their children, and their entire family, now and forever. In your Holy Name, we pray. Amen.

JANUARY 5TH

THE WORD OF GOD CLEANSES US –
LET THE WORD OF GOD CLEANSE YOU TODAY

Today's Scripture reading:

"So the Lord God caused the man to fall into a deep sleep; and while he was sleeping, he took one of the man's ribs and closed up the place with flesh. Then the Lord God made a woman from the rib he had taken out of the man, and he brought her to the man."
(Genesis 2:21-22) NIV

The Lord God is another name for God. It is the general name for God, which emphasizes his greatness and power. It is a name by which God reveals himself to his own people. It is inherent in the revelation of God's covenant name displaying his loving kindness in his redemptive concern for the human race, and his nearness, to include his faithful presence with his own people. This personal name is used in situations where he is seen in direct relationship to his people, or to nature. Where the words "Lord God" are coupled together, they point to God as the all-powerful Creator who has entered into a caring covenant relationship with humankind. Therefore, man and woman were created in God's image. The woman was created by God to be someone who will be reminding a man of the love of God at all times by showing him kindness, and the man will be seeing the kindness of God in the woman. Moreover, she was to share and try to solve problems which the man was not patient enough to solve. She was to share his responsibility and she must be cooperative with him in order to fulfill God's Will, desires, and purposes for his and her life and the life of the Universe. God Almighty ordained marriage, and most importantly, the institution of marriages on earth.

Prayer:

Lord Jesus Christ, you were present at the wedding in Canaan during your earthly ministry. Help us to continue to join people of this earth together in Holy Matrimony in order that their life will be what you want it to be, a life of peace, joy, and love, a marriage that no one can put asunder, or break by any form of evil. Lord Jesus Christ let them use their life in the honor of your Holy Name. Help and direct them to help the poor and the needy among them, according to your commandment with faithfulness to you and to themselves bless and guide them to your everlasting arm with joy throughout their life. In your great mighty Holy Name, we pray. Amen.

JANUARY 6TH

THE WORD OF GOD CLEANSES US –
LET THE WORD OF GOD CLEANSE YOU TODAY

Today's Scripture reading:

"The man said, 'This is now bone of my bones and flesh of my flesh; she shall be called woman, for she was taken out of man."
(Genesis 2:23) NIV

God's plan for marriage consists of one male and one female who become one flesh, which means both of them were united physically and spiritually. The wife is a given to her husband, her task is to help her husband and submit to her husband; her primary duty to her husband is to love, respect, bring assistance, purity and the most important that was required of her is the development of a gentle and quiet spirit, as well as see herself as a mother of the house - a loving mother to her children and to her husband. She must be a good mother, making sure that she is capable of her role. God the Father, the Creator sees a wife's submission to her husband as an actual part of her obedience to Christ Jesus as her Lord and Savior.

Prayer:

Lord Jesus Christ we come here today in your presence. Hold us together our Holy God, we praise you. Let the heavens be glad and joyful and the earth rejoice. We bless you for creating this world, for your promises to your people in this world and for Jesus Christ in whom your fullness dwells. Lift up our hearts; let us be joyful that you created us for your glory with your Holy hands. Help us to live a life that is pleasing and justifying in your sight, help us to live a life of submission, respect for each other, for our friends, our partners, our husbands, our wives, and all other people around us. God our Father, you are the source of all light. Today you have revealed to the world your light which enlightens all nations. Fill our hearts with the light of faith, that we who bear the candles may walk in the path of your goodness, and come to the light that shines forever through your Son Jesus Christ, our Lord. Help us to live a life that will bring great glory to your Holy Name. Be with us always and forever. In Jesus' great Holy Name, we pray. Amen.

JANUARY 7TH

THE WORD OF GOD CLEANSES US –
LET THE WORD OF GOD CLEANSE YOU TODAY

Today's Scripture Reading:

"Then God said, 'Let us make a man in our image, in our likeness, and let them rule over the fish of the sea and the birds of the air, over the livestock, over all the earth, and over all the creatures that move along the ground:' " (Genesis 1:26)NIV

All human life is derived from the beginning from Adam and Eve. Adam called and named his wife Eve which means "living because she was the first mother of all the humanity of all generations in the Universe. God has established the family as the basic unit in the society. Therefore, in every family there must be a leader of the family. God has assigned to the husband the responsibility of being the head of the household and his entire family. Husband headship must be exercised in love, with gentleness and consideration of his wife and his family children, grandchildren, and great grandchildren.

Prayer:

God the Father Almighty, compassionate gracious God, Jesus Christ his only Son Holy Spirit ever one God, let the people of this earth know that you are the Creator; you created us in your likeness. Help us to love you as you love us, and sent your Son to redeem us from our sins, so that we may be able to get close to you, and be able to maintain intimate communion with you from this earth to heaven. Help us to love you with all our hearts and love our neighbor as we love ourselves. Lord Jesus, our Lord and our Savior, look down from heaven and bless those men and women, who call unto you sincerely from the bottom of their heart, strengthen their hearts with your power and with the power of the indwelling of the Holy Spirit. Help them to live a life that will bring great honor to your Holy Name, and that will also bring honor to their family. Teach them to know your word and to use your word in everything they might be going through now and forever. In your great Holy Name , we pray. Amen.

JANUARY 8ᵀᴴ

THE WORD OF GOD CLEANSE US –
LET THE WORD OF GOD CLEANSE YOU TODAY

Today's Scripture Reading:

"The man and his wife were both naked, and they felt no shame."
(Genesis 2:25) NIV

God Almighty created Adam and Eve in His own image so that He could have a loving personal relationship with them for all of Eternity. God designed human beings as triumphant beings, which means: that the body, soul, and spirit that they possess in mind, emotion, and will respond to God freely with the worship of him and service to him as their Lord and Savior. He designed them to serve him with the heart of faith, loyalty, and with gratefulness. Adam and Eve were not ashamed because they both loved the Lord. In the same way, today we are never ashamed of what we are going through because we know that our Lord is with us, always and forever. Jesus Christ is in control and he has got the whole world in His hands.

Prayer:

Lord Jesus Christ, compassionate gracious loving God, fill us with Your full presence on this earth everywhere we may be, guide us and lead us in everything we do. Do not let us be ashamed, no matter how we look, or in whatever work we do. Help us to live forever for your glory. Lord Jesus Christ, you are the one and only the Son of the living God. We pray to you now and in the hour of our death have mercy and grace, give pardon and rest to the dead and strength to the living. Give to your Holy Church peace and concord, and to the sinners everlasting life and glory. You are with the Father and the Holy Spirit. You live and reign forever. Our Lord and Savior, who has taught us that all our doings without love are nothing. In your mercy send us your Holy Spirit, empower us, and pour into our hearts love for you and for the people in the whole world. Grant us the light of your Son Jesus Christ to shine upon us and may His glory fill the sky. Hear our prayers O' Lord and let our cry come unto you always. Preserve us for your eternal glory. Solve all our problems; fulfill all our needs with the glory and with the honor of Your Holy Name, we pray. Amen.

JANUARY 9TH

THE WORD OF GOD CLEANSES US –
LET THE WORD OF GOD CLEANS YOU TODAY

Today's Scripture Reading:

"Then the servant told Isaac all he had done. Isaac brought her into the tent of his mother Sarah, and he married Rebecca. So she became his wife, and he loved her, and Isaac was comforted after his mother's death." (Genesis 24:66-67) NIV

A man and a woman were charged to be fruitful over all God's creations. They were also therefore created to form family relationships. This makes clear and started the purpose of God in our lives. He considers a godly family and especially in the raising of children which is the utmost priority in the Universe. God expected men and women to consecrate all things in the Universe to him and to manage it in a God-glorifying way that will fulfill his divine purpose. The wife is also a comforter to her husband, especially after the death of the husband's mother.

Prayer:

God Almighty, gracious loving God, show all those who believe in your ways O' Merciful and mighty God, teach them your ways with the power of your Holy Spirit. Lead those who put their trust in you into truth; your Word is true, teach them the truth of your Word. You are the God of our salvation; in you we trust throughout our lives. Lord Jesus Christ you are the eternal Word of God; you are the comforter through the power of the Holy Spirit, the giver of life, who through the Father and the Son, he is being glorified and worship, grant us comfort after the death of our loved ones. When that happens help us to feel your full presence in our hearts, bless all the newlyweds, and provide children for them. Let them trust and hold each other in everything they do, and be at the center of their hearts, now and forever in Jesus Christ's mighty and Holy Name, we pray. Amen.

JANUARY 10TH

THE WORD OF GOD CLEANSES US –
LET THE WORD OF GOD CLEANSE YOU TODAY.

Today's Scripture Reading:

"You shall not covet your neighbor's house. You shall not covet your neighbor's wife, or his manservant or maidservant, his ox or donkey, or anything that belongs to your neighbor."
(Exodus 20:17) NIV

The Lord God commands us to live in peace with our neighbors. God's commandment goes beyond the external sin of word or deed, to condemn evil motives and desires. Coveting means we must not get involved, or love our neighbor's properties to the point of a desire or lust for it. It is wrong, Christians must not lust after anything that belongs to another person. We must not jealous, or envy about other people's goods, including their wife or their husband. The Lord God said it is wrong and evil. This is the beginning and the depth of human sinfulness in the entire world. Our Lord said: This Law, as well as the others, exposes the depravity of men and women which calls for them to seek grace and moral power with contentment from God. Greed signified the thirst for having more, and more, while covetousness does not refer to providing for one's own needs and those of one's family while we work for our needs, however, we just are rich toward God by seeking first his kingdom and his righteousness. Believers should harken to the Lord Jesus Christ's warning and examine whether selfishness and greed exist in our own hearts.

Prayer:

Lord Jesus Christ, bless all the people of this Universe with the Spirit of contentment in order that they will be pleased with everything you have given them. Let them focus on your unfailing love. Lord God Almighty Father, Son and Holy Spirit keep us saved in mind, spirit, soul, so that we do not have desire, or lust for what does not belongs to us. This could only be done through the power of the indwelling of the Holy Spirit and Daily Reading of the Word of God. The Word of God empowers and strengthens us from all unrighteousness and all sins. Merciful God, who has made all men, you have never hated what you have made, and you did not desire the death of a sinner, but that he or she should be converted and live. Have mercy upon all who do not know you as you revealed in the Gospel of your Son. Take from them all ignorance, hardness of heart and mind, and contempt of your Word, and let them know you are our Lord and Savior. God Almighty call the sinners and lost to you, so that they may be made one flock under one Shepherd, Jesus Christ our Lord, who lives and reigns with you and the Holy Spirit one God, world without end. Amen.

JANUARY 11ᵀᴴ

THE WORD OF GOD CLEANSES US –
LET THE WORD OF GOD CLEANSE YOU TODAY

Today's Scripture Reading:

"Do not seek revenge or bear a grudge against one of your people, but love your neighbor as yourself. I am the Lord.
(Leviticus 19:18) NIV

The neighbor does not mean people that live close to us, or people that live with us in the same building, "neighbor" refers to all the people that we come across, that we contact with, or a business partner. This commandment of God was to correct and regulate the way we treat each other. Christian believers must derive a pleasant way to show our love and care to all the people around us.

Prayer:

Lord God Almighty you are the eternal God, our heavenly Father, you have graciously accepted us as a living member of your Son our Lord and Savior Jesus Christ continues to bless all those who believed in you with your mercy and with your unending love throughout our days on this universe. Help us to love our neighbor as we loved ourselves. Guide us in all the areas of our lives and make us to be useful for you O'Lord, and at the end help us to gain eternal life which you alone offer. Grant husband and wife with strength and courage to love and serve you with gladness and singleness of heart through Jesus Christ our Lord and Savior God the Father, the Creator of heaven and earth who wants us to care, love, and help our neighbors. Lord Jesus, you are the one whose mercy is unfailing and whose compassion was even greater than the contrition of the penitent thief, forgive us miserable sinners, you are our Lord though we are guiltless of such sins; Look have mercy upon us, O' Lord God our redeemer King, and grant us your grace that when this our life on earth ended we may live with you forever in heaven. You are the Savior of this universe, who through the cross and your precious blood you redeemed us from our past, present, future sins; continue to save all those who will call unto you from their heart and give their life to you. Lord Jesus Christ blessed are those people that you wash clean from any unrighteousness and you forgive them their sins; you alone can save us, and you alone saved us. You are worthy of our praises and thankfulness. In your Holy Name , we pray. Amen

JANUARY 12TH

THE WORD OF GOD CLEANSES US – LET THE WORD OF GOD CLEANSE YOU TODAY

Today's Scripture Reading:

"Let the morning bring me word of your unfailing love, for I have put my trust in you. Show me the way I should go, for to you I lift up my soul." (Psalm 143:8) NIV

We must pray to God in the morning and at night, we must always trust the Lord for who he is, also at all-time ask him for guidance, control, direction of our lives. The psalmist praise God for his unfailing love and his hope that God will revive him again and deliver him out of his great trial, and from all overwhelming adversity and testing so that he did not reach the end of his endurance. Husband and wife must hold each other tight during the time of trials and tribulations they might be going through. They must remember that they are one in Spirit and make God an immovable rock, stronghold, shield, and deliverer from their enemies.

Prayer:

Lord Jesus Christ our Lord and Savior blessed all the couple that were going through problems in their marriage be their rock of salvation, solve all their problems, fulfill all their need, help them to pray together, call onto you in everything, they might be going through now and forever. Almighty God, who has drawn man and woman together in the bonds of natural affection, grant them wisdom, self-mastery, and pure devotion in the ordering of their common lives, that each may be to the other a strength in need, a counselor in perplexity, a comfort in sorrow, and a companion in every joy. And so knit their will together in your will, and their spirit in your Spirit, that they may enter together your kingdom, in which love is the fulfilling of the Law; through Jesus Christ our Lord; O' Savior of the world who by the cross and precious blood has redeemed us save us help us we humbly call onto you O' Lord. Amen.

JANUARY 13ᵀᴴ

THE WORD OF GOD CLEANSES US –
LET THE WORD OF GOD CLEANSE YOU TODAY

Today's Scripture Reading:

"Let love and faithfulness never leave you; bind them around your neck, write them on the tablet of your heart." *(Proverbs 3:3) NIV*

Christian's believers who are obeying God and living by his Holy principles will result in better and good health with a longer life; full of happiness and maintain a perfect prosperous life. Christians, who have a strong faith in the Lord, will enjoy this life more than those who have no steady faith. Trusting in the Lord with a faithful heart, without doubting his Word men and women must use the word of God to bind themselves together in Holy matrimony. They must stand on the Word of God. Eat the Word of God as food and Drink the Word of God as water; they must let the Word of God stand at the center of their hearts.

Prayer:

God the Father Almighty you are the maker of heaven and earth sea and everything that dwell in it, Jesus Christ his only Son,

Holy Spirit ever one God; have mercy on all the believing Christians that were calling unto you sincerely from the bottom of their hearts. Lord God Almighty, Jesus Christ our Lord and Savior, have mercy upon us. Lord God Almighty Father of all creations, help us to forgive our enemies those who persecuted us and those who do all forms of evils to us, turn them around from evil to good, turn their hearts and minds to follow your ways and to stop their evil ways and live a good life, life of peace in the Holy Spirit. Lord Jesus Christ our Lord and our Savior, have great compassion upon all those who call unto you faithfully, sincerely from their hearts, have mercy upon them, strengthens, comfort, help them, especially those who are weak, those who fall and finally those who are under the Satanic attack. Let your Word be our immortal food, as you are the Word of God who came down from heaven fill men and women with your full presence, be their immortal food. Help them and bless them with your sufficiency now and forever. Let them stands on God's unfailing love and confidently approach the thrown of Grace, let them be the doer of your Word, not only the hearer. In your mighty Holy Name, we pray. Amen.

JANUARY 14TH

THE WORD OF GOD CLEANSES US
LET THE WORD OF GOD CLEANSES YOU TODAY

Today's Scripture Reading:

"Let love and faithfulness never leave you; bind them around your neck, write them on the tablet of your heart." (Proverbs 3:3-4) NIV

Husband and wife must learn how to gain the blessings of the Lord and his wisdom by learning how to fear the Lord and thereby, guarded themselves from any form of evil along their life's path. They must also acquire the ability to discern good from evil by constantly reading and staying in the Word of God. It will help them to control anger against each other, and avoiding any tragedies of sin, such as fornication and all such of sexual immoralities that usually damage a good marriage; as well as troubles that can dissolve their relationship. The Word of God will help them not to desire evil things nor associate with those people who practice evil; they will associate themselves with good and righteous people. They will live a faithful life to God and to themselves.

Prayer:

Lord God Almighty, our Father in heaven, compassionate and ever-loving God, manifest your Word to the husband and wife, the men and women who are single, and dating each other. Lord Jesus Christ let them put in remembrance that the world and everything in it belongs to you and you are the sole owner of this Universe. Lord Jesus Christ help us to put stop to wars among the nations in all the world, give all the nations the blessing of your peace, unity, and let there be freedom upon all the people in all the nations of earth. Help us to take care of the injustice that is going on in all the nations, let the truth prevail, and set those who are in prisons free of what they did not do and there being punished. Bless all those who believe in you with their hearts desires if you know that it is good for them. Let there be more and more government programs that will help people to change their live to the better. Whatever that we loose on earth will be loosed in heaven, and whatever that we bind on earth will be bound in heaven; therefore, Lord Jesus Christ, let your Will be done in our lives not our Will but yours be done in our lives now and forever. In your Holy great and mighty Holy Name, we pray. Amen.

JANUARY 15TH

THE WORD OF GOD CLEANSES US –
LET THE WORD OF GOD CLEANSES YOU TODAY

Today's Scripture Reading:

"And so we know and rely on the love God has for us. God is love whoever lives in love lives in God, and God in him."
(1st John 4:16) NIV

John called all Christians to demonstrate love for three reasons: (a) Love is the very nature of God which he showed by giving us his own Son for us, we share his nature because we are born of him. (b) God loved us, we have experienced his love, through the forgiveness and we are obligated to help other, even if it is at great personal lost to us. (c) If we love one another, God will continue to live in us, and his love is made complete in us. God is love and his love is always with us, if we abide in him, we will continue to have the fullness of his love.

Prayer:

Lord God Almighty Father, Son and Holy Spirit; Lord Jesus Christ the great shepherd of the sheep fill us with your love and mercy , we pray. Lord God, the compassionate gracious loving God, you alone can turn sinners to you O' Lord, you alone can guides the humble spirit in all they do and the righteous to the right way, Lord Jesus Christ, you alone can teach us your way to the lowly and the weak. You bless the poor, and the hunger with good food, your goodness fill all the people on earth, you rain to the just and unjust, you feed the wicked with good food, you shine your Sun to the just and unjust, you continually correct and turning evil into a great good; no one like you our Lord, None Like you. Let your love fill us up as the water fills that sea and flow through us to millions of millions of people who does not know you our Lord. Bound men and women, husband, and wives with their children with your bond of love and peace. Let your full presence be in every household, and let your love manifest, spread like a wildfire in the wilderness in the heart, mind and spirit soul of every human being on this earth in Jesus Christ Holy Name, we pray amen, amen.

JANUARY 16TH

THE WORD OF GOD CLEANSES US –
LET HIS WORD CLEANSES YOU TODAY.

Today's Scripture Reading:

"Submit to one another out of reverence for Christ."
(Ephesians 5:21) NIV

God ordained husband and wife to submit to each other. Our Lord and Savior require a mutual submission in him as a general spiritual principle. This principle is to be applied first of all to the Christian families. Submission, humility, gentleness, patience, and respect must be the characteristic of each other, or each member of the household. Wife must submit by yielding in love to her husband's responsibility as the head of the household and as the leadership in the family. As well as the husband must submit to the need of his wife in an attitude of love and self-giving. Children must submit to the authority of their parents in obedience and respect. Parents must also submit to the needs of their children and bring them up in the instruction of our Lord Jesus Christ.

Prayer:

Lord God Almighty you are the creator of all things, in you all things consists, you are the sustainer of the universe together with all the people that live in it. God the Father almighty it is right and good as well as joyful to give thanks to you always wherever we may be and in everything we do, let us see that we give thanks to you and we are doing it for you, for your glory and for your Holy Name. Father almighty, the creator of heaven and earth, we praise you through Jesus Christ our Lord and Savior, who live and reign with you forever. Change us, mold us, and shape us to be what you want us to be for your glory on this earth. Bless us with your full presence throughout our lives on earth. Create in us a new heart, new minds, a new spirit, and a new name that will praise your Holy Name and gives thanks to you, and honor your Holy Name every day, every second on this earth. We pray that you bring all the family to you, clothe us with your righteousness, keep us safe from any and all the earthly troubles help the husband and wife to take care of their children with love according to your Holy instruction now and forever. In your mighty and matchless Holy Name , we pray. Amen.

JANUARY 17ᵀᴴ

THE WORD OF GOD CLEANSES US –
LET HIS WORD CLEANSES YOU TODAY.

Today's Scripture Reading:

"Do not get drunk on wine which leads to debauchery. Instead, be filled with the Spirit. Speak to one another with psalms, hymns and spiritual songs. Sing and make music in your heart to the Lord."
(Ephesians 5:18-19) NIV

God's children must experience a constant renewal of the power of the Holy Spirit in their lives. Christians are to be baptized in the Holy Spirit after their conversion both husband and wife must be baptized in the Holy Spirit; not that one is religious and the other did not, this type of marriage will create confusion and argument. They must be filled with the Holy Spirit in order to be able to live a Christian life together and raised their children with the admonition and instruction of God. Being filled with the God's Word, praying together in the spirit, and giving thanks and singing to the Lord, serving one another; speaking with joy to God.

Prayer:

Lord Jesus Christ you bless us with your Spirit, Spirit of Holiness, let your Spirit live in us forever; controlling, directing, structuring our path in this life; join all the family on earth together with the power of your Holy Spirit. Bring us the day of Pentecost whereby the Holy Spirit will rush like a rushing wind to the hearts and minds of everyone on this universe, without the power of the Holy Spirit no one can serve you according to your Will. Fill us up with the power of the Holy Spirit, help us to serve you with the Holy Spirit empowerment, and help us to worship you with love and joy through all the days of our life. Filled us with your Spirit the Paraclete heavenly guest, the comforter who will comfort us at the time of earthly troubles. Purified the family on earth with the power of the Holy Spirit. Without the Holy Spirit living within us we cannot live a Christian life that God requires from us. We thank you for blessing us with your Spirit, which is the Spirit of Holiness. In Jesus Christ's mighty, Holy Name , we pray. Amen

JANUARY 18TH

THE WORD OF GOD CLEANSES US –
LET HIS WORD CLEANSES YOU TODAY.

Today's Scripture Reading:

"Always giving thanks to God the Father for everything, in the name of our Lord Jesus Christ." (Ephesians 5:20th) NIV

The language of the heart of a believing Christians must be thankfulness for everything that is going on in their lives and faithfulness with praises. Believers must worship the Lord with thanksgiving and praises to our redeemer King. Husband and wife must praise the Lord Jesus Christ with all gentleness, honor sing praises to His Holy Name. When husband and wife daily engage themselves with praises and thankfulness, they will receive the peace of God that surpasses all understanding from one another; they will live together in love with the peace of God without argument and quarreling and without temptation.

Prayer:

Lord Jesus Christ, you are the God of mercy, Merciful and Mighty God, true Son of God, you are worthy of all our praises and thankfulness O' Lord, None like you in heaven and in this earth. Fill the hearts and minds, spirit, souls, and body of men and women, husbands, and wives with peace of God that surpasses all understanding to rule their hearts. Fill them with praises and thankfulness to you from heaven above. Help us to focus on you in all what we do or say and in all our undertaking day and night keep us away from any unrighteousness fill us with your righteousness, holiness, peace, and shine your great glory upon us at all times every day of our life. Lord Jesus Christ we offered ourselves to you, sanctify us with your Holy Spirit so that we may faithfully receive your life in us and serve you with all our hearts, minds, soul, and body, and be faithfully following you, and worship you in Spirit and in truth throughout our life. In Jesus Christ great Holy Name , we pray. Amen

JANUARY 19TH

THE WORD OF GOD CLEANSES US – LET HIS WORD CLEANSES YOU TODAY.

Today's Scripture Reading:

"Let us therefore make every effort to do what leads to peace and mutual edification. Do not destroy the work of God for the sake of food. All food is clean, but it is wrong for a man to eat anything that causes someone else to stumble."
(Romans 14:19-20) NIV

All the believing Christian's husband and wives, men and women must consider how to encourage each other in true holiness, Christ likeness and love with a concern faith, holiness and moral behavior is very important in Christian's daily lives. We must correct with love sincerely when it comes to food and drinking. They must try not to engage in any form of behavior that will destroy their relationship with the Lord or anything that can grieve the Holy Spirit that indwells them. Husband and wife must learn how to correct, rebuke one another in love and with the Spirit of humility. There should be mutual understanding when it comes to food and drinking.

Prayer:

Lord Jesus Christ do not let husband and wife engage themselves in any food or sexual immorality that will run their relationship with you, or that might grief the Spirit of God that indwell them; if the wife knows that certain food is not good for her husband, protect, guide and lead their hearts to stay away from cooking food that can make each other sick, or give them health problems. Our Lord Jesus Christ, the Holy one of Israel, the seed of David, the one and only incarnate Son of the Father, you have baptized us with your Spirit, the Holy Spirit of power and mighty, You have feed us with yourself as our immortal food, which will help us to grow in you more and more, that we may live with you forever. Keep us save in this world of chaos, bless us with peace, grant us with strength, courage, love, and help us to serve you with gladness and singleness of heart through the power of the Holy Spirit. In your Holy Name , we pray. Amen.

JANUARY 20ᵀᴴ

THE WORD OF GOD CLEANSES US –
LET HIS WORD CLEANSES YOU TODAY.

Today's Scripture Reading:

"For even Christ did not please himself but, as it is written: The insults of those who insult you have fallen on me. For everything that was written in the past was written to teach us, so that through endurance and the encouragement of the Scripture we might have hope." (Romans 15:3-4) NIV

The Scripture is telling us that Christ did not come to the world to please himself men and women, husband and wives who disregard the convictions of others in order to please themselves are destroying the work of God. Living a sacrificial life in order to help others will strengthen God's Kingdom. It will also, help to increase the wisdom and moral laws of God concerning every aspect of the life of husband and wife together as well as the revelation of God concerning himself, such as salvation and return of the coming of Christ, which will help them to value each other permanently.

Prayer:

Lord Jesus Christ you are the true Son of God, you are the Alpha and Omega, you are the beginning and the end, you are the first and the last; No one like you, No one before you and no one after you. We give you praise our Lord; you are worthy to be praise. Help us and teach us to be able to live a sacrificial life, as you live a sacrificial life for us, help and sustain the husband and wife together in their marriage as you are the husband of the church. We pray that the peace of our Lord and Savior Jesus Christ, the one and only true Son of God, which surpasses all understanding, his great wisdom and mercy, keep our hearts and minds, soul, Spirit in the knowledge and understanding of Jesus Christ the Son of God and the power of the Holy Spirit be with us and remain with us always throughout the days of our life. In your Holy Name , we pray. Amen

JANUARY 21ST

THE WORD OF GOD CLEANSES US –
LET HIS WORD CLEANSES YOU TODAY.

Today's Scripture Reading:

"It is better not to eat or drink wine, or do anything else that will cause your brother to fall. So whatever you believe about those things keep between yourself and God."
(Romans 14: 21-22) NIV

All the Christian believers must make this Word of God very important with three guidelines about drinking wine fermented wine and all other alcohol drinks and beverages.

Drunkenness is a serious sin that will exclude one from the kingdom of God. Believing Christians must know that the kingdom of God is not a matter that is primarily subject to territory, or to extent; rather it is a matter of the king's power, authority, and rules. it is not a kingdom as in eating and drinking. Rather, the evidence that God is our King and that he truly reigns in our lives and in the lives of husbands and wives, to include all the people in the world in righteousness, peace, joy in the Spirit of Holiness and Joy in the Holy Spirit.

Prayer:

We praise you our Lord for helping us by blessing us with your Holy Spirit. Without the power of the Holy Spirit we cannot live a Christian life, nor do what is pleasing in your sight. Help all the people of this world to live together with the power of the Holy Spirit. Keep us safe at all times, so that we may be able to raise godly children, raise them in your direction, so that the children of the world which are the next generation, will be able to live in this world with the fear of God, with the Love of God, and with the blessings of God, and moreover, they will be able to live a life of love that you ordained from heaven above before the foundation of the world and that you required from every living soul in this Universe. In Your mighty matchless Holy Name , we pray. Amen.

JANUARY 22ND

THE WORD OF GOD CLEANSES US –
LET HIS WORD CLEANSES YOU TODAY.

Today's Scripture Reading:

"In him we have redemption through his blood, the forgiveness of sins, in accordance with the riches of God's grace that he lavished on us with all wisdom and understanding."
(Ephesians 1:7-8) NIV

In Jesus Christ every faithful believing Christians husband and wives, men and women every members of the house hold who lives in union with Jesus Christ are the redeemed Christians, they have conscious communion with their Lord and Savior, in this relationship their very lives are seen as the life of Christ living inside them. The price paid by Jesus Christ was very costly - through his blood he redeemed believers. Redemptive work of Christ Jesus covers all the full range of human need humanity in need of forgiveness, deliverance, reconciliation, peace, love, new life, wisdom, understanding, community, acceptance, order, security, hope, and victory in their conflict with Satan and his forces. Husband and wives believing Christians must maintain personal fellowship with Jesus Christ this is the most important thing in this life and is the Christian experience. Union with Jesus Christ comes as a gift of God through faith.

Prayer:

O' Merciful and Mighty God Father all our Lord Jesus Christ, with your love we were redeemed from our sins. Sin does not have dominion over us anymore; we become your children forever. You are the only one who redeemed us from our sins, and bless us with a new life that is only in you. Lord Jesus Christ delivers all those who believe in you, who put their trust in you, from the life of sin and death. Open their heart, minds to your grace and to your truth. The Scripture says that grace and truth came through Jesus Christ; fill us up with faith and truth. Bless all the people of the earth with a new life; revive all the Souls of human being to your direction. Blessed the people of this earth with a new Spirit, a new mind, a new heart so that they may be able to live together in peace and in your true love; in your Mighty Holy Name , we pray. Amen.

JANUARY 23ᴿᴰ

THE WORD OF GOD CLEANSES US –
LET HIS WORD CLEANSES YOU TODAY.

Today's Scripture Reading:

*"A wife of noble character who can find? she is worth far more
than rubies. Her husband has full confidence in her and
lacks nothing of value."*
(Proverbs 31:10-11) NIV

This Scripture revealed and described the ideal wife and mother that God expected from family in the world. People of this world especially women a mother of our next generation of the people of this earth; their entire life must be centered on a reverent fear of God. She must have a compassion for those who are in need and faithfulness and love towards her family.

All the ideals set forth here might probably not be fulfilled in any one wife and mother. But each wife and mother can seek to serve the Lord, her family, and others in these kinds of ways with the ability of material resources that God the Father has given her. A women's position on this earth is a position of true feminine dignity is a as a godly wife and mother. No greater joy, blessing, honor, or fulfillment can come to her than when a Christians wife and mother, bears children, loves her children, and brings them up to love Jesus Christ and to live like him for God's glory. Honor and dignity of childbearing must not be depreciated by the Christians, or by the Christians husband. It was the childbearing of Mary that became the channel of the salvation of the people in the world.

Prayer:

Lord Jesus Christ, our Lord and Savior; open the womb of wives that were looking unto your Holy hands for a child. Bless them as you blessed Anna, Sara, Elizabeth, and Virgin Mary with yourself. Performed your miracle of childbearing to all the women looking for children that comes from their womb; answer their prayer of child-bearing if you know is according to your will, and is good for them both physically and also good for their health. In your Matchless, Mighty Holy Name, we pray. Amen.

JANUARY 24TH

THE WORD OF GOD CLEANSES US – LET HIS WORD CLEANSES YOU TODAY.

Today's Scripture Reading:

"But may the righteous be glad and rejoice before God; may they be happy and joyful. Sing to God, sing praise to his name, extol him who rides on the clouds his Name is the Lord and rejoice before him. A Father to the Fatherless, a defender of widows, is God in his Holy dwelling." (Psalm 68:3-5) NIV

God rules over his creations and cares for his people. The children of Israel, sing his victory over his enemies, which foreshadow of Christ's destruction of evil and all the evil at his Second Coming. The triumph of all believers, in Christ Jesus as they rejoice eternally in God's presence. Believing Christians must know the Fatherhood of God which was emphasized in both the Old Testament and the New Testament. God delights in protecting the weak, disadvantaged, mistreated and lonely among the people of this world. If the people of this world feel that they were alone and lonely, they should ask God to put them under his special-care and protection.

Prayer:

Lord Jesus Christ you are the Father to the Fatherless; you are the provider of those who are in need; you are the deliverer of those who are in all various kinds of bondage with drugs, sin, alcohol, and all forms of immoralities. You love us so much, more than what we can imagine. We pray that you will continue your full presence in the life of those who are in bondage of sin, oppression, trials, and persecution. Almighty God, we beseech you graciously to behold all the family in this world for which our Lord Jesus Christ died on the cross and raise to life for our sins. Help us to live with you from this earth to heaven world without end. We pray that Jesus Christ the Son of God, be manifest upon us, that our lives may be a light to the world; and the blessings of God the Father Almighty, Father, Son, and the Holy Spirit live in us, be among us and remain with us always and forever. Amen.

JANUARY 25ᵀᴴ

THE WORD OF GOD CLEANSES US –
LET HIS WORD CLEANSES YOU TODAY.

Today's Scripture Reading:

"In those days when the number of disciples was increasing, the Grecian Jews among them complained against the Hebraic Jews because their widows were being overlooked in the daily distribution of food." (Acts 6:1) NIV

The Apostles who were full of the Holy Spirit give orders about the distribution of the food to the widows; they discern through the Spirit of God that widows among them were being overlooked on a daily basis in terms of the food distributions. Even, it is the same today in our society some widows are being neglected and they suffer want, especially those widows with no children. Husband and wife must make a strong provision that will help care for one another if one should die before the other. Jesus Christ wants all the widows to be cared for wherever they are living. All the believers of Jesus Christ must care and make it their responsibility to care for the Senior Citizens, their mother and father, as well as their grandfather and grandmothers. It will be pleasing to our Lord and Savior, whereby he turns around and blesses the giver and the caretaker more and more.

Prayer:

Lord Jesus Christ in your mercy helps us to provide for the fatherless and the widows. Send help to them wherever they may be on the universe, in the villages of the earth, in the mountains, in the wilderness, in the valley, on the islands of the earth. Guide them and keep them safe. Especially those who are in the rural areas and remote parts of this world. Lord Jesus Christ do not stop caring for them. Do not stop providing for their needs medically, food, and clothing. Holy Spirit, the creator, from the foundation of the world; you moved on the surface of the waters from your breathe all the creations draw their life. Without you, there is no life, life will go back to dust. Holy Spirit of God, you are the counselor, by your inspiration, the prophets and all the messengers of God spoke and acted in faith. You clothed the messengers with your power to be able to bear and speak your Word. God the Holy Spirit descend, bless your people with power. Baptize us with your Holy Spirit, our Lord and Savior. In your mighty Holy Name , we pray. Amen.

JANUARY 26TH

THE WORD OF GOD CLEANSES US –
LET HIS WORD CLEANSES YOU TODAY.

Today's Scripture Reading:

"Now to the unmarried and the widows I say: It is good for them to stay unmarried, as I am. But if they cannot control themselves, they should marry, for it is better to marry then to burn with passion. To the married I give this command (not I, but the Lord) A wife must not separate from her husband. But if she does she must remain unmarried or else be reconciled to her husband. And a husband must not divorce his wife."
(1st Corinthians 7:8-11) NIV

Paul recognizes that God wants marriage to be permanent. He also, acknowledges, however, that sometimes in a marriage relationship may become so unbearable that separation from the partner is necessary. It is not that God permitted divorce, but it is because that God hates adultery, or abandonment of a marriage partner. Husband and wife must work out their differences thoroughly before divorcing themselves. They must consider the effect of divorce in the life of their children. Children suffer when father and mother separate, or divorce because children love their mother and father.

Prayer:

Lord Jesus Christ, compassionate gracious loving God, You are the husband of the Church, the cornerstone of the Church. Let the husbands love their wives and their children, as you love the Church and gave your life to the Church. Lord Jesus Christ empower and fill the hearts of husband and wife with communion of your Holy Spirit. You are the husband of the Church, our Lord and Savior. Teach them to love one another in the power of the Holy Spirit and the command of your Word. All those who believe in you, purify their hearts and minds; send them into the world with your love to witness of your love to the sinner and the lost. Lord Jesus Christ, in your mercy bring your people that believe in you the fullness of your peace and glory of your Holy Name. Almighty God let your peace be upon us now and forever. Let the people of this earth seek you and let them find you and give their lives to you in spirit, soul, and body, in order that they may live a peaceful life from this earth to heaven. In Your great, mighty, and Holy Name , we pray, a Name above all names. Amen.

JANUARY 27TH

THE WORD OF GOD CLEANSES US – LET HIS WORD CLEANSES YOU TODAY.

Today's Scripture Reading:

"Give proper recognition to those widows who are really in need. But if a widow has children or grandchildren, these should learn first of all to put their religion into practice by caring for their family and so repaying their parents and grandparents, for this is pleasing to God." (1st Timothy 5:3-4) NIV

We have a widow named Anna who never left the temple but worshiped day and night, fasting and praying for the coming of the Messiah. Anna a prophetess, daughter of Phanuel, of the tribe of Asher, she was very old. She had lived with her husband seven years after her marriage, and she became a widow until she was at the age of eighty-four. Anna never left the temple, she worshipped day and night, fasting, and praying. She gave thanks to God when Mary and Joseph brought Baby Jesus to the temple. Up till today we have many widows that devoted their lives to God and pray day and night for the Gospel of God to reach the unreachable in their language. The church in Ephesus had a list of widows who were entitled to material support from the Church.

Prayer:

God the Father Almighty, the creator of all things, Merciful and Mighty God full of truth and righteousness, Father of our Lord Jesus Christ, we pray to you, in your mercy and love, answer the prayers of all the widows that were praying to you day and night, send help to them, all the Senior Citizens in their home, or at the Senior Citizen's facilities in all the nations of earth; send help to them in all the areas of their lives where they were in need of help. Those who have children touch the heart of their children and move them to take care of their elderly, parents, and grandparents. Protect, guide and lead, feed them, clothe them, make your face shine upon them, and bless them with your abundant peace that surpasses all understanding. O' Merciful and mighty God, have mercy upon all the widows, single parent and their children. In your Holy Name, we pray. Amen.

JANUARY 28TH

THE WORD OF GOD CLEANSES US –
LET HIS WORD CLEANSES YOU TODAY.

Today's Scripture Reading:

"Therefore, get rid of all moral filth and the evil that is so prevalent and humbly accept the word planted in you, which can save you.   Do not merely listen to the Word, and so deceive yourselves.   Do what the Word says." (James 1:21-22) NIV

All the believing Christians, husband and wife, people of the world must listen to the word of God and be the doer of the word of God. The word of God, either in teaching, preaching written, cannot effectively take hold of a person's life, if he or she is not separated from moral filth and evil. God commands all the Christians believers to set aside the ungodly filth that corrupt society and seeks to influence families. The filth of lives can defile the Souls and separated them from the love of God which is in Christ Jesus our Lord. Believing husband and wife and the people of this earth, must not engage in any kind of impurity, or obscenity, they must not allow any form of moral filth into their lives which can break their homes, and mess up their life, this include all the filthy languages, through Videos and Televisions, or Internet, Pornography Movies and immoral behavior shows on Television;

which can grieves the Spirit of Jesus Christ that lives the life of Jesus Christ in you.

Prayer:

Lord God Almighty Father, Son and Holy Spirit the giver of life, the sustainer of all things and our redeemer King; help all us to live a clean life by putting all the filthy languages that can break us away from your Holy Spirit, language that can break marriages, and good relationship with our friends and our co-workers and especially filthy language that can break our spiritual relationship with you; when Spirit is grieved by what we say out of our mouth. Cleanse our mouth, our tongue as you cleanse Isaiah's tongue our Lord. Help us to focus on your redeeming love for us every day of our lives, in order that we may live a peaceful life that will bring honor and glory to your Holy Name. Amen.

JANUARY 29TH

THE WORD OF GOD CLEANSES US – LET HIS WORD CLEANSES YOU TODAY.

Today's Scripture Reading:

*"Do not take advantage of a widow or an orphan.
If you do and they cry out to me, I will certainly hear their
cry." (Exodus 22:22-23) NIV*

The regulations reveal that God was deeply concerned about the hardships of the widow, the poor and the disadvantaged, and he was moved with compassion for them. The husband and wife all believers and the people of this world must know that when divorce happen, it is a tragedy, and it is the result of human sin. God gives guidelines to regulate divorce; God was deeply concerned about the poor and the needy. Therefore, when marriage broke up women and children suffered from the impact of divorce. They will be forced to rely on their mother or their father where two people take care of them together; one person will be caring for them. It caused poverty and distresses for the entire family; it also causes hatred and violence in the mind of the children as they grow up. Some Children will grow up not to love anyone, or they might grow up with a revengeful heart.

Prayer:

Lord Jesus Christ you love the little children and you told them to let them come unto you; you held them in your arms and blessed them. We pray that you comfort children of divorced parents, and those children whose parents are going through divorce, or have already divorced, separated, to include either the father or mother who have moved out of the home. Children feel lonely without the father, or without the mother, and a mother cannot replace the love of the father in the children's heart. A father cannot replace the love of the mother in the children's heart. Father, Son, and Holy Spirit, ever one God, help us to also take care of widows and orphan, among us; answer their prayers whenever they cry to you in prayer. Straighten out the life of the orphan and children of divorced parents. In your mighty Holy Name have mercy upon us O' Lord. Jesus Christ, you are the Son of the living God, we pray that you have great compassion on all the children that are or have suffered through their parent's divorce. In Your Holy Name, we pray. Amen.

JANUARY 30TH

THE WORD OF GOD CLEANSES US –
LET HIS WORD CLEANSES YOU TODAY.

Today's Scripture Reading:

*"For the Lord your God is God of gods and Lord of lords,
the great God, mighty and awesome, who shows no partiality and
accepts no bribes. He defends the cause of the fatherless and
widows, and loves the alien, giving him food and clothing."*
(Deuteronomy 10:17-18) NIV

God Almighty always emphasized the necessity of love that comes from a pure heart. Jesus Christ is the same yesterday, today, and forever he never show any partiality to any of his created beings. God the Father, Son and God the Holy Spirit did not want anyone, of his children and the people of this world to substitute passion and heartfelt love for him with mere mouth and not from their pure heart, or showing love with outward religious forms, such as keeping the commandment, making an offering sacrifices, calling on his Name every minute but they did not give their life to him. It is necessary that men and women believers and the people of this earth obey God from their heart with sincere, love and honor God in Jesus Christ; so that our lives will be well pleasing to him, and God will smile at us when we do what is pleasing on his sight.

Prayer:

Our heavenly Father, Father of our Lord Jesus Christ, Compassionate Gracious Loving God, Father of all Mercies, one God who lives forever more; , we pray that you help us to live a life that will bring great honor to your Holy Name a life that will constantly exalted your Holy Name from this earth to heaven, a life that will be full of the love of Jesus Christ and bring the Gospel to the end of the earth and reach the unreachable in their own language. Come Holy Spirit into our lives with the power of a mighty wind. Open our minds and our hearts with the flame fire of your wisdom and knowledge. Holy Spirit of God loose our tongues to show your praises, for only in your spirit can we voice your words of peace and claim Jesus Christ as our Lord and Savior, come to us Holy Spirit in dwell us and live the life of Jesus Christ in our hearts and minds with power. In Jesus Christ great Holy Name, we pray. Amen.

JANUARY 31ST

THE WORD OF GOD CLEANSES US – LET HIS WORD CLEANSES YOU TODAY.

Today's Scripture Reading:

"He upholds the cause of the oppressed and gives food to the hungry. The Lord sets prisoners free; the Lord gives light to the blind, the Lord lifts up those who are bowed down, the Lord loves the righteous. The Lord watches over the alien and sustains the fatherless and widow, but he frustrates the ways of the wicked. The Lord reigns forever, your God, O Zion, for all generations. Praise the Lord." (Psalm 146:7-10) NIV

All the believers must praise the Lord for he is good for his steadfast love endure forever. Every church service must be full of big proclamation of his Holy Name with praises and thankfulness from all the people of this earth, especially the Christian families all over the world. Parents must teach their children how to praise the Lord at all times, and full of joy. All the believing Christians must praise and gives thanks to God when they wake up every morning with the praises of God the Father, Son and God the Holy Spirit in their mouth. Because of his blessings that never fail and his mercies that always flows to us his people, his children and all the people of the world. The Lord rain to the just and to unjust, he provides for the righteous and unrighteous. His blessings always flow to us every minute and every second.

Prayer:

Lord God Almighty, Compassionate gracious loving and merciful and mighty God: We give you glory praises and thankfulness because you are the only true God who have unconditional love for us on this earth. We pray for your continue presence in our lives will never fail, we pray that you will always listen to our prayers and answer our prayers. Therefore, we must give God the glory for all our past, present, and our future deliverances and give him the honor and glory throughout our lives. We must always look unto Jesus the author and the finisher of our faith. We give you thanks O' God for the goodness and love which you have made known to us since the beginning of creation; , we pray that you bless us immeasurably, abundantly that we will be able to offer you our wealth for the glory of your Holy Name, we will be able to bring sinners and the lost, people of all other regions unto you. Let those who does not know you, seek you and find you our Lord and our great redeemer, let those who seek you find you, reveal yourself to the people of this world who does not know you our Lord, let them know there is God, who is in charge of all good things for his goodness. In Jesus Christ's mighty Holy Name, I pray. Amen.

DAILY REFLECTION NOTES

FEBRUARY

FEBRUARY 1ST

THE WORD OF GOD CLEANSES US –
LET HIS WORD CLEANSES YOU TODAY.

Today's Scripture Reading:

"Sanctify them by the truth; your word is truth." (John 17:17) NIV

Our Lord and Savior Jesus Christ, our redeemer King; pray for the disciples when his time of his crucifixion is coming nearer. He pray that God the Father almighty to sanctify them and also those who will believe in his word through their ministry. Sanctify means to make them Holy, and separated, or set them apart. The evening before our Lord's crucifixion Jesus Christ prays that his disciples will be a Holy people, separated from the world of sin for the purpose of worshiping and serving God. Our Lord pray that all the believing Christians must be set apart in order to get close, near to God, to live for him and to be like him. This sanctification can only be accomplished through believers devotion to the truth revealed to them by the Spirit of truth.

Prayer:

Lord God Almighty Father Son and Holy Spirit sanctify all the believing Christians today and forever. Let your purpose be achieved in our lives, let your full presence be known in our lives, let the word of truth fills us up as the water fills the sea, let your abiding presence be known in our lives every day of our life. Let the people that did not know you, see your great light shining upon us and be converted unto you our Savior Lord. Sanctify all our children with your grace and mercy, protect them from Bully Kids when they are in school, Let them focus on their studies, and concentrate on their education in order that they may be able to be useful for you as they grow up. Comfort the children of divorce parents; bless them with peace of God that surpasses all understanding to deal with the violent kids in their classroom and in their neighborhood. Put in their mind to follow all the government rules and regulations in order to be able to live a life of peace and joy. Almighty God have mercy on all our children, forgive us if we did not take care of them as you want, or according to your will; strength then in all goodness, anointed them with the power of the Holy Spirit and keep them for eternal life. You are our great intercessor in heaven, do not stop your prayer, continuous pouring your blessings upon us, and let your prayer continuously rushing down upon us like a rushing wind from heaven. In your great, matchless, Holy Name, we pray. Amen.

FEBRUARY 2ND

THE WORD OF GOD CLEANSES US –
LET HIS WORD CLEANSES YOU TODAY.

Today's Scripture Reading:

"And you also were included in Christ when you heard the word of truth, the gospel of your salvation. Having believed, you were marked in him with a seal, the promised Holy Spirit. Who is a deposit guaranteeing our inheritance until the redemption of those who are God's possession to the praise of his glory."
(Ephesians 1:13-14) NIV

We have to know that the Holy Spirit and his place in the believers' redemption is a central emphasis in the book of Ephesians. The Holy Spirit is the mark, or seal of God's ownership. Holy Spirit is a deposit; it is the first installment, or down payment, guaranteeing our inheritance. Today and till Christ our Lord returns, Holy Spirit is given to believers as a down payment of what we are going to have in greater fullness in the future. It is the presence and his work in our lives is a pledge of our future inheritance.

Prayer:

Lord Jesus Christ, you are the one and only who baptized with the Holy Spirit. Baptize all those who call on your Holy Name from the bottom of their heart with the power of the Holy Spirit, so that we can live and serve you with singleness of heart and with the empowerment of the Holy Spirit. O' lord, Holy Father, giver of health and salvation; send your Holy Spirit to sanctify, so that by faith we may be able serve you faithfully, follow you without doubting and without wavering. Let the power of your anointing of the Holy Spirit heal all who are sick, those are suffering from diseases, those who are disable among us. Lord Jesus Christ pray for us the prayer that can never be uttered , that the Holy Spirit will work in us in greater measure, so that we may receive more wisdom, understanding, revelation and knowledge concerning God's redemptive purpose for this present life; and in our future salvation. We pray that your salvation will flow through us to other people who do not know you in this world. In Jesus Christ's Holy Name, we pray. Amen

FEBRUARY 3RD

THE WORD OF GOD CLEANSES US – LET HIS WORD CLEANSES YOU TODAY.

Today's Scripture Reading:

*"Learn to do right! Seek justice, encourage the oppressed.
Defend the cause of the fatherless, plead the case of the
widow. Come now, let us reason together, says the Lord.
Though your sins are like scarlet, they shall be as
white as snow; though they are red as crimson,
they shall be like wool." (Isaiah 1: 17-18) NIV*

All believing Christians must learn how to do the right thing at all times, they must also seek justice where justice is needed, defend the fatherless and widow, and the single parents people that might be neglected and encourage one another with love and compassion. We must try our best to help those who are in need of our help. God did not want to condemn and destroy his people. He came down from heaven and offered us full forgiveness and pardon if people will repent their sins, put away evil and strive to do right as well as obey the word of God. God's forgiveness is now available for all who, though they have sinned, confess their sins, repent, and accept God's cleansing through the precious blood of Jesus Christ.

Prayer:

Almighty God, you are the giver of life and love, bless us with wisdom and devotion in the ordering of our common life with you, counselor in perplexity, a comfort in time of sorrow, and a sincere companion in the time of joy. That we may live together in this life with love and peace; all the days of our life; through our Lord and Savior Jesus Christ. Lord Jesus Christ from whom all the goodness flows. You are the channels of blessings. We have erred and strayed from your ways like a lost sheep, we have followed devices and desires of our own hearts, we have offended, and against your Holy Laws, we have left undone those which we out to have done, and we have done those things which we should not have done. Lord God almighty in your mercy O' Lord forgives those who confess their sins restore us, according to your promises you gave us through Jesus our Lord. O' most Merciful Father, for the sake of your Son, help us to live a godly, righteous, sober life to the glory and honor of your Holy Name. Amen

FEBRUARY 4TH

THE WORD OF GOD CLEANSES US –
LET HIS WORD CLEANSES YOU TODAY.

Today's Scripture Reading:

"As he looked up, Jesus saw the rich putting their gifts into the temple treasury. He also saw a poor widow put in two very small copper coins. I tell you the truth, he said, this poor widow has put in more than all the others. All these people gave their gifts out of their wealth; but she out of her poverty put in all she had to live on." (Luke 21: 1-4) NIV

Our Lord Jesus Christ gives a lesson on how God evaluates giving since this reference to the widow is not as it may seem on the surface. The significance of a person's gift is determined not by the amount of giving, but by the measure of sacrifice or true generosity involved in the giving. The rich sometimes will give only a token from the abundance of their wealth that involves neither sacrifice, nor generosity. Though the widow gave only a very small amount, her giving represented a heart of extravagant generosity, as it was all she had to live on. She gave as much as she possibly could. Our Lord's assessment can be applied to the totality of our relationship with him and our services for him.

Prayer:

Lord Jesus, our Lord and our Savior, our redeemer King, you are the immortal, the invisible the only wise God; help us to give all we have on this earth to you faithfully and sincerely, including our spirit, soul and body, so that you may be able to use us for the work of the Gospel of God, and for the work of the Kingdom. O' eternal God, you have promised to be a Father to a thousand generations of those who have known you, love you, and fear you. Bless them and preserve their life, receive them, and enable them to receive you that through the power of the Holy Spirit to worship you with the spirit of holiness. Help us to give our money, our wealth, to enhance the work of the Kingdom on this earth. Help us to live a life that will honor, adore, and glorify your Holy Name. Amen

FEBRUARY 5TH

THE WORD OF GOD CLEANSES US –
LET HIS WORD CLEANSES YOU TODAY.

Today's Scripture Reading:

"They devoted themselves to the apostles teaching and to the fellowship, to the breaking of bread and to prayer. Everyone was filled with awe, and many wonders and miraculous signs were done by the apostles. All believers were together and had everything in common Selling their possessions and goods, they gave to anyone as he had need." (Acts 2:42-45) NIV

This Scripture reveals seven important characteristics of a Spirit-filled church immediately after Pentecost. (a) The apostles engaged in the teaching of the Gospel and the people were nourished in the Word taught by the apostles, some of which later became the words of our New Testament Scriptures which were church centered teaching. Same till today, the teaching of the Gospel of God is very important to the unsaved people in the world. (b) The apostles fellowship together with new believers, and old believers, encouraging them and helping them; they developed a vertical relationship to God, but also nourished horizontally a warm, honest, open, healing, redeeming fellowship based on a common life of God together in Jesus Christ, pursued of fellowship of Christ the Holy Spirit. The apostle were breaking bread just as our Lord instructed them, which all the church of Christ are doing up till today the Lord's Supper. (c) The apostles and all the believers were engaging in prayer, in an unceasing prayer which is a priority and integral part of our life as a Christian together, the more , we pray the more we put the Holy Spirit to work in our lives. (d) The apostles engaged in the righteous influence and witness of new people in the community, in the towns and everywhere, Jesus Christ's ministry our flow up till today from the apostles to us by the power of the Holy Spirit. Therefore, the Lord continues to add new converts into the church daily.

Prayer:

All mighty God Father of our Lord Jesus Christ - you call us from darkness into your marvelous light continues to take care of all the believing Christians who are calling unto you every minute and every second, hear our prayers as we witness, teach, and proclaim the Gospel every day to the people of this world who does not know you. O' gracious God, we give you humble and anxiety as a servant who desires now to offer you praises and thanksgiving, most merciful and mighty Father, that by your mercy and assistance we may live faithfully according to your will in this life, and finally partake of everlasting glory in the life to come through Jesus Christ our Lord. You do not want anyone to perish, you want them the come to the knowledge of repentance and pray for forgiveness which is only in you. Strengthens us in all the areas of our lives, so that we can be able to call the sinners and the lost unto you. Turn around those who are persecuting the Christians all over the world from evil to good, from violent to peace, from hatred to love. Let them be converted unto you our Lord and Savior. You are our Father in heaven; wash us and cleanse us from any unrighteousness; clothe us with your righteousness now and forever. In Jesus Christ's great and Holy Name, we pray. Amen

FEBRUARY 6ᵀᴴ

THE WORD OF GOD CLEANSES US –
LET HIS WORD CLEANSES YOU TODAY.

Today's Scripture Reading:

"When the Lord began to speak through Hosea, the Lord said to him, Go; take to yourself an adulterous wife and children of unfaithfulness, because the Land is guilty of the vilest adultery in departing from the Lord. So he married Gomer daughter of Diblaim, and she conceived and bore him a son."
*(Hosea 1:2-3)*NIV

The Scripture revealed to us that: God's relationship with the children of Israel is frequently compared to a marriage contract. Children of Israel constantly departing from the Lord in order to worship Idols and other Pagan gods; was treated by God as spiritual infidelity or prostitution. Hosea's marriage was an object lesson for the unfaithful northern Kingdom. Gomer later turned to physical adultery and immorality, her departure from the Lord led not only to false worship, but also to lower moral standards. The same pattern of immoral living can be seen today wherever God's people turn away from true commitment to the Lord.

Prayer:

O' Most blessed light divine, shine within our hearts and our innermost being fill us! Where you are not, we have nothing there, nothing good in our deed or thought when you are not in our heart. Come Holy Spirit and heal our wounds; renew our strength in you; on our dryness pour out your living water that sprinkle up to eternal life. Help us to be a faithful follower that will follow you faithfully, sincerely, take away any Idol that might want to be on our way of worshiping you in spirit and in truth. Help us to get close to you more and more everyday of our life. Wash us clean from any unrighteousness, and clothe us with your righteousness. Lord Jesus Christ, Father, Son, and the Holy Spirit, help us to focus in your faithfulness to us, be at the center of our hearts; do not let us see anything that will turn us away from your unfailing love and compassion for us. O' Lord our God; hold us tithe with your Holy hands. Drive away any thing that can contaminate our spirit, soul, body that we will not be able to get close to you. Wash us clean from any unrighteousness; clothe us with your Holiness now and forever. In Jesus Christ's mighty great Holy Name, we pray. Amen

FEBRUARY 7ᵀᴴ

THE WORD OF GOD CLEANSES US –
LET HIS WORD CLEANSES YOU TODAY.

Today's Scripture Reading:

"You ask, Why? It is because the Lord is acting as the witness between you and the wife of your youth, because you have broken faith with her, though she is your partner, the wife of your marriage covenant. Has not the lord, made them one? in flesh and spirit they are his. And why one? Because he was seeking godly offspring. So guard yourself in your spirit, and do not break faith with the wife of your youth."
(Malachi 2:14-15) NIV

God Almighty is telling us that men and women and the people of this earth, believers, and unbelievers, they have been unfaithful to their wives and to their husbands whom they had married when they were young. They were seeking to divorce them, only because they wanted to marry someone else. The Lord God was against this kind of selfish action, he said he made husband and wife one. God hates divorce that is initiated and based for selfish purposes; this kind of divorce is like one covering himself with violence; God indicating that unjust divorce is equal in God's sight to gross injustice, cruelty, and murder.

Prayer:

Our Father in heaven, Father of our Lord Jesus Christ, most Merciful and mighty God; , we pray that you open the heart of husband and wife, let them know that divorce is a sin in the sight of God, especially, if they wanted to replace themselves with someone else. Let them know that the children suffer when the marriage broke up and divorce cause a lot of evil against each other. Lord Jesus Christ, wash the stains of guilt away, and bend our stubborn heart to do your Will; melt our frozen heart, warm our heart with your love and mercy, guide the steps of those who go astray. Have mercy on the faithful one who adores you, confess you, to all people. God the Holy Spirit in your sevenfold gift descend to give us the virtue's sure reward; give them salvation O' Lord, give them joy that never end. Lord Jesus who attended the wedding in Canaan and blessed them, help us to bless people of this earth's marriage, keep them together in good harmony and let them follow your commandment. In your Holy Name, we pray. Amen.

FEBRUARY 8TH

THE WORD OF GOD CLEANSES US – LET HIS WORD CLEANSES YOU TODAY.

Today's Scripture Reading:

"But after he had considered this, an angel of the Lord appeared to him in a dream and said, Joseph son of David, do not be afraid to take Mary home as your wife, because what is conceived in her is from the Holy Spirit. She will give birth to a Son, and you are to give him the Name Jesus, because he will save his people from their sins." (Matthew 1:20-21) NIV

The importance of the Virgin birth cannot be over emphasized. In order for our redeemer to be qualified to pay for our sins and bring Salvation, he must be, in one person, fully human, sinless, and fully divine. Mary's virgin birth satisfies all three of these requirements. The only way that our Lord and Savior Jesus Christ could be sinless was to be conceived by the Holy Spirit. And the only way he could be divine was to have God as his Father. As a result: Christ conception was not by natural; but by the supernatural work of God. And that is why the Angel said: "The Holy one to be born will be called the Son of God," (Luke 1:35).

Prayer:

Lord Jesus Christ you came down from heaven to redeem us from our past, present, and future sins, you revealed to us as one divine person with two natures, you are divine and sinless human being help us to know you better as we walk with you every day of our lives. Reveal yourself to those people on this earth who has never known you and never experience your redeeming love for the humanity. God the Father Almighty you are the maker of heaven and earth Sea and everything that dwell in it, Holy Spirit ever one God. You are the one and only Eternal Father, strong and mighty to save, your arm have bound the storm, you bid the mighty Ocean deep in storm to keep its appointed limits; Oh our Father in heaven, hear our prayers when we cry to you. Have mercy on those who are in danger all over the world, Jesus Christ you are the one and only that walked on the ocean, and calm the storm. Bless us who believes in you with your divine power, purified our hearts and mind to worship you in Spirit and in truth, help us to pray to you in spirit and in truth, love you forever our Lord Jesus Christ make us to live forever in Spirit and in truth. In your mighty Holy Name, we pray. Amen.

FEBRUARY 9TH

THE WORD OF GOD CLEANSES US – LET HIS WORD CLEANSES YOU TODAY.

Today's Scripture Reading:

"Some Pharisees came to him to test him. They asked, is it lawful for a man to divorce his wife for any and every reason. Haven't you read, the creator made them male and female, and said, for this reason a man will leave his father and mother and be united to his wife, and the two will become one flesh. So they are no longer two, but one. Therefore, what God has joined together, let man not separate." (Matthew 19:3-6) NIV

God's plan for standard marriage is one man and one woman joined together for life and dissolved only by death. Jesus Christ gives an exception which was based on marital unfaithfulness. Marital unfaithfulness includes adultery and any other kinds of sexual immorality. Therefore, divorce is to be permitted whenever sexual immorality is involved. Christ said that divorce is permitted in the Old Testament in cases where a husband discovered premarital un-chastity after the marriage ceremony had taken place, but permitted divorce due to premarital un-chastity because of the hardness of the people's heart. Old Testament Law on immorality after marriage executing of the offending party so that the innocent parties will be free to remarry without problem.

Prayer:

Lord God Almighty have mercy upon all the couple; let them set their mind to live in good harmony throughout the rest of their life. Forgive the adulterer, and spare his life, so that he can live for you forever. Lord Jesus Christ let the husband and wife be faithful to one another with the fear of God and live righteously. Oh, Lord hears our cry when we cry to you. Hear the cry of those who are in problems disasters, wars, and diverse diseases. Most Holy Spirit, you that you calm the chaos dark and rude, and you bid the angry tumult to cease, you give wild confusion, peace, Oh Lord hear our cry when we cry to you. Holy Spirit you the trinity of love and the power, have mercy on those who are in danger help them every hour; from rock and tempest, fire and enemy, protect them wherever they go now and forever more they shall rise to you with the hymns of praises and thankfulness. O' Lord our God in your mercy hear our prayer when we call and cry to you. In Jesus Christ's great and Holy Name, we pray. Amen.

FEBRUARY 10TH

THE WORD OF GOD CLEANSES US –
LET HIS WORD CLEANSES YOU TODAY.

Today's Scripture Reading:

"Remember Lot's wife! Whoever tries to keep his life will lose it, and whoever loses his life will preserve it." (Luke 17:32) NIV

Lot's wife made a tragic mistake; she placed her affections on society and earthly material things, rather than on heavenly things. She turned back because her heart was still in Sodom. Every believing Christians should ask themselves whether their heart is more attached to the earthly things than to Jesus and the hope of his returning to earth, to set up his Kingdom. Believers must make Jesus Christ their problem solver, their great physician, the deliverer, provider, and the sustainer of their life. Jesus Christ will not take anyone who is divided in half; you must give your total being to him. Those who waver like a shadow cannot have the fullness of Christ. Christ will not share your heart with a pagan God.

Prayer:

God the Father, God the Son, and God the Holy Spirit, we call on to you today and forever to manifest yourself in the heart of those who fully belong to you. Those who call unto you sincerely every minute and every second from their pure heart. O' God, you have taught us through your blessed Son that whoever receives a little child in the Name of Jesus Christ receives Jesus Christ himself; we give you praises and adoration for the blessing you have bestowed upon us , for everything you have given us, we pray that you confirm our joy by a lively sense of your presence with us and give us strength and patient, wisdom to live our life for your glory, help us to love all what is true and noble, just and pure, lovable and gracious, all what is excellent and admirable. Continuously pouring your favor upon us everywhere we go and in everything we do, in our home, office, and when we are in the house of worship.

Shine your great light from heaven upon us, made us alive in your spirit, soul, and body. Pour out your Holy Spirit upon us, Spirit of power, Spirit of knowledge, so that we can live our life completely for you without waiver. In Jesus Christ's Holy Name, we pray. Amen.

FEBRUARY 11TH

THE WORD OF GOD CLEANSES US –
LET THE WORD OF GOD CLEANSES YOU TODAY.

Today's Scripture Reading:

"I tell you the truth, Jesus said to them, no one who has left home or wife or brother or parents or children for the sake of the Kingdom of God will fail to receive many times as much in this age and, in the age to come, eternal life."
(Luke 18:29-30) NIV

Jesus Christ explained clearly to his disciples and to us today that there is a reward promised to those leave their mother and father and go for missionary journey, spend their money to enhance the work of the Lord; there is reward for those who faithfully and sincerely serve the Lord in all various work of the Gospel preaching teaching, writing, singing, proclaiming the Gospel to all the people in all the nations of this world. Christ said that they will receive blessings in hundred fold from this earth to heaven; a heavenly inheritance is awaiting those who serve the Lord faithfully.

Prayer:

Lord Jesus Christ, you are the one that save us from our past, present and future sins. Bless us with everything that we may need, that will help us to serve you on this earth faithfully. Teach us, call us, ordain us, let us know how to serve you, with the spirit of holiness, so that at the end we will be able to receive a reward an inheritance that the Father promise through Jesus Christ, most important to be able to receive the Crown of righteousness that you gave to those who love your appearing. Almighty God Father of all mercies sustainer of all things, we praise your Holy Name and give you glory, because of your blessings that are pouring unto us every day of our lives, especially the blessing of all those who serve you, faithfully and sincerely such as: pastors, ministers, and missionaries, to include those continuously calling the laborers into the harvest field. You said that the: "Harvest is plenty, and the laborer is few, that we should pray that you send more laborers into the harvest field." Touch our hearts and minds to love you more and more and serve you according to your will for us. So that we will be able to receive the reward of eternal life. In Jesus Christ's Holy Name, we pray. Amen.

FEBRUARY 12ᵀᴴ

THE WORD OF GOD CLEANSES US –
LET THE WORD OF GOD CLEANSES YOU TODAY.

Today's Scripture Reading:

"But since there is so much immorality,
each man should have his own wife,
and each woman her own husband.
The husband should fulfill his marital
duty to his wife, and like wise the wife
to her husband." (1st Corinthians 7:2-3) NIV

The Scripture made it clear that the commitment of marriage means that each partner relinquishes the exclusive right to his or her own body and gives the other a claim to it. That is, neither marriage partner may fail to submit to the normal sexual desires of the other. Such desiring within marriage are natural and God given, and to refuse to carry out one's responsibility in fulfilling the other's needs is to open up the marriage to Satan's temptation of adultery. Apostle Paul was teaching those who are couples to learn how to submit to one another in everything with respect and with no arrogance. Husband must respect, and the wife must respect her husband without any doubt.

Prayer:

Lord God Almighty, you are the one that ordained marriage from the foundation of the universe in the Garden of Eden. Our everlasting Father, whose will it is to restore all thing in your well-beloved Son, Jesus Christ, the Lord of lords, the King of kings, the God of gods; in your infinite mercy grant that your people of this universe, who are enslaved by sin, live in the bondage of sin, may be free and brought together under your most glorious rule; who lives and reigns with you and the Holy Spirit, one God, now and forever, help us to be one in you as you and your Father are one, help us to know you and worship you with the spirit of holiness. You have redeemed us from any unrighteousness; use us for your great glory. Bind the husband and wife together with your power of true love, you are the husband of the church our Lord, help them to love each other with a true heart. Take care of our children, solve all our problems, fulfill all our needs, according to your heart desires and Will for our life. Help husband and wife to take good care of their children, anointed them with the oil that you alone use, and baptized them with the power of your Holy Spirit now and forever. Help the man and woman to have the union from this earth to heaven in their heavenly home above. Protect and guide them, do not let them be a bully and a violent person. Let them have joy that you alone supply throughout their life. In Jesus Christ's Holy Name. Amen.

FEBRUARY 13TH

THE WORD OF GOD CLEANSES US –
LET THE WORD OF GOD CLEANSES YOU TODAY.

Today's Scripture Reading:

"I would like you to be free from concern.
An unmarried man is concerned about the
Lord's affairs - how he can please the Lord. But a married
man is concerned about the affairs of this world - how
he can please his wife-- and his interests are divided.
An unmarried woman or virgin is concerned about
the Lord's affairs: Her aim is to be devoted to the Lord in both
body and spirit.
But a married woman is concerned about the affairs
of this world - how she can please her husband."
(1st Corinthians 7:32-34) NIV

We live in the period when all worldly things are hastening toward an end. Therefore, life in this world should not be a believing Christian concern; we should direct our utmost concern, goal, and our greatest attention towards our heavenly home above. Scripture clearly saying there an unmarried is not that the person is inferior to be married or that the person is not beautiful enough. In fact, it is better into her most important way of all the possibility of offering undistracted service to God. The unmarried men and women will be able to concentrate on the things that belong to the Lord in a greater way than the married.

Prayer:

God the Father Almighty Father of our Lord Jesus Christ, the true Son of God, and the Holy Spirit ever one God. Help us to be content with the way that you want us to live our lives for you. Help us by opening our hearts to do what is pleasing and justify in your sight every day of our life. Help us to live a life that is pleasing to you, to please you in all the areas of our lives bring us close to you now and forever. Our Father in heaven, whose blessed Son our Lord Jesus Christ before his passion prayed for his disciples that they might be one, as you are one with the Father; bound us together in love and obedience to you, may be united in one body by the one Spirit, that the world may believe in him whom you have sent, your Son Jesus Christ our Lord; who lives and reigns with you, in the unity of the Holy Spirit one God, the Holy Trinity forever and ever. Bless us as , we pray, with confidence approaching the throne of grace. In Jesus Christ's Holy Name, we pray. Amen.

FEBRUARY 14TH

THE WORD OF GOD CLEANSES US –
LET THE WORD OF GOD CLEANSES YOU TODAY.

Today's Scripture Reading:

"For the husband is the head of the wife as Christ is the head of the church, his body, of which he is the Savior. Now as the church submits to Christ, so also wives should submit to their husbands in everything." (Ephesians 5:23-24) NIV

God Almighty, Jesus Christ his only begotten Son has established the family as the basic unit in society. Every family must have a leader. Therefore, God has assigned to the husband the responsibility of being the head of the wife and children. Husband's responsibility that God the Father gave him from the beginning of the creation is that he must be the head of his wife and make a provision for his family's spiritual and domestic needs. The wife is also given responsibility as task to help her husband and to submit to her husband. The wife important duty is love and respects her husband. Wife must try her best to live in good harmony with her husband no matter what circumstances they were going through in their lives.

Prayer:

Lord Jesus Christ, you are the husband of the church , we pray that you sustained the husband and the wife so that they can live together in good harmony; by respecting, honoring and focus on you our Lord. O' our heavenly Father in you we live and move and have our being: We humbly pray that you guide the husband and wife in the way wisdom, knowledge and understanding, to live together in good matrimony; be the governor of their finances, and all their properties with the power of your Holy Spirit, that in all the cares and occupations of our life we may not forget you, but we may remember that we will walk and do everything we said and done in your sight; through the power and the word of Jesus Christ our Lord.

God the Father almighty you are the only sustainer of the universe; Revived and renewed our marriage, manifest your life in us and let us call unto you in everything we might be going through. In your Holy Name, we pray. Amen.

FEBRUARY 15ᵀᴴ

THE WORD OF GOD CLEANSES US –
LET THE WORD OF GOD CLEANSES YOU TODAY.

Today's Scripture Reading:

"Now the overseer must be above reproach, the husband of but one wife, temperate, self-controlled, respectable, hospitable, able to teach, not given to drunkenness, not violent but gentle, not quarrelsome, not lover of money. He must manage his own family well and see that his children obey him with proper respect."
(1st Timothy 2:3-4) NIV.

Those who want to be an elder in the church or overseer, they must be above reproach means, and they must have excellent behavior to their family, wife, children as well as their parents, if they still have parents. The must be able to set good example in the church to new believers and other believing Christians in the congregation. They must prove a conduct that is blameless in their marital life, family life, and social life and in their business life. No elder or overseers should have a justifiable charge of any form of immorality or misconduct against him or her.

Prayer:

Lord Jesus Christ you are the foundation of the church, the head of the church, you are the corner stone of the church, you are the life of the church, you gave your life to us on the cross, on the cross our salvation is completed we give you thanks and praises our Lord, Most Merciful and Mighty God. Help us to call and chose an elder or overseer that will set a good standard as a good conduct toward the service of the Lord. O' God, our Father in heaven, Compassionate gracious loving God, from you all desires, all good counsels, and all just work proceed; Give us all those who believe in you, and all your servants on this earth with the success and courage to serve you better. You are the source of eternal light; shine your unending light upon us who look for you, that our lips may be full of your praises and thankfulness throughout our lives and our worship to you will give you glory, through Jesus Christ our Lord. Help us to call and chose those who will serve you with moral excellency with good reputation now and forever. In Jesus Christ's great and Holy Name, we pray. Amen .

FEBRUARY 16TH

THE WORD OF GOD CLEANSES US –
LET THE WORD OF GOD CLEANSES YOU TODAY.

Today's Scripture Reading:

"One of the seven angels who had the seven bowls
full of the seven last plagues came and said to me,
come, I will show you the bride, the wife of the Lamb.
And he carried me away in the Spirit to a mountain
great and high, and showed me the Holy City.
Jerusalem, coming down out of heaven from God."
(Revelation 21:9-10)NIV

When the angel said to John come, I will show you the bride, the wife of the Lamb, he showed John the Holy City, Jerusalem - the City was there, but a city with walls and gates cannot be the bride. When Jesus wept over Jerusalem, the city was there, but it was really the people he was weeping over. The Scripture says the new Jerusalem is prepared as a bride beautifully dressed for her husband. Apostle John used symbolic language to describe the Holy City, whose glory cannot be totally comprehended by human understanding. Bride is part of the wedding of the Lamb and marriage of the Lamb means the people in the Holy City who's their names are written in the Book of Life. They will see his face; Jesus presents the church to himself, the church is Jesus's bride, even though the word bride is hardly used. All the believing Christians are the church and we are the body of Body of Jesus Christ, Jesus Christ is the Head of his Church in heaven and on this earth.

Prayer:

God the Father Almighty, Jesus Christ his only Son, Holy Spirit the giver of life, who proceeded from the Father, and whom through Father and the Son he was glorified; we pray that you fill us with Holy food which is yourself, you are the husband of the church we are the church, we are the part of your body, your flesh and your bones, we are the bones of your bones. Let your full presence be always known in our lives; be our immortal food forever. O' Merciful and mighty God, we give you most humble and with the heart of love, thank you for all the goodness and loving kind to us on this universe, we thank you for all your creation, preservation and all the blessings of this life and the life to come; but above all we give you thanks for your inestimable, infinite love in the work of redemption of the earth through our Lord Jesus Christ, for the means of the gift of grace, and for our blessed hope of glory for your return. Help us to make our hearts and minds are thankful to you more and more every day of our life.

Provide for all our needs, direct, control and make us your bride from this earth to heaven, so that we can live with you in the new Jerusalem which one day will be coming down from heaven. In Jesus Christ's Holy Name, we pray. Amen.

FEBRUARY 17TH

THE WORD OF GOD CLEANSES US –
LET THE WORD OF GOD CLEANSES YOU TODAY.

Today's Scripture Reading:

"Love is patient, love is kind. It does not envy, it does not boast, it is not proud. It does not boast, it is not rude, it is not self-seeking, it is not easily angered, it keeps no record of wrongs. Love does not delight in evil but rejoices with the truth. It always protects, always trust, always hopes, always perseveres."
(1st Corinthians 13:4-7) NIV

All the believing Christians must exercise love wherever they may be, in all they do, and with all the people in the world. Love is an activity and a behavior, not just as an inner feeling or motivation. Various aspects of love included here the characterizes God the Father, God the Son, and God the Holy Spirit; our Lord Jesus Christ said: "Love your neighbor, do unto others as you wants other to do unto you, love one another, as the Father love me, so, I love you continue in my love". In so many areas of our lives we find out that love is very important. For God so loved the world, he gave his only begotten Son, that those who believe in him will have internal life.

Prayer:

Lord God, God of Mercy and Love compassionate gracious loving God. plant your love in our heart and mind of those who call unto you in Spirit and in Truth, from the bottom of their hearts. Purified them with your Word, your Word is true. Let your love for us flow through us to those who do not know you our Lord and Savior, in your mighty Holy Name , we pray. Almighty God our everlasting Father let our prayer in your presence be as incense, the lifting up of our hands as the sacrifice. Give us grace to behold you, present in your Word, your commandment, and help us to know you in the lives of those around us. Stir up in us the flame fire of your love which binds in the heart of your Son Jesus Christ as he bore his passion, and let your light burn in us to eternal life in you to all the people of all ages in this world and the world to come. Help us to love our neighbor as we love ourselves, let the love that perfect all the bound of perfect peace prevails in our life, help us to serve you with our love, and follow you forever with love, continuously pouring your love upon our life, and let your love flow through us to those who has never know you in their own language. In your Mighty matchless Holy Name, we pray. Amen.

FEBRUARY 18TH

THE WORD OF GOD CLEANSES US –
LET THE WORD OF GOD CLEANSES YOU TODAY.

Today's Scripture Reading:

"Let the morning bring me Word of your unfailing love, for I have put my trust in you. Show me the way, I should go, for to you I lift up my Soul. Rescue me from my enemies, O Lord for I hide myself in you. Teach me to do your Will, for you are my God; may your good Spirit lead me on level ground."
(Psalm 143:8-10) NIV

All the believing Christians who are facing all forms of adversity and testing, and those who feel that they have reached the end of their endurance must exercise patient and hope in the Lord Jesus Christ, who never fail and who will never fail them. What our Lord wants all the believers to know is that they must be a hard working individual, as a Christian realizing that they must set example of a good citizen. Christians are not to be idle; the devil will soon find them something to do. The mind of man is a busy thing; It fit be not employed in doing good, it will be doing evil; the mind will engage in evil manners. This command was given to apostle Paul to be given to all the Christians it is the command of our Lord Himself, the authority of Christ should awe our minds to obedience, and his grace and goodness should help us. This command is for the whole church their behavior towards the disorderly persons. They must feed their hearts with prayers and supplications to the Lord. Believing Christians must boldly approach the thrown of grace with confidence; send their petition, scroll, and table their case and put all their problems in the hands of the Lord who has the power and authority to solve their problems and fulfilled their needs.

Prayer:

Lord Jesus Christ you are our rock of salvation. impart in our hearts and minds that whatever the enemies are throwing to us we can put it in your hands; you are the one O' Lord who can destroy the plan of the enemies in our lives. You have the power to destroy the work of the enemies who rise up against us, who does not want us to have peace of mind to serve you. We thank you our Lord for your love and faithfulness for us now and forever. Blessed are you, O Lord our God, the creator of all things in heaven and in this earth; bless us with your eternal peace as you have given rest to the weary, renew the strength of all who put their hope in you, bestow upon them the spirit of obedience, which is the ultimate key to serve you on this earth. Protect those who seek you faithfully from the bottom of their hearts, as you protected the children of Israel in the wilderness. Keep us save from any form of sin and sin nature and keep us from every form of evil, and every fear; for you O' Lord is our light of salvation, and the strength of our life. We give you the glory and honor now and forever. For your Holy and in your Holy Name , we pray. Amen.

FEBRUARY 19TH

THE WORD OF GOD CLEANSES US – LET THE WORD OF GOD CLEANSES YOU TODAY.

Today's Scripture Reading:

"If I have the gift of prophecy and can fathom all mysteries and all knowledge, and if I have a faith that can move mountains, but have not love, I am nothing. If I give all I possess to the poor and surrender my body to the flames, but have not love, I gain nothing. Love is patient, love is kind, it does not envy, it does not boast, it is not proud. It is not rude, it is not self-seeking, it is not easily angered, it keeps no record of wrongs. Love does not delight in evil but rejoices with the truth."
(1st Corinthians 13:2-6) NIV

Those whose lives are filled with religious activities, including speaking in tongues, prophecy and with great work of faith but have no love for one another are lacking in a knowledge of true spiritually. Jesus Christ in God the Father does not impress with religious works; without love it all adds up to nothing in his Holy eyes. Believers who are in Christ Jesus and filled with his love for people are in full recognition of him and are welcome in his kingdom.

Prayer:

Lord God Almighty, our gracious, merciful and mighty God, to you alone we put our trust, to you alone we put our hope, be our light in darkness, O' Lord, and in your infinite mercy keep us save in time of dangers. Let your full presence be known in our life, keep us save at all-time wherever we may be, control our thought, our mind, our hearts, look down from heaven our Lord Jesus Christ, hear our prayer and answer our prayers from your heavenly throne, and illuminate our hearts with the light of your knowledge and understanding of the Scripture. Lord builds us up with your unfailing love for you and for other people around us. Help us to love everyone and with your love help those who are in need of your love with great compassion. Lord Jesus Christ we love you because you love us first and came down from to us to redeemed us from our past, present, and future sins; have mercy upon us as we call unto you every day of our lives. In your infinite mercy, continue to shed your love in our hearts and mind every day of our life so that at the end we can live with you in heaven. In your mighty Holy Name, we pray. Amen.

FEBRUARY 20TH

THE WORD OF GOD CLEANSES US –
LET THE WORD OF GOD CLEANSES YOU TODAY.

Today's Scripture Reading:

"Love must be sincere. Hate what is evil; cling to what is good. Be devoted to one another in brotherly love. Honor one another above yourselves. Never be lacking in Zeal, but keep your spiritual fervor, serving the Lord. Be joyful in hope, patient in affliction, faithful in prayer. Share with God's people who are in need. Practice hospitality. Bless those who persecute you; bless and do not curse." (Romans 12:9-14) NIV

All the believing Christians who devoted in faith to Jesus Christ must be devoted to one another as brothers and sisters in Christ with a sincere, kindness and tender affections. We must be faithful in prayer means to present continuously, tense of a very strong word, it implies persistence, perseverance, and insistence in our prayers to the Lord. Scripture recognized that most believers would have struggle, not only in keeping the attitude of prayer, but also to spend real time in prayer. We are exhorted to be diligent and faithful in prayer since it is our access to God through Jesus Christ for a life of spiritual intimacy and this is the way whereby God advances his kingdom.

Prayer:

Lord Jesus Christ you are our great intercessor in heaven pray through us the prayer that cannot be uttered; shed your light upon us, pour out your spirit upon us, pour it out, rain your blessings upon us according to our needs. You alone know what we needed and the right time we needed it, you alone are the true God, the very God, the King of kings, the Lord of lords, the Light of this world, the true light that shine forever and no darkness can overcome it. Let our life glorified your Holy Name, let our life exalted your Holy Name and enhance your kingdom of light. Guide us when we are walking on the street O' Lord, keep watch on all the senior citizens walking slowly to cross the street in the day time, and guard them when they sleep in their homes, help them to sleep in peace and wake up in peace. Let them be able to know you and worship you, give their life to you before the last day of their lives in this universe. Protect all the senior citizens in Nursing home, and in their homes. In your mighty Holy Name, we pray. Amen.

FEBRUARY 21ST

THE WORD OF GOD CLEANSES US –
LET THE WORD OF GOD CLEANSES YOU TODAY.

Today's Scripture Reading:

"I pray that out of his glorious riches he may strengthen you with power through his Spirit in your inner being, so that Christ may dwell in your hearts through faith. And I pray that you, being rooted and established in love."
(Ephesians 3:16-17) NIV

It is an important and valuable prayer to have a believer's inner being strengthened by the Holy Spirit is to have our spirit energized with the life of Christ and to bring our soul, feelings, thoughts and purposes more and more under Jesus' influence and under his direction in order that the Holy Spirit can manifest his power through believer, or us in greater measure. The purpose of this strengthening is three fold: (a) Jesus Christ will establish his full presence in our hearts; (b) We as the children of God through Jesus Christ his Son may be rooted and established in the revelation of Christ's love for us, together with all the saints with full comprehension; (c) As believers of Jesus Christ, we must be filled with all the fullness of God to the point that God's presence will so fill us that we will reflect from our innermost being the character and stature that belongs to the Lord Jesus Christ our Savior and redeemer King.

Prayer:

Lord God Almighty Father, Son and the Holy Spirit in your mercy fill us with the fullness of your Son Jesus Christ, that we may be able to live with him forever doing what is pleasing in his sight. Bless us with your full presence from this earth to heaven that we may be able to witness of your love to all the people in the whole world, that the Gospel of God will reach the ends of the earth, under the earth, and utmost part of the earth; that the people in the world will know the power of the Holy Spirit, the giver of life. Almighty God, you are the fountain of wisdom, you know all our necessary things that we needed before we ask. You said that before we kneel down, you have already answered our prayers. In your mercy have compassion. We pray to you about our infirmities, even those things that are unworthy, and worthless, that we ask for in prayer blindly, for the sake of your only begotten Son Jesus Christ our Lord, fulfill our prayer request if you know that what we ask for in prayer is good for us, and especially in according to your will. In Jesus Christ's Holy Name, we pray who lives and reigns with you with the power of the Holy Spirit, forever one God. In your Holy Name, we pray. Amen.

FEBRUARY 22ND

THE WORD OF GOD CLEANSES US –
LET THE WORD OF GOD CLEANSES YOU TODAY.

Today's Scripture Reading:

"Let love and faithfulness never leave you; bind them around your neck, write them on the tablet of your heart. Then you will win favor and a good Name in the sight of God and man."
(Proverbs 3:3-4) NIV

Our trusting in the Lord Jesus Christ our whole heart is the opposite of doubting the Lord and doubting his Word. Trust is the fundamental principle to our relationship with our Lord and Savior and this trust is based on the promise that our Lord is trustworthy and always trustworthy. As children of God, we can be assured that our heavenly Father loves us and will faithfully care for our needs; his compassion and his faithfulness never fail and will never change. Our Lord guides us rightly, he give us grace to be able to abound in all the areas of our lives, and most assuredly he keep his promises in the most difficult times of our lives, we can commit our ways to the hands of our Lord, and trust him to work and do what is justified on our behalf in any circumstances of this life.

Prayer:

Lord Jesus Christ, our Lord and Savior, compassionate gracious loving God, you are the Holy one of Israel the seed of David, the incarnate Son of God - we loved you with our whole heart, and abide in your Word, because your Word is true. O' Lord our God, you have taught us to keep all your word and your commandments which is the sign of our love for you, and you told us to love our neighbor as we love ourselves; grant us the grace and mercy of the Holy Spirit, we will be focus, with all our hearts and minds, so that we may be united with all the believers and nonbeliever of this world with pure affection and love through Jesus Christ our Lord and Savior. Let your love and faithfulness abide with us now and forever. Bind your Word on our neck, write it on our heart and put it on our food, so that it will strengthened us and help us to grow in wisdom, knowledge and understanding of you and of the Holy Scripture, let your word grow in our heart, with reflection that those who sees us will know that we belongs to you spirit, Soul and body forever. Let your glory shine upon us, protect us and bless us with God's favor from above, in your Holy Name , we pray. Make our heart be the temple of the Holy Spirit where your glory shines forever. Amen.

FEBRUARY 23ᴿᴰ

THE WORD OF GOD CLEANSES US – LET THE WORD OF GOD CLEANSES YOU TODAY.

Today's Scripture Reading:

*"And so we know and rely on the love God has for us.
God is love. Whoever lives in love lives in God, and God in him. In
this way, love is made complete among us so that we will have
confidence on the day of judgment, because in this world we are
like him."*
(1st John 4:16-17) NIV

God love us we who have experienced God's love in our life through the forgiveness of our sins must be able to help others who lack the love of God. If we remain in Jesus Christ, we automatically have fellowship with the Father; sincerely endeavor to obey his commands and we will also be able to separate ourselves from the spirit of the world. We will remain in the truth and love other people around us. moreover, we will have confidence that Jesus Christ life and love are in us, we are in him, as he is in the Father. We will not be condemned on the day of judgment because we have the assurance of salvation. Love is the very nature of God; we have to love one another, because the blood of Jesus Christ cleanses us from any unrighteousness.

Prayer:

Jesus Christ the Lamb of God, worthy is your Name from this earth to heaven you are the only one whose glory fills the skies; Jesus you are the truth, and the only light of this world. Create in us a new heart, anew mind, a new soul that will be filled with your love. Our merciful and mighty God, from you all the goodness flows, grant that we may abide in you and in your word by your command, that we may be able to think about those good things that will exalted your Holy Name, and spread the Gospel to the end of the earth. Let your glory be revealed among all the nations in this world, so that the church and all the believers will persevere with steadfast faith in the proclamation of your Holy Name and the witnessing of the Gospel more and more. By your merciful and mighty guardians show people of this earth the way of salvation. Love for you and love for everyone around us. Fill us with the love of God that surpasses all understanding, and make us to know the true love that will set us free. Bless us with your unfailing infinite love and great compassion forever and forever, in your Holy Name, we pray. Amen.

FEBRUARY 24TH

THE WORD OF GOD CLEANSES US – LET THE WORD OF GOD CLEANSES YOU TODAY.

Today's Scripture Reading:

"If anyone says, I love God, yet hates his brother, he is a liar.
For anyone who does not love his brother, whom he has
seen, cannot love God, whom he has not seen. And he has given
us this command: Whoever loves God must also love his brother."
(1st John 4:20-21) NIV

The Love of God cleanses us from any unrighteousness, if we love our brother, and do good to our brother, we have demonstrated the love of God in our heart, if we love our neighbor, do good to our neighbor the love of God is in us. If it is possible to say, you love God, if you do not love your brother. God Almighty, Father Son and Holy Spirit shed his love upon us in our heart through our Lord Jesus Christ's redemptive work of salvation; that love flows through us to other people around us and to the entire people in the world, and in everything we do, and where we go. Love for others is the second commandment Christian's believer's love; if it is accompanied by love for God which is the greatest commandment as well as obedience to Christ commands prove that we have the love of God in us.

Prayer:

Our Lord Jesus Christ, you loved us so much, you came down from heaven to seek that which was lost, and save the sinners, you pardon and purchased us with your precious blood on the Calvary. Help us to love one another, to love you as we ought to love you and to love our neighbor as ourselves throughout our journey on this earth. Baptize us with your unending love and with the power of the Holy Spirit.

Lord Jesus Christ, we pray that by your grace and mercy you will always follow us, and make us continually to be a good servant, a faithful servant in all the area of our service to you, that we may be able to sing praises to your Holy Name at the end that we have finish the race, and we have completed the work that you assigned for us on this earth. We pray that you will continue to call sinners and the lost unto you, and the people of all other religions, including the Idol worshipers and Pagans. Bless us with everything that we need to be able to call sinners and the lost to you, and that you will help us to live a glorifying live that will be pleasing in your sight. Amen.

FEBRUARY 25TH

THE WORD OF GOD CLEANSES US –
LET THE WORD OF GOD CLEANSES YOU TODAY.

Today's Scripture Reading:

"However, as it is written: No eye has seen, no ear has heard, no mind has conceived what God has prepared for those who love him; but God has revealed it to us by his Spirit. The Spirit searches all things, even the deep things of God."
(1st Corinthians 2:9-10) NIV

Nobody knows the Spirit of except God himself. The things that God has prepared for those who love him can be understood by believers through the power of the Holy Spirit's revelation and illumination. The more the believers read and study the Scriptures, the more the Holy Spirit illuminates their understanding of the truth of the Gospel. Through the Spirit what the believer reads is made clear, even if he or she lacks the knowledge, the Spirit will make it clear. The Holy Spirit also gives to every faithful believer a strong assurance of the divine knowledge of the origin of the Scripture. Our Lord Said: "But when he, the Spirit of truth, comes, he will guide you into all truth. He will not speak on his own; he will speak only what he hears, and he will tell you what is yet to come," (John 16:13). All believing Christians must abide with the teaching and the power of the Holy Spirit in order to grow in the Lord.

Prayer

Lord God Almighty let the Spirit of Truth make plain to us what is hidden in our life that we need to know. Let the Spirit of Truth teach us all the truth that we need to know that will help us love you more and more, and love ourselves as well as love our neighbor. You are always ready to hear our prayers Lord; we pray that in your mercy, with your infinite love, you will continue to listen to our prayers and answer our prayers, without you we are nothing. Let your Holy hand hold us tight, and let your merciful eyes watch us grow. Pour down upon us the abundance of your mercy, forgiving us those things whereby our conscience is afraid, and giving us those good things which we are not worthy to ask, but through your love, the work of redemption of our Lord Jesus Christ you gave us eternal life resurrection of the body and life everlasting. We meditate on your goodness, at all-times our Lord; you are the biggest giver - you give yourself to us, so that we may live and worship you, love you, and have strong faith in you throughout our life on earth. Let the Spirit of Truth, lead and guide us into all truth throughout our life on this Universe with your Holy Name, a Name above all Names, we pray. Amen.

FEBRUARY 26TH

THE WORD OF GOD CLEANSES US –
LET THE WORD OF GOD CLEANSES YOU TODAY.

Today's Scripture Reading:

"How great is the love the Father has lavished on us, that we should be called children of God! And that is what we are! The reason the world does not know us is that it did not know him." (1st John 3:1) NIV

God is our heavenly Father and, we are his children is one of the greatest revelations in the New Testament. Being a child of God, adopted in Christ as his very own is a high honor and privilege of our salvation. Being a child of God is the basis for our faith and the basis for our trust in God; and our hope of glory for the future to come. As God's children, we are heirs of God and joint heir with Jesus Christ. God the Father wants us to be increasingly made aware through the power of the Holy Spirit which is the "Spirit of Sonship" that we are God's children. The Spirit produces the cry "Abba Father" in our hearts and gives us the desire to be led by the Spirit. Being a child of God is the basis for our discipline by the Father and also the basis for the reason we live to please him and do what is pleasing in his sight.

Prayer:

God the Father, Son and Holy Spirit ever one God. We pray that you make everyone that believes in you, your children. Make it your ultimate goal in making all the Christian believers your children, so that you can save them forever into your Holy hands. Conform us to the likeness of your one and only Son whom his glory will forever we share. Lord Jesus Christ, our Lord and Savior, you declare to us your almighty power by showing mercy and sympathizing with us; mercifully grant unto us a measure your grace, that we may obtain your promises, most especially that we may be made a partakers of your heavenly treasure and inheritance; through our Lord Jesus Christ, who live and reign with you and the Holy Spirit, forever one God. Let the people of this world see the great things you have done in our lives and turn to you, let them give their life to you faithfully and sincerely, Let them know that you are Lord there is no other, let those who are suffering from alcohol, drug, and any form of addiction forsake their addicted habit and turn to you, in order that you may be able to heal them, you are the great healer, all power belongs to you our Lord. In your Holy Name, we pray. Amen.

FEBRUARY 27ᵀᴴ

THE WORD OF GOD CLEANSES US – LET THE WORD OF GOD CLEANSES YOU TODAY.

Today's Scripture Reading:

"For everyone born of God overcomes the world
This is the victory that has overcome the world,
even our faith. Who is it that overcomes the world?
Only he who believes that Jesus is the Son of God."
(1st John 5: 4-5) NIV

This is the one who came by water and blood - Jesus Christ our Lord. He did not come by water only, but by water and by blood. And it is the spirit who testifies because the spirit is the truth. The faith that overcomes the world is a faith that sees eternal realities, that experiences God's Power and loves Jesus Christ to such an extent that the world's sinful pleasures, secular values, ungodly ways and selfish materialism not only lose their attraction for believers but also looked with aversion and grief. Water and blood may probably refer to Christ baptism at the beginning of his ministry and to his death on the cross. Jesus Christ death as the God-man is thereby made fully the atonement for our sins; the Spirit of God bears witness to this truth. We share in the nature of Jesus Christ because we are born of him, who loved us and died for us on the cross; so that we can overcome the world of sin and sin nature.

Prayer:

Lord God Almighty, God of compassion, God of Mercy, The Merciful and Mighty God who dwells above the heavens; Father Son and the Holy Spirit forever one God; , we pray that you sanctify all the believing Christians with your power, Mercy and Love. Pour out your Holy Spirit upon us; so that we can be born of God the Father in order to overcome the world of sin and claim the victory for you by faith, hear our prayers and answer our prayers O Lord, you are the one who can save us. Lord Jesus Christ our gracious master and our Savior, you are a great God above all gods, you give unto us the increase of faith, you increase our blessed hope, and love; that we may obtain your promises, help us and make us to love which you command us to do, help us to be able to grow in grace and grow in your sanctification every day of our lives. Help us to get closer and closer to you, and be useful for you in all the area of the work of the Gospel. Help us to proclaim your Holy Name and help us to walk with you from this earth to heaven. Light up our life, so that we may be able to discern between the spirit of truth and the spirit of error; you are our great shepherd, do not let us stray away from you. Lift us up in all the areas of our life. In your mighty, matchless Holy Name, we pray. Amen.

FEBRUARY 28ᵀᴴ

THE WORD OF GOD CLEANSES US –
LET THE WORD OF GOD CLEANSES YOU TODAY.

Today's Scripture Reading:

"Above all, love each other deeply, because love covers over multitude of sins. Offer hospitality to one another without grumbling. Each one should use whatever gift he has received to serve others, faithfully administering God's grace in its various forms." (1st Peter 4:8-10) NIV

The Scripture is telling us to be able to love one another deeply, from our hearts. We must be concern for other people's suffering and find any way possibly to help them. Believers must be hospitable and kind, tender hearted to those in need; to serve other believers through the use of spiritual gifts given to us by the Holy Spirit. We must use the Spirit of Prayer that the Spirit of the Lord gave us to pray for those who are sick in the hospital and at home. We must use the Spirit of prayer to pray for those who lost their jobs, or the loss of their loved ones. Believers must use the Spirit of prayer to pray for all those who are in distress, weak, those who are in bondage of so many things such as alcohol, drug, and addiction of many things in their life. Believers must use all the gift of the Holy Spirit to enhance the work of the Lord on this earth such as preaching the Gospel, teach, witnessing in so many ways that will bring sinners and the lost to his Holy hands.

Prayer:

Lord Jesus Christ our Lord and our Savior, show all those who believe in you your ways O' Merciful and mighty God, teach us your ways with the power of the Holy Spirit lead those who put their trust in you into your truth, your word is true, teach us the truth of your word; you are God of our salvation in you we know the truth and the truth set us free throughout our lives. Do not let your great compassion fail upon us. Sanctify us with your word, your word is true; O Lord do not let us put our mind on worldly things, but to fix our mind on heavenly things, help us to look into what is permanent, not what is temporary, not things that is passing away, help us to cleave to those things that shall abide and endure forever, through the love of Christ our Savior. Stretch your Holy hands and bless us abundantly, immeasurable in all the areas of our lives. Your love for us is from everlasting to everlasting forgiving us all our sins, you are the only one that we offended, and you are the only one that offered us forgiveness of our sins. Remember your children O' Lord according to your loving kindness and your goodness for the people in the world, turn them to know you and worship you, in the Spirit of Holiness so that our world will be more peaceful in your Holy Name, we pray. Amen.

FEBRUARY 29TH

THE WORD OF GOD CLEANSES US –
LET THE WORD OF GOD CLEANSES YOU TODAY.

Today's Scripture Reading:

*"This is the confidence we have in approaching God:
that if we ask anything according to his will, he hears us.
And if we know that he hears us - whatever we ask - we know
that we have what we asked of him." (1st John 5:14-15) NIV*

Believing Christians must pray according to the will of God. Our prayers in our lives it must be presented to God in submission and with confidence according to the will of Jesus Christ as it is revealed in the Scripture, by the Holy Spirit. We as the children of God, adopted by Christ Jesus, we know God's will for our lives in many instances, and in many circumstances because it is revealed in the Scripture that the Holy Bible that we read day and night. The will of God becomes clear only as we earnestly are seeking his face and his Will. Once we know his will about any given issue, then we can ask in confidence and with faith. When we do this, we know that Jesus Christ hears us and that his purposes for us will be accomplished. Obedience to the command of Jesus Christ and doing what is pleasing in his sight are some of the indispensable conditions in order to receive what we ask for in prayer. Believers must be confidently approaching the throne of grace, in order to receive mercy and for the grace of God from the Father to abound in all areas of our lives. The sword of the Spirit is the Word of God with our prayer, the Holy Spirit uses the Word of God which cleanses us from any unrighteousness. We must pray without ceasing until we get answer to our prayers. Our Lord and Savior gave us the parable of importunity prayers in the Holy Scripture we have you use the example of it. Jesus Christ our Lord and Savior is the only one that listens to prayer and answer prayers.

Prayer:

Lord God Merciful and Mighty God hear our prayers and in your infinite mercy answer our prayers. You said ask and you shall be given; answer all our prayers if what we asked is good for us, give it to us our Lord. You said knock on the door, the door is going to open; Lord Jesus Christ, we pray that you open all the great doors of our blessings that the enemies closed because our enemies did not want the children of God to receive the blessings of God. Lord Jesus Christ you said seek, you shall find. We seek your face in everything that we are doing every day of our life, direct, control, provide and make it happen according to your will, and mercy. Rain down all what can make us to serve you on this earth with joy, rain down financial blessing in so many areas of our lives, rain down spiritual blessing through the baptism of the Holy Spirit, rain down your great wisdom, knowledge and understanding of the Scripture and your Word to help us to get closer and closer to you, to be able to be useful to you, and to be able to take the Gospel to the ends of the earth with your glory, in your glory and by your glory so that your Holy Name will be exalted higher and higher, more than ever before in the history of this earth. God the Father Almighty Most

Merciful and Mighty God in Jesus Christ's great Holy Name, we pray. Amen.

145

DAILY REFLECTION NOTES

MARCH

MARCH 1ST

THE WORD OF GOD CLEANSES US –
LET THE WORD OF GOD CLEANSES YOU TODAY.

Today's Scripture Reading

"In fact, everyone who wants to live a godly life in Christ Jesus will be persecuted, while evil men and impostors will go from bad to worse, deceiving and being deceived. But as for you, continue in what you have learned and have become convinced of, because you know those from whom you learned it, and how from infancy you have known the Holy Scriptures, which are able to make you wise for salvation through faith in Jesus Christ." (2nd Timothy 3:12-15) NIV

Persecution of Christians comes in so many ways, physically and spiritually body Soul and Spirit; but our Lord and Savior is always there to deliver us. persecution comes in one form or another is the inevitable for those who want to live a godly life in Jesus Christ. Believer's loyalty to Jesus Christ, his truth, and his righteous standards involves a constant determination not to compromise our faith or give in to the deluge of voices calling us to conform to the world and to lay aside the Word of truth. Because of believer's godly standards, the faithful will be deprived of privilege and they will be ridiculed; they will experience grief at seeing godliness rejected by the majority of the people of this world. Believing Christians should be happy that we suffered persecution because of our commitment to live in a godly manner, and we have stood firmly for Jesus Christ and his redemptive work of salvation.

Prayer:

God the Father Almighty, compassionate, gracious loving God, Jesus Christ his only Son Holy Spirit forever one God, you blessed us washed us clean by the power of your Holy Spirit, God of mercy come quickly to help us who are going through many temptations and diverse troubles, Lord Jesus you know the weakness of all of us, and each of us, help us to seek you and find your mighty power to save souls through Jesus Christ your one and only begotten Son; who lives and reign with you and the Holy Spirit the giver of life who proceed from the Father and the Son, one God, now and forever, O' Lord our God, we lift up our soul to you our God, we put our trust in you, let us not be put to shame, let all those who believe in you, rejoice in you. Do not let those who put their trust in you be put to shame, do not let our enemies triumph over us, do not let them continue laughing and rejoicing of their evil work against your children. Let all the evil doer be disappointed in all their work against your children prosper. Lord Jesus Christ let them know that there is no power but the power of God. We love you; we worship you, and we give you praises and thankfullness forever. Amen.

MARCH 2ND

THE WORD OF GOD CLEANSES US –
LET THE WORD OF GOD CLEANSES YOU TODAY.

Today's Scripture Reading:

"Greater love has no one than this that he lay down his life for his friends. You are my friends if you do what I command. I no longer call you servants, because a servant does not know his master's business. Instead, I have called you friends, for everything that I learned from my Father I have made known to you."
(John 15: 13-15) NIV

Jesus Christ our Lord and Savior calls us to a life of holiness, intimacy and personal devoted love that will follow his commandments. He gave his life for us, he lay it down because of his love for us. He calls us his friends because he wants to have intimate relationship and personal relationship with us. Christ Jesus does not want to call us servants because we are more than a servant on his eye; instead, he wants to call us his friend because he blessed us with his Spirit. The Spirit of Jesus Christ made us to be one in Jesus Christ, because Christ dwells in our heart, and live his Holy life through us. The Holy Spirit made known to believers everything of God and Jesus Christ. The Spirit of Christ is our teacher, counselor, comforter, comforting us in all the areas of our lives.

Prayer:

Our heavenly Father, you sent your only begotten Son into this universe; to come and redeemed us from our sins, and save us from the bondage of oppression, and from the dominion of darkness, we entrusted our life into your care. Help us to remember that we are all your children, and to continue to love you to the desires of your heart, how you want us to live this earth for your glory and purpose, help us to attain to that full stature that you intended for us to live in order to give your eternal kingdom and we eternally live with you forever. Lord Jesus Christ we love you and pray that you continue to dwell in us forever, and you will dwell in the heart of all those who believe in you and we thank you that you made us your friend, you call us friend. Lord Jesus brings us close to you and pray for us the prayer that cannot be uttered. Continue to pour out your Spirit upon us as , we pray to you, bless us abundantly, exceedingly, protect us, guide us, and heal all our diseases, knowing and unknown. You are our divine deliverer, deliver us from any trouble, and problems and keep us save for your glory. In Jesus' marvelous, great and Holy Name, we pray. Amen.

MARCH 3RD

THE WORD OF GOD CLEANSES US –
LET THE WORD OF GOD CLEANSES YOU TODAY.

Today's Scripture Reading:

"Can a mother forget the baby of her breast and have no compassion on the child she has borne? Though she may forget, I will not forget you! see, I have engraved you on the palms of my hands; your walls are ever before me."
(Isaiah 49:15-16) NIV

God the Father, God the Son and God the Holy Spirit was telling all the believing Christians who are going through problems, afflictions, persecutions, adversity, or maybe they felt that God forsake them. God's response in this Scripture gives them divine assurance to any believer going through trial times. Our Lord said that his love for us is greater than the natural affection of a loving mother for her children; it is, therefore, unthinkable that our Lord will forget us; especially in our times of despair, grief, and troubles. Christ compassion for us will never fail, regardless of life's circumstances; he watches over us with great tenderness and love, and we may rest in the conviction that Christ will never leave us, nor forsake us. The evidence and assurance of God's great love is that he has engraved us on the palms of his own hands, so that he can never forget us; the scars of nails in his hands are always before his eye as a reminder of the great love he has showered on us and his desire to care for us.

Prayer:

Most Holy, and most gracious God, by you we obtain knowledge and wisdom to the point that we can live in this world for the glory of your Holy Name. We praise you with all our hearts for everything that you bless us with, you provide for our food, the crops yield more and more so that we may eat and also give to others who have problems with their land and the crop did not comes out; but you increase and bless our ground and the gathering of its fruits, and for all the other blessings of your merciful providence that you bestowed upon all the people in all the nations of this earth. Lord Jesus Christ we give you thanks O' Lord, you are worthy to be praise from now to eternity, and we give you thanks and all glory for everything that you have gone through us in order to save us. we give you thanks and honor for your hands of nails; you are worthy of all our praises and thankfulness. Create us with yourselves so that we may continue to love you forever with our heart, our mind, and our soul forever. In Jesus' great, mighty, and Holy Name, we pray. Amen.

MARCH 4ᵀᴴ

THE WORD OF GOD CLEANSES US –
LET THE WORD OF GOD CLEANSES YOU TODAY.

Today's Scripture Reading:

"May the Lord direct your hearts into God's love and Christ's perseverance. In the Name of the Lord Jesus Christ, we command you, brothers, to keep away from every brother who is idle and does not live according to the teaching you received from us."
(2nd Thessalonians 3:5) NIV

The Spirit of the Lord Jesus Christ is great and mighty; he is the one directing our hearts into God's love and Jesus Christ perseverance. Without the Spirit, the Holy Spirit of God directing, controlling, guiding, leading, we believers of Jesus Christ will not be able to live a Christian life. The Spirit of the Lord takes total control when , we pray earnestly. We are sure that God will protect us in all the areas of our life, and he will strengthen us in time of any temptation that might assail us as well as protect us from the powerful forces of evil. Those who were living idle lives were the people who were loafing and unwilling to work. They practice laziness and they take advantage of the church's generosity, because they were receiving support from the brothers and sisters in the congregation. Apostle Paul says that people like that must be disciplined by keeping them away from and not to be associated with other people in the Church. Help must be given to those who are really in need in the congregation.

Prayer:

Lord God Almighty most gracious, most compassionate loving God, full of truth and upright in mercy, you alone can turn sinners to you; you alone can turn those who have the spirit of laziness among us to a dedicated, hardworking people. O' Lord guide our humble spirit in all we do and the righteous to the right way. Lord Jesus, teach us your way to the lowly and weak. You bless the poor, and the hunger with good food. Your goodness fills all the people on earth. You give rain to the just and unjust; you feed the wicked, and your sun shines to the just and to the unjust. You continually correct, and turn evil into a great good. There is no one like you, our Lord. Lord, Jesus Christ, bless us with the spirit of discernment in order to be able to discern and know those who are really in need of the church, and help them. Those who unwilling to work for their daily bread, wash them clean from laziness and any unrighteousness, so that they can be used for their family, the work of the ministry, and for your kingdom. In Jesus' great and Mighty, Holy Name, we pray. Amen.

MARCH 5TH

THE WORD OF GOD CLEANSES US –
LET THE WORD OF GOD CLEANSES YOU TODAY.

Today's Scripture Reading:

"We love because he first loved us" (1st John 4:19) NIV

Jesus Christ showed his love to us - the Scripture says " For God so loved the world that he gave his one and only Son, that whoever believes in him shall not perish but have eternal life" John 3:16 God's love is so wide enough to embrace all the people on earth. God gave his Son as an offering for our past, present and future sins on the cross. Christ showed his love to us first, the atonement of Jesus Christ proceeds from the loving heart of God the Father. It was not forced on him; he laid down his life so that we may have life, and have it abundantly. He does not want anyone to perish, he wants them to come to the knowledge of repentance and pray for forgiveness which is only in him. All the Christian believers must love Jesus Christ because he gave his life for us, and those of us that we believes in him must not live for ourselves, we must live for him forever. Jesus Christ is the mediator of a new covenant, and our advocate of a new covenant, his love for us is infinite.

Prayer:

Lord Jesus Christ we give you praises and thankfulness for coming down from heaven and give your life for us, so that we may live and worship you Hallelujah. Lord Jesus make us alive in you, make us one in you as you and Father are one, bless us with a new heart, a new Spirit, and a New Soul that will love you to eternity from this earth. Lord Jesus Christ, you are tempted in every way as we are, and did not sin, who by your grace we are able to get victory of all the work of evil, and who by your Son Jesus Christ we are no longer living a selfish life, but we live for you who died and gave his live for us on the cross. We give you our unceasing praises and worship you with a joyful spirit joining our voices with the Angels and archangels and with the entire heavenly host who forever sing praises to your Holy Name and proclaim the glory of your Holy Name on earth. You are worthy O' Lord of our praises and adoration, the fruits of our lips is giving praises to your Holy Name forever. In Jesus' great Holy Name, we pray. Amen.

MARCH 6TH

THE WORD OF GOD CLEANSES US –
LET THE WORD OF GOD CLEANSES YOU TODAY.

Today's Scripture Reading:

"Husbands, love your wives, just as Christ loved the church and gave himself up for her to make her Holy, cleansing her by the washing with water through the Word."
(Ephesians 5:25-26) NIV

God our Father gave the husband responsibility as the head of the wife. He must be able to make a provision for the family's welfare, both spiritually by introducing them to the Word of God; going to church on Sundays, and being active in Church. He must be able to care for his family's domestic needs such as food, clothing, education, and shelter. Husbands must be love, protect, and maintain a deeper interest in his wife and his entire family's welfare. In the same way that our Lord Jesus Christ loved the Church and gave himself to her without blemish, with the Word and water, and with His precious blood. Husbands must be faithful to their wife and to their children. They must live in good harmony with happiness at all times; this is Christ's command concerning husbands and wives.

Prayer:

Lord God Almighty, we give you humble thanks because you have graciously pleased to deliver us from evil, and keep us safe from any danger. Keep all the men and women, husband and wives from sickness, and all diseases that are plaguing people in this world. Let them give their lives to you faithfully and sincerely for the glory of your Holy Name. You are our redeemer King. Lord Jesus Christ; open the heart and minds of husbands and wives, let their marriage be a union. They must live together in unity both in body and in the Spirit. Lord Jesus Christ drive away temptation from them, let them live together with a faithful strong faith, and trust. Keep them safe in your Holy hands; let them be able to abide in you forever and forever. We pray that the peace of our Lord and Savior Jesus Christ, the one only and only true Son of God, which surpasses all understanding, his great wisdom and mercy, keep our hearts and minds, soul, spirit and body in the knowledge and understanding love of Jesus Christ. The wisdom of God and the power of God, the Holy Spirit, be with all men and women of all ages who remain in Christ Jesus forever. In Jesus Christ's great and Holy Name, we pray. Amen.

MARCH 7TH

THE WORD OF GOD CLEANSES US – LET THE WORD OF GOD CLEANSES YOU TODAY.

Today's Scripture Reading:

"Since you are precious and honored in my sight, and because I love you, I will give men in exchange for you, and people in exchange for your life. Do not be afraid, for I am with you; I will bring your children from the East and gather you from the West."
(Isaiah 43:4-5) NIV

God the Father Almighty expresses his love for the children of Israel and the benefit of that love. All the blessings for the children of Israel then, apply even more to all those who are God's children today through faith in Jesus Christ. God has created and has redeemed believers we belong to him, and he knows every one that belongs to him by their names. When we pass through troubles and afflictions, we will not be destroyed, for he loved us, and he is with us. All the believing Christians are precious and honored in the sight of God. Jesus Christ has the power and authority over any circumstances we might be going through; he gave us a new life.

Prayer:

Lord Jesus Christ you are our deliverer in any troubles and afflictions. O' Lord you created all the people in this world in your image; we give you the wonderful diversity of people in the world, and races and cultures in this world. Enrich our lives by ever increasing our fellowship, and show us your presence in those who differ most from us, until our knowledge of your love is made perfect in our love for all our children, through our Lord and Savior. We give you praise and thankfulness for your unfailing, and steadfast love for those who belongs to you; those who gave their life to you faithfully and sincerely. You are our ever living Savior, eternal life is in you, and you promise all those who belongs to you with an infinite love for us thank you our Lord for your love and compassion; now and forever. In Jesus Holy Name, we pray. Amen.

MARCH 8ᵀᴴ

THE WORD OF GOD CLEANSES US –
LET THE WORD OF GOD CLEANSES YOU TODAY.

Today's Scripture Reading:

"The Lord replied, 'My presence will go with you, I will give you rest.' And the Lord said to Moses, 'I will do the very thing you have asked, because I am pleased with you and I know you by Name,' "
(Exodus 33:14, 17) NIV

All God's children should constantly and fervently pray to know God's ways, his heart, purpose, wisdom, his Holy principles, and even his suffering; by this prayer we will come to know God the Father, Son and the Holy Spirit himself better and better every day. For example: God answered Moses' prayer because he respected Moses, and considered him a friend, and moreover, he was pleased with him, because Moses was doing what is pleasing in his sight. He consulted the Lord before he did anything, or moved the Israelites from place-to-place. Moses found favor in the eyes of God, while Aaron and the nation of Israel disobeyed God, Moses remained loyal to the Lord and mediated between the Lord and the children of Israel. All believing Christians that know the Lord and are loyal to the Lord enjoyed the same preference and favor in the eyes of the Lord and forever.

Prayer:

Lord Jesus Christ helps us to live a life that honors you, loyal to you and pleasing in your sight. Bless us with favor in everything we do and help us to serve you faithfully, sincerely so that at the end eternal life will be ours forever, we will live with you in heaven with love for God the Father with the Holy Spirit the giver of life Lord God Almighty always let your Fatherly care reached to the uttermost parts of the earth: We humbly beseech you graciously to behold and bless those who we love, grant that they may draw nearer and nearer unto you through the power of the Holy Spirit, and in the fellowship of all the saints in heaven and in this earth. Help us to bear more and more fruits into your kingdom. Strengthens us in all the areas where we are weak and help us to walk with you throughout our lives to heaven. In the honor of your Holy Name, we pray. Amen.

MARCH 9TH

THE WORD OF GOD CLEANSES US –
LET THE WORD OF GOD CLEANSES YOU TODAY.

Today's Scripture Reading:

"Therefore, since we have been justified through faith, we have peace with God through our Lord Jesus Christ, through whom we have gained access by faith into this grace in which we now stand. And rejoice in the hope of the glory of God."
(Romans 5:1-2) NIV

Since we have been justified, some of the benefits of justification through faith are mentioned here: peace with God through our Lord and Savior, grace, hope assurance, perseverance, the love of God, the gift of the Holy Spirit, Salvation from the wrath of God, the ministry of reconciliation to God, our salvation by the life and the presence of Jesus Christ, and with the joy of God in our hearts. Believers have hope in our Lord and Savior which is a confidence from God concerning his promises. It is sure because it is based on the integrity of God's Word. Believers will experience the reality of hope because God is the God of hope, the object, and the assurance of our hope. Christ Jesus is our hope of glory, he is coming back to judge the dead and the living and all the eyes shall see him.

Prayer:

Lord Jesus Christ in you alone we put our trust and our hope, do not let our faith, our hope, and our trust in you shaky. Purify our mind, our hearts, let our hearts stay with you, let our mind focus on your unfailing love for us. O' blessed Lord; you ministered to all who came to you: Look with great compassion upon all who through addiction have lost their health and freedom. Restore to them the assurance of your unfailing mercy; remove from them the fears that beset them, strengthen them in the work of their recovery and to those who care for them, give patient, understanding and persevering love.

Let your full presence be known in our lives, let the people of this earth see you clearly through us, let them know that we belongs to you spirit, soul, and body forever, we worship you in Spirit and in truth forever, you are worthy to be praise; in your mighty Holy Name, we pray. Amen

MARCH 10TH

THE WORD OF GOD CLEANSES US –
LET THE WORD OF GOD CLEANSES YOU TODAY.

Today's Scripture Reading:

*"The Lord himself goes before you and will be with you he will
never leave you nor for sake you.
Do not be afraid; do not be discouraged."
(Deuteronomy 31:8) NIV*

The Lord God Almighty promised the children of Israel that he will not leave them, nor forsake them; he will be with them and they should not be discouraged. The same promise of God in the Old Testament also applied to the New Testament believers in Jesus Christ. This promise is to all who sincerely receive Christ as their Lord and Savior. Believers are assured that if they love God above all else and depend on him father than on any worldly material security, the Lord will never desert nor forsake them, but will be their helper in times of troubles and afflictions. Because of this promise, we must be strong and courageous, we must persevere in all trials. We must resist any form of temptation that they enemy wanted to throw on our path; and continue to be steadfast trusting in the Lord and fully obeying his commandments; he will go before us and make any crooked ways straight.

Prayer:

Lord Jesus Christ, you said that we should go and makes the disciples of all nations and you said that you will not leave us, nor forsake us; you will be with us till the end of the age. Lord Jesus Christ live your life through us and fulfill the great commission through us take the Gospel to the end of the earth through us under the earth through us, preach, teach, write the Gospel through us, witness the Gospel through us, use all those who believe in you in a mighty way so that your Holy Name will be exulted, the Gospel will reach the unreachable in their own language in all the remote areas of this world, perform your big miracle through us on this earth in a such a way that the Gospel will be spreading like wild fire, the wind of the Holy Spirit will be rushing into the hearts and minds of the people of this earth. They will live the life of God, love one another, wars and the rumors of war will be no more. Your Holy Name will be praise forever. Hear our prayers and answer our prayer O' Lord our God. In Jesus Christ's mighty Holy Name, we pray. Amen.

MARCH 11TH

THE WORD OF GOD CLEANSES US –
LET THE WORD OF GOD CLEANSES YOU TODAY.

Today's Scripture Reading:

"I have set the Lord always before me. Because he is at my right hand, I will not be shaken. Therefore my heart is glad and my body also will rest secure, because you will not abandon me to the grave, nor will you let your Holy One see decay. You have made known to me the path of life; you will fill me with joy in your presence, with eternal pleasures at your right hand."
(Psalm 16: 18-11) NIV

All believing Christians should seek the Lord and cherish him above all else, to include a maintaining of intimate fellowship with the Savior. Our Lord manifests himself to all those who love him with continual presence at his right hand; thus, he brings his love, guidance, reassurance, protection, resurrection, and eternal pleasures. A believer's prayer will help him or her to develop a personal relationship with Christ, and it will also give confidence in a future life with God with the certainty that will let him, or her, know that he will not abandon them in the grave. There is no death in the believer; it is a change of place, departed from, or absent from the body on earth and presence with the Lord. All believing

Christians should rejoice that Jesus Christ the Son of God has conquered the grave forever. He is the author of salvation.

Prayer:

Lord Jesus Christ, our Lord and our Savior, we praise you and have adored you. You are alive forevermore; you have defeated the enemy; you have conquered the grave. Victory is ours in you O' Lord. Your presence is like heaven to us our Lord. You are our deliverer. You let us know that in returning to you and putting all faith in you, that we can have rest and be saved, in quietness and in confidence shall be our strength and peace. We pray that you bless us with your full presence; bless us with everlasting salvation. That among all the changes and chances of this mortal life, bless us with your life our Lord; help us to worship you in spirit and in truth. Help us to forever be close to you and seek your face in everything that we do and say. Help us to abide in you and in your Word forever; always let your full presence be known in our lives. We pray that you will continue to fill us with your full presence because in your presence there is joy unspeakable, joy forever in your great and Holy Name, we pray. Amen.

MARCH 12TH

THE WORD OF GOD TRANSFORMS SOULS; LET THE WORD OF GOD BE YOUR TRANSFORMATION TODAY.

Today's Scripture Reading:

"The Lord is my light and my salvation whom shall I fear? The Lord is the strong hold of my life - of whom shall I be afraid? Though an army besiege me, even then will I be confident. One thing I ask of the Lord, this is what we seek: that we may dwell in the house of the Lord all the days of my life, to gaze upon the beauty of the Lord and to seek him in his Temple."
(Psalm 27: 1, 3-4) NIV

Believers that gave their life to the Lord should be able to live confidently in this life no matter what they were going through, they must seeks God's presence; it is the most important thing, most one thing to be treasured in the believer's life; and he prays for it with singleness of purpose: Our Lord Jesus Christ himself calls all the believers to this same purpose. We must seek his face. Those who seek his face, strive to dwell in God's Holy presence, are given the firm assurance that no matter what trials comes to them, the Lord will never forsake them, they have no reason to fear, God's goodness is reserved for them. Trusting in the Lord and being confident in his love and compassion, goodness are indispensable for persevering in faith.

Prayer:

Lord Jesus Christ, you are our light of salvation; Lord make us an instrument of your peace. Where there is hatred, let us sow love, where there is injury, pardon, where pardon is needed, where there is violence, help us to sow peace, where there is darkness, help us to sow light. Where there is sorrow help us to sow joy. Grant us that we may not fall into any temptation, and despair, help us to be able to give to the poor and the needy, to those in distress and to the homeless, as well as those who are sick around us. Restore unto us the joy of your salvation and do not take you Holy Spirit from us that leads us to the way everlasting. Lord Jesus Christ our Lord and our Savior, the true Son of God, we pray that your continuous presence will never cease. We pray that we that belong to you are blessed with immeasurable blessings of your presence which is heaven to us. If your presence is with us, who can beat us down, and who can destroy us, no one. Thank you, Lord Jesus, for your full presence in our lives now and forever. In Jesus Christ's only Name, we pray. Amen.

MARCH 13TH

THE WORD OF GOD TRANSFORMS SOULS; LET THE WORD OF GOD BE YOUR TRANSFORMATION TODAY.

Today's Scripture Reading:

"The righteous cry out, and the Lord hears them;
he delivers them from all their troubles.
The Lord is close to the broken hearted and
saves those who are crushed in spirit.
A righteous man may have many troubles,
but the Lord delivers him from them all;
he protects all his bones, not one of them
will be broken." (Psalm 34: 17-20) NIV

God almighty father of all mercies right from the Old Testament he promised blessings and prosperity for those who obeyed his command - yet alongside this promise is the reality that the righteous may have many troubles. Believers' beliefs, as well as living righteously for the Lord will not keep us from troubles and earthly trials, moreover, our commitment to the Trinity often brings testing and persecution that God has ordained that we must go through many hardships to enter his kingdom. When his purpose in permitting affliction is accomplished, he then delivers us from them either by direct supernatural intervention in this life, or by victorious death and transference to the life hereafter - eternity. Believers must be confident that our Lord and Savior answer his prayers and he is a deliverer, protector, provider, the great healer, the great physician, a problem solver, the compassionate gracious God.

Prayer:

God the Father Almighty, Jesus Christ his only son, our Lord and Savior, our redeemer King, the sustainer of all his creation; help us to get closer and closer to you every day of our lives. You have the power and authority and control to solve all our problems, to put stop to the work of the enemy in our lives honor and glorified your Holy Name. Almighty and merciful God grant us absolution and the remission of all our sins, true repentance, and amendment of life, and the grace and the consolation of your Holy Spirit; Lord Jesus Christ we call on to you our almighty God, to purify our consciences by your daily visitation to us, that when your Son our Lord shall come, we may find in him a mansion prepared for himself; through Jesus Christ our Lord and Savior. Direct us O' Lord, in all our doing with your most gracious favor, and further us with you continual help that in all our works we may continue to abide in you and at the end to glorify your name. Finally, help us to reach our goal which is everlasting life in heaven. In your great mighty, Holy Name, we pray. Amen.

MARCH 14TH

THE WORD OF GOD TRANSFORMS SOULS; LET THE WORD OF GOD BE YOUR TRANSFORMATION TODAY.

Today's Scripture Reading:

"Trust in the Lord and do good; dwell in the Lord and enjoy safe pasture. Delight yourself in the Lord and he will give you the desires of your heart. Commit your way to the Lord; trust in him and he will do this: He will make your righteousness shine like the dawn, the justice of your cause like the noonday sun. Be Still before the Lord and wait patiently for him."
(Psalm 37:3-7a) NIV

Believers in Jesus Christ should be able to take delight in the Lord and in his great abundant peace, blessing of good health, and well-being that he gives. Christian believers must be able to express God's genuine pleasure in what makes them smile and happy. King David, the writer of this scripture, is telling all those who believe in the Lord to delight themselves in the Lord, which means to desire and enjoy nearness of his presence and the truth and righteousness of his Word. We must know that those who delight themselves in the Lord, God gives them the desires of their hearts. God will always answer the cry of our hearts, and God will always answer the cry of our hearts if our heart's desire are in accordance with his will. When believers delight themselves in God and his Will, God himself places desires within our hearts that he then sets out to fulfill for his purpose for our life.

Prayer:

Lord Jesus Christ, bless us with a heart that will delight in your will, that will love you as we ought to love you help us and guide us so that the desires that you laid on our hearts, you will be able to fulfill it according to your desire and plans for our life. Lord Jesus Christ helps us to put all our trust in you, all our hope in you, and put all our live in your Holy hands. O' Lord our God, in you we are able to live a meekness and guided life, be our guide in the world of uncertainties by your grace and mercy, help us to confidently approach the throne of grace, pour on us the spirit of wisdom, knowledge and understanding in everything we are doing and everywhere we may be, lead us to the narrow path of life that we may see the light and forever staying in the light. Assist us in all our supplications and prayers and lead us to life everlasting. Shine your great glory upon us wherever we may be on this earth, help us to live with you from this earth to heaven. In your great, mighty, Holy Name, we pray. Amen

MARCH 15TH

THE WORD OF GOD TRANSFORMS SOULS; LET THE WORD OF GOD BE YOUR TRANSFORMATION TODAY.

Today's Scripture Reading:

"Why are you downcast, o my Soul? Why so disturbed within me? Put your hope in God, for we will yet praise him, my Savior, and my God. By day the Lord directs his love, at night his song is with me - a prayer to the God of my life." (Psalm 42: 5, 8) NIV

In you O' Lord we put our hope do not let us be ashamed. Those who thirst for God and yearn for a greater manifestation of his presence may experience delay. Yet the faithful believing Christians will continue thirsting for and seeking God. Our Lord and Savior Jesus Christ promises to bless those who hunger and thirst for righteousness rather than settle for less than his full blessings. In the midst of God's silence, we must continue to press onto know God and to experience a greater measure of the Holy spirit. Believers must not be despair, but they must put their hope in God and trust in his unfailing love. The Lord is always ready to help his people, straightened out their lives, forgive them their past, present and future sins. Christ is able to pardon all the sinners, revive their souls and make them alive in him.

Prayer:

Lord God Almighty Father, Son and the Holy Spirit wash us clean from any unrighteousness and clothe us with your righteousness do not let us be ashamed Lord Jesus Christ you are our Savior and our redeemer, bring us close to you every day of our lives. help us to know you and get near, to you direct your love to us wherever we may be on this earth. Lord Jesus Christ, pour out on all who believe in you, pour out your spirit on all who desire the Holy Spirit; the spirit of grace and supplication; deliver us when we draw near to you from our coldness of heart and from our wandering of minds, help us to be steadfast in thoughts and kindness affections we may worship you in spirit and in truth through our Lord and Savior. Now to God who is able to do more than what we expected, who is also strengthens us according to the Gospel and according to the proclamation of Jesus Christ, and according to the revelation of the mystery of God that was kept secret for all ages but is now revealed, and through the prophetic writings made known to all the Gentiles according to the command of the eternal God. In your great mighty Holy Name, we pray. Amen

MARCH 16TH

THE WORD OF GOD TRANSFORMS SOULS; LET THE WORD OF GOD BE YOUR TRANSFORMATION TODAY.

Today's Scripture Reading:

"Hear my cry, O God; listen to my prayer from the ends of the earth I call to you, I call as my heart grows faint; lead me to the rock that is higher than I. For you have been my refuge, a strong tower against the foe. I long to dwell in your tent forever and take refuge in the shelter of your wing."
(Psalm 61:1-4) NIV

Believing Christians were teaching and taught to forgive their enemies and pray for their enemy's salvation, the Scripture also says that, sometimes we need to pray for evil to cease and for justice to be done for the innocent. We should be vitally concerned for the victims of cruelty, oppression and evil. We must cry to the Lord on the afflictions of our enemies that is casting down our Souls, that our Soul should take refuge in the Lord, who has always been our refuge and our strong tower in time of trouble and against our enemies. We should open our hearts be strong and not to grow weary or faint, believers must be able to stand on the mighty rock of our Savior who is the leader, the director, and the controller of our lives. Our prayer is to constantly pray without ceasing to God who is the author and finisher of our faith.

Prayer:

Lord God Almighty you will always our mighty rock and our shelter; there is no one like you in all the Earth. Lord Jesus Christ help us to bring to reality the obedience of faith to the only wise God. God Almighty draw our hearts to you guide our minds, fill our imaginations, control our hearts and minds, our wills, that we may truthfully belong to you, and be able to dedicated unto the Lord spirit, soul and body use us, we pray and always to the glory and welfare of the people, help us in our daily work, in the office or at our home; give us grateful hearts, that we may appreciate all what you have done for us in our lives and what you are still doing and what you will still do in our lives. We bless you our Lord for given us our food at the right time to sustain our lives and to make our heart your throne. Deliver us from all the work of our enemies; turn them around from evil to good, and also from violence to peace. Destroy their wicked plans against us. Wash us clean from any unrighteousness and clothe us with your righteousness in your mighty Holy Name, we pray. Amen

MARCH 17TH

THE WORD OF GOD TRANSFORMS SOULS; LET THE WORD OF GOD BE YOUR TRANSFORMATION TODAY.

Today's Scripture Reading:

"My soul finds rest in God alone; my salvation comes from him. He alone is my rock and my salvation; he is my fortress, I will never be shaken." (Psalm 62:1-2) NIV

Our salvation according to the Scripture; expresses the fundamental truth by which every believing Christians must abide and should live on this earth; our salvation comes from only Jesus Christ no one else. Jesus Christ is the source of our salvation through his atonement blood on the cross. Therefore, in times adversity, afflictions and earthly trouble, or any opposition from the enemies, we should turn to the Lord as our rock of salvation and our fortress. he will never let us be shaken or lose hope in him. Christ is our ultimate refuge and our deliverer. All the believing Christians who trusts in the Lord, should be able to say: I never be shaken" they will not allow trouble, or suffering to shake their confidence in the Lord. he is the mighty rock of our salvation; they must commit themselves to him and earnestly praying and let him know in prayer what is in their heart, in other words; pour out the desires of their heart to him.

Prayer:

Lord Jesus Christ our Lord and our Savior in your mercy and love help us to know you more and more with the power of your Holy-spirit. Be at the center of our heart help us to commit ourselves to your service on this earth, so that Souls may be saved into your Holy hands Gospel be preach boldly clearly in the nations. Let those who seek you find you, when people of this earth pray to you sincerely from the bottom of their heart answer their prayer and forgive them all their sins. Bless us with a grateful heart, our Father; make us to be mindful of the needs of other people around us. Lord Jesus Christ accept our thanks and praises for all that you have done for us, we gives you thanks for the splendor of the whole creation, for the beauty of this world, for the wonder of life and for the mystery of your love for us. Let your peace that surpasses all understanding rules our hearts and minds forever. In Jesus great Holy Name, we pray. Amen.

MARCH 18TH

THE WORD OF GOD TRANSFORMS SOULS; LET THE WORD OF GOD BE YOUR TRANSFORMATION TODAY.

Today's Scripture Reading:

"He who dwells in the shelter of the most high will rest in the shadow of the Almighty. I will say of the Lord, He is my refuge and my fortress, my God, in whom I trust." (Psalm 91:1-2) NIV

The Scripture says that God Almighty expresses the security of those who trust him fully, and it says that God assures all the believers that he will be our refuge and our protector. God Almighty wants us to dwell in his shelter, an unfailing shelter, an unending shelter, and an un-destroyable shelter, so that we will be able to have full rest in his shadow forever. Jesus Christ wants us to seek his unfailing and protection in times of our spiritual and our physical danger. God's security for his children never fails for those who fully committed their lives to the will and to the protection of the almighty as well as daily dwell in his presence. The more a believing Christian abide in Jesus Christ and in his word, and make him their life and a dwelling place, the more Christ's protection and provisions for their lives grows. We must always be the doer of the Word of God not the hearer alone. The Word of God purifies and brings us to the presence of God daily with our prayers.

Prayer:

Lord Jesus Christ you are the compassionate gracious loving God, full of truth and righteousness abiding in truth and forgiveness. Helps us to know you more and more, help us to abide on your love, on your blessings and on your compassion from now and forever more. Christ Jesus our Lord all honor and glory to you our risen Lord, you conquered the grave, Christ our Lord is risen today hallelujah. We give you praise that you died for us to save our souls you have opened paradise, we have the cross, the grave and the skies, the battle is won. Your redeeming work is done and completed we glorified your Holy Name, no one before you and no one after, you delivered us from death an sin you bless us with the gift of grace and salvation Holy is your Name forever, you are our eternal hope of glory – worthy is the Lamb that was slain, whose precious blood set us free to be the people of God. We offer our thankful praises a lamb, sheep redeems; Christ Jesus, who is sinless, reconciles us sinners to the Father, we give you thanks and praises forever. In your mighty Holy Name, we pray. Amen.

MARCH 19TH

THE WORD OF GOD TRANSFORMS SOULS; LET THE WORD OF GOD BE YOUR TRANSFORMATION TODAY.

Today's Scripture Reading:

"Because he loves me, says the Lord, I will rescue him; I will protect him for he acknowledges my Name. He will call upon me, and I will answer him; I will be with him in trouble; I will deliver him and honor him. With long life will I satisfy him and show him my salvation." (Psalm 91:14-16) NIV

Our Lord Jesus Christ addressed the believing Christians, those who are faithful followers. The Lord knows that they truthfully love him, he himself promises to come to their aid in times of troubles, danger, and afflictions. The secret for receiving God's protective care is a heart that is intimately attached to the Lord in gratitude and affection. The Lord Jesus Christ is the only one who knows the true believers, and he will always be with them in all their earthly troubles, the Lord will hear their prayers, even before they call unto him, he hears their prayers before they kneel down, he has answered their prayers and give them lives full of his divine presence and provisions.

Prayer:

Our Father in heaven, Merciful and mighty God, compassionate, gracious loving, a great God above all gods, Jesus Christ our Lord and Savior, you are the Father to the Fatherless, husband to the widows. provider for those who are in need; Father Son and Holy Spirit forever one God. Hear our prayers and fulfills all our supplications and our needs. Protect and guide and lead those true believers who truthfully put their trust in you and keep your commandment. Lord Jesus Christ do not stop loving us, and please in your infinite mercy rescue us in times of danger. We thank you Lord for setting us and your designed for how we should serve you, you demand the best from us, and help us to give you the best, and do what is justify and pleasing in your sight. We praise you for your blessings for our family and friends, and for the loving care which surrounds us every day, with affection and love.

Bless us with the power of your Holy Spirit and keep us save at all times, so that we may be useful for your glory, for the work of the kingdom, for the work of the Gospel help us to live in your glory for your glory now and forever. In Jesus Christ Holy Name , we pray. Amen.

MARCH 20TH

THE WORD OF GOD TRANSFORMS SOULS; LET THE WORD OF GOD BE YOUR TRANSFORMATION TODAY.

Today's Scripture Reading:

"Praise the Lord O my Soul; all my inmost being, praise his Holy Name. Praise the Lord, O my soul, and forget not all his benefits - who forgives all your sins and heals all your diseases, who redeems your life from the pit and Crowns you with love and compassion, who satisfies your desires with good things so that your youth is renewed like the eagles." (Psalm 103:2-5) NIV

All the believing Christians must express thanksgiving and praises to the Lord for all his benefits and blessings that he bestows upon us as a believing covenant people. We must never forget God's goodness and mercies for us. We must not stop thanking him for his blessings showered on us through the Holy Spirit. We must thank him for healing all our diseases, delivering us from the bondage of sin, sickness and death, and the gift of redemption and eternal life. Forgiveness is the first and most important gift we receive from the Lord; through it we are restored to God and redeemed from destruction. Healing of our diseases that come to us because of sin and Satan is likewise part of the salvation that

God makes available to his people. Our Lord shows his mercy to those who truly fear him.

Prayer:

Lord Jesus Christ let the fruit of our lips is giving praises and thankfulness to your Holy Name. Bless us with the Spirit of praises and thankfulness to your Holy Name; Above all, we give you thanks our Lord for the great mercies and promises given to us in Christ Jesus our Lord, bless us with your life, our Lord and forever, bless us with mind to think, and hearts to love our neighbor, love our enemies, love our neighbors as ourselves, love our families, friends, community members, government officials, and all the people. We give you thanks for the beauty of the world and wonder of your creation in this world and in the sky and sea. We give you thanks for the good health and strength and work which is a blessing from the Lord. Lord Jesus Christ you are the great healer, heal us from all our diseases, and sickness. Bless us with our hearts desires if you know that our hearts desire is good for us and is according to you will for our life. Help us to always remember all what you have done in our lives and what you are still doing in our lives and what you are still going to do in our lives; in your great mighty Holy Name , we pray. Amen.

MARCH 21ST

THE WORD OF GOD TRANSFORMS SOULS; LET THE WORD OF GOD BE YOUR TRANSFORMATION TODAY.

Today's Scripture Reading:

"Praise the Lord. Blessed is the man who fears the Lord who finds great delight in his commands. He will have no fear of bad news; his heart is steadfast, trusting in the Lord. His heart is secure; he will have no fear; in the end he will look in triumph on his foes"(Psalm 112:1a, 7-8) NIV

All the believing Christians who are living confidently in the Lord have no fear of any bad news, because they know that God have the power to take care any bad news either personally or publicly, or nationwide. Christians should not live in fear, fear is not of God; they should put their trust, hope, and faith in the Lord at all times. In so many ways and at so many circumstances, the devil want to put fear in our heart, want us to think that the Lord is not near, or he has abandoned us. When this type of thought comes to our mind, we must rebuke it in the mighty Name of Jesus Christ, and tell the devil that he is a liar, he cannot win. Victory is ours in Jesus Christ, Jesus Christ is able and more than able to fulfill our needs, and solved all our problems. Christ is our deliverer because we put our trust in him and not on ourselves, or any material, things on this earth, or any circumstances that wanted to raise themselves up against the will of the Lord.

Prayer:

Lord Jesus, the compassionate, gracious loving God; bless us with your full presence, help us to live a blessed life ; blessing you every minute and every second of our life on earth, open our hearts, make it steadfast, trusting your Holy Name in everything we do, or say. Lord God Almighty, Father Son and the Holy Spirit, eternal God, our heavenly Father; you forgive us our past present future sins and you bless us with your Holy Spirit. continuously delivering us from all evils of the enemy and from the power of Satan; lead us not into any temptation of the enemies; and deliver us from evil ones, and people. Grant us, most Merciful God your faithful people pardon and your peace that surpasses all understanding, that we may be made perfect by your grace, and serve you with quiet Spirit and gentle mind through the power of the Holy Spirit and our Lord Jesus Christ. Amen.

MARCH 22ND

THE WORD OF GOD TRANSFORMS SOULS;
LET THE WORD OF GOD BE YOUR TRANSFORMATION TODAY.

Today's Scripture Reading:

"Unless the Lord builds the house, its builders labor in vain. unless the Lord watches over the city, the watchmen stand guard in vain. In vain we rise early and stay up late, toiling for food to eat - for he grants sleep to those he loves." (Psalm 127:1-2) NIV

This Scripture is revealing to us, all the believers that we need the approval of our Lord and Savior in everything we are doing, or about to do. God's blessing is truly valuable in life; conversely, if God is not in our lives, activities, goals, to include without our families, all will be in vain, and will end in frustration and by disappointment. Therefore, believers should seek God's blessings and guidance in all things from the very beginning of our lives. As we labor to build God's house on earth, we must make sure that we build it according to his pattern and by his Spirit, not according to mere human ideas, or plans, and efforts. We must put all our daily activities in the hands of the Lord before we approach, buying, or selling, in all our businesses we must put it in the hands of the Lord. We need the absolute approval of our heavenly Father in everything, before it is done; otherwise, it will be in vain. Our Lord and Savior knows what is good for us. He knows we can live, with no violence, or problems, and he knows the food that is good for us to eat.

Prayer:

Our Lord and Savior, Jesus Christ, the true Son of God. Help us to shape our lives, plan our lives, and structure our lives according to your grace and mercy. We give you thanks for the courage you gave us and patient in time of suffering and faithful in adversity, we thanks the Lord and praise him for his mercy and love upon us. Bless us with the power of your Holy Spirit that we may know Jesus Christ and make him known to other people to know him at all time and in all places on earth. Touch our hearts and mind before we do anything so that we will put it in your hands. Bless us with your power of the Holy Spirit, controlling, directing, instructing us in everything we do ; live your life in us forever, you are the Emmanuel God with us, God in us. Bless us abundantly, immeasurable, with all the blessings that you know that we needed in all the areas of our live. Bless us with great success in everything we do, or about to do, Bless us with peace so that we may live in peace from this earth to heaven. In your Holy Name , we pray. Amen.

MARCH 23ʳᵈ

THE WORD OF GOD TRANSFORMS SOULS; LET THE WORD OF GOD BE YOUR TRANSFORMATION TODAY.

Today's Scripture Reading:

"Where can I go from your Spirit? Where can I flee from your presence? If I rise on the wings of the dawn, If I settle on the far side of the Sea, even there your hand will guide me, your right hand will hold me fast. Search me, O God, and know my heart; test me and know my anxious thoughts. See if there is any offensive way in me, and lead me in the way everlasting."
(Psalm139:7, 9-10, 23-24) NIV

Our Father in heaven knows our inward thoughts, motive, desires, fears, as well as our outward habits and actions. He knows all we do from the beginning of the day to the end of the day. In everything we do, God encircles us with his care and lays his hands of favor upon our heads. As a child of God, Christ blesses us with his Spirit, we can never go away from his Spirit, and we can never move beyond God's care, guidance and from his supporting strength, this is the key to understand our God operations. Our Lord and Savior, he is with us in all our situations in this life, and in whatever the present, now and the future will bring.

Prayer:

Jesus Christ our Lord, the ever living Savior, chosen of the Father full of grace and compassion. Hold us with your Holy hands that we may not stray away from your presence. Bless us with the empowerment of the Holy Spirit, and bring us close to you; Lord Jesus Christ there is no where we can go from your presence we are in your garden. The heavens is your throne, the earth is your footstool. Lord God Almighty you are the Omnipotent, omnipresent, and Omniscient, you know everything and see everything, you are all powerful, all merciful, all knowing, and most especially you are everywhere, nothing is close from you, we are in your garden; bless all the children in the villages of the world who have no food to eat and no proper clothe to wear and no clean water to drink; in your infinite mercy send help to them our Lord in a miraculous way send help to them, feed them, clothe them and provide clean water for them to drink. Continuously pouring your knowledge and wisdom to people of this earth so that they can be able to reach the unreachable in their own language, bless them with the preaching and teaching of the Gospel and bless them with the gift of grace and salvation. Let your right hands hold us tight and your merciful eye watches us grow now and forever. Amen.

MARCH 24TH

THE WORD OF GOD TRANSFORMS SOULS; LET THE WORD OF GOD BE YOUR TRANSFORMATION TODAY.

Today's Scripture Reading:

"The Lord is righteous in all his ways and loving toward all he has made. The Lord is near to all who call on him, to all who call on him in truth. He fulfills the desires of those who fear him. He hears their cry and saves them. The Lord watches over all who love him, but all the wicked he will destroy." (Psalm 145:17-20) NIV

God the Father, Almighty, God the Son, and God the Holy Spirit; the only one God and true God of the universe a righteous God, his righteousness is incomprehensible and incomparable. he rain to the just and to unjust. He shines his glory on those who loves him and those that does not love him. All who call unto him in truth, with sincere and upright of heart may be assured that the Lord is near to them and he takes good care of them. The Lord hears the prayers of those who call unto him from the bottom of their heart, he will fulfill their heart's desires, if their desires are good for them, and Jesus Christ will deliver all those who love him from the work of the enemies. All the believing Christians should know that our Lord and Savior are always there to take care of our needs and save us from any troubles.

Prayer:

Lord Jesus Christ no one, like you, none like you, no one like you. No one has loves us the way you loved us, and no one care for us, the way you care for us. Our merciful and mighty God, you taught us your Holy Word that we might be able to live righteously with you from now to the glory of your Holy Name, from this earth to heaven. Our Lord and Savior, nourish the soul of all those who believe in you and gave their life to you; lift up your countenance upon us and give us peace of God that surpasses all understanding in all the areas of our lives. Help us to call all the sinners and the lost unto you; forgive them their sins, clothe them with your righteousness, and bless us with your Spirit indwelling power. O' Lord our God who lives and reign now and forever, in the powerful Holy Name of Jesus, we pray. Amen.

MARCH 25TH

THE WORD OF GOD TRANSFORMS SOULS; LET THE WORD OF GOD BE YOUR TRANSFORMATION TODAY.

Today's Scripture Reading:

"Trust in the Lord with all your heart and lean not on your own understand, in all your ways acknowledge him, and he will make your path straight." (Proverbs 3:5-6) NIV

Our own understanding is limited, fallible and subject to error; all the believers must, therefore, be enlightened by God's Word and the Holy Spirit. To lean on our own understanding, rather than to trust God according to his Word and according to the Holy Spirit, magnifies the human mind while it diminishes the human spirit. Dependence on human reasoning rather than trusting in God leads to pride and spiritual arrogance and leanness. Instead of being wise in our own eyes, we should demonstrate our trust in the Lord asking him continually for wisdom and knowledge of his will in all spheres of our life. In all our ways we must acknowledge in all our plans, decision, and activities, we should acknowledge the Lord, awareness of who God is in our lives, he is our Lord and Savior, His will must be our supreme desires of our heart. We must live in close relationship with our Lord asking him for the direction of our life.

Prayer:

Lord Jesus Christ help us to trust you more and more in all our decision making that can have great impact in our lives. Empower us to seek your face, and follow your commandment. Almighty God, Father of all mercies sustainer of all things, we entrust all the believing Christians into your Holy hands; you never fail caring for those who believe in you and you have never stop loving us, bless us with a new life in you and help us to live for you forever. Fill our hearts and minds with your love and love for others around us now and forever, help us to live and abide in your presence and in your Word. Let your life be manifest in our lives, let the people of this earth see you clearly through us and let them know that we belongs to you spirit, soul, and body, faithfully, and sincerely. Help us to focus on your redeeming love for us, be at the center of our hearts controlling, directing, instructing, teaching, guiding, correcting, and forgiving us our sins, protecting and make us yours forever. In your Holy Name, we pray. Amen .

MARCH 26TH

THE WORD OF GOD TRANSFORMS SOULS; LET THE WORD OF GOD BE YOUR TRANSFORMATION TODAY.

Today's Scripture Reading:

"Surely God is my salvation; I will trust and not be afraid.
The Lord, the Lord, is my strength and my song; he
has become my salvation. With joy you will draw water from the
wells of salvation. In that day you will say: Give thanks to the
Lord, call on his Name; make known among the nations what he
has done, and proclaim that his Name is exalted."
(Isaiah 12:2-4) NIV

God's people will praise him when the universal reign of the Messiah begins. The Scripture reveals that: the salvation of God to the people of Israel during his days on earth but they did not believe him. All the believing Christians must be praying for God's salvation for the children of Israel before Christ return to set up his Kingdom. Even now all the believers must pray for the anticipate faith and hope for our Lord's return and the establishment of his eternal reign in the righteousness and with truth. When that day comes, we will sing a song of praise and a song of rejoicing; for the Lord fulfills his promise for those who believe in him and love him. Christ return to the earth will be the beginning of a new heaven and a new earth where righteousness reigns forever.

Prayer:

Lord Jesus Christ we are waiting and praying patiently for your glorious return unto this earth to set up your kingdom of light and love; where righteousness will reign forever, guide us to this truth, and make us to be worthy to live with you there and serve you forever where there is no darkness. Lord Jesus Christ bless us with the heart of compassion for those who are suffering from addiction and lost their good health from through the daily usage of drug and alcohol, in your mercy take away the fears that beset them and strengthen them in the process of recovery, and give them patient, understanding and persevering love to pray to you more and more so that they will completely recover and be useful for you. Give them the understanding, and help them to be willingly accepting help; so that they may live a righteous life that you approve and that will help them to walk with you from this earth to heaven. In your great Holy Name, we pray accept our prayer. Amen.

MARCH 27TH

THE WORD OF GOD TRANSFORMS SOULS; LET THE WORD OF GOD BE YOUR TRANSFORMATION TODAY.

Today's Scripture Reading:

"You will keep in perfect peace him whose mind is steadfast, because they trust in you. Trust in the Lord forever, for the Lord, the Lord, is the Rock eternal." (Isaiah 26: 3-4) NIV

All the believing Christians must be confident that our Lord and Savior will accomplish his redemptive purpose; all the believers must break out in prayer and praises. God will destroy all the power of evil on this earth and the establishment of his kingdom. As the trying and stressful days of the earth are coming nearer and nearer; God will keep in perfect peace the remnant that remain steadfast and faithful to him. In times of persecution and virtue believers in all nations must continually strive to keep their heart and minds in perfect peace as well as turned to the Lord in prayer. Believers must trust and hope in the Lord, they must place their trust in him because he is the mighty Rock who endures forever; he is the sure and firm foundation. He will open the door that the enemy closed ad closed the door that the enemy opened that is given us trouble.

Prayer:

Lord Jesus you are our lord and Savior the compassionate gracious loving God. We pray for your unfailing love, and the power of your Holy Spirit in the lives of those who believe in you. Gracious God, pour out your Holy Spirit upon us and upon your gifts of bread and wine, that the bread we break every Sunday and the cup we bless may be the communion of the body and the blood of Jesus Christ, we are your body Lord Jesus Christ, help us to be one in you, as you and Father are one. By your Spirit make us with the living Christ Jesus and with all who are baptized in his Name, that we may be one in the ministry in every place as this bread is Christ's body for us, send us out to be the body of Christ in the world. Give us strength to serve you faithfully truthfully with all our hearts, unit us with the promised of the day of resurrection, when with the redeemed of all the ages will feast with you at your table in glory, through Jesus Christ, and with Christ, in Christ , we pray in the unity of the Holy Spirit all glory and honor are yours, our Lord and Savior; bind us together until the day you return back to the world. Let your full presence be known in our lives; let the people of this earth, see you clearly in our lives, let all those who love you rejoices in you now and forever. In Jesus Christ's mighty, Holy Name, we pray. Amen.

MARCH 28TH

THE WORD OF GOD TRANSFORMED SOULS; LET THE WORD OF GOD BE YOUR TRANSFORMATION TODAY.

Today's Scripture Reading:

"This is what the Sovereign Lord, the Holy One of Israel says: 'In repentance and rest is your salvation, in quietness and trust is your strength, but you would have none of it.' " (Isaiah 30:15) NIV

Beginning from the Old Testament God takes repentance of our sins seriously, he continuously sending messengers, his prophets to the people of Israel so that they can repent their sins. He was telling them that the repentance bring salvation, without repentance, no one can have salvation. Our Lord and Savior came to this world gave his life to us so that through the repentance of our sins. The people of Judah could be saved if only its rulers and the people would return to God and put their confidence in him. Since they did not, however, they would be defeated and standalone a banner on the hill, a stark example of all the consequences they will face because they forsake their God. Same with all the believing Christians today, they must live a life that is justified in the eye of the Lord at all times.

Prayer:

O Merciful and gracious God, our Lord Jesus Christ one and only our redeemer King, one and only the true and faithful Holy one of Israel, the Seed of David, our Lord and Savior, the very God, the King of kings, the Lord of lords, the God of gods, the Light of this world, the true light that shines forever and no darkness can comprehended it. We call unto you to bring peace into this world, your peace that surpasses all understanding into the heart and mind of every living soul on this earth. Pray for us the prayer that cannot be uttered. Guide us with your mercy and love, forgive us our sins and bless us with the power of your resurrection. Help us to forgive those who do wrong against us, and lead us to your eternal kingdom so that we can live with you there forever and ever. O heavenly Father, have mercy upon us, blesses us with the Spirit of forgiveness, help us to forgive as Christ forgive on the cross. Clean our hearts and pour out your Holy Spirit upon us, so that we can forgive those who trespass against us. You are the mighty warriors, all power belongs to you in heaven and in this earth, you said that vengeance is yours you will repay therefore, in your mercy help us to forgive those who do wrong to us physically and spiritually and help us to live a peaceful life. In your Holy Name , we pray. Amen.

MARCH 29TH

THE WORD OF GOD TRANSFORMED SOULS; LET THE WORD OF GOD BE YOUR TRANSFORMATION TODAY.

Today's Scripture Reading:

"Do you not know? have you not heard? The Lord is the everlasting God, the creator of the end of the earth. He will not grow tired or weary, and his understanding no one can fathom. He gives strength to the weary and increases the power of the weak. Even youths grow tired and weary, and young men stumble and fall; but those who hope in the Lord will renew their strength. They will soar on wings like eagles; they will run and not grow weary, they will walk and not be faint." (Isaiah 40:28-31) NIV

All believers should develop their hope in the Lord, we must trust him fully with our lives; it involves looking to him as our source of help and grace in times of need. Those who hope in the Lord are promised with the constant renewal of their faith in the Lord. The Promise of God's strength that will constantly revive them in the midst of exhaustion and weakness; suffering and trials. The Lord will bless them with the ability to rise above their difficulties like the eagles that soars into the sky; and the ability to run spiritually without tiring and to walk steadily forward without fainting at God's delays. God promises that if his people will patiently trust him, he will provide whatever is needed to sustain them constantly.

Prayer:

Lord Jesus Christ blesses us with the Spirit of patience so that we may be able to have strength to wait patiently for your promise for our lives. Help us to know you better in all the areas of our life. Bless us with your peace that surpasses all understanding, to live for you and wait with prayer for all your promise in all the areas of our lives, you are the one that knows what is good for us, you give the best for your children, do not let us settle for less. Let all the young men and women focus on you, do not let them fall into sin our Lord, there the next generation that will take the Gospel to the end of the earth before your return to earth to judge the dead and the living, therefore, Lord Jesus Christ continuously calling all the young men and women unto you, all the college students, high school students, junior high school and all the people of all ages. Do not let us rush and pick up what does not belong to us, or anything that can cause us big financial problems. Do not let us rush to pick a husband, a woman, having a child, buying properties that can cause a great deal of trouble for us. Bless us with the spirit of patience so that we may be able to live our life for you according to your will for us from this earth to heaven. Hear our prayer Lord, have mercy, in your mighty matchless Holy Name, a Name above all Name in heaven and in earth , we pray. Amen.

MARCH 30TH

THE WORD OF GOD TRANSFORMED SOULS; LET THE WORD OF GOD BE YOUR TRANSFORMATION TODAY.

Today's Scripture Reading:

"So do not fear, for I am with you; do not be dismayed for I am your God. I will strengthen you and help you; I will uphold you with my righteous right hand. All who rage against you will surely be ashamed and disgraced; those who oppose you will be as nothing and perish." (Isaiah 41:10) NIV

All the Christian believers must not lie in fear because the grace of God is never failing, and Christ is all sufficient in our lives. There is nothing Jesus Christ cannot do for those who love him, and call unto him from the bottom of their heart. Fear is not of God; there is no fear in God. believers must not live in fear, or in worries. As the children of God, we also become God's chosen servants. We can, therefore, claim the promises of God for ourselves. We must not fear other human beings because God is with us to give us his grace and strength that we need to face all of this life's circumstances. Christ is with us and he will help us through times of crises as our source of peace; and to sustain us. He is there at the right hand of God to be our advocate. Our Lord Jesus Christ is praying for us and interceding with God the Father on our behalf the moment we give our life to Jesus Christ. He is in control; he has the power and authority to take care of his own.

Prayer:

Lord Jesus Christ our gracious master and our God, our Rock of salvation, our great intercessor in heaven; pray for us and interceded for us the prayer that no one can hear, that is only between you and the Father, that we may live a life that is pleasing and justifying in your sight, that we may live a life that will bring great honor to your Holy Name, that we may live a life that will exalt your Holy Name more than ever before, that we may live a life that will bring the Gospel to the end of the earth, under the earth utmost part of the earth, in the mountain, in the valley, in the wilderness, in the Ocean, that the sinner, the lost, and the people of all other religion, the Idol worshipers and Pagan worshipers will turn unto you. Help us to live a life that will take the Gospel to all the four corners of the earth. You know what we needed our Lord and Savior and you know the right time that we need it, the time that you have set for everything in our lives do not let it fail our Lord have mercy upon us, have mercy upon us, let your love and mercy flows through us to other people in the world that did not know you. We praise your Holy Name, glorify your Holy Name, magnify your Holy Name, and adore you honor you forever. In your mighty Holy Name , we pray. Amen.

MARCH 31ST

THE WORD OF GOD TRANSFORMS SOULS; LET THE WORD OF GOD BE YOUR TRANSFORMATION TODAY.

Today's Scripture Reading:

"Fear not, for I have redeemed you; I have summoned you by Name: you are mine. For I am the Lord, your God, the Holy One of Israel, your Savior." (Isaiah 43:1b, 3a) NIV

God the Father Almighty showed his love to the children of Israel by delivering them from the Babylonian's Captivity because God loves the people of Israel. They are the descendant of Abraham, Jacob, and Isaac. God the Father expresses his love for Israelites and the benefits of that love revealed up till today in Jesus Christ redemptive work on the cross for all the people on earth. All the blessings mentioned here for the people of Israel apply even more to those who are God's children through faith in Jesus Christ. God has created and has redeemed believers; we belong to him, and he knows each one of us by Name. When we pass through trouble and affliction, we will not be destroyed, for he is with us; we are precious and honored in his sight; we are the object of his great love. The Lord God Almighty is the great I am no one before him no one after, he is the Holy One of Israel and he is our blessed Savior and our redeemer King.

Prayer:

Lord Jesus Christ our blessed Savior and our great redeemer. Almighty God the compassionate and everlasting God, you made the world with all its marvelous order, the Moon, the Sun, the Galaxies of the Stars, and the infinite complexity of all the living creature, bless us as we are trying to fathom the mysteries of your creation, let our curiosity make us to come to know you more and more truthfully, and more surely fulfill our service as your servant in the design of your eternal purpose; we love you our Lord and Savior the creator of heaven and earth, Sea and everything that dwell in the ocean, and under the earth, we adore you and praises your Holy Name with thankfulness forever. We pray that you bless us immeasurable, abundantly in all the areas of our lives. Create in us a new life, a new mind, a new spirit, a new soul, in order that we may be able to serve you with singleness of heart with an unending love for you. Lord Jesus Christ our Lord, manifest your full presence in our lives, bless us with the power of the Holy Spirit, that we may live and serve you according to your will for our life. Do not leave us nor forsake us our Lord. Let your full presence be with us throughout our lives, be our immortal food, live your life through us, help us to be complete in you, you are our sufficiency, and the source of our eternal life. In Jesus Christ great Holy Name , we pray. Amen.

DAILY REFLECTION NOTES

APRIL

APRIL 1ST

THE WORD OF GOD TRANSFORMS LIFE – LET THE WORD OF GOD BE YOUR TRANSFORMATION TODAY

Today's Scripture Reading:

"O Lord, my strength and my fortress, my refuge in time of distress, to you the nations will come from the ends of the earth and say; our Fathers possessed nothing but false gods, worthless Idols that did them no goods! Therefore, I will teach them this time I will teach them my power and might. Then they will know that my Name is the Lord." (Jeremiah 16:19-21)NIV

Prophet Jeremiah foresaw a day when the nations of the earth would come and worship the Lord and will renounce their false gods as worthless, Idols that cannot talk. All the people on earth will put down their Idols, they will stop worshiping a pagan God such as moon, Sun, the ocean, God of Iron, God of thunder God of the dead, or worshiping of their dead father and mother, or God of the mountain. They will worship the God of the living who lives forever more, who created the earth and everything that is in it. They will worship the true God, who loves us and gave us his

Son to redeem us from our sins in order that we may live and serve him forever.

Prayer:

Lord God Almighty; Father, Son and Holy Spirit, be with us forever; let your full presence be known in our lives. Let the people of this earth, worship you and honor you in spirit and in truth. Let them know you are the one and only the true God, no one before you and no one after, you alone are God we adored you forever O'Lord. With all our heart and mind we adore you and , we pray for the peace that comes from above the heavens of heavens to rest upon all the people in all the nations of this world; for your loving kindness and your salvation of the souls of all the people in this world to be manifest, that they will be saved; and the blessings of your goodness, blessings of good health, and the blessings of good life for the people in all the nations of this world. In Jesus Christ loving Spirit , we pray. Amen

APRIL 2ND

THE WORD OF GOD TRANSFORMS LIFE – LET THE WORD OF GOD BE YOUR TRANSFORMATION TODAY

Today's Scripture Reading:

"You will seek me and find me when you seek me with all your heart. I will be found by you, declares the Lord, and will bring you back from captivity. I will gather you from all the nations and places where I have banished you, declares the Lord, and will bring you back to the place from which I carried you into exile."
(Jeremiah 29:13-14) NIV

When the people of Israel stray away from God, his desires and purpose did not change for them. Same with all the believing Christians today; if we seek the Lord in prayer with all our heart and mind, he will answer us and fulfill his promise in our lives. Because when God desires to do great things for his children, he will move his children to great level of prayers so that the timing of God's answer to their prayers is often linked to God's purposes for all his people. God would listen, and answer our prayers from heaven and he will fulfill all his promises of restoration, and established his children that call unto him; every minute and every second. God said if we seek him with all our heart, we will find him, he declared, and he promises to change our lives to the better.

Prayer:

Lord Jesus Christ you are the only one that can change our lives, from violent to peace, the peace of God that surpasses all understanding, we give you thanks guide us and lead us into the righteous way. When we call unto you, in prayer, seeking your face in everything we may be struggling with, and going through, battling with, Lord Jesus answer our prayers, and help us to be found in you. Let the hearts of all the people in all the nations rejoice in you our Lord, let them know that you the sustainers of this universe, let them seek you and find you, let them seek you with all their heart. You are the one and only that change life, turn the life of those who call unto you faithfully and sincerely around for the better and let the praises of your Holy Name full their mouth; Let them give you thanks for all you begin to do in their lives and for you will continue to do in their lives. In Jesus Christ great mighty Holy , we pray. Amen

APRIL 3ᴿᴰ

THE WORD OF GOD TRANSFORMS LIFE –
LET THE WORD OF GOD BE YOUR TRANSFORMATION TODAY

Today's Scripture Reading:

*"As the rain and the snow come down from heaven,
and do not return to it without watering the earth and
making it bud and flourish, so that it yields seed for the
sower and bread for the eater, so is my Word that goes
out from my mouth; it will not return to me empty, but will
accomplish what I desire and achieve the purpose for which
I sent It." (Isaiah 55:10-11) NIV*

The Word of God is God; God created the Universe with is Word, he created us with his Word. He sent his Son to this world with his Word through the Holy Spirit which indwells virgin Mary. The Word of God become flesh and dwell among us, we beheld his glory, the glory of the only begotten Son of God - Jesus Christ the anointed Messiah and the Savior of the world. The Word of God stands firm in the heavens and came down as a rushing wind on the day of Pentecost when God pouring his Holy Spirit to the hearts and minds of all the apostle, and the people in Jerusalem on that day; Three Thousand people were saved into the hands of the Lord. The Word of God is dynamic and powerful, and it accomplishes great things the Word of God is the creative Word, God spoke the earth into being - He said let there be Light and there is light.

Prayer:

Lord Jesus Christ let your Word be manifest in our lives, feed us with your Word, your Word is true, cleanses us from any unrighteousness , Cleanses us with your Word from anything that can contaminate Spirit, Soul and Body. Let your Word penetrate into the darkest heart and light it up with the illumination of the Holy Spirit, Let the heart and minds and souls of the people on this earth receive your Word which will bring peace to this world of sin. Let your Word, your living Word abide in us and make us alive in our hearts, and minds and in you forever for the glory of your Holy Name. Amen.

APRIL 4TH

THE WORD OF GOD TRANSFORMS LIFE – LET THE WORD OF GOD BE YOUR TRANSFORMATION TODAY

Today's Scripture Reading:

"But someone may ask, how are the dead raised? with what kind of body will they come? How foolish! what you sow does not come to life unless it dies. When you sow, you do not plant the body that will be, but just a seed, perhaps of wheat or something else. But God gives it a body as he has determined, and to each kind of seed he gives its own body." (1st Corinthians 15:35-39) NIV

Apostle Paul was referring to the resurrection of the body which is an essential; in the New Testament Scripture ; resurrection of the body refers to God's raising a human body from the dead and reuniting it with the person's Soul and Spirit, which when a person die it was separated. When believers receive their new bodies, they put on immortality and they will become all that God intended for humans at creation. Believers may come to know God in the fullness as God wants them to know him as he desires. The faithful who will be alive when Christ return for his people will experience the same bodily transformation as those who have died in Christ before the day of resurrection. They will be given a new body identical to the body given to those raised from the dead at that time.

Prayer:

Lord Jesus Christ, you gave your life to us, so that those of us that lives, we will not live for ourselves, we will live for you forever. Blesses us with the new body, a new Spirit, a new heart, and a new Name to live for you, and to serve you in singleness of heart. Bless us with abundant love for you from this earth to heaven; fill us up with your word, to worship you, praise you, and pray to you and to give you great glory and thanks every day of our lives. Amen.

APRIL 5TH

THE WORD OF GOD TRANSFORMS LIFE – LET THE WORD OF GOD BE YOUR TRANSFORMATION TODAY

Today's Scripture Reading:

"Ah, Sovereign Lord, you have made the heavens and the earth by your great power and outstretched arm. Nothing is too hard for you. You show love to thousands but bring the punishment for the fathers' sins into the laps of their children after them. O great and powerful God, whose Name is the Lord Almighty, great are your purposes and mighty are your deeds. Your eyes are open to all the ways of men; you reward everyone according to his conduct as his deeds deserve." (Jeremiah 32:17-19) NIV

Our Lord and Savior want us to demonstrate strong faith in him; just as he tested prophet Jeremiah during the captivity of Babylonian forces. Jeremiah was instructed by the Lord to go and buy a field of land in his hometown village a place that has already controlled by the Babylonian army. Jeremiah exercised his strong faith in God by purchasing the land, Jeremiah demonstrated faith in God' promise, and believed that some of the children of Israel will return to the land and build houses there. It was clearly prophet Jeremiah's sign of hope and trust in the Lord. In a similar manner, our situations may at times seem hopeless and desperate;

yet if we belong to God, we have the promise and hope of a better future in life.

Prayer:

Lord God Almighty compassionate gracious loving God, continuously increase your faith in us, you are our hope of glory compassionate merciful and mighty God, you are our life, we have no life without you, without you we are nothing and we cannot do anything. Fulfill your promise in our lives exercise your mercy and power in our life, make way where there is no way, and help us to be completely surrender to your lordship, and help us to serve you till the end of our life On this earth. In Jesus Christ Holy Name , we pray. Amen.

APRIL 6TH

THE WORD OF GOD TRANSFORMS LIFE – LET THE WORD OF GOD BE YOUR TRANSFORMATION TODAY

Today's Scripture Reading:

"Do not be life them, for your Father knows what you need before you ask him. So do not worry, saying, what shall we eat? or what shall we drink? or what shall we wear? For the pagans run after all those things, and your heavenly Father knows that you need them. But seek first his kingdom and his righteousness, and all these things will be given to you as well. Therefore, do not worry about tomorrow, for tomorrow will worry about itself. Each day has enough trouble of its own." (Matthew 6:31-34) NIV

Our Lord Jesus says do not worries to the point that you will develop lack of faith in God's Fatherly care and love. God Almighty, Father, Son and the Holy Spirit have promised all his children in the time of troubles and violence. God promised to provide our daily bread, clothing and all our necessities. Believing Christians need not to worry; if we seek and call unto God, to let him reign in our lives. We can be sure that he will assume full responsibility for all those who wholly yielded to him in prayer. Those who follow

Christ Jesus are urged to seek above all else God's kingdom and his righteousness. Believer must diligently seek his face for everything in our lives.

Prayer:

Our Father in heaven, you are the source of our lives; you have the love and power to provide for all our provisions, because you are the God of provisions. You are our great Physician, the Healer, you have the power and mercy to heal us from any sickness, from all our diseases, and all divers disease; plant your Word in our heart that will make us to grow in grace and grow in sanctification, help us to seek your heavenly kingdom and your righteousness above all things in this world. In your matchless Holy Name , we pray. Amen.

APRIL 7TH

THE WORD OF GOD TRANSFORMS LIFE – LET THE WORD OF GOD BE YOUR TRANSFORMATION TODAY

Today's Scripture Reading:

"I am the Lord, the God of all mankind. Is anything too hard for me? "(Jeremiah 32:27) NIV

God is the God of all the people on this earth. Awareness and acknowledgment of who God is in our lives is very important. Nothing is impossible for him to do in heaven above and on earth below, God is all powerful, all mighty, and merciful God, nothing beyond his reach. God's Word promises a blessed life and future for all the believing Christians in Christ Jesus. We can depend on his Word, even though we might know what he said is going to happens, or the specific manner in which, it will be accomplished. We still have to stand, and trust God's Word for our lives. Again and again we read in the Scripture, that God the Father, Son and Holy Spirit ever one God; confirmed, affirmed to us his Holy Name, he is the creator, no one before him and no one after. Nothing is too hard for him to do; and nothing is impossible for him to accomplish. He knows us more than we know ourselves. He is the all-powerful, all knowing, the immortal, the invisible, the only wise God. God is our omnipresent, omniscience - God is exalted beyond our reach in his power. God's people should not be afraid because God is with them.

Prayer:

Lord God Almighty, you alone have the power to change our lives to the better, to rescue us from any danger, to bless us in all our needs at the right time. You alone can save us, You alone are the all-knowing and all merciful and mighty, you alone can protect, guide and lead us to life everlasting, You are our great intercessor in heaven, pray for us the prayer that no one can hear, and ask the Father for all that we needed to live a life that is justify and pleasing in your sight. Help us to live a life of soul winner, winning millions, and millions of sinners and the lost into your Holy hands. You alone O' Lord forgive us all our sins, you are the God of resurrection eternal life, no one has ever given; you gave us eternal life so that we may live with you forever in heaven; thank you Jesus. Amen.

APRIL 8TH

THE WORD OF GOD TRANSFORMS LIFE – LET THE WORD OF GOD BE YOUR TRANSFORMATION TODAY

Today's Scripture Reading:

"Come to me, all you who are weary and burdened, and I will give you rest. Take my yoke upon you and learn from me, for I am gentle and humble in heart and you will find rest for your souls. For my yoke is easy and my burden is light." (Matthew 11:28-30) NIV

Our Lord Jesus Christ was calling all the sinners and the loss to himself during his earthly ministry. He gave an invitation that was irresistible to his hearers. Our Lord's invitation still available for the sinners and the lost up till today. Jesus Christ's gracious invitation comes to all who are weary and burdened with the troubles of this life and the sins of their own human nature. By coming to Jesus, and becoming his servant obeying and following his commandments, his directions, his Will free us from our insurmountable burdens and give you rest; peace and his Holy Spirit to lead us through life. Whatever trials and cares you carry will be borne with his help and grace. Jesus Christ is the Lord of life; he will carry all our burdens, our problems, our headaches.

Give your life to him today, he will take care of you, his yoke is very easy, and his burden is very light.

Prayer:

Our Savior Lord, come to us, carry all our problems, fulfill all our heart desires, if you know that our heart's desires is good for us and it is according to your Holy Will and it will bring great glory to your Holy Name; that it will exult your Holy Name in so much that all the sinners and the lost of this world will come to you for forgiveness of their sins, and they will have life in you from this earth to heaven. In your Mighty Holy Name , we pray. Amen.

APRIL 9TH

THE WORD OF GOD TRANSFORMS LIFE –
LET THE WORD OF GOD BE YOUR TRANSFORMATION TODAY

Today's Scripture Reading:

"Are not five sparrows sold for two pennies? Yet not one of them is forgotten by God. Indeed, the very hairs of your head are all numbered. Don't be afraid; you are worth more than many sparrows." (Luke 12:6-7) NIV

Our Lord and Savior Jesus Christ teach that God's faithful children are of great worth to our heavenly Father. God values us more than we can imagine. He point out here how valuable we are that the very hairs in our head are all numbered - God knows how many hairs in our head. There are no devices that ever count the hair on people's head but God in his infinite love know how much the number is of hair on every one of us head. God values us and our personal needs; he desires your love and fellowship so much that he sent his only Son Jesus Christ to die on the cross for you and me. We are never away from his presence, his care, and his concern. Jesus Christ knows all our needs trials and our sorrows. WE are so important to God that he treasures your faithfulness, love, and your loyalty above all earthly things. Our Lord and Savior gave his life for us; on the cross there is no greater love than that, our faith and unwavering faith and love in Jesus

Christ proved genuine in the midst of trials and tribulations, this is his glory and honor.

Prayer:

Lord Jesus Christ, you are worthy of all our praises and thankfulness because of what you have done for us, how you call us into your eternal glory. Lord Jesus Christ do not let your love fail for us. Continue to call sinners and the lost unto you, made them alive in you now and forever. Amen.

APRIL 10TH

THE WORD OF GOD TRANSFORMS LIFE – LET THE WORD OF GOD BE YOUR TRANSFORMATION TODAY

Today's Scripture Reading:

"Be dressed ready for and keep your lamps burning, like men waiting for their master to return from a wedding banquet, so that when he comes and knocks they can immediately open the door for him It will be good for those servants when he comes, I tell you the truth, have them recline at the table and will come and wait on them." (Luke 12:35-37) NIV

This Scripture reveals our Lord' Second Coming to earth; it concerns our Lord' coming for his faithful people, the churches know no other attitude than that it was near, and it could happen at any time. All the believing Christians was called to be spiritually ready at all times and to wait for the return of the Lord. All true believers must be enjoined on the truth in Christ Jesus; they must be so bound to the Lord as their greatest treasure that their hope and longing is the return of Jesus. All the believing Christians must be dressed and be ready, waiting for the uncertain time of Christ coming. Jesus Christ coming back to this world is imminent; he could come back at any time. Believers must be waiting and looking for Christ himself, not for a complex of events that might begin at any time.

Prayer:

Lord God Almighty Jesus Christ our Lord and Savior - you are our hope of glory; you are the one who have eternal life. Pour out your blessing to your people in abundant and immeasurably with your eternal life, mold us shape us, bless us with your infinite love, love of grace that you bestow upon us on the cross. Help us to worship you with the Holy Spirit empowerment. Help us to know you from this earth to heaven and continue to live with you heaven. Amen.

APRIL 11TH

THE WORD OF GOD TRANSFORMS LIFE –
LET THE WORD OF GOD BE YOUR TRANSFORMATION
TODAY

Today's Scripture Reading:

"Therefore, I urge you, brothers, in view of God's mercy to offer your bodies as a living sacrifice, Holy and pleasing to God This is your spiritual act of worship. Do not conform any longer to the pattern of this world, but be transformed by the renewing of your mind. Then you will be able to test and approve what God's Will is - his good, pleasing and perfect Will."(Romans 12:1-2) NIV

God's profound mercy to believers in Jesus Christ, believers should be willingly offering their bodies to God as a living sacrifice for his honor, praise and for his glory. Our greatest desire should be to live the life of the Holy worship and devotion to God in Christ. The sacrifice requires separating ourselves from the pattern of this world; and pursuing God in Holy passion with focus of our mind on him. Our bodies are to be consecrated to God, our Lord Jesus for a lifetime of worship and service. Believers must offer their bodies as dead to sin, and as the instruments of righteousness and as the temple of the Holy Spirit. Do not be conformed because there is a very real pressure to conform to the pattern of the present world system and be squeezed into its mold on many different levels. This pressure must be firmly resisted by all true believers. The alternative to conforming to the world's values and lifestyle is transformation. Transformation results when Christ and his Word renew our minds so that our visions, values and plans are governed by God's revelation and his eternal truth, rather than by the world's temporal and deceptive pattern.

Prayer:

Lord Jesus Christ transform us, by the renew of our minds. Protect us from the worldly lust, do not let us be conform to this world of deception, transform us, by your power and love with your great compassion through the power of the indwelling of the Holy Spirit now and forever. God the Father Almighty, Father of all people in heaven and in this earth, Father of our Lord Jesus Christ, we praise you for your infinite love, calling us to be a Holy people in the kingdom of your begotten Son Jesus, who is the likeness of your eternal and invisible glory, the first born of all creations, God the Father, through our Lord Jesus Christ, we thank you for the resurrection of the body and life everlasting. In Jesus Christ Holy Name , we pray. Amen.

APRIL 12TH

THE WORD OF GOD TRANSFORMS LIFE –
LET THE WORD OF GOD BE YOUR TRANSFORMATION TODAY

Today's Scripture Reading:

"All this I have spoken while still with you, But the counselor, the Holy Spirit, whom the Father will send in my Name, will teach you all things and will remind you of everything I have said to you. Peace I leave with you; my peace I give you. I do not give to you as the world gives. Do not let your hearts be troubled and do not be afraid." (John 14:25-27) NIV

Those who do not obey Christ's teachings do not have personal love for him, and without love for Jesus himself, true saving faith will not exist. To say that people remain saved even though they cease to love Christ, they start living in sin contradicts the words of Jesus Christ concerning love, obedience, and the indwelling of the Holy Spirit. Holy Spirit - the counselor, our helper, our comforter, as a friend coming alongside to help. As Jesus Christ as the helper of his disciples, he touched the weakness of Peter's mother-in-law and gave her strength for service. Holy Spirit is very important in the life of all the Christian believers, without the indwelling of the Holy Spirit; we cannot live a Christian life. Holy Spirit teaches, direct, help us to live a Holy life and plant his Holy character, along with the ministration of that Holy character in the lives of believers which is what matter most. Holy Spirit abides in us, we abide in him, lives in us, and we live in him. He tell us what is going to happen, before it happens, he teaches us the Scriptures just as Jesus taught the apostle. Holy Spirit strengthens us in all the areas of our weakness.

Prayer:

God the Father, God the Son and God the Holy Spirit , we pray to you, that you will continue to live your life in us, directing and take total control of our lives because you are the one that knows what is the best for us. You are a friend, the true friend, the paraclete heavenly guest who proceeded from the Father and the Son, you are the giver of life, abide in us forever. Holy Spirit our comforter, counselor, the almighty God, you are the giver of live, you proceeded from the Father and the Son, and you are our helper in all the areas of our lives. We give you praises and thankfulness from now and forevermore, In Jesus Holy Name, we pray. Amen.

APRIL 13TH

THE WORD OF GOD TRANSFORMS LIFE –
LET THE WORD OF GOD BE YOUR TRANSFORMATION TODAY

Today's Scripture Reading:

"Remain in me; and I will remain in you. No branch can bear fruit by itself; it must remain in the vine. Neither can you bear fruit unless you remain in me. I am the vine, you are the branches. If a man remains in me and I in him, he will bear much fruit; apart from me you can do nothing. If you remain in me and my words remain in you, ask whatever you wish, and it will be given you. If you obey my commands, you will remain in my love, just as I have obeyed my Father's commands and remain in his love"(John 15:4-5, 7, 10) NIV

After a person believers and people of this earth believes in Jesus Christ and their sins forgiven, he or she receives eternal life and the power to remain in Christ. Given that power, the believer must then accept that responsibility in salvation and remain in Christ. Believer continue to abide, or live just as the branch has life only as long as the life of the vine flows into it, so believers have Christ's life only as long as Christ's life flows into them through their remaining in Christ. The conditions by which we remain in Christ are: (a) Keeping God's Word in our hearts continually and in our minds and making it the guide for our actions. (b) Maintaining the habit of constant intimate communion with Christ in order to draw strength from him. (c) Obeying his command, remaining in his love and loving each other. (d) Keeping our lives clean through the Word. (e) Resisting all form of sins and yielding to the Holy Spirit's direction.

Prayer:

Lord Jesus Christ our Lord and our Savior, you are the vine we are the branches, without you we are nothing. Baptized us with the Holy Spirit so that we may be able to be one in you, as you and the Father are one. Be at the center of our hearts and take total control of our lives, help us to worship you in the Spirit and in truth; at the end help us to live with you in heaven. Amen.

APRIL 14TH

THE WORD OF GOD TRANSFORMS LIFE – LET THE WORD OF GOD BE YOUR TRANSFORMATION TODAY

Today's Scripture Reading:

"And we know that in all things God works for the good of those who love him, who have been called according to his purpose"(Romans 8:28) NIV

God Almighty Father of our Lord Jesus Christ always look for our good in all things in this world because we loved him and do what is pleasing to him. Go called us according to his eternal glory and according to his purpose for our lives. Therefore, in all things God works for our good the assurance of the word of God greatly encourages all the believers when we must endure suffering in this life. God will bring good out of all our affliction, trials, and persecution and suffering; God always turn evil that people for his children to a great good - the good that God works is conforming us to the image of Jesus Christ and ultimately bringing about our glorification. This promise of our Lord and Savior is limited to those who love him and have submitted to him through faith in Christ. All things that the Scripture mention does not include our sins and negligence, no one can excuse sin by maintaining that God will work it out for good. God only turn evil to good for those who love him, those who abide in his Words and follow his commandments not those who practice evil and live in sin.

Prayer:

Lord Jesus Christ protects all those who faithfully sincerely give their life to you those people that submitted their lives into our Holy hands. Lord Jesus Christ in your mercy and love turn all the work of the enemy into your great good, and bless us with the manifestation of the Holy Spirit, that we may serve you with all our hearts throughout our life on this earth. In the power and mercy of Jesus Christ, the one and only who gave us the great commission I pray. Amen.

APRIL 15TH

THE WORD OF GOD TRANSFORMS LIFE –
LET THE WORD OF GOD BE YOUR TRANSFORMATION TODAY

Today's Scripture Reading:

"What, then, shall we say in response to this? If God is for us, Who can be against us? Who shall separate us from the love of Christ? Shall trouble or hardship or persecution or famine or nakedness or danger or sword? No, in all these things we are more than conquerors through him who loved us. I am convinced that neither death nor life, neither angels nor demons, neither the present or the future, nor any powers, neither height nor depth, nor anything else in all creation, will be able to separate us from the love of God that is in Christ Jesus our Lord."
(Romans 8:35, 37-39) NIV

All the believing Christians being a victims, in this fallen world; in Jesus Christ we are over and above in victory; instead of barely getting by in life's difficult experiences, in and through Jesus Christ we are over whelming a conquerors. Christ has gained the decisive victory for us at the cross! because of his victory and the power of the Holy Spirit within us, we are empowered to be more than conquerors in our struggle of life. If anyone fails in his or her spiritual life, it will neither be from lack of divine grace and love, nor from any external force or over whelming adversity but from their own neglect to remain in Jesus; our Lord have the certainty that we will never be separated from God's love.

Prayer:

Our Lord and Savior, Jesus Christ the Son of God, the true God, the very God: , we pray to you; do not let us see anything that will separate us from your love, help us to be able to remain in your love from this earth to heaven, help us to be able to love you more and more every day of our life. Help us to be able to love everyone around us both believers and unbelievers around the world, and strive to let them know the love of God the Father that it is in Jesus Christ his only Son, with the help of the Holy Spirit indwelling power, help us to show and teach and witness to the people - the sinners and the lost the way of salvation by grace alone and in Christ alone so that they may rejoice in your love, as we rejoice in your love. Hear our prayer and answer our prayers O' Lord our blessed redeemer King. Amen.

APRIL 16TH

THE WORD OF GOD TRANSFORMS LIFE – LET THE WORD OF GOD BE YOUR TRANSFORMATION TODAY

Today's Scripture Reading:

"But he said to me, 'My grace is sufficient for you, for my power is made perfect in weakness.' Therefore, I will boast all the more gladly about my weaknesses, so that Christ's power may rest on me. That is why, for Christ's sake, I delight in weaknesses, in insults, in hardships, in persecutions, in difficulties, for when I am weak, then I am strong." (2nd Corinthians 12:9-10) NIV

Grace is God's presence, favor and power. God's grace and power are most dearly seen and profoundly revealed in the midst of our human weaknesses. The greater our weakness and trials for Christ, the more the grace of God will give to accomplish his Will. What he gives is always sufficient for us to live our daily lives, to work for him, and to endure our suffering, and the thorns in our flesh. As long as we draw near to Jesus Christ, Christ will give us his heavenly strength and comfort. WE should boast and see the eternal value in our weaknesses, for they cause Christ's power to rest on us and live within us as we walk through this life toward our heavenly home.

Prayer:

Lord Jesus Christ empowers us to be able to have your strength during the time of weakness. Almighty and most merciful Father have mercy upon us. Fulfill all your promise unto mankind in Christ Jesus our Lord, and grant us, O most merciful Father that you may strengths us in all the areas of our lives where we are experiencing weakness, that we may hereafter live a godly, righteous, and sober life, to the glory of your Holy Name, be our immortal food live your life in us now and forever and ever. In your marvelous Holy Name , we pray. Amen.

APRIL 17TH

THE WORD OF GOD TRANSFORMS LIFE –
LET THE WORD OF GOD BE YOUR TRANSFORMATION TODAY

Today's Scripture Reading:

"Rejoice in the Lord always. I will say it again: Rejoice let your gentleness be evident to all. The Lord is near. Do not be anxious about anything, but in everything, by prayer and petition, with thanksgiving, present your requests to God. And the peace of God, which transcends all understanding; will guard your hearts and your minds in Christ Jesus." (Philippians 4: 4-7) NIV

All the believing Christians must rejoice and gain strength by recalling the Lord's grace, nearness and promises. We must believe that the Lord may come at any time. Christ's return as imminent; therefore, we must be ready working and watching at all times. The one essential cure for worry is prayer, for the following reasons, through prayer we renew our trust in the Lord's faithfulness by casting all our anxieties and problems on him, who care for us. God's peace comes to guard our hearts and minds as a result, or our communion prayers with Jesus Christ. God strengthens us to do all the things he desires for us to do for him.

Prayer:

God Almighty Merciful and mighty God compassionate gracious loving God, full of truth and righteousness; help us to rejoice in your ways, to live a gentle life, not to worry or anxious about anything in our lives. Help us by programing us that in everything we might be going through that you have the power to strengthens us and turn our problems in to a great good that will bring you great glory to you. Lord Jesus Christ guides us, do not live us nor forsake us, live your life in our hearts and minds that we may live and serve you from this earth to heaven. Amen.

APRIL 18TH

THE WORD OF GOD TRANSFORMS LIFE – LET THE WORD OF GOD BE YOUR TRANSFORMATION TODAY

Today's Scripture Reading:

"For this reason I remind you to fan into flame the gift of God, which is in you through the laying on of my hands. For God did not give us a spirit of timidity, but a spirit of power, of love and of self-discipline." (2nd Timothy 1:6-7) NIV

The gift that God gave to Timothy was compared to a fire that he must fan into flame. The gift was probably a special anointing and power from the Holy Spirit to fulfill his ministry. The gift and the power bestowed on all the believing Christians by the Holy Spirit do not automatically remain strong and vital. They must be fueled by the grace of God through our prayer, faith, obedience, and diligence. The empowerment of the Holy Spirit helps the pastors, ministers, pastoral staff, and leaders to guard and defend the Gospel committed to them even in a day when many depart from the faith. They must defend the Gospel with strong Word of God not with timidity; they must defend the Gospel of God from any attack of the enemy and against the false teachers and challenge the Church if it is tempted to lay aside the truth. This duty is very essential for all the true believers of Jesus Christ to ensure the salvation of God for themselves and for those who are under their charge as the congregation.

Prayer:

Lord God Almighty most Merciful and compassionate loving God. Father of our Lord Jesus Christ, who gave us his Son for our sins on the cross; we pray that you bless us with empowerment of the Holy Spirit, baptize us with power of the Holy Spirit from above, so that we may boldly proclaim your Holy Name, take the Gospel to the ends of the earth in their own language, magnify your Holy Name. Let us serve you with the empowerment of the Holy Spirit; cast away the spirit of timidity and help us to be bold, confident, joyful, to preach and teach the Gospel to the people in all the nations throughout our life on earth and in heaven. Bless us with the Crown of Rejoicing. In your mighty great Holy Name, we pray. Amen.

APRIL 19TH

THE WORD OF GOD TRANSFORMS LIFE –
LET THE WORD OF GOD BE YOUR TRANSFORMATION TODAY

Today's Scripture Reading:

"Let us then approach the throne of grace with confidence, so that we may receive mercy and find grace to help us in our time of need." (Hebrews4:16) NIV

Believers in Jesus Christ after they have given their life to Jesus Christ our Lord and Savior; they must approach the throne of grace confidently, faithfully, and sincerely - because Jesus Christ sympathizes with our weaknesses. We can confidently approach the heavenly throne, knowing that our prayers and petitions are welcomed and desired by our heavenly Father. The throne of grace is called the throne of grace because from it flows God' love, help, mercy, and forgiveness of our sins, wisdom to live this world; spiritual power to fight against the forces of evil - Satan and all the demonic power of darkness. The throne of grace is where all the spiritual gifts, all the fruit of the Spirit, and all that we need in any circumstances started and manifest. One of the great blessings of salvation is that our Lord Jesus Christ is now our high priest of the new covenant and our mediator of the new covenant, who opens the way for us to come to the Father with confidence for all the areas of needs in our lives.

Prayer:

Jesus Christ our Lord; , we pray that you listen to our prayers and you answer our prayers as we confidently approaching the throne of grace where you sited at the right hand of God the Father Almighty. As we boldly and confidently approach the throne of grace bless us with your mercy and grace to abound more and more in our lives. You are the shepherd of the sheep, the great shepherd, and the chief shepherd; in your infinite mercy bless your sheep who are calling unto you day and night without ceasing. Amen.

APRIL 20TH

THE WORD OF GOD TRANSFORMS LIFE –
LET THE WORD OF GOD BE YOUR TRANSFORMATION TODAY

Today's Scripture Reading:

"Keep your lives free from the love of money and be content with what you have, because God has said, never will I leave you; never will I forsake you. So we say with confidence, The Lord is my helper; I will not be afraid. What can man do to me?"
(Hebrews 13:5-6) NIV

Believers must discipline themselves to be able to focus on the Lord at all time without worry about money. The warning against the love of money is a concern of every believing Christians even the pastors and the ministers. Greed and immorality are closely connected with each other. All too often the love of abundance and luxury and constant desire for wealth up a person to sexual sins. No matter how limited our earthly possessions may be, or how trying our circumstances, we must never need to fear that God will desert or forsake us. Our heavenly Father cares for us. Therefore, we can say with author of the book of Hebrews - the Lord is my helper, I will not be afraid. This can generally and confidently be affirmed with confidence in times of distress, in times of trials or in times any form of earthly troubles.

Prayer:

Lord God almighty, our Father in heaven, compassionate loving God. You are the channels of blessings, the provider of all who put their trust in you. You know what we needed before we ask. You are the source of our financial blessings. Bless us with all what we needed in or to live a life that is pleasing unto you our Lord. Do not let the love of money, greed, and any immoral characters that people put on to get money come to our way. Do not let us get into any crooked business of the world. In your mercy help us, and provide for our financial needs, do not let the power of your provision cease upon us. In your Holy Name , we pray. Amen.

APRIL 21ST

THE WORD OF GOD TRANSFORMS LIFE –
LET THE WORD OF GOD BE YOUR TRANSFORMATION TODAY

Today's Scripture Reading:

"If any of you lacks wisdom, he should ask God, who gives generously to all without finding fault and it will be given to him. But when he asks, he must believe and not doubt, because he who doubts is like a wave of the sea, blown and tossed by the wind." (James 1:5-6) NIV

Divine wisdom from heaven is one of the great gifts that the Spirit of the Lord gave all his children. The Holy Spirit bestows wisdom; this wisdom is directly from God to us for He is the God of wisdom, knowledge, and understanding. Believers are to ask for God's wisdom for coping with all our earthly trials and tribulations, not just for deliverance from them. The wisdom of God brings, or creates the spiritual capacity to see and evaluate our life and our conduct from God's point of view. The wisdom of God will open our hearts and mind through the power of the Holy Spirit to know if we are living our life for the glory of God or not. It involves making the right choices and doing the right things according to God's Will which was revealed in his Word, or if you are doing the right thing in our lives and to other people according to the leading of the indwelling of the Holy Spirit. Believers can receive godly wisdom by coming to God and asking for it by faith.

Prayer

Lord God Almighty, Jesus Christ his only Son - God of wisdom and mercy - bless us, anoint us with your godly wisdom and mercy so that we can live a godly life that will be pleasing in your sight at all times. Answer our prayer when we ask prayer for the blessing of your godly wisdom upon us. With your godly wisdom, we will not lack the understanding of the Scripture and all other things that we need to know in order to serve you better. Lord Jesus Christ, we need great wisdom to live in this world, and help us to bear more and more fruit and be fruitful for your kingdom. Amen.

APRIL 22ND

THE WORD OF GOD TRANSFORMS LIFE –
LET THE WORD OF GOD BE YOUR TRANSFORMATION TODAY

Today's Scripture Reading:

"Cast all your anxiety on him because he cares for you. Be self-controlled and alert. Your enemy the Devil prowls around like a roaring lion looking for someone to devour. Resist him, standing firm in the faith, because you know that your brothers throughout the world are undergoing the same kind of suffering. And the God of all grace, who called you to his eternal glory in Christ, after you have suffered a little while will himself restore you and make you strong, firm and steadfast. To him be the power for ever and ever. Amen" (1st Peter 5:7-11) NIV

All the believing Christians, in all circumstances must cast all what they were going through in the hands of Jesus Christ with no form of anxiety or fear because Christ care for us, and he never stop caring for all those who believe in him. We must pray for self-control of foods, of our money, our financial spending, we must be able to control our spending habit, our angers, and all other behavioral problems that we are struggling with as a Christian. God cares for the troubles of every one of his children;

this truth is emphasized throughout his Word. All our fears and all forms of anxieties and concerns must be decisively given to God.

Prayer:

Lord God Almighty Father, Son, and the Holy Spirit one God and the very God of the universe. Do not cease your caring for us. Solve all our problems, fulfills all our needs help us to cast all our problems into your Holy hands. Let those who believe in you, rejoices in you. let your Holy Name be exulted in all the earth. Continuously helping us to make provision for all that we may need even before , we pray to you. Help us to confidently boldly cast all our problems into your Holy hands, without doubts. Amen.

APRIL 23RD

THE WORD OF GOD TRANSFORMS LIFE –
LET THE WORD OF GOD BE YOUR TRANSFORMATION TODAY

Today's Scripture Reading:

"Moses answered the people, Do not be afraid stand firm and you will see the deliverance the Lord will bring you today. The Lord will fight for you; you need only to be still."
(Exodus 14:13a, 14) NIV

Our Lord and Savior the great shepherd of the sheep - always fight our battle, he fight the battle of the people of Israel then in the Old Testament, he is fighting our battle today. Our Lord still fighting for us up till now, and fill Christ return to establish his kingdom on earth. We see in the darkness the cloud miraculously protected the Israelites, by moving between the Egyptians and the children of Israel. At the same time God's Pillar of fire flooded with light the way across the sea so that the Israelites could cross over. God assured the people that he will fight for them, but they had to move forward to the sea in faith. God almighty fights for his people as they walk in faith and in obedience to his Word. Believing Christians must be still and put their trust in the Lord, who called them from darkness to his marvelous light, he has the power and authority to fight our battle, nothing is impossible for him to do in his loving kindness to us.

Prayer:

Lord God Almighty, God of mercy and love we give you great glory and honor, because you are always be, and you will always be in the life of those who put their trust and faith in you. Hold us in your Holy hands so that in whatever we are going through in life we will not be afraid because we are in your mighty, powerful Holy hands. You have the power to fight our battle, in sickness or in health, we know that you will fight our battle, even the battle we do not know that was ranging in our inmost being, all glory and honor be yours forever. Amen.

APRIL 24TH

THE WORD OF GOD TRANSFORMS LIFE –
LET THE WORD OF GOD BE YOUR TRANSFORMATION
TODAY

Today's Scripture Reading:

"So he went down and dipped himself in the Jordan river seven times, as the man of God had told him and his flesh was restored and became clean like that of a young boy. Then Naaman and all his attendants went back to the man of God. He stood before him and said, Now I know that there is no God in all the world except in Israel." (2nd King 5:14-15)) NIV

This Old Testament story is a prophetic of Jesus Christ, God's promised Messiah. It is amazing that Naaman, a foreigner, was miraculously delivered from leprosy and apparently converted to the true God, while many lepers in Israel remained unclean. Jesus Christ himself mentioned this story of Naaman in order to emphasize that when God's people disobey him and his Word, he will take his kingdom from them and raise up others to experience his love, salvation, and his kingdom power. Naaman's faith cleansed him from his leprosy. The unbelieving Israelites will not be able to receive their blessing from the Lord. Because Jesus Christ is the only Messiah that God promised the Israelites that he is to come but they did not believe, and he was crucified according to the Scripture. The story also warns us that we may be excluded from what God's doing by adhering to human traditions or by failing to believe in the power of God's kingdom.

Prayer:

Lord Jesus Christ helps us to believe in the power of your resurrection as you sited at the right hand of God. Sanctify us with your power and mercy to believe in you and in your Word, which abide and live forever. Lord Jesus Christ calls us unto you so that we may be with you now and forever. Wash us clean with your precious blood from our past, present, and future sins, as you cleanse Naaman from all his leprosy. Sin is like a leprosy that needs to be cleanse from our spirit, soul and body, your blood shed on the cross is only the remedy that can atone for our sins. We give you thanks Lord Jesus Christ for your precious blood that wash us clean and make us white as snow forever to be with you in eternity. Amen.

APRIL 25TH

THE WORD OF GOD TRANSFORMS LIFE –
LET THE WORD OF GOD BE YOUR TRANSFORMATION TODAY

Today's Scripture Reading:

"Do not let this book of Law depart from your mouth; meditate on it day and night, so that you may be careful to do everything written in it. Then you will be prosperous and successful. Have I not commanded you? be strong and courageous. Do not be terrified; do not be discouraged, for the Lord your God will be with you wherever you go."(Joshua 1:8-9) NIV

The Scripture revealed to us that after the death of Moses God Almighty appointed Joshua to take over the service of Moses. Joshua was to be faithful to God's Word by talking about it, meditating on God's Word, obeying all the commandment of God's Word fully. To meditate on the Word of God means to read the Holy Scripture quietly, or talk to yourself as you think. It involves reflecting on God's Words and always applying them to every areas of our Life. God stated that, if Joshua do what he said, he will be prosper and greatly successful. Those who know the Word of God and obey God's Word and his Law will be prosperous and successful, because they possess the wisdom to live righteously and to achieve God's goal for their lives. The requirements for prosperity and success are as follows: (a) we must be strong, courageous, and diligent; (b) we must make God's Word our authoritative guide for all our beliefs and our actions. (c) we must study and meditate daily on God's Word, (d) we must be determined to seek earnestly God's presence throughout our life.

Prayer:

Lord Jesus Christ, we pray that you bring emersion into your Word, make it our daily bread, feed us with your Word; Your Word is true. Help us by directing our hearts and minds to stay in your Word. Bless us with the knowledge and understanding of your Word, anoint our hearts to study the Scripture, meditate on your Word so that we may be courageous, and have great success and most importantly, so that we may be proper in your service of the work of the Gospel. You are our everlasting, ever living God. We live for you, in all the areas of our lives now and forever. In matchless Holy Name, we pray, a Name above all names in heaven and on earth. Amen.

APRIL 26TH

THE WORD OF GOD TRANSFORMS LIFE – LET THE WORD OF GOD BE YOUR TRANSFORMATION TODAY

Today's Scripture Reading

"The Lord is a refuge for the oppressed, a stronghold, in times of trouble. Those who know your Name will trust in you, for you Lord, have never forsaken those who seek you. Sing praises to the Lord, enthroned in Zion, proclaim among the nations what he has done." (Psalm 9:9-11) NIV

The Lord our God is always a refuge for all those who are oppressed from the Old Testament to the New Testament believer. Christ Jesus is our stronghold and our fortress in times of affliction, distresses, tribulations, sicknesses. He is our divine deliverer, before he ascended to heaven, Jesus Christ gave us his Word, he said, he will never leave us, or forsake us; he will be with us till the end of the age. Christ will one day deliver those who seek him, and he will bring judgment against his enemies. In order to prevent discouragement and despair at the apparent success of evil in the world, God's children must firmly believe and confess that the Lord will one day vindicate those who, in spite of affliction, persevere against all who would destroy their faith in God, this also apply to the haters of God, the enemies of God and his church as well as haters of the cross of Jesus Christ. There will be conflict between the forces of evil and the forces of righteousness. Faithful believers will be opposed by Satan, the world and false teachers, false believers with the church.

Prayer:

Lord Jesus Christ you are our refuge, to those who oppress us; they cannot win. because you are our deliverer from the power of the enemy. You dwell above the heavens, heavens is your throne, the earth is your foot stool, keep us safe from the power of the enemy who want you to forsake us, and wants us to forsake you, make us strong to stay in your Word, and to follow your command, your word is true. Do not let us be ashamed, be our stronghold and our fortress every day of our lives.

APRIL 27TH

THE WORD OF GOD TRANSFORMS LIFE – LET THE WORD OF GOD BE YOUR TRANSFORMATION TODAY

Today's Scripture Reading:

"I pray that out of his glorious riches he may strengthen you with power through his Spirit in your inner being, so that Christ may dwell in your hearts through faith. And I pray that you, being rooted and established in love."(Ephesians 3:16-17) NIV

To all the believing Christians, God's love in Jesus Christ is like a tree or a plant with deep roots inside the soil, which is established in his love, is like a building with strong foundation which is laid on a solid rock. This illustration emphasize a deep love of Christ with no Superficiality, it also convey that the revelation of the love of Christ is necessary in our life for a deep solid relationship that issue or enough forth in powerful fruit and life to the glory of God. To have our being our inner-being strengthened by the Holy Spirit is to have our spirit energized, empowered with Christ life and to bring our soul, feelings, thoughts and our purposes more and more under Jesus Christ influence and directions so that the Holy Spirit will be able to manifest his power through us in a greater measure. The purpose of strengthening is of three fold: (1) Jesus Christ may establish his presence in our hearts and minds, (2) We may be rooted and established in the revelation of Christ's love for us with all the saints with full comprehension, (3) We may be filled with all the fullness of God.

Prayer:

God Almighty Father, Son and the Holy Spirit fills us with your full presence through the empowerment of the Holy Spirit that it may empower us in so much that it will reflect from our innermost being the character, behavior and the statures that belong to our Lord Jesus Christ. Lord Jesus Christ our one and only the Savior of the people in this world, baptizes us with the Holy Spirit with fire so that we may be able to do great things for the work of the Gospel, and take the Gospel to where the Gospel has never been heard before in their language. In your great, great mighty Holy Name , we pray. Amen.

APRIL 28TH

THE WORD OF GOD TRANSFORMS LIFE – LET THE WORD OF GOD BE YOUR TRANSFORMATION TODAY

Today's Scripture Reading:

"For we know in part and we prophesy in part, but when perfection comes, the imperfect disappears. When I was a child, I talk like a child, I thought like a child, I reasoned like a child, when I became a man, I put childish ways behind me. Now we see put a poor reflections as in a mirror, then we shall see face to face. Now I know in part; then I shall know fully, even as I am fully known. And now these three remain; faith hope and love. But the greatest of these is love" (1st Corinthians 13:9-13) NIV

These Scriptures are telling us that when we were a child, we lived a different life. We do not know everything that was going on in our lives then because we acted and behaved like a child. We thought like a child, as well as reasoned like a child; the same happens when we are a baby in Christ. We are in need of the milk of the Word of God, not the solid Word. God comes in our life and exalts childlike character more than ministry, faith, or the possession of spiritual gifts. God the Father values and emphasizes character that acts in love, patience, kindness, unselfishness honesty, endurance in righteousness much more that faith to move mountains, or to perform great achievements in the Church. The greatest in the kingdom of God will be those who are great in inward godliness and who demonstrate a genuine love for God and people, and surprisingly, not those who are greatest in outward accomplishments. God's love poured out within believers hearts through the Holy Spirit is always greater than, faith, hope, or any things else.

Prayer:

Lord God Almighty compassionate gracious loving God, you are our deliverer; you deliver us from any earthly troubles. As we grow up be our teacher take all the childish things away from us, and bless us with your full presence and love, your presence is heaven to us. Fill us with your Spirit, Spirit of holiness, protect and guide and lead us. Help us to put all this that can contaminate our spirit, soul, body, and that may grieve the Holy Spirit away from us. In your mercy and love, we pray. Amen

APRIL 29TH

THE WORD OF GOD TRANSFORMS LIFE – LET THE WORD OF GOD BE YOUR TRANSFORMATION TODAY

Today's Scripture Reading:

"The Spirit himself testifies with our spirit that we are God's children. Now if we are children then we are heirs - heirs of God co-heirs with Christ, if indeed we share in his sufferings in order that we may also share in his glory. I consider that our present sufferings are not worth comparing with the glory that will be revealed in us."(Romans 8:16-17) NIV

The Holy Spirit empowers us and also imparts to us confidence that through Jesus Christ and with Jesus Christ, in Jesus Christ we are now children of God. The Spirit of God makes real the truth that Christ Jesus loved all those who believe in him with everlasting and unceasing love. Up till this present moment Jesus Christ still loves us, and he continues to live for us in heaven at the right hand of God the Father Almighty. Christ is the believer's mediator, intercessor, and our advocate in heaven. The Holy Spirit also shows us that the Father loves us as his adopted children, no less than he love his one and only begotten Son. Most important, the Holy Spirit creates in us the love and confidence by which we cry to our heavenly Father as, Abba Father who can fathom your love in our life.

Prayer:

Lord Jesus Christ our gracious and merciful God, help us to know you, more and more every day of our life, help us to worship and honor you in Spirit and in truth throughout our life, and at the end help us to live with you in heaven. Lord Jesus Christ, we belong to you spirit, soul and body, whatever we might be going through in all the areas of our lives; we know that you are with us, do not let your blessing fail for us now and forever. Amen.

APRIL 30ᵀᴴ

THE WORD OF GOD TRANSFORMS LIFE –
LET THE WORD OF GOD BE YOUR TRANSFORMATION TODAY

Today's Scripture Reading:

"As you come to him, the living stone - rejected by men but chosen by God and precious to him you also, like living stones, are being built into a spiritual house to be a Holy priesthood, offering spiritual sacrifices acceptable to God through Jesus Christ - for in Scripture it says: See, I lay a stone in Zion, a chosen and precious cornerstone, and the one who trust in him will never be put to shame." (1st Peter 2: 4-6) NIV

The Old Testament Priesthood was based on descendants of Aaron alone. Whereby their distinctive activities was to offer sacrifices and intercession to God on behalf of his people and to communicate with God. Now, through Jesus Christ's atonement for our sins, every born again believing Christians has been made a priest before God. The priesthood of all believers is as follows: (1) All believers have direct access to God the Father through Jesus Christ. (2) All believers are under the obligation to live Holy lives, (3) All believers are to offer up spiritual sacrifices to God, including being a living sacrifice of joy and obedience to God and nonconformity to the world. (4) Believers' offering and petitions, sacrifices of praises to God must continue throughout their life. (5) Believers must serve the Lord with their whole hearts and willing hands. (6) Believers must perform good deeds giving of our material possession; (8) presenting our bodies to God as instrument of righteousness.

Prayer:

Lord Jesus Christ you are our one and only corner-stone, chosen by God and sent to this world to redeem us from our sins. You are the living stone and our Holy priesthood forever. Almighty Father, maker of heaven and earth and everything that dwells in it. You created man and woman and every soul of human being in your own image, draw them together in the bonds of natural affections, grant them wisdom, and pure devotion in the order of their common lives, that each of them may be to each other a strength in need, a counselor in time of grief or sorrow and in perplexity, a comfort in every struggle of lives, and a companion in every joy, in sickness and in good health, join our will together with your will O' Lord our God, and let our spirit be one with your Spirit; in order that we may be able to enter your kingdom of light in which love is the fulfilling of the Law, through Jesus Christ our redeemer King. Let your light shine upon us always and forever. Hear and answer all our prayers for sinners and the lost, touch the hearts and mind of unbelievers and turn them to you, and make them to be useful in your kingdom now and forever. Amen.

DAILY REFLECTION NOTES

MAY

MAY 1ST

THE WORD OF GOD TRANSFORMS LIFE – LET THE WORD OF GOD BE YOUR TRANSFORMATION TODAY

Today's Scripture Reading:

"One thing I ask of the Lord, this is what I seek; that I may dwell in the house of the Lord all the days of my life, to gaze upon the beauty of the Lord and to seek him in his temple. For in the day of trouble he will keep me safe in his dwelling he will hide me in the shelter of his tabernacle and set me high upon a rock. I am still confident of this, I will see the goodness of the Lord in the land of the living. Wait for the Lord; be strong and take heart and wait for the Lord."(Psalm 27:4, 13-14) NIV

All believing Christians must always seek God's presence; it is the one important, and one most treasured in this life. God almighty call us for this purpose. We must be confident, trusting in God's love and goodness, the most important thing is to dwell in the house of the Lord and behold the beauty of God's house, and his presence throughout our life here on earth. The Lord takes pleasure in keeping us safe, so that we do not have to divide attention, but we focus on him and him only. We must seek him in his temple worship him in spirit and in truth. Our Lord and Savior always keep us safe in any earthly troubles and deliver us from any unrighteousness even when we do not aware of it, or know it. God's activities in the life of a believing Christians are incomprehensible.

Prayer:

Lord Jesus Christ compassionate, gracious loving God full of truth and righteousness abounding in mercy and forgiveness bless us with your full presence at all times and use us in a mighty way in the work of your kingdom; for your glory now and forever, provide everything we may need to serve you with big proclamation of your Holy Name by witnessing the Gospel to the unsaved and people of all other religion. In your matchless Holy Name , we pray. Amen.

MAY 2ND

THE WORD OF GOD TRANSFORMS LIFE – LET THE WORD OF GOD BE YOUR TRANSFORMATION TODAY

Today's Scripture Reading:

"The Word of the Lord came to me, saying,
Before I formed you in the womb I knew you,
before you were born I set you apart;
I appointed you as a prophet to the nations."
(Jeremiah 1:4-5) NIV

Jeremiah was called by God to be a prophet to the southern kingdom of Judah. His ministry was over forty years; the Lord God almighty used him faithfully for his service. God was instructing prophet Jeremiah in the Old Testament that he has a plan for him even before he put him in his mother's womb, and when he was born, he made him a prophet to the nation of Israel. In the same way, today in the New Testament, the Lord has a plan for those he loves. Our Lord and Savior will answer our prayers and intercede for us at the right hand of God. God almighty always fulfill his promises; when he said it - it is done. He said, there is no word that comes out of his mouth will be void. The word will go to where he sends it, and it will achieve the purpose that he sent it for. God never fails; He restored back the children of Israel to their nation which no one or any nation of this world can take it away from them. God fulfills his Word and promise when the time fully comes both in relation to the fullness of his redemptive purposes, in response to his faithful people's earnest prayers.

Prayer:

Lord God Almighty, Father of our Lord Jesus Christ, do not let the plan you have for us in this life fails. You are the great I am all power belongs to you, you have the power, love, and mercy to restore those who stray away from you through the earthy troubles draw them back to you and keep them safe for eternity. You are the everlasting Savior; you have the power and control over any circumstances we might be going through in this world; in your mercy continuously calling the lost unto you for your glory and for their gift of eternal life in you forever. You are the God of blessings, from you all the goodness flows; bless us abundantly, immeasurably, and exceedingly now and forever. In your mighty Holy Name , we pray. Amen.

MAY 3ᴿᴰ

THE WORD OF GOD TRANSFORMS LIFE – LET THE WORD OF GOD BE YOUR TRANSFORMATION TODAY

Today's Scripture Reading:

"For all have sinned and fall short of the glory of God, and are justified freely by his grace through the redemption that came by Christ Jesus. God presented him as a sacrifice of atonement, through faith in his blood. He did this to demonstrate his justice, because in his forbearance he had left the sins committed before hand unpunished" (Romans 3:23-25) NIV

Faith in the Lord Jesus Christ as our Lord and Savior is the only condition that God requires for salvation, Christ came to the world as a sacrifice offering for our sin, he died not for his own sake, but for the sake of sinners. Christ is our substitution, he suffered death as the result of humanity sins, as our substitute, and he offered himself for atonement for our sins. Christ is our propitiator his death for sinners satisfied God's righteousness and his moral order, thereby, removing his wrath against the repentant sinner. God's integrity requires that sin be punished, and propitiation be made for our sinners' sake. Through propitiation by Jesus Christ's blood, God's holiness remained uncompromising and he was able to justify and reveal his grace and love in salvation. It must be emphasized that God himself set forth Christ as propitiation. God did not need to be persuaded to show mercy and love, for already God was reconciling the world to himself in Jesus Christ.

Prayer:

Lord God Father of all mercies and love, sustainer of all things, you are in Jesus Christ reconciling the people of this world to yourself through our Lord Jesus Christ who is the propitiator for our sins, we give you thanks and give you praise for your love for us through the atonement of your Son Jesus Christ. We give you thanks our Lord you are worthy to be praise. In your mighty Holy Name , we pray. Amen.

MAY 4TH

THE WORD OF GOD TRANSFORMS LIFE – LET THE WORD OF GOD BE YOUR TRANSFORMATION TODAY

Today's Scripture Reading:

"For God so loved the world that he gave his one and only Son, that whoever believes in him shall not perish but have eternal life"
(John 3:16) NIV

This particular Scripture reveals the heart of God and the purpose of God for the humanity. God's love is wide enough to embrace all the people in the world. God Almighty Father of our Lord Jesus Christ gave his Son as an offering for sin on the cross. The atonement proceeds from the loving heart of God. It was not something forced on him. Jesus Christ is God's only begotten Son and the only Savior of the people in the world, and for the loss of humanity, or human race. Believer's self-surrendering fellowship with him and obedience to Christ. A fully assured trust in Jesus Christ that he is both able and willing to bring you a final salvation and to fellowship with God in heaven. The "word" perish points not to physical death but to the dreadful reality of eternal punishment. Eternal life is the gift God bestows on all the believers when we are a born - again Christians after we have repented of our sins and gave our life to him faithfully and sincerely. Eternal life expresses perpetuity but also quality of life a divine quality of life, a life that is free us from the power of sin, death and Satan, a life that removes us from what is merely earthly in order to know God and get close to him and be in his house throughout the days of our life.

Prayer:

Lord Jesus Christ you are the God eternal, the invisible the only wise God, bless us with eternal life so that at the end of this life we may be able to live with you now and forever. Continuously bringing, calling, moving sinners and the lost unto you. You do not want anyone to perish, you want them to come to the knowledge of repentance and pray for the forgiveness that is only in you, our Lord, fulfill the great commission through all the believers in this world. Help us to take the great commission to the four corners of the earth, auto-most part of the earth, under the earth, let the Gospel of God continuously spreading like a wildfire in the heart and mind of all the living souls on earth. In your great Holy Name , we pray. Amen.

MAY 5ᵀᴴ

THE WORD OF GOD TRANSFORMS LIFE – LET THE WORD OF GOD BE YOUR TRANSFORMATION TODAY

Today's Scripture Reading:

"And you also were included in Christ when you heard the Word of truth, the gospel of your salvation. Having believed, you were marked in him with a seal, the promised Holy Spirit, who is a deposit guaranteeing our inheritance until the redemption of those who are God's possession to the praise of his glory."
(Ephesians 1:13-14) NIV

The Holy Spirit and his place in the believing Christians is life and, in the believers, redemption is the central emphasis in the Scripture the Book of Ephesians. The Holy Spirit is the mark, or seal of God's ownership, is the first installment of the believers inheritance. The Holy Spirit is the wisdom of the revelation that helps the believers of Jesus Christ when he or she draws near to God. The believer is automatically included in the Christ Jesus after repentance of their sins; the Holy Spirit take over and dwell in the believer's heart and mind, living the life of Jesus in him or her. Building the body of the believer into the Holy Temple where God the Father, Son and Holy Spirit dwell and abode forever. Holy Spirit responsibility is to reveals the mystery of Jesus Christ before the foundation of the world to the believer; strengthens the believer with power in the inner being, motivate the unity in the

Christians faith in full Christ likeness. The Holy Spirit is grieving when there is sin in the life of the believer.

Prayer:

Lord Jesus Christ brings all the believers to you by the baptism of your Holy Spirit. Clothe us with the power of the Holy Spirit to serve you faithfully from this earth to heaven. Do not let anything of this world trouble us to the point that it will take us away from your presence; strengthens us where we are weak and help us to live with you and for your glory now and forever. Amen.

MAY 6TH

THE WORD OF GOD TRANSFORMS LIFE –
LET THE WORD OF GOD BE YOUR TRANSFORMATION TODAY

Today's Scripture Reading:

"Therefore, get rid of all moral filth and the evil that is so prevalent and humbly accept the Word planted in you, which can save you." (James 1:21)NIV

The Word of God, either preached, or written, cannot effectively take hold of a person's life if he or she is not separated from moral filth and evil. God Almighty Jesus Christ our Savior commands us as believers to set aside all the ungodly filth that permeates a corrupt society, and which influences us and our families. This filth will defile our souls and blight our lives. The Scripture says that what is improper for God's Holy people. Accordingly, we must not engage in any kind of impurity or obscenity. We must be aware that allowing any kind of moral filth into our lives or into our homes, including filthy language, or obscenity through televisions, video, or some Internet, grieves the Holy Spirit and violates God's Holy standards for his people. God's Word warns believers; "Let no one deceive you with empty Words, for because of such things God's wrath comes; therefore, do not be partners with them" Believers must take righteousness and holiness seriously. Our houses and our offices must be swept clean and filled with the Word of God and the holiness of Jesus Christ.

Prayer:

Lord Jesus Christ you revealed yourself to us, in your mercy manifest your full presence in our lives. Help us to seek you and find you every day of our life. Lord Jesus Christ wash us clean from any filthiness of the world, and make us your own forever. Purified us from all our sin, help us to live a life that is justify in your sight. Bless us with the power of your Holy Spirit so that we may love you more and more everyday of our life. Amen.

MAY 7TH

THE WORD OF GOD TRANSFORMS LIFE –
LET THE WORD OF GOD BE YOUR TRANSFORMATION TODAY

Today's Scripture Reading

"But you are a shield around me, O' Lord, you bestow glory on me and lift up my head. To the Lord I cry aloud, and he answers me from his Holy hill. I lie down and sleep; I wake again, because the Lord sustains me. I will not fear the tens of thousands drawn up against me on every side" (Psalm 3:3-6) NIV

All the believing Christians who live according to God's Will, but find themselves confronting affliction and opposition may call on God with the confidence that he will act on their behalf according to his divine purpose. The Scripture mentioned - shield, it referring to God's protection - God Almighty is our shield and sources of our protection and where we may be on this earth, he is always there, his light is shining upon us where ever we may go, he always put his shield around us, as well as bestow his glory on us and lift up our head. When we don't expect something great is always happen in our lives that lift our hope and our head up so that the greater things happens in our lives, the more we cry aloud to him, who only the source of our life. God will always answer the prayer of his people from his Holy hill, he is our sustainer he sustains us in all the areas of our lives.

Prayer:

Lord Jesus Christ Father, Son, and the Holy Spirit, your Holy hands, deliver us from any obstacles of life. Help us to maintain good relationship with you and call unto you for everything we need, or we may need. you are the giver of life; bless us with your life. Open our heart and mind so that we can see all the good things you have prepared for us from this earth to heaven, especially our heavenly inheritance. Amen.

MAY 8ᵀᴴ

THE WORD OF GOD TRANSFORMS LIFE – LET THE WORD OF GOD BE YOUR TRANSFORMATION TODAY

Today's Scripture Reading:

"Lift up your heads, O you gates; be lifted up, you ancient doors, that the King of glory may come in. Who is this King of glory? The Lord strong and mighty, the Lord mighty in battle. Lift up your heads, O you gates; lift them up, you ancient doors, that the King of glory may come in. Who is he, this King of glory? The Lord Almighty he is King of glory." (Psalm 24:7-10) NIV

Jesus Christ is the one and only the compassionate gracious living God is the King of glory, because his glory fills the sky, he is the King of glory because his great glory shine in our hearts and minds of all those who beliefs in him. The King of glory is the Lord Jesus Christ our Lord and Savior. Christ is the King of glory because the generation of those who seek him, faithfully, believers must pray that the King of glory will come, and manifest himself to us in this world without delay. This prayer of concerns of God's kingdom to come; anticipating Christ's eternal reign and the final destruction of evil, the Devil and his devilish angels. Jesus Christ is the King Eternal and the King of glory because Eternal Life dwell in him Those who belongs to the King Eternal, have received eternal life which bestows by the King of glory, King Eternal.

Prayer:

Lord Jesus Christ you are the King of glory, Eternal Life, bless the people of this earth so that they can be able to open their hearts and minds to you so that you may bless them with Eternal Life which comes only from you our one and only the King of glory. Come to our life and live in us forever. Amen.

MAY 9TH

THE WORD OF GOD TRANSFORMS LIFE – LET THE WORD OF GOD BE YOUR TRANSFORMATION TODAY

Today's Scripture Reading:

"But the eyes of the Lord are on those who fear him, on those whose hope is in his unfailing love, to deliver them from death and keep them alive in famine." (Psalm 33:18-19) NIV

Naturalistically, hope is wishful thinking about something good happening in the future, or tomorrow. The Scripture says: hope is a firm confidence from God about future issues because they are based on God's promises and revelation; in other words, hope is connected and is inseparably with a firm faith and a confident trust in the Lord. The foundation for the believer's confident hope derives from the nature of God, of Jesus Christ and of God's Word. Believer's hope must be in God who made the heavens and earth and the things that dwell in it. Our hope must also be in his Son Jesus Christ, our redeemer King, our gracious Master, and our God and in his Word. Believing Christians' hope must be based on God's love and on God's grace in the midst of our sufferings in our lives and we may be able to stand in his presence. We have hope that our suffering will be over when we get to leave this earth and also receive our resurrection bodies. With these great promises in store for those who hope in God and in his Son Jesus Christ, we must rejoice.

Prayer:

Lord Jesus Christ our Lord and Savior, you are our hope of glory, our eternal life. Teach us, equip us, change us in this life so that we may seek you and find you if we seek you with our hearts and minds. create in us a new Spirit, a new heart, a new Name, that will live for you forever and worship you with hope and your glory that will shine upon us forever. Amen.

MAY 10TH

THE WORD OF GOD TRANSFORMS LIFE –
LET THE WORD OF GOD BE YOUR TRANSFORMATION TODAY

Today's Scripture Reading:

"Teach me your way, O Lord, and I will walk in your truth; give me an undivided heart, that I may fear your Name. I will praise you, O lord my God, with all my heart; I will glorify your Name forever. For great is your love toward me; you have delivered me from the depts. of the grave" (Psalm 86:11-13) NIV

Lord God Almighty you are the greatest teacher on earth during your earthly ministry, you opened the Scripture to them, and they rejoice in your teaching greatly, they passed your teaching unto us, and we believe in you. Continue to teach us your way on this earth, your way is the best way. We will walk in your truth with undivided heart that will bring glory and honor to your Holy Name. In the midst of our troubles, afflictions, persecutions and tribulation including all the earthly troubles and adversities we ask in humble spirit to teach us your ways and your truth so that we can be able to teach others that does not know you and they may, or might not have the fear of God in their heart. When we are experiencing trials and going through all forms of difficulties, teach us to cry out to God for wisdom and to be able to walk in Christ ways with a heart that truly fears and delight in your truth.

Prayer:

Our Lord and Savior Jesus Christ, I pray that you continuously filling us with your truth teaching us your way, showing us the right path, so that we may be able to walk in your ways, and help us to know your way because you are the way, the truth, and the life. All life dwell in you, show us your way so that we can walk with you forever. During your earthly ministry, and up till today Lord Jesus Christ, the greatest teach, in loving kindness and mercy, teach us how to live a good life that will bring honor to your Holy Name. Amen.

MAY 11ᵀᴴ

THE WORD OF GOD TRANSFORMS LIFE – LET THE WORD OF GOD BE YOUR TRANSFORMATION TODAY

Today's Scripture Reading:

"And if I go and prepare a place for you, I will come back and take you to be with me that you also may be where I am know the way to the place where I am going"(John14:3-4) NIV

Jesus Christ our Savior Lord promised all the believing Christians and he gave us the Word of assurance when he was about to live this world and go the heaven, he will return from his Father's right hand presence and take his people to live with him in heaven; to the place where he prepared for them. This is all the believing Christians hope of glory because Christ is coming back for his own. This is the Word of assurance of hope of all the believers today and till Christ return. Jesus Christ will be coming back for his faithful in order for them to escape the world future trials and tribulations that is going to happens at ends time. Jesus Christ is coming back to take all those who call unto him faithfully and sincerely to live with him forever. Jesus Christ promised that where he is that where we will be in heaven, he said in his Father's house there are many mansions, he has gone ahead of us, through the resurrection and ascension in order to prepare a place for us, we will all be raptured into heaven and live with Christ forever.

Prayer:

Lord Jesus Christ, you loved us with an everlasting love from the beginning of the creation of this world. Help us guide us, to live a life that will bring great glory to your Holy Name, a life that we will be able to live with you in heaven and serve you; and be useful for you, you are the only way, Lord Jesus Christ show us the way, you are the one who have Eternal Life, bless us with eternal life. In your mighty Holy Name , we pray now and forever. Amen.

MAY 12TH

THE WORD OF GOD TRANSFORMS LIFE – LET THE WORD OF GOD BE YOUR TRANSFORMATION TODAY

Today's Scripture Reading:

"In the beginning was the Word, and the Word was with God, and the Word was God. He was with God in the beginning. Through him all things were made, without him nothing was made that has been made. In him was life, and that life was the light of men. The light shines in the darkness, but the darkness has not understood it." (John 1:1-5) NIV

Apostle John begins his Gospel message by calling Jesus Christ the Word. In using this designation for Jesus Christ, John presented Christ as the personal Word of God as well as indicates that in these last days God has spoken to us though his Son. Jesus Christ is the manifold wisdom of God and he is the perfect revelation of the nature and person of God. Just as a person's Words reveal his or her heart and mind of God. This is one of the main things that characterized Jesus Christ as the Word. (a) Jesus Christ is the Word in relation to God the Father, Christ pre-existence with God the Father before the creation of the universe. (b) Jesus Christ was a person existing from eternity, distinct from, but in eternal fellowship with God the Father. (c)

Christ Jesus was fully divine and fully human; having the same nature and essence as the Father.

Prayer:

Lord Jesus Christ, O' Merciful and mighty God, you are the God of glory Son forever more, you are the immortal, the invisible, the only wise God. You are the incarnate Son of God full of grace and truth, Jesus the Lamb of God who took away the sin of the people of the whole world. Jesus Christ you are the Word of God became flesh and dwell among us; we beheld your glory, the glory of the only begotten Son of the Father full of love and kindness. Stretch your Holy hands from heaven and bring the people of this world close to you, that we may see you clearly, love you more dearly, follow you more nearly, praises your Holy Name, and praise your Holy Name from this earth to heaven. Feed us with your Word, your Word is true. Help us to seek your full presence in our lives every day in this world. Amen.

MAY 13TH

THE WORD OF GOD TRANSFORMS LIFE –
LET THE WORD OF GOD BE YOUR TRANSFORMATION TODAY

Today's Scripture Reading:

"There came a man who was sent from God; his Name is John. He came as a witness to testify concerning that light, so that through him all men might believe. He himself was not the light, he came only as a witness to the light. The true light that gives light to every man was coming into the world." (John 1:6-9) NIV

Jesus Christ is the Word of God in relation to the world. Jesus Christ is the light that shines in this evil and sinful world that is controlled by Satan. The majority of the people in the world have not accepted Jesus's life or his light, but the darkness has not mastered it or won it over. It was through Jesus Christ that God the Father created and sustains the universe. Jesus Christ is the Word became flesh and took on human nature but without sin. Jesus Christ illumines all who hear his Gospel by imparting a measure of grace and understanding in, or that they may freely choose to accept or reject the Gospel message. Apart from the light of Jesus Christ, there is no other light by which we may see the truth and be saved. The basic Word of the incarnation - is that Christ left heaven and entered the condition of human life through the human birth and became the God man. Jesus Christ was not created; he is eternal, and he has always been in loving fellowship with the Father and the Holy Spirit - the Holy Trinity forever one God.

Prayer:

Lord Jesus Christ, no one has ever loved like you and no one has ever cared like you. You came down from heaven to save us and to give us life in you, life everlasting, and eternal life, we give you thanks and praises, we glorified your Holy Name now and forever, for what you have done for us on the cross, you are the one and only the light of the world, the light that shine forever, let your life shine upon us every day of our lives in everything we do, and everywhere we are, if we have a thousand tongues is not enough to thank you and praises your Holy Name for your infinite love for us. Amen.

MAY 14ᵀᴴ

THE WORD OF GOD TRANSFORMS LIFE – LET THE WORD OF GOD BE YOUR TRANSFORMATION TODAY

Today's Scripture Reading:

"Though you have not seen him, you love him; and even though you do not see him now, you believe in him and are filled with an in expressible and glorious joy, for you are receiving the goal of your faith, the salvation of your souls." (1st Peter 1:8-9) NIV

God the Father considers the faith of believers today as a greater wonder than the faith of those who saw and heard Jesus in person, even after his resurrection. Believing Christians now, although they have never seen him, love him and believe in him According to Jesus Christ, there is a special blessing for those who have not seen and yet have believed. As we live by faith, we are given joy as God's gift to us. Our faith is based not only on God's Word in the New Testament, but also on God's Word in the Old Testament. Where the Holy Spirit through the prophets predicted Jesus Christ's sufferings and the glories that will follow. The Scripture says that Jesus is God; this is the foundation of the Christian faith and is of utmost importance for our salvation. Without Christ being divine he could not have made atonement for the sins of the people in the world.

Prayer:

Lord Jesus Christ continue in your mercy to call the sinners and the lost to you, bless them with the Spirit of believe in order that they may believe the Scripture. You said blessed are they that are not see but believe; bless them even, as they were not there with you during your earthly ministry. They will love you and believe in you through the ministry of the Pastors, Ministers, and missionaries proclaiming the Gospel all over the world; through the power of the Holy Spirit indwelling. Amen.

MAY 15TH

THE WORD OF GOD TRANSFORMS LIFE – LET THE WORD OF GOD BE YOUR TRANSFORMATION TODAY

Today's Scripture Reading:

"Then Jesus Declared, I am the bread of life; He who comes to me will never go hungry, and he who believe in me will never, be thirsty. But as I told you, you have seen me and still you do not believe. All that the Father gives me will come to me, and whoever comes to me I will never drive away. For I have come down from heaven not to do my will but to do the will of him who sent me" (John 6:35-38) NIV

Jesus Christ our Lord and Savior, the one and only the bread of life, he said: "I am the bread of life" this is the first of the seven "I Am" statement of our Lord recorded in the Gospel of John, each one emphasizing an important aspect of the personal ministry of Jesus Christ. Jesus Christ was telling his disciples during his earthly ministry that he is the sustenance that nourishes spiritual life of everyone that believes in him and gave their life to him. Jesus Christ affirmed clearly that, and promised to welcome all who come to him in repentance of their sins and in faith. Those who come to Jesus Christ, all the believing Christians who come in response to the grace given to them by God, Christ will not and will never drive away. Jesus Christ did not want anyone to be perished, he wants them to come to the knowledge of repentance and ask for the forgiveness which is only in him.

Prayer:

Lord God Almighty, Father, Son, and Holy Spirit forever one God; , we pray that in your infinite mercy you will continue to call the sinners and the lost unto you. You do not want them to perish, bless them with the Spirit of repentance so that they can repent of their sins, and be one in your Spirit, Soul, and Body. Be our bread of life now and forever, so that we may be able to be useful for the work of the kingdom. Amen.

MAY 16TH

THE WORD OF GOD TRANSFORMS LIFE – LET THE WORD OF GOD BE YOUR TRANSFORMATION TODAY

Today's Scripture Reading:

"Be very careful, then, how you live not as unwise but as wise, making the most of every opportunity, because the days are evil. Therefore, do not be foolish, but understand what the Lord's Will is." (Ephesians 5:15-16) NIV

This is a remedy against sin and circumspection; if you are to reprove others for their sins, you must look well to yourselves, and to your own behavior and conduct. We have here another preservative from the before - mentioned sins; it being impossible to maintain purity and holiness of heart and life without great circumspection, exactly in the right way, in order to which we must be frequently consulting our rule. Not as fools, who walk at all adventures, and who through neglect, and want of care; fall into sin, and destroy themselves, but we must walk as wise, as persons taught of God. Circumspect walking is the effect of tree wisdom, but the contrary is the effect of folly. Believers must remember the time; time is very important in everything we do in this life. For example, a trader who diligently observes and improves the seasons for his merchandise and trade. Good believing Christians must be good husbands and good wives, parents, sisters, and brothers at all time. They should make the best use they can of the present seasons of grace. Our time is a talent given to us by God for some good end, and it is misspent and lost when it is not employed according to God's design.

Prayer:

Lord Jesus Christ our Lord and Savior help us to see clearly, that we need to use our time in a godly way on this earth. Help us so that we do not lose our time here; help us to endure to redeem our time, and double it diligently for the future service for you. In your Name, we pray. Amen.

MAY 17TH

THE WORD OF GOD TRANSFORMS LIFE –
LET THE WORD OF GOD BE YOUR TRANSFORMATION TODAY

Today's Scripture Reading:

"Do not get drunk on wine, which lead to debauchery. Instead, be filled with the Spirit speak to one another with psalms, hymns and spiritual songs. Sing and make music in your heart to the Lord, always giving thanks to God the Father for everything, in the Name of our Lord Jesus Christ. Submit to one another out of reverence for Christ."(Ephesians 5:18) NIV

The Scripture reveals that all the believing Christians must repeatedly being filled by the Spirit. God's children must experience constant renewal of the Holy Spirit. Christians are to be baptized in the Holy Spirit after conversion, yet they are to be filled with the Spirit repeatedly for worship, service, and witness. Drunkenness is a sin that seldom goes alone, but often involves men in other stances of guilt; it is a great hindrance to the spiritual life. Instead of being filled with wine, the apostle Paul, exhorts believers to be filled with the Holy Spirit. Those who are full of drink are not likely to be full of the Holy Spirit. Men and women should make every effort to labor for a plentiful measure of the graces of the Spirit, because a plentiful measure of the grace of the Spirit will fill the souls with greater joy, and courage. Believes should not be satisfied with a little of the spirit, but to be fully filled with the Spirit.

Prayer:

Lord Jesus Christ compassionate great God above all gods. Fill us with your Spirit, you are the one that save us, in order that we may dwell in you and you may dwell in us by your Spirit; in order that we may be able to worship you; serve you in the Spirit of holiness throughout our days on this earth, and also, we will continue to service you in heaven. Amen.

MAY 18TH

THE WORD OF GOD TRANSFORMS LIFE –
LET THE WORD OF GOD BE YOUR TRANSFORMATION
TODAY

Today's Scripture Reading:

"I have made you known to them; and will continue to make you known in order that the love you have for me may be in them and that I myself may be in them." (John 17:26) NIV

During our Lord Jesus Christ earthly ministry, he showed his respect for his disciples. His teaching that he has led the apostles to the knowledge of the Scripture and understanding of the knowledge of Christ what Christ had done for them; declaring the Name of the Lord of the disciples in greater details and measure. This he had done for all those who believe in him. All the believing Christians are indebted to Jesus Christ for all the knowledge we have of the Father's Name. Those whom Christ recommends being favored of God he first leads into an acquaintance with God. What he intended to do yet further for them; declaring of their names to God the Father. Christ designed to give further instruction after his resurrection by the outpouring of the Holy Spirit after his ascension; to all believers, into whose hearts he hath shined, he shines more and more. This is to secure and advance their real happiness in two ways: Christ designed that all the believing Christians to have communion with God the

Father: Therefore, he gave them the knowledge of God's Name by pointing out that the love which the Father gave to him, he has given the same love to those who believe in him.

Prayer:

God the Father Almighty compassionate gracious loving God, Jesus Christ his only Son Holy Spirit forever one God - the Holy Trinity. In your infinite Mercy and love for all the people on this earth, continue to pour out your Holy Spirit on us so that we will be able to witness, worship and serve with the Holy Spirit empowerment in all the areas of our lives. O Merciful and mighty God, have mercy upon us now and forever. Amen.

MAY 19TH

THE WORD OF GOD TRANSFORMS LIFE –
LET THE WORD OF GOD BE YOUR TRANSFORMATION TODAY

Today's Scripture Reading:

"If any of you has a dispute with another, dare he take it before the ungodly for judgment instead of before the saints? Do you not know that the saints will judge the world? and if you are to judge the world, are you not competent to judge trivial cases? Do you not know that we will judge the angels? How much more the things of this life!?" (1st Corinthians 6:1-3) NIV

Whenever there is a dispute between Christians, they should be able to settle within the church and not in courts of Law. The church must judge the right or wrong involved, render a verdict and exercise discipline if needed. This does not mean that a believer may not use courts in serious cases with unbelievers. The church must not allow mistreatment, or abuse of widows, children, and the people who are weak. The Scripture is based strictly on the issues where there was no clear right or wrong, sinful actions must not be tolerated, in the church of God, it must be handled according to the Christ's instruction. In cases of divorced or deserted of family, or the refusal to support his wife and children with alimony, the mother with the right motives and concern for children may take the case to court.

Prayer:

Lord Jesus Christ our Lord and Savior, Most Holy, the Holy One of Israel, the true Son of God, we pray that you bless us with peace in the church, you yourself deal with a greedy, and destructive person in the church, while on earth, by taken the right action on the person. Lord Jesus, live your life through us forever, Let the husband and wife, all those who believe in you solve their problems with the knowledge and wisdom of God, instead of rushing to court, and destroying each other, because one wanted to win the case especially in the area of divorce, child support, and dividing of properties; let them use your wisdom instead of falling into sin, or destroying each other's life. Protect, guide, lead, and control all the families of God. In your great Holy Name I pray. Amen.

MAY 20TH

THE WORD OF GOD TRANSFORMS LIFE –
LET THE WORD OF GOD BE YOUR TRANSFORMATION TODAY

Today's Scripture Reading:

"For in Christ Jesus neither circumcision, nor un-circumcision has any value. The only thing that counts is faith expressing itself through love."(Galatians 5:6) NIV

Jesus Christ is the end of the Law, having come, now it was neither here nor there whether a man were circumcised or uncircumcised; he was neither the better for the one, nor the worse for the other, nor would either the one, or the other recommend him to God. Yet he informs that what would do so is faith, which worked by love. Without faith nothing else would stand them in any way. Faith where it is true is a working grace; it works by love, love for God the Father, Son and the Holy Spirit, love for our brothers and sister; and with faith working by love is all in all in the lives of all Christians. The life of a believing Christians is a race, wherein he must run, and hold on, if he would obtain the prize. It is not enough that we run the race, but we must run well to win the race and to receive a crown of righteousness at the end in heaven saving faith is a living faith in a living Savior, a faith so vital that it cannot avoid expressing itself in love motivated by deeds. Faith that does not sincerely love and obey Christ Jesus or show a real concern for the work of God's kingdom does not qualify as saving faith.

Prayer:

Lord God Almighty, Father, Son, and the Holy Spirit, Father of love and mercy, let the people of this earth know that everyone is the same in your Holy hands, uncircumcision, and circumcision we are all one in Spirit. Let love prevail and perfect all what is lacking in our lives, let your love, increase in our heart and flow through us to other people in this world. Hear our prayers and have mercy upon us, O' Lord, the one and only the creator of all things. Lord Jesus Christ bless all those who believe in you with a saving faith, a steadfast faith, help all believers to run a race for the work of the kingdom and win the crown of righteousness when we get back to heaven - hear our prayers O' Lord. Amen.

MAY 21ST

THE WORD OF GOD TRANSFORMS LIFE –
LET THE WORD OF GOD BE YOUR TRANSFORMATION TODAY

Today's Scripture Reading:

"If you obey my commands, you will remain in my love, just as have obeyed my Father's commands and remain in his love."
(John 15:10) NIV

"Jesus Christ our Lord and Savior call us to a life of Holy intimacy and personal devotion to his Lordship. This is possible for all those who believe in him. Christ Jesus cannot, and will never tell us to do what it is impossible for us to do. As a loving Savior, who loved us so much that he came down from heaven and gave his life for us, he know what is good for us, he wants us all the believing Christians to be with him in heaven and live with him forever. Jesus Christ knows that this is possible because of his Father's love for us, which he has poured into our hearts by the power of the Holy Spirit. God demonstrated his great love through Jesus Christ's dying for us while we were still sinners. The condition of remaining in Jesus is that we will remain in Jesus's love by pursuing spiritual intimacy and communion with him, and by obeying his word that he commands, just as he did with the Father. All the believing

Christians must then accept that responsibility in salvation and remain in Christ Jesus.

Prayer:

Lord God Almighty the compassionate, gracious loving God we thank you for all what you have done through us, doing through us, and still going to do through us in other for the people of this world to receive your gift of grace, and be saved into your Holy hands. accept our prayers O Lord, let those who do not know you seek you, find you, and give their life to you faithfully and sincerely; let them call on your Holy Name, let them put their faith in you, let them worship you with all their spirit, soul, and body now and forever. Amen.

MAY 22ND

THE WORD OF GOD TRANSFORMS LIFE – LET THE WORD OF GOD BE YOUR TRANSFORMATION TODAY

Today's Scripture Reading:

"The Lord will keep you from all harm - he will watch over your life; the Lord will watch over your coming and going both now and forevermore." (Psalm 121:7-8) NIV

This Scripture reveals and applied to our Christian lives; from our spiritual birth until we leave this earth to rest God always preserve us. Our physical lives as we go out in the morning to work and come home in the evening; he is our constant guard; He is our spiritual strength. Our Lord is our shade; he not only protects those whom belongs to him by keeping them safe at all times, but he refreshes; he is always near to his people for their protection and refreshment, he has never at a distance from them; Christ is our keeper and shade on our right hand; so that he is never far to seek. Believers will never be hurt either by the open assaults of their enemies, which are very visible as the scorching beams of the sun, or by their secret treacherous attempts which are like the insensible insinuations of the cold by night. The Lord Jesus Christ preserves his own people from any evil, the evil of sin and the evil of trouble. It is the spiritual life, especially, that God will take under his protection; Christ shall preserve all believer' soul. He will keep them save in all their ways; he shall also preserve their going out, and their coming in. Believing Christians are under Christ protection in all their journeys and voyages, outward bond or homeward bound. Christ will keep them alive in him on this earth and he will keep them alive in him when they died and with him in heaven

Prayer:

Our Lord and Savior we give you thanks and glorified your Holy Name for being our heavenly Father and our protector, provider, and our keeper from all harms. We give you praises and thankfulness for watching   over us wherever we go, no one like you our Lord, you are worthy of our praises; and thankfulness. Continuously keeping us save from any danger and afflictions, and any weapon of evil people of this world. In your great mighty Holy Name , we pray. Amen.

MAY 23RD

THE WORD OF GOD TRANSFORMS LIFE – LET THE WORD OF GOD BE YOUR TRANSFORMATION TODAY

Today's Scripture Reading:

"Whatever you do, work at it with all your heart, as working for the Lord, not for men, since you know that you will receive an inheritance from the Lord as a reward. It is the Lord Christ you are serving. Anyone who does wrong will be repaid for his wrong, and there is no favoritism." (Colossians 3:23-25) NIV

All the believing Christians were exhorted and urged to regard all labor as a service rendered to the Lord. WE must work as though Christ were our employer, knowing that any work performed for the Lord will someday be rewarded. Believing Christians must know that anyone who does wrong will be repaid for their wrongdoing either within the family, church, or employment place. Christians must demonstrate the love of Jesus Christ in them; they must show concern for justice and fairness to one another. Mistreatment of other people of a believing Christians is a serious matter that will affect their future glory in heaven. Those who treat other people, on their job, their family, their relatives, friends with love and goodness will receive reward from the Lord. Anyone who mistreats and does wrong to another believer will be repaid for his wrong. The guilty will carry that wrong to judgment and bear the consequences without partiality.

Prayer:

Our Lord and Savior, our Father in heaven, no one like you, you see everything, and you know everything help us to live a life of love, let your Holy Spirit manifest his power and mercy upon us, so that we will be able to live a clean life that does not do wrong to anyone, a life that look for good of others and full of the love of God now and forever more. Amen.

MAY 24TH

THE WORD OF GOD TRANSFORMS LIFE – LET THE WORD OF GOD BE YOUR TRANSFORMATION TODAY

Today's Scripture Reading:

"He who guards his lips guards his life, but he who speaks rashly will come to ruin." (Proverbs 13:3) NIV

We Christians must be aware that a guard upon our lips is a guard to our soul. He that is cautions, and thinks twice before he speaks once, keeps his soul from a great deal of guilt and grief and saves himself the trouble of many bitter reflections. There is a one ruined by an ungoverned tongue. Our Lord and our Father in heaven wants us to keep our lips away from careless speech. Speech that ties people, down, demeaning people speech that destroys people's life, and ruined our relationship with other people at work, and within our families. Believing Christians must keep guards on their lips which will automatically guards their life from destruction and all other earthly troubles. An undrilled tongue can undermine our influence for righteousness, cause us to sin and affect our relationship with God. A perfect person will carefully control his or her speech. We should ask God in prayer for help in controlling our tongue.

Prayer:

Lord God Almighty Father, Son, and the Holy Spirit, help us to guard our tongue, train us and help us to think before we say anything out of our mouth that can destroy other people around us. Lord Jesus Christ, help us to control our angers, emotions, our behavior, and our characteristic manner of speaking to our husband, children, our parents and our co-worker, our Boss in the office, our friends do not let us return evil for evil, let us return good for evil. In Jesus Christ's mighty, Holy Name, we pray. Amen.

MAY 25TH

THE WORD OF GOD TRANSFORMS LIFE – LET THE WORD OF GOD BE YOUR TRANSFORMATION TODAY

Today's Scripture Reading:

"In reply Jesus declared, 'I tell you the truth, no one can see the kingdom of God unless he is born again.' Jesus answered, 'I tell you the truth, no one can enter the kingdom of God unless he is born of water and of the Spirit. Flesh gives birth to flesh, but the Spirit gives birth to spirit. You should not be surprised at my saying, You must be born again. The wind blows wherever it pleases. You hear its sound, but you cannot tell where it comes from or where it is going. So it is with everyone born of the Spirit.'" (John 3: 3, 5-8) NIV

Nicodemus was getting the knowledge from Jesus Christ when the other disciples were sleeping. He knew not how soon Jesus would leave the town. Therefore, he came to see Jesus at night. Jesus accepted him joyfully and accepted his integrity, as well as pardoned his infirmity and hereby taught his ministers to encourage good beginnings, though he was weak.

There is hope for those who have a respect for Jesus Christ in this world because Jesus Christ will touch them and open their understanding as he did to Nicodemus. As the wind, though unseen, is identified by its activity and sound, so also the Holy Spirit is observed by his activity in our lives and also teaches those who are born again the Word of God.

Let us Pray:

Lord Jesus Christ you are the lord of life, open our heart and mind to the Scripture, teach us the Scripture as you aught Nicodemus during your earthly ministry, feed us with your truth and unchanging Word that we may be close to you and live in you and you in us forever. You are the life changer, change our life to the better, move our life to go on in your direction and lift up our spirit to abide in you now and forever in the power of your Holy Name, we pray.

MAY 26TH

THE WORD OF GOD TRANSFORMS LIFE –
LET THE WORD OF GOD BE YOUR TRANSFORMATION TODAY

Today's Scripture Reading:

"Do not repay evil with evil or insult with insult, but with blessing, because to this you were called so that you may inherit a blessing. For whoever would love life and see good days must keep his tongue from evil and his lips from deceitful speech. He must turn from evil and do good; he must seek peace and pursue it."
(1st Peter 3: 9-11) NIV

All the believing Christians should endeavor to be all of one mind in the great points of faith, in real affection, and in the Christian practices. Although Christians cannot be exactly of the same mind, yet they should have compassion for one another, and love as brothers, Christian's doctrine requires pity to the distressed, and civility to all. Christians must maintain good relationship towards one another and towards their enemies. When unbeliever give you evil words, give them good words; for Christ has called us to bless those that curse us, and has settled a blessing on you as your everlasting inheritance. The commands of our Lord and Savior say that we must return blessing for railing, we must pity, pray for and love those who rail at us. Apostle Peter emphasize that those who turn away from evil in both word and deed and pursue peace will experience lives full of God's blessing and favor.

Prayer:

Lord God Almighty, Jesus Christ the only Son of God, we pray that you live your life through us, bless us with abundant blessing so that we may live and love you forever from this earth to heaven. Lord Jesus Christ helps us to experience your full presence with the help of the Holy Spirit living your life through us and shedding your light upon us ever y day of our life. You are the Alpha and Omega we give you praise our Lord; you are worthy of all our praises and adorations. Amen.

MAY 27TH

THE WORD OF GOD TRANSFORMS LIFE – LET THE WORD OF GOD BE YOUR TRANSFORMATION TODAY

Today's Scripture Reading:

"Who is wise and understanding among you? Let him show it by his good life, by deeds done in the humility that comes from wisdom. But if you harbor bitter envy and selfish ambition in your hearts, do not boast about it or deny the truth."
(James 3:13-14)NIV

The Scripture is telling us that a wise man will not value him merely upon knowing things, if he value himself; he has no wisdom to make a right application of that knowledge. these two things must be put together in order to make us for the account of the true wisdom. A good conversation by a Christians believer, if we are wiser than others, this evidenced by the goodness of our conversation, not by the roughness or vanity of it. True wisdom may be known by its work. When we are mild and calm, we are best able to hear reason and best able to speak it. Wisdom produces meekness, and meekness increases wisdom. Selfish ambition refers to the vice that prompts us to promote our own interest. Selfish ambition in the church is equated with humanistic wisdom. Humanistic wisdom is earthly it defile that which his Holy and of the spirit, it is unspiritual without the Holy spirit. A person with selfish ambition does not love God, or give God the glory for his life.

Prayer:

Jesus Christ our Lord and Savior, in your mercy , love and compassion, bless us with godly wisdom to serve you, honor you and worship you in spirit and in truth, help us to honor you throughout our life, created a new heart in us. let your Holy Name be glorified now and forever; let the people of this earth see you clearly through us, let them see the great things you have done for us, in us, and let them know that we belongs to you spirit, soul and body forever; and be converted onto you, so that they can as well live a peaceful life and a godly life that you approved. Amen.

MAY 28TH

THE WORD OF GOD TRANSFORMS LIFE – LET THE WORD OF GOD BE YOUR TRANSFORMATION TODAY

Today's Scripture Reading:

"However, I consider my life worth nothing to me, if only I may finish the race and complete the task the Lord Jesus has given me - the task of testifying to the gospel of God's grace. Now I know that none of you among whom I have gone about preaching the kingdom will ever see me again. Therefore, I declare to you today that I am innocent of the blood of all men."
(Acts 20:24-26) NIV

Apostle Paul gave all the believing Christians a concern of himself, his main concern was not preserving his own life; what counted most to him and to all believers of Jesus Christ is that he might finish the ministry to which God had called him wherever it ended, even if it is in the sacrifice of his life, he would finish his course with Joy and he prayed that Christ will be exalted higher and higher in our mortal body, whether by life, or death. Life and service for Jesus Christ represent a race that one must run with absolute fullness of faith for our Lord. The word "blood" is used normally in the sense of bloodshed, the crime of causing someone's death; it also means that if anyone should die spiritually the person will be lost forever. Preachers of the Word must not be blamed because they were as instructed by God faithfully sharing faith in Christ with unbelievers, sinners, and the lost.

Prayer:

Lord God Almighty, our gracious Master and our God, we pray that you bless us with your Holy Spirit, to the fullness so that we may worship you and daily do what we can to be a blessing to other people, also to be doing what is pleasing in your sight at all times. We praise you; we honor and give you adoration, and we thank you for your sanctification. Our Lord Jesus Christ you are our one and only Lord, no other. Let your glory fill the sky and manifest on earth. In your great Holy Name, we pray. Amen.

MAY 29TH

THE WORD OF GOD TRANSFORMS LIFE –
LET THE WORD OF GOD BE YOUR TRANSFORMATION TODAY

Today's Scripture Reading:

"The lips of the righteous nourish many, but fools die for lack of judgment. The blessing of the Lord brings wealth, and he adds no trouble to it." (Proverbs 10:21-22) NIV

The reason why the lips of the righteous nourishes many people is because they are full of the Word of God, which is the bread of life, where with souls are nourished up While the heart of the wicked worth nothing. His principles, his notions, his thoughts, his purposes and all the things that fill him and affect him are worldly and carnal, and therefore, of no value. Worldly wealth is that which most men and women have their hearts very much upon, but generally mistake both the nature of the thing they desire and the way by which they hope to obtain it. Desirable wealth is to be expected, not by making ourselves drudges to the world but by the blessing of God. All too often material wealth in this world is gained through wickedness and greed and is therefore, not from God. True riches consist in the blessing of the Lord whether we are materially poor or rich, the Lord's presence and favor are our greatest wealth. What comes from the love of God has the sign of God to preserve his soul from those turbulent lusts and passions of which the increase of riches is commonly the incentive.

Prayer:

Lord Jesus Christ you are our Lord there is no other. We pray that you baptize all the believing Christians with the power of the Holy Spirit now and forever so that we may bear more and more fruits into your kingdom, Lord Jesus Christ help us to watch what we say out of our mouth, help us to say good things that we be an inspiration to other people and that will turn their life around, and they will be converted to you, and give their life to you; now and forever. Amen.

MAY 30TH

THE WORD OF GOD TRANSFORMS LIFE – LET THE WORD OF GOD BE YOUR TRANSFORMATION TODAY

Today's Scripture Reading:

"Because he loves me, says the Lord, I will rescue him; I will protect him, for he acknowledges my Name. He will call upon me, and I will answer him; I will be with him in trouble, I will deliver him and honor him with long life will I satisfy him and show him my salvation." (Psalm 91:14-16) NIV

Our Lord and Savior himself addresses his faithful followers because they truly love him. He himself promises to come to their aid in times of trouble. The secret of receiving God's protection is by a heart that is intimately attached to the Lord in gratitude and affection. Our Lord Jesus Christ knows who such believers are, and he will be with them in trouble, hear their prayers, and give them lives that are full of his divine presence and provisions. Jesus Christ is a deliverer in trouble, and he delivers, the living, and the dying; Christ is our deliverer. Our Lord and Savior, call us unto him, and he will answer our prayers. Christ is the one who pours out the Holy Spirit, the spirit of prayer upon us that is why we can pray to him. He also pours out the Spirit of his grace and favor. With the spirit of prayer that the Lord blesses us, that is the reason why he listens to our prayer when we pray to him, and when we call upon him in prayer. He will answer.

Prayer:

Lord God Almighty, Father Son and Holy Spirit, the giver of life, the beginning and the end, the First and the Last, the seed of David, the incarnate begotten Son of God; you are our Lord and Savior, when we call to you in prayer, you answer our prayer. We give you thanks, our Lord; you are worthy of all our worship, and adoration, you are our Great Intercessor in heaven, the Mediator of a new covenant. You are our advocate of a new covenant in heaven; pray for us the prayer that can never be uttered. Ask the Father for what we need that we did not mention in our prayers to you, because you know what is good for us, and you know what we need in our life. Bring us close to you every day of our lives, and help us to be worthy of your Kingdom, where at the end we will be able to live with you there, with the Father and the Holy Spirit forever. In your gracious, marvelous, Holy Name, we pray. Amen.

MAY 31ST

THE WORD OF GOD TRANSFORMS LIFE –
LET THE WORD OF GOD BE YOUR TRANSFORMATION TODAY

Today's Scripture Reading:

"Now we know that if the earthly tent we live in is destroy, we have a building from God, and eternal house in heaven, not built by the human hands. Meanwhile we groan, longing to be clothed with our heavenly dwelling, because when we are clothed, we will not be found naked."(2nd Corinthians 5:1-3) NIV

The term earthly tent refers either to the believer's earthly body or to the believer's earthly life. The building from God, an eternal house in the heavens, not built by human hands likely refers either to a temporary body prepared for believers in heaven while they await their resurrection body, or to the environment of the heavenly existence. All the believing Christians have a building of God - they have a firm expectation of the future felicity. Heaven in the looking eye and it is the hope of the believers. We look upon it as a house, or habitations, our father's house, and our everlasting home. It is a house in the heavens. It is a building of God. It is eternal in the heavens, not like the earthly tabernacles, the poor cottages of clay in which our souls now dwell. When it is expected this happiness shall be enjoyed. Those who have walk with God shall dwell with God forever.

Prayer:

Lord Jesus Christ our Lord and our Savior, I give you thanks for your preservation of our lives and for everything you have given us to enjoy in this world. We give you thanks for clothing us with your righteousness and holiness so that we will not be found naked but be clothe with your mercy and love. Continue Our Lord to shine your great glory upon us now and forever. Make our heart your home, abode in us forever, live your life through us forever, heal the sick through us, shelter the homeless through us, make disciples of all people in all the nations through us, preach and teach the Gospel through us, let your kingdom come and let your will be done through us as it is written in heaven. We love you; we praise you and we give you thanks forever and ever. Amen.

DAILY REFLECTION NOTES

JUNE

JUNE 1ST

THE WORD OF GOD CLEANSES US -
LET THE WORD OF GOD CLEANSES YOU TODAY.

Today's Scripture Reading:

"For it is God who works in you to will and to act according to his good purposes. Do everything without complaining or arguing, so that you may become blameless and pure, children of God without fault in a crooked and depraved generation, in which you shine like stars in the universe as you hold out the word of life- in order that I may boast on the day of Christ that I did not run or labor for nothing." (Philippians 2:13-16) NIV

God's grace works in his children to produce in them both the desire and power to do his will. However, God's work is not one of compulsion, or irresistible grace. The work of grace within us is always dependent on our cooperation and our response of faith. Jesus Christ and his apostles emphasized that the world we live in is an unbelieving and perverse generation. The people of the world are deception and in darkness, and therefore, they have distorted the view of life, values, and religion; they follow immoral ways of life and reject the norms of God's word. God's children have a different world view and values and are separate from the world. In loyalty to the Lord Jesus; we are to be blameless, pure and without fault, in order to proclaim his glorious redemption to the lost world. Our Lord and Savior opened the gates of heaven by salvation of God, so that we can come straight to him. Christian believers who are obeying God and living by his Holy principles will result in better health with a longer life; that is full of happiness and maintains a perfect prosperous life. Christians, who have a strong faith in the Lord, will enjoy this life more than those who have no steady faith. Believers must practice daily the trusting in the Lord with a faithful heart.

Prayer:

Lord God Almighty, Jesus Christ our Lord and Savior, Most Compassionate, Most Merciful Mighty Gracious Loving God. help us to know you more and more every day of our life. Help us to worship you in Spirit and in Truth, to give you great honor and serve you; do all what is pleasing and justifying in your sight, direct us through the power of the Holy Spirit which indwells and abide in us forever. Let your word be our immortal food, as you are the word of God came down from heaven feels men and women with your full presence, be their immortal food. help them and bless them with your sufficiency now and forever. Let those stands on the unfailing love and confidently approach the throne of grace boldly and sincerely with your unending joy. Amen.

JUNE 2ND

THE WORD OF GOD CLEANSES US - LET THE WORD OF GOD CLEANSES YOU TODAY.

Today's Scripture Reading:

"What good will it be for a man if he gains the whole world, yet forfeits his soul? Or what can a man give in exchange for his soul? For the Son of Man is going to come in his Father's glory with his angels, and then he will reward each person according to what he has done. I tell you the truth, some who are standing here will not taste death before they see the Son of Man coming in his kingdom" (Matthew 16:26-28) NIV

Jesus Christ was telling his disciples about his Second Coming whereby, he will set up his kingdom. "The Son of Man" coming in his kingdom refers to the event of Pentecost when Christ baptized his followers with the Holy Spirit and with great power, accompanied by miraculous signs and wonders as the demonstration of Jesus Christ's exaltations and the kingdom's presence on the earth. People of this earth focus on the money and material things of this world; without thinking of their soul or eternity our Lord Jesus was pointing out to them during one of his teaching on earth that the kingdom of heaven is more important than the earthly things. They must seek the Kingdom of God first before any other things because they cannot lose their soul. Jesus

Christ is coming back to set up his Kingdom and all the eyes shall see him.

Prayer:

Lord Jesus Christ our Lord and Savior, you are the God of resurrection eternal life, all life dwell in you our Lord. Help us through the power of your Holy Spirit to seek your kingdom and righteousness before any other things on this earth. Lord Jesus Christ you are God of glory, you are the eternal life. Equip us with all what we needed, that will make us a good preacher of the Gospel and that will make us to belong to you completely, to be full in Christ. Amen.

JUNE 3RD

THE WORD OF GOD CLEANSES US -
LET THE WORD OF GOD CLEANSES YOU TODAY.

Today's Scripture Reading:

"Therefore, I tell you, do not worry about your life, what you will eat or drink; or about your body, what you will wear. Is not life more important than food, and the body more important than clothes? Look at the birds of the air, they do not sow or reap or store away in barns, and yet your heavenly Father feeds them. Are you not much more valuable than they? who of you by worrying can add a single hour to his life?"(Matthew 6:25-27)NIV

Our Lord Jesus Christ did not tell us not to make provisions for our physical needs, he was telling all those who belongs to him, not to worry about our physical needs, because he know what we needed and he is in control of all our needs physically and spiritually. Christ did not want believers to have anxiety or worry that will shows a lack of faith in God's Fatherly care and love. God Almighty that clothes, provide food for the birds of the air have the power to provide for all our needs. God's promise to all is children in this world of trouble and uncertainty. God has promised to provide for our food, clothing, and other necessities of life. We need not to worry; if we seek to let God reign in our lives; we can be sure that he will assume full responsibility for those wholly yielded to him.

Prayer:

Lord Jesus Christ you are the God of provisions, provide for us what we needed in this life , physically and spiritually, do not let us worry; help us to be strong in faith that you are powerful enough to move the mountain. No one before you and no one after you that care and love as you care hear our prayers, our Lord, and our redeemer King. In your great mighty Holy Name , we pray. Amen.

JUNE 4ᵀᴴ

THE WORD OF GOD CLEANSES US - LET THE WORD OF GOD CLEANSES YOU TODAY.

Today's Scripture Reading:

"For this is what the high and lofty One says - he who lives forever, whose Name is Holy; I live in a high and Holy place, but also with him who is contrite and lowly in Spirit, to revive the Spirit of the lowly and to revive the heart of the contrite. I will not accuse forever, nor will I always be angry, for then the Spirit of man would grow faint before me - the breath of man that I have created." (Isaiah 57:15-16) NIV

God the Father Almighty; our Father in heaven, Father of our Lord Jesus Christ, the Messiah, and the mediator of a New Covenant. God who lives in a high and Holy place above the heavens, promise to dwell with those who are contrite and lowly in the spirit. Contrite or crushed, refers to those people the believing Christians who are broken hearted because of their sinfulness, or because of the enemies' oppression - these are the people who cry out to the Lord day and night for deliverance. Those believers who lowly in spirit are those who are humble or bowed down by all sorts of diverse adversity - God respond to the cry of these people in order to revive them with the light and life of his presence.

Prayer:

Lord God Almighty Father Son and the Holy Spirit revive our trouble souls when we are going through diverse diseases, earthly troubles, worriedness, and sorrows. Lord Jesus Christ, a Name above all names in heaven and on earth; you have the power to solve all our problems and you have the power to fulfill all our needs. Let your love and light come down from heaven and fill us with your joy. Joy everlasting today and forever. help us to love you more and more with the power of your Spirit. Amen.

JUNE 5TH

THE WORD OF GOD CLEANSES US - LET THE WORD OF GOD CLEANSES YOU TODAY.

Today's Scripture Reading:

"I am torn between the two: I desire to depart and be with Christ, which is better by far; but it is more necessary for you that I remain in the body.   Convinced of this, I know that I will remain, and I will continue with all of you for your progress and joy in the faith, so that through my being with you again your joy in Christ Jesus will overflow on account of me."
(Philippians 1:23-26)NIV

To all the believing Christians to die is gain because we are going to see the Lord; true Christian believers in Jesus Christ need not to fear death. They must know that absent in the body present with the Lord. They also know that our Lord and Savior have a purpose for the living and that death when it comes is simply the end of their earthly mission, and the beginning of a greater life with Jesus Christ our Lord. Believing Christians must do their best to serve the Lord on this earth and be useful to him Spirit, Soul, Body. Apostle Paul said: that he will continue to live in the flesh so that he can be able to give glory to the Lord, and to be able to witness to the sinners and the lost, and convert them to the Lord. All the believing Christians must strive to make their life useful for the Lord.

Prayer:

Lord Jesus Christ, great is your faithfulness, you are the one and only our Lord and Savior, compassionate gracious living God, we pray to you, call unto you, to create a new heart unto us, so that we will be able to serve you, be useful for you, throughout our life on this earth. Help us merciful and mighty God to be what you want us to be on this earth, your glory and the glory of God the Father be with us now and forever. Amen.

JUNE 6TH

THE WORD OF GOD CLEANSES US - LET THE WORD OF GOD CLEANSES YOU TODAY.

Today's Scripture Reading:

"Now we know that if the earthly tent we live in is destroyed, we have a building from God, an eternal house in heaven, not built by human hands. Meanwhile we groan, longing to be clothed with our heavenly dwelling, because when we are clothed, we will not be found naked. For while we are in this tent, we groan and are burdened, because we do not wish to be unclothed but to be clothed with our heavenly dwelling, so that what is mortal may be swallowed up by life." (2nd Corinthian 5:1-4) NIV

The term earth tent refers to either to the believer's earthly body or to the believer's earthly life. The building of God is an eternal house of God in heaven, not built by any human hands. All the believers of Jesus Christ who are full in him are in Christ heavenly building from this earth to heaven. They are in the presence of God, and nothing can take them out of the hands of the Lord. Because when we are clothed with Jesus ' love, Jesus power that no human efforts, or any earthly troubles can take us away from him. While we are in this body, we go through troubles but in Christ there is a perfect peace because he is the Prince of Peace.

Prayer:

Lord Jesus Christ our Lord and our Savior. , we pray for your mercy and love, for your Holy Spirit , we pray that you come to us and live your life through us and in us now and forever from this earth to heaven; , we pray that you clothe us with the power of your resurrection that no earthly trouble can destroy in us. We pray for your full presence to be manifest in our spirit; soul body now till you come again to set up your kingdom. Amen.

JUNE 7TH

THE WORD OF GOD CLEANSES US - LET THE WORD OF GOD CLEANSES YOU TODAY.

Today's Scripture Reading:

"For though we live in the world, we do not wage war as the world, we do not wage war as the world does. The weapons we fight with are not the weapons of the world. On the contrary, they have divine power to demolish strongholds. We demolish arguments and every pretension that sets itself up against the knowledge of God, and we take captive every though to make it obedient to Christ. And we will be ready to punish every act of disobedience, once your obedience is complete."
(2nd Corinthians 10:3-6)NIV

Believers warfare is against spiritual forces of evil, therefore, worldly weapons such as aggression, violence, wealth, organizations, political solutions, human ingenuity, eloquence, propaganda, Charisma, and personality are in themselves inadequate, to pull down Satan's strongholds. The only weapons that is adequate to destroy the fortresses of Satan, unrighteousness and false teaching are those that God gives; such as the blood of Jesus, the authority of Jesus's Name, the power of the Holy Spirit and spiritual gifts. These weapons are very powerful because they are spiritual and come from God; whereby, Godly weapons are: the Word of God, Commitment to the truth of God, righteous living, Gospel proclamation, faith, love, hope of salvation, and persevering in prayer. By using these weapons against the enemy, believers will emerge victoriously on this earth. God's presence, his kingdom will be powerfully revealed in order to save sinners and the lost, drive away Demons, Sanctify believers, baptized them with the Holy Spirit.

Prayer:

Lord Jesus Christ our Lord and our Savior, we pray to you that you empower us by the power of the Holy Spirit, let your power of the Holy Spirit, let your power and mercy be manifest, let your glory shine upon those who believers in you; let your mercies flows to the hearts and minds of those who love you now and to eternity in heaven. In your matchless mighty Holy Name , we pray now and forever. Amen.

JUNE 8TH

THE WORD OF GOD CLEANSES US -
LET THE WORD OF GOD CLEANSES YOU TODAY.

Today's Scripture Reading:

"The mind of sinful man is death, but the mind controlled by the Spirit is life and peace; the sinful mind is hostile to God. It does not submit to God's Law, nor can it do so. Those control by the sinful nature cannot please God. You, however, are controlled not by the sinful nature but by the Spirit, if the Spirit of God lives in you. And if anyone does not have the Spirit of Christ, he does not belong to Christ. But if Christ is in you, your body is dead because of sin, yet your spirit is alive because of righteousness."
(Romans 8:6-10) NIV

In this Scripture passage, reveals and describes two classes of people: Those who live according to the sinful nature and those who live according to the Spirit. To lie according to the sinful nature is to be occupied with its desires, thoughts, emotions, and physical gratification; which includes all forms of immorality, adultery, hatred out busts of anger, with drug and allowed addition. To live according with the Spirit is to submit and seek to the Holy Spirit's direction and control, and to focus one's attention, thoughts, energy, and values on the things of God. it is to live consciously at all times in God's presence, trusting him to give us the help and grace we need to accomplish his will in us and through us.

Prayer:

Lord Jesus Christ, the one and only true God. , we pray that you turn every believing Christians with the power of the Holy Spirit unto you, help us to know you, abide in your word, and in your commandment. Lord Jesus Christ you are a living Savior full of truth and righteousness, compassionate living God, who alone sit at the right hand of God the Father Almighty; , we pray that you listen to our prayers and answer all our prayer now and forever in the beauty of your holiness. In your Holy Name , we pray. Amen.

JUNE 9TH

THE WORD OF GOD CLEANSES US - LET THE WORD OF GOD CLEANSES YOU TODAY.

Today's Scripture Reading:

"For in him we live and move and have our being. As some of your own poets have said, we are his offspring. Therefore, since we are God's offspring, we should not think that the divine being is like gold or silver or stone - an image made by man's design and skill. In the past God over looked such ignorant, but now he commands all people everywhere to repent."(Acts 17:28-30) NIV

In the beginning, before the full knowledge of God came through our Lord Jesus Christ, God the Father almighty always overlooked much of human sins and ignorance of himself. Now that his full and perfect revelation has come with Jesus Christ's appearing, all are commanded to repent and believe in Jesus as their Lord and Savior. There are no exceptions, for God will not overlook anyone's sins. All must repent and turn away from their sins to God, or be condemned. Repentance, in other words, is an essential posture for receiving the gift of salvation. All the believing Christians live and move, and we have our being in Jesus Christ, he is our live, without him we are noting. Christ is our life without him we have no life. he came down from heaven to give us his life, and he gives us his life in full and in truth.

Prayer:

Lord Jesus Christ you are the giver of life from you all the goodness flows, you are the channels of our blessings. Listen to our prayers and answer our prayers as , we pray to you concerning all the things that is going on in this world, all the violent and chaos, of the nation's hear our prayers and answer our prayers, you are the one who save us you are the one who can save us, you are the one who call us and most importantly and especially you are the one who indwell us. Do not let your mercy fail; continue to bless us with your everlasting love. Amen.

JUNE 10TH

THE WORD OF GOD CLEANSES US - LET THE WORD OF GOD CLEANSES YOU TODAY.

Today's Scripture Reading:

"Therefore, since we are surrounded by such a great cloud of witnesses, let us throw off everything that hinders and the sin that so easily entangles, and let us run with perseverance the race marked out for us. Let us fix our eyes on Jesus, the author and perfecter of our faith, who for the joy set before him endured the cross, scorning its shame, and set down at the right hand of the throne of God. Consider him who endured such opposition from sinful men, so that you will not grow weary and lose heart."
(Hebrews 12:1-3) NIV

Believing Christian's race is the lifelong test of faith in this world; the race must be run with perseverance, with patience and endurance; is the way to victory is the same as that of the Saints. The race must be run by throwing off the sin that so easily entangles us, or most be setting sin; by fixing our eyes on our Lord Jesus Christ who persevered to the end by enduring the cross. The race must be run by throwing off the sin that so easily entangles us. The race must be run with an awareness that our greatest danger is the temptation to give up and yielded to sin, or to return to the country we had left, and to once again become citizens of the world - fixing our eyes on Jesus in our race of faith we look to

Jesus as our example of trusting God, of commitment to his will, of prayer, of overcoming temptation and suffering of enduring loyalty to the Father seeking the joy to complete the work that he assigned for us.

Prayer:

Lord God Almighty our Father in heaven, one and only the Merciful and gracious living God. Be with us in all the areas of our lives, guide us and lead us with the power of the Holy Spirit; lead us to the way everlasting now and forever. Help us to be complete in you, and to be able to do great things that will exalt your Holy Name higher and higher more than ever before in this world.   In your great mighty matchless Holy Name , we pray. Amen.

JUNE 11ᵀᴴ

THE WORD OF GOD CLEANSES US -
LET THE WORD OF GOD CLEANSES YOU TODAY.

Today's Scripture Reading:

"Endure hardship as discipline; God is treating you as sons. For what son is not discipline by his father? If you are not disciplined and everyone under goes discipline? Then you are illegitimate children and not true sons. Moreover, we have all had human fathers who disciplined us and we respected them for it. How much more should we submit to the father of our spirits and live! our father disciplined us for a little while as they thought best; but God disciplines us for our good, that we may share in his holiness."
(Hebrews 12:7-10) NIV

Our Lord and Savior discipline all the children he owns - There are so many ways that the Lord uses to discipline his children. The facts about God's discipline of believers and the hardships and troubles, he allows to suffer. They are a sign that we are God's children; They are the assurance of God's love and concern for us. The Lord's discipline has two purposes that we might not be finally condemned with the world and that we might share God's holiness and continue to live sanctified lives without which we will never see that Lord. These are two possible consequences of the Lord's discipline that we may endure the hardships God leads us through, submit to God's will and continue to remain faithful. By doing this we will continue to live as God's spiritual children and share in his holiness which will yield the harvest of righteousness.

Prayer:

Lord God Almighty we glorify you, and we adored you, for everything you made possible in our lives; for the work of the Gospel that is spreading into all the nations of earth. We give you praises for your mercy, love, joy that will help us to get close to you so that you may be able to shape us, mold us, purified us as silver and gold been purified; and make us to be fit for your eternal life where righteousness dwell and reign forever Amen.

JUNE 12TH

THE WORD OF GOD CLEANSES US - LET THE WORD OF GOD CLEANSES YOU TODAY.

Today's Scripture Reading:

"You who are trying to be justified by the Law have been alienated from Christ; you have fallen away from grace. But by faith we eagerly await through the Spirit the righteousness for which we hope. For in Christ Jesus neither circumcision nor uncircumcision has any value. The only thing that counts is faith expressing itself through love." (Galatian 5:4-6) NIV

All the believers in Jesus Christ possess the Spirit and they are the children of God who are born by the power of the Spirit. The Scripture revealed that some of the early Christians believers in Galatia, called the Galatians, had transferred their faith in Christ to faith in legalistic observances of the Law; they had fallen away from grace. To fall from grace is to be alienated from Christ and to abandon the principle of remaining in God's grace, which provides life and salvation. The Scripture maintains that a person is saved through faith in Jesus Christ. In this passage defines the exact nature of that faith. Saving faith is a living faith in a living Savior, a faith so vital that it cannot avoid to expressing itself in love - motivated by deeds. Faith that does not sincerely love and obey Jesus Christ and does not show a real concern for the work of God's kingdom, and does actively resist sin and the world of sin, it does not qualify as a saving faith.

Prayer:

Lord Jesus Christ, our Lord and Savior, who alone offers us forgiveness of our sins and resurrection of the body, help us to have a saving faith for you, a saving faith that will love you and serve you with all our minds and hearts, now and forever. Build us up with a saving faith that will honor you and love you forever from this earth to eternity; we give you praises and thankfulness, our Lord and our redeemer King, now and for ever and ever. Amen.

JUNE 13TH

THE WORD OF GOD CLEANSES US - LET THE WORD OF GOD CLEANSES YOU TODAY.

Today's Scripture Reading:

"I have been crucified with Christ and I no longer live, but Christ lives in me, The life I live in the body, I live by faith in the Son of God, who love me and gave himself for me. I do not set aside the grace of God, for if righteousness could be gained through the Law, Christ died for nothing!" (Galatian 2:20-21)NIV

Believer's relationship must be the same as of Paul; we have been crucified with Christ in terms of a profound personal attachment to and reliance on his Word. those who have faith in Christ live their lives in intimate union with their Lord, both in his death and in his resurrection. All the believing Christians have been crucified with Christ on the cross. They have died to the Law as a means of salvation and now live through Jesus Christ for God because of the salvation which is in Christ Jesus; sin no longer has control over them. He who has been crucified with Christ Jesus now lives with him in his resurrection life. Christ and his strength live within us, becoming the source of all life and the center of all our thoughts, words, and deeds. It is through the Holy Spirit that Christ's risen life is continually communicated to us. Our sharing of Christ death and resurrection is appropriated through our faith confident in our belief, love, devotion, and the loyalty we have in the true Son of God, who loved us and gave himself for us on the Cross.

Prayer:

Lord Jesus Christ, we all the believers has been crucified with you, we share in your death and in your resurrection, let your life manifested in our mortal body; let your full presence be known in our lives now and forever. Lord Jesus Christ live your life in us forever, be our immortal food, feed us to the fullness with yourself throughout our life in this world. Exalted your Holy Name through us, baptize us with the empowerment of the Holy Spirit so that we may be strong and be strengthens with all might and serve you, take the Gospel to the end of the universe in everyone's language. In your great Holy Name , we pray now and forever. Amen.

JUNE 14TH

THE WORD OF GOD CLEANSES US - LET THE WORD OF GOD CLEANSES YOU TODAY.

Today's Scripture Reading:

"What shall we say, then? shall we go on sinning so that grace may increase? by no means we died to sin; how can we live in it any longer? Or don't you know that all of us who were baptized into Christ Jesus were baptized into his death? We were therefore, buried with him through the glory of the Father we too may live a new life." (Romans 6:1-4) NIV

Can believers of Jesus Christ continue to live a life of sin, so that grace may abound? No. The idea that believers may continue in sin and yet remain secure in Jesus Christ because of God's grace is not true. True believing Christian are identified as being in Christ, one in Jesus Christ as he is one with the Father. emphasizing, one fundamental truth by virtue of being baptized into Christ and into his death so that their old life of sin is buried, moreover, believers has been translated from sin's realm into another realm, which is the realm of life in Jesus Christ. Since true believers have died to sin and therefore, made definitive separation from the past life of sin, they will not continue to live in sin. If they continue to live a life of sin, they are not truly a believer of Jesus Christ or they are not yet been converted. Individual cannot be slaves to sin and as well be slaves to Christ at the same time.

Prayer:

Lord Jesus, our Lord and Savior help us to be totally surrendered to your lordship; do not let sin get hold of us, do not let sin take us away from you. Wash us clean from any unrighteousness and clothe us with your righteousness, do not let sin have dominion over us our Lord. Get rid of all our sins, nature, clothe us with your righteousness, and do not let sin have dominion over us, controlling us our Lord. Get rid of all our sin nature clothe us with your righteousness and grace. Amen.

JUNE 15TH

THE WORD OF GOD CLEANSES US - LET THE WORD OF GOD CLEANSES YOU TODAY.

Today's Scripture Reading:

"If we live, we live to the Lord; and if we die, we die for the Lord. So, whether we live or die we belong to the Lord. For this very reason, Christ died and returned to life so that he might be the Lord of both the dead and the living. You, then, why do you judge your brother? or why do you look down on your brother? for we will all stand before God's judgment seat." (Romans 14: 8-10) NIV

All the believing Christians must know that the moment they gave their life to Jesus Christ, they are living in Jesus Christ, everything they do or say is Christ, we must live a life that we know that our Lord and Savior will approve, a life that is going to bring great glory to his Holy Name. The Scripture says Christ in us the hope of glory. If we die, we die for our Lord Jesus Christ, we are going to heaven to live with him there, so therefore, whether we live, or die for Christ our efforts and prayer is to do what is pleasing to him at all times. Believers must refrain from judging each other in trivial matters; believers should consider how to encourage each other to true Christ likeness and holiness when it concerns faith. We must be able to correct and rebuke each other in love and humility, and when necessary exercising discipline through the direction of the Holy Spirit.

Prayer:

Lord Jesus Christ live your life through all the believing Christians forever. help us to live a life of discipline, take correction with love and correct with love and be able to correct one another with the glory of your Holy Name. Help us to focus on your redeeming love for us, so that we can grow in grace and grow in sanctification throughout our lives and help us to love you as you love us. Amen.

JUNE 16TH

THE WORD OF GOD CLEANSES US - LET THE WORD OF GOD CLEANSES YOU TODAY.

Today's Scripture Reading:

"It is written: As surely as I live, says the Lord every knee will bow before me; every tongue will confess to God. So then, each of us will give an account of himself to God. For the kingdom of God is not a matter of eating and drinking, but of righteousness, peace, and joy in the Holy Spirit, because anyone who serves Christ in this way is pleasing to God and approved by men. Let us therefore make every effort to do what leads to peace and to mutual edification. Do not destroy the work of God for the sake of food. All food is clean, but it is wrong for a man to eat anything that causes someone else to stumble." (Romans 8:11, 17-21) NIV

The kingdom of God is not a matter primarily of subjects, territory, or extent. Rather it is a matter of the King's power, authority, and rule. It is not a mundane kingdom as in eating and drinking; rather, it is the evidence that God is our King and that he truly reigns in our lives in righteousness, peace, joy, and in the Holy Spirit. There are three important guidelines about drinking and eating in the Scripture, concerning fermented wine and other alcoholic beverages: Drunkenness is a serious sin that will exclude one from the Church and from the Kingdom of God. An act of abstinence is commanded because of the seriousness and the dangers inherently associated with drug and alcohol; Christ's love must make a believer to abstain from what might cause another person to be laid into sin and fall into sin.

Prayer:

Lord Jesus Christ, through the power of the Holy Spirit, help us to control what we put in our mouth, help us to help others to get closer to you, not to make themselves fall into sin. Control our habits and our character concerning food and alcohol beverages drinking, which can easily take us away from you, or grieve the Holy Spirit who is our counselor, comforter, paraclete, and heavenly guest. Uphold us in your Holy hands; do not let food control us to the point that it damages our body. Help us to control all the food that we eat in order to be able to live a strong healthy life for your glory. Amen.

JUNE 17ᵀᴴ

THE WORD OF GOD CLEANSES US - LET THE WORD OF GOD CLEANSES YOU TODAY.

Today's Scripture Reading:

"Known, yet regarded as unknown; dying, and yet we live on; beaten, and yet not killed; sorrowful, yet always rejoicing; poor, yet making many rich; having nothing, and yet possessing everything." (2nd Corinthians 6:9-10)NIV

All the believing Christians were given the ability to accomplish God's Will, is an energizing strength that flows from our risen Christ and operates through the Holy Spirit indwelling to the believer. It is not contradictory to the Gospel for a truly dedicated Christian to be financially poor. Paul affirms that he possessed little of this world's goods, yet as God's servant he made others spiritually rich. Same with today's Christians, we must continue the work of the Lord as long as we are still alive; the reward is from our Lord and Savior. Believers stand in need of the grace of God to arm us against the temptations of honor on the one hand, so as to bear good report without pride, and of dishonor on the other hand, so as to bear reproaches without recrimination. Some represented them as the best; and others at the worst, of men: by some they were counted deceivers, by other as true. They were slighted by the men of the world as unknown, not worth taking notice of; yet in all the churches of Christ they were well know, and of great account; they were looked upon a dying, and yet behold, we live because we live for Christ. Believers' face chastened, and often fell under the lash of the Law, yet not killed, God's protect his own, and though it was thought that they were sorrowful, a company of believers that were always rejoicing in the Lord. Believers were despised as poor, and yet in the services of the Lord, they we made many sinners and the lost rich, by preaching the unsearchable riches of Jesus Christ in God the Father to them. Even though they have nothing, yet they possessed all things, they had noting in themselves, but possessed all things in Christ- this is the paradox of a Christian life all for Jesus.

Prayer:

Lord Jesus Christ our compassionate gracious loving God, you are God of miracle, you save us from our past, present, and future sins, so that we may live and have live in you, live everlasting. You are a great God, above all gods, you are the God of infinite love and mercy, you are our healer, and we praise you for healing us from all our diseases, feeding us with heavenly food which refreshes us, and make us alive in you. All glory, majesty, power everlasting to you our Lord and Savior; now and forever more. Amen.

JUNE 18TH

THE WORD OF GOD CLEANSES US - LET THE WORD OF GOD CLEANSES YOU TODAY.

Today's Scripture Reading:

"Though you have not seen him, you love him; and even though you do not see him, now, you believe in him and are filled with an in expressible and glorious joy, for you are receiving the goal of your faith, the salvation of your souls." (1stPeter 1:8-9) NIV

Our Lord Jesus Christ gave us his word before he ascended into heaven; he said: "blessed are those who have not seen and yet have believed" John 20:29. In eternal glory they shall reign. All the believers of Jesus Christ must rejoice because of his unchanging blessings for us. God Almighty Father of our Lord Jesus Christ considers the faith of all the believing Christians today as a greater wonder than the faith of those who saw him and heard in him in person, even after his resurrection. Believers now, although they have never seen him, love him and believe in him. That, this is the reason why our Lord Jesus said; there is a special blessing in heaven for those who have not seen and yet believed. As we live by faith, we are given joy as God' gift to us. True Christian has a sincere love for Jesus Christ because they believe in him. Where there is a true faith for Jesus Christ and true love there is always joy unspeakable and full of the glory of our Lord. Full of glory means full of heaven;

there is more of heaven and the future glory in the present joys of Christians.

Prayer:

Lord Jesus you are our life, you are our joy, you are the true and the living Savior. You blessed us before we even come to know you and you loved us with an unending love. You clothe us with your goodness and righteousness, we praise you and give great thanks to your Holy Name our Lord; in your Holy Name , we pray, and we pray that you will always and forever living your life through us. Amen.

JUNE 19TH

THE WORD OF GOD CLEANSES US -
LET THE WORD OF GOD CLEANSES YOU TODAY.

Today's Scripture Reading:

"Who has saved us and called us to a Holy life - not because of his own purpose and grace. This grace was given us in Christ Jesus before the beginning of time but it has now been revealed through the appearing of our Savior, Christ Jesus, who has destroyed death and has brought life and immortality to light through the gospel." (2nd Timothy 1:9-10) NIV

Jesus Christ is the only Savior, who has saved us from the agony of sin and death. God has done great things for believers by the Gospel of Christ. The nature of the Gospel and the glorious design of it is the Gospel which aims at our salvation. It is designed for our sanctification. All who shall be saved here after are sanctified. Wherever the Gospel of God is preached and taught, witnessing it is an effectual call that is found to be a Holy call. The origin of it is the free grace and the eternal purpose of God in Christ Jesus. The Gospel is the manifestation of the purpose of God and the grace of God. By the Gospel of Jesus Christ, death is abolished. Death that was once an enemy has become a friend; it has become the gate by which we pass out of a troublesome, sinful world, into a world of perfect peace and purity. Believers triumph over death; he has brought it to the light, not only set it before us, but offered it to us, by the Gospel.

Prayer:

Lord Jesus Christ, the immortal, the invisible and the only wise God. You have saved us, and you called us to a Holy life which is only in you - sanctify us with your mercy and love. We pray to you Lord that you will continue calling the sinner and the lost unto you. Do not leave us, and do not forsake us. We ask that you solve all of our needs. Help us to be in your presence in all the days of our lives; protect us, guide us, keep us safe at all times, now and forever. Amen.

JUNE 20TH

THE WORD OF GOD CLEANSES US -
LET THE WORD OF GOD CLEANSES YOU TODAY.

Today's Scripture Reading:

"Salvation is found in no one else, for there is no other Name under heaven give to men by which we must be saved. When they saw the courage of Peter and John and realized that they were unschooled, ordinary men, they were astonished and they took note that these men had been with Jesus."(Acts4:12) NIV

The work of the Gospel was given to all the believing Christians before the foundation of the world. Disciples were also convinced that the greatest need of every individual was salvation from sin and the wrath of God, and they preached that this need could be met by no one other than the person of Jesus Christ. This truth reveals the exclusive nature of the Gospel and the church's heavy responsibility of preaching the Gospel to every person. If there were other ways of salvation, the church could be at ease, but according to Jesus Christ himself - there is no hope for anyone apart from salvation through him. This is no hope for any one apart from salvation through him. This is also the basis for the missionary imperative. As there is no other Name by which diseased bodies can be cured, so there is no other Name by which a sinful soul can be saved. We cannot be saved but by Jesus Christ, Christ alone. Our Salvation is not in ourselves; we can destroy ourselves, but we cannot save ourselves. This is the honor of Jesus Christ's Name that it is the only Name whereby we must be saved. This Name is given - God has appointed it - it is given under heaven. He has all both in the upper and in the lower world.

Prayer:

Lord Jesus Christ your Name is above all names, your Holy Name wake up the dead, healed the sick, and cleans all diseases from the Leper; put your Holy Name in our mouth, touch our tongue with your power through the Holy Spirit to perform miracles, do great things through us by waking up the dead, and by call sinners and the lost unto you. Cleans us from any filthiness of the spirit, soul, and body, and use us for your eternal glory now and forever. Amen.

JUNE 21ST

THE WORD OF GOD CLEANSES US -
LET THE WORD OF GOD CLEANSES YOU TODAY.

Today's Scripture Reading:

"For I will pour water on the thirsty land, and streams on the dry ground; I will pour out my Spirit on your offspring, and my blessing on your descendants. They will spring up like grass in a meadow, like poplar trees by flowing streams. One will say, I belong to the Lord; another will call himself by the Name of Jacob; still another will write on is hand, The Lord's and will take the Name of Israel." (Isaiah 44:3-5) NIV

Although Israelites were largely an apostate nation - people in prophet Isaiah's time, but he prophesied that the day would come when the Holy Spirit would be poured out on the future generation. This prophecy was fulfilled on the day of Pentecost, and is also waiting for the full fulfillment when they will accept Christ as the Messiah. The outpouring of God's Spirit upon his people is associated with restoration, blessing, and fruitfulness. If we give a prominent result of the Spirit being poured out upon us as our testimony and prove that we belong to the Lord and that he is our heavenly Father. The Spirit will create in us the confidence that we belong to God and that we have all the rights and privileges of being his children. God's blessings never fail - the water that God will pour out is his Spirit just as Jesus Christ said during his earthly ministry that: whoever believes in me, as the Scripture has said, streams of living water will flow within him John 7:38 When Jesus refer to the Scripture it because it is the very word of the Father through prophet Isaiah.

Prayer:

Lord God Almighty, Father, Son, and the Holy Spirit, we pray that you fill us with your Spirit as the water fills the sea, let the power of the indwelling of the Holy Spirit help us to grow in grace and grow in your sanctification and glorification. Let the supreme authority of your Word make us alive in you now and forever. Amen.

JUNE 22ND

THE WORD OF GOD CLEANSES US - LET THE WORD OF GOD CLEANSES YOU TODAY.

Today's Scripture Reading:

"I am not ashamed of the gospel, because it is the power of God for the salvation of everyone who believes; first for the Jew, then for the gentile. For in the gospel a righteousness from God is revealed, a righteousness that is by faith from first to last, just as it is written: The righteous will live by faith."(Romans 1:16-17) NIV

The wrath of God is an expression of his righteousness and his holiness. The righteous person continues to live by faith, and in so doing grows from one level of maturity to another. In this way, the believer progresses along the path of righteousness to live a rich and full spiritual life. God almighty freely offers the humanity and those that believes in him eternal life in Jesus Christ. The Gospel of God is the only path to believer's salvation through Jesus Christ. Salvation is a gift of God's grace received through faith in Jesus Christ - who is the only way to the Father. Salvation is provided for us by God's grace which he gives freely in Christ Jesus, based on his death and resurrection, as well as a continued intercession for believers in heaven. The salvation of believers is the power of God unto salvation - no believer of Jesus should be ashamed of the Gospel which shows us the way to salvation, without the power of God to salvation there will be no Gospel. The Gospel that show us the way of salvation also makes known the righteousness, therefore, the righteousness of God was revealed in the Gospel.

Prayer:

Lord Jesus, you are the righteousness of God, the wisdom of God, and the power of God. Bless us with the power of your word that we may live and worship you in Spirit and in truth. Accept our praises adoration, blessings, magnification, and glorification, you are worthy of all our blessings from this earth to heaven; help us to love you more and more and worship you with the spirit of holiness, there is no one like you our Savior. Do not be silent to our prayers our Lord, make yourself known to those who does not know you through our lives and through our love for you and your infinite love for us. In your marvelous gracious Holy Name, we pray. Amen.

JUNE 23RD

THE WORD OF GOD CLEANSES US - LET THE WORD OF GOD CLEANSES YOU TODAY.

Today's Scripture Reading:

Enter through the narrow gate. For wider is the gate and broad is the road that leads to destruction, and many enter through it. But small is the gate and narrow the road that leads to life, and only few find it." (Matthew 7:13-14)NIV

Jesus Christ our Lord and Savior during his earthly ministry; told us that majority of the multitudes would not follow him on the road that leads to life because they like things of this world than things in heaven. Whereby, those who enter the humble gate of true repentance and deny themselves to follow Christ, sincerely endeavor to obey is commands, earnestly seek his kingdom and his righteousness, and persevere until the end of true faith, purity and love are not the many but the few. Our Lord taught that following him involves bearing obligations concerning righteousness acceptance of persecution, love for enemy and self-denial. There is a choice of sinful ways, but all paths in this: you will have abundance of company in a broad way, because many people like to go through that way; following the multitude will be to do evil, if we go with the crowd, it will be the wrong way. The way of holiness many did not find it. The gate is straight conversion and regeneration are the gates, which means out of the state of sin into a state of grace, we must go through this gate, by the new birth, this is a straight gate which is very hard to find, and hard to get through we must become as a little children, we must deny ourselves, put off the world, we must be willing to forsake all for our interest in Christ.

Prayer:

Lord Jesus Christ our Lord and Savior in your mercy from heaven lead us to a narrow way; help us to seek your way, walk in your way from this earth to heaven. lead us to the right path, control all our ways through the power of your Holy Spirit which indwell us and abide in us from this earth to heaven in your mighty Holy Name , we pray. Amen.

JUNE 24TH

THE WORD OF GOD CLEANSES US - LET THE WORD OF GOD CLEANSES YOU TODAY.

Today's Scripture Reading:

"Yet I will rejoice in the Lord, I will be joyful in God my Savior, The sovereign Lord is my strength; he makes my feet like the feet of a deer, he enables me to go on the heights."
(Habakkuk 3:18-10) NIV

Prophet Habakkuk testifies that he served the Lord not for what he gave, but because he was God. Acknowledgment of God's power, God's revelation in his life. Habakkuk commune with God, and he realized that God is always present in his life. Even in the midst of God's judgment on Judah. Habakkuk chose to rejoice in the Lord; God would be his Savior and an unfailing source of strength. he knew beyond a doubt that a righteous remnant would survive the Babylonian invasion, and he proclaimed with confidence the ultimate victory of all who live by faith in God. Habakkuk said: "yet will I rejoice in the Lord' those who, are when they were full, enjoyed God in all, when they are emptied can enjoy all in God, and can sit down, upon the heap of the ruins and even then sing to the praise of God, and the glory of God. This is the principal ground of our joy in God that he is the God of our eternal salvation, the salvation of the soul; and, if he be so, we may rejoice in him in our greatest distresses, since by them our salvation cannot be hindered but may furthered. Joy in God is near in our off season, no, it is in a special manner seasonable when we meet with losses and crosses in the world, that may then appear that our hearts are not set upon this things nor our happiness bound up in them.

Prayer:

Lord God almighty helps us to rejoice in you and to be build up with your covenant for our lives, you are our strength and our salvation in you our heart rejoices. Lord Jesus Christ, in you there is joy, joy everlasting, you are the only source of joy of every human soul on this earth, you are the bundle of joy to all those who believe in you and follow you, you are the channels of our joy and our blessing, we acknowledge you, in your infinite love and mercy bless us with your joy that never ends, and we praise your Holy Name forever. Amen.

JUNE 25TH

THE WORD OF GOD CLEANSES US - LET THE WORD OF GOD CLEANSES YOU TODAY.

Today's Scripture Reading:

*"Jesus looked at them and said, 'with man this is impossible,
but not with God; all things are possible with God."
(Mark 10:27) NIV*

Jesus Christ is our life; he is the rock of our salvation in him there is life, life everlasting. Nothing is impossible for him to do in heaven and on this earth. He gave us life, life in abundance; he blesses us with his Spirit. Christ sees everything and knows everything. In him we move we have our being. Jesus Christ is life and the giver of life. The grace of God can do what we think is impossible to do, because with Jesus Christ all things are possible. The greatness of the salvation of those that have but a little of this world, and leave it for Christ. The people knew what the abundance of promises that were, in the Old Testament temperate good things, they knew likewise that they who are rich have so much larger opportunities of doing good; and therefore, were amazed to hear that it should be so hard for rich people to go to heaven, but Jesus Christ referred it to the hands of the Almighty power of God, to help the unbelievers and the rich people over the difficulties of the understanding that lies in the way of salvation.

Prayer:

Lord God Almighty from you all the goodness flows, help us to understand the Scripture because nothing is impossible for you to do, in heaven above, and in the earth below. Open our hearts to you, so that we may know you more and more every day of our life, worship you and let the sinner and the lost turn to you, and be converted unto you in faithfulness and sincerity with the power of your Holy Name, now and forever. Amen.

JUNE 26TH

THE WORD OF GOD CLEANSES US - LET THE WORD OF GOD CLEANSES YOU TODAY.

Today's Scripture Reading:

"Go, said Jesus, your faith has healed you. Immediately he received his sight and followed Jesus along the road."
(Mark 10:52) NIV

All those who believed in Jesus Christ, and gave their life to him; some of them were converted after experiencing the power of healing of Jesus Christ. In so many way the Scripture revealed how Jesus healed the sick, open the eye of the man born blind, raised the dead on the road to Nain, raised Jairus' daughter, raised Lazarus from the grave by the power of his word, No one has ever heal as Jesus healed, Christ power of healing is incomparable and it is in comprehensible. The Scripture said that: "The Father love, the Son and put everything in his hands" Christ is the word of God, the power of God to those who believe "through him the righteousness of God is being revealed from faith to faith, the just shall live by faith" when believers exercised strong faith in the Lord Jesus Christ, he put Christ to work, and the power of Jesus Christ will be manifest in him. Faith in Christ is setting on work, or rather Christ setting our faith on work. When the man receive his sight, he became the follower of Jesus he was once blind but now he sees clearly, then he came to Christ for spiritual healing, when he was healed spiritually.

Prayer:

Lord Jesus Christ, bless us with spiritual eyesight, in order that we may be able to follow you faithfully and sincerely. Open our eyes so that we can behold your beauty that draws us effectually to run after you now and forever. Continuously purge us clean from any unrighteousness, so that we can be able to follow your ways, abide in your word, and are faithful to follow your commandment. Amen.

JUNE 27TH

THE WORD OF GOD CLEANSES US -
LET THE WORD OF GOD CLEANSES YOU TODAY.

Today's Scripture Reading:

"I love you, O Lord, my strength. The Lord is my rock, my fortress and my deliverer; my God is my rock, in whom I take refuge. He is my shield and the horn of my salvation, my stronghold. I call to the Lord, who is worthy of praise, and I am saved from my enemies." (Psalm 18:1-3) NIV

The Scripture was referring to Jesus Christ which means through the messiah all the nations will praise the Name of God. Believers might struggle against any sort of earthly trouble, but Jesus Christ is our strength, our stronghold, and our fortress. Christ gave all those who believe in him victory over the work of the enemies. Jesus Christ is our rock the rock that never changes, or weak, Christ is our shield in any areas of our lives. We struggle against the physical and spiritual forces of this world. God's care for us never fails. Christ is our rock, safety and security in God's immovable strength; our fortress - a place of refuge and safety where the enemy cannot penetrate; Christ our deliverer a living protector our shield God stepping between us and harm, our horn of my salvation - strength and victorious power to deliver and save us, my stronghold - high place among the rocks, safe from plunder and from destruction.

Prayer:

Lord Jesus Christ our Lord and Savior, our shield, and our deliverer in any earthly troubles. Listen to our prayers and answer our prayer, in you all the power of the evil disappear in our lives; you are the rock of salvation, you save us from sin and death and from the power of darkness we praises your Holy Name now and forever. Amen.

JUNE 28TH

THE WORD OF GOD CLEANSES US -
LET THE WORD OF GOD CLEANSES YOU TODAY.

Today's Scripture Reading:

"So Christ was sacrificed once to take away the sins of many people; and he will appear a second time, not to bear sin, but to bring salvation to those who are waiting for him."
(Hebrews 9:28) NIV

Under the Old Testament, and the old covenant, the children of Israel watched intensely for the reappearance of the high priest after he had gone into the sanctuary to make atonement, likewise believers, knowing that their high priest has entered the heavenly sanctuary as their advocate, wait with earnest hope for his reappearing to bring salvation to its completion. The Scripture said that God was in Jesus Christ, reconciling the people of this world to himself, that those who believes in him will not be condemn, Christ was sacrificed for our sins once and for all on the cross. This is the matter of comfort to the godly, that they shall die well and die but once; but it is matter of terror to the wicked who die in their sin. After death comes the judgment. God' commandment is that the sinner must die and must be judged Jesus Christ bear our sin, he offered to bear the sins of the people in the world, he was wounded for our transgressions, he came from heaven to take away our sins, he is coming back again to judge the dead and the living and all the eye shall see him.

Prayer:

Lord Jesus Christ compassionate gracious loving God. You love us first, you gave your life for us and you bear all our sins on the cross, we praise and give you thanks. Help us to love you as you love us, to teach other about you and let your love flow through us to other sinners and the lost and the people of all other religions that they may be saved and receive eternal life which is only in you. Amen.

JUNE 29TH

THE WORD OF GOD CLEANSES US -
LET THE WORD OF GOD CLEANSES YOU TODAY.

Today's Scripture Reading:

"Therefore, he is able to completely those who come to God through him, because he always lives to intercede for them. Such a high Priest meets our need - one who is Holy, blameless, pure, set apart from sinners, exalted above the heavens." (Hebrews 7:25-26) NIV

Jesus Christ lives in heaven in his Father's presence interceding for every believer according to the Father's Will. Through Jesus Christ ministry, of intercession, we experience God's love and God's presence, and believers find mercy and grace to help us in times of need and troubles, weakness temptations, and trials. Jesus Christ is our high priest in heaven and his high priestly prayer for all those who believes then and those who will believes on the witness of the Gospel. Christ desire to pour out the Spirit on all believers, the Holy Spirit help believers to understand the content of Jesus Christ ministry of intercession. WE as a sinner, we need the high priest to make satisfaction and intercession for us. No priest could be suitable or sufficient for our reconciliation to God the Father but one who was perfectly righteous. The Lord Jesus was exactly such a high priest as we wanted, for he has a personal holiness, absolutely perfect. Christ is Holy. No sin dwell sin him, he show his love by dying on the cross for us.

Prayer:

Lord God Almighty Father of our Lord Jesus Christ we give you thanks for helping us by sending your Son for our sin, and to reconcile us to you. We give thanks to you O' Lord our God the Father; through your Son Jesus Christ, and we pray that you will baptizes us with your Holy Spirit through your Son. Amen.

JUNE 30TH

THE WORD OF GOD CLEANSES US - LET THE WORD OF GOD CLEANSES YOU TODAY.

Today's Scripture Reading:

"How beautiful on the mountains are the feet of those who bring good news, who proclaim peace, who bring good tidings, who proclaim salvation, who say to Zion; your God reigns."
(Isaiah 52:7) NIV

The Scripture revealed that the word of Prophet Isaiah fore shadows the announcement of salvation through the coming of Messiah. The focus of the proclaimed message is that our God reigns the kingdom of God has come to earth. The preaching of the Gospel plainly intimates that, the deliverance was a type and figure of the redemption of mankind by Jesus Christ. The good news is the spoken of a great blessing, which ought to be welcomed with a great joy. Those that bring the tidings of their release shall be very acceptable as they come over the mountains is found about Jerusalem. They say unto Zion" thy God reigns" applied to the preaching of the Gospel, which is a proclamation of peace and salvation; it is the Gospel indeed, good news of victory over our spiritual enemies and liberty from our spiritual bondage. The good news is that the Lord Jesus reigns. Christ himself brought these tidings first and of him the word speaks "How beautiful are his feet!

his feet that were nailed to the cross, how beautiful upon mount Calvary all the believing Christians shall rejoice in the Lord.

Prayer:

Lord Jesus Christ we glorified your Holy Name, you saved us, and you brought us the good news of the Gospel forever. We also bring the good news of the Gospel to those who do not know you, those who sit in the shadow of darkness. Help us to continue to spread the good news of the Gospel to all the people in all the nations by the power of the Holy Spirit. Amen.

DAILY REFLECTION NOTES

JULY

JULY 1ST

THE WORD OF GOD IS A TRANSFORMATION
LET THE WORD TRANSFORM YOU TODAY.

Today's Scripture Reading:

"He who pursues righteousness and love finds life, prosperity and honor. A wise man attacks the City of the mighty and pulls down the strong hold in which they trust. He who guards his mouth and his tongue keeps himself from calamity."
(Proverbs 21:21-23) NIV

Believers must do justly and love mercy, and though they cannot attain perfection, yet it will be a comfort to believers if they aim at it; believing Christians who follow righteousness shall surely find righteousness. They will be proper in everything they do as well they will be honor. Those who have wisdom, they often perform great things and they were confident of their strength. People that are wise will gain the affections of the people around them and they will conquer them by strength of reason, which is a more noble conquest than that obtain by strength of arms. Those believing Christians that keep their souls must also keep watch before the door of their lips, and they must keep the mouth by temperance, that nothing be eating or drink to an excess. They must keep their tongue also, that no for bidden word should go out of the door of their lips, no corrupt communication, they keep their heart, and tongue from sin, and they must keep the tongue their tongue also, that no forbidden word should go out of the door of their lips, no corrupt communication, they keep their heart, and tongue from sin, and they just keep the tongue and the heart out of trouble.

Prayer:

Lord God Almighty, Father of all mercies sustainer of all thing; let the words of our mouth, the meditation of our heart be acceptable in your sight; do not let us say a word out of our mouth that will tear, demeaning, downgrading, pull anyone down, discourage any one in what they are doing or about to do. Plant in our hearts the inspirational words; words of wisdom, words of knowledge and understanding ; word of the Holy Scripture that we read every day, word that will convert souls into your Holy hands, words of life, that will make people alive in you and rejoice in you, let the words of encouragement comes out of our mouth at all times, words that will build people up, lift up their spirit , soul and body. Lord Jesus Christ help us to keep our hearts, our minds and our tongues out of trouble, do not let corrupt communication comes from our heart to our tongue; keep us save and clean so that you can be able to use us for your glory now and forever. In your great might Holy Name , we pray now and forever. Amen.

JULY 2ND

THE WORD OF GOD IS A TRANSFORMATION LET THE WORD TRANSFORM YOU TODAY

Today's Scripture Reading:

"Praise the Lord, O my Soul, all my inmost being, praise his Holy Name. Praise the Lord, O my Soul, and forget not his benefits, who forgives all your diseases, who redeems your life from the pit and crown you with love and compassion, who satisfies your desires with good things so that your youth is renewed like the eagles." (Psalm 103:1-5) NIV

All the believing Christians must learn how to live a life of praises and thanksgiving to the Lord for all the benefits and blessings that he bestows on all the believing covenant people. Believers must never forget God's goodness to us and is compassion over our lives. Believers must not fail to be thankful for his blessings that the Lord is showing on us through the empowerment of the Holy Spirit. David in this Scripture pouring and communicating with his own heart, and stirs up himself to make it his duty of praising the Lord. We must bless the Lord with our Soul at all times with everything he created us with, blessed the Lord with all our being, all our inward being. We must remember all what God almighty has done in our life. He pardon our sins, he forgives all our iniquities, we are restored to the favor of God, which bestows good things on us; he is still forgiving, as we are still sinning and repenting.

Prayer:

Lord Jesus Christ, our gracious master and our deliverer help us to call unto you in everything we might be going through. We give you thanks for everything you have done in our lives; we adored you and honor you now and forever. We give you praises and thankfulness now and forever. Amen.

JULY 3RD

THE WORD OF GOD IS A TRANSFORMATION LET THE WORD TRANSFORM YOU TODAY

Today's Scripture Reading:

"They will put you out of the Synagogue; in fact, a time is coming when anyone who kill you will think he is offering service to God. They will do such things because they have not known the Father or me. I have told you this, so that when the time comes you will remember that I warned you. I did not tell you this at first because I was with you." (John 16:2-4) NIV

Our Lord and Savior were speaking about the hostility from the religious authorities and congregations. Jesus Christ was making reference to those who hate believing Christians; They also include some religious people and false prophets. All profess churches that do not adhere to Jesus' teaching and apostolic revelation, or that do not seek to remain separated from the corrupt systems of society, belong to the world. These so called professed believers have value so different from the true New Testament Gospel that when they persecute, or kill true followers of Christ, they think they are serving God. It is possible for those that are real enemies of God's service to pretend a mighty zeal for it; the devil's work has many a time been done in God's livery.

God's people have suffered the greatest hardships from conscientious persecutors. Many that pretend to know God are wretchedly ignorant of him. Those that are ignorant of Jesus Christ cannot have any right knowledge of God.

Prayer:

Lord Jesus Christ protects your people, remember your people O' Lord that are going through persecution in the world. Turn all the haters of God to the lovers of God; turn all the haters of the Cross of Christ to the lovers of the Cross of Christ; turn them from evil to good, from hatred to love, from violent to peace, from wickedness to good, from jealousy to love. In your powerful Holy Name , we pray. Amen.

JULY 4TH

THE WORD OF GOD IS A TRANSFORMATION LET THE WORD TRANSFORM YOU TODAY

Today's Scripture Reading:

"He who dwells in the shelter of the most high will rest in the shadow of the Almighty. I will say of the Lord, he is my refuge and my fortress, my God, in whom I trust. If you make the most high your dwelling even the Lord, who is my refuge then no harm will befall you, no disaster will come near your tent. For he will command his angels concerning you to guard you in all your ways; They will lift you up in their hands, so that you will not strike your foot against a stone." (Psalm 91: 9-12) NIV

Those who commit themselves to the will and the protection of the Lord Jesus Christ, expresses the security and trust full in the Lord, it this assurance that God the Father our refuge and our fortress whom we seek for protection in our lives. Believers must be strong in the word of the Lord. The more fully we abide in Christ Jesus and his word, and making him our life and our dwelling place forever, the fuller will be our peace and the greater will be our deliverance in times of danger. It is a great truth that was laid down in general sense for all the believers that all those who live a life of communion with God are constantly safe under his protection, and may therefore, preserve a Holy serenity of mind at all times. It is the character of true believer that he dwells in the secret place of the highest God; he is at home in God, returns to

God, and reposes in him as his rest, and they will have a residence, under God's protection.

Prayer:

Lord God almighty Father, Son and Holy Spirit keep us under the shadow of your wings. Protect, guard, and lead us to the righteous place. Hold us in your Holy hands preserve us and dwell in us, and we will dwell in you forever. Amen.

JULY 5TH

THE WORD OF GOD IS A TRANSFORMATION LET THE WORD TRANSFORM YOU TODAY

Today's Scripture Reading:

"Each of you should look not only to your own interests, but also to the interest of others. You attitude should be the same as that of Christ Jesus; Who, being in very nature of God, did not consider equality with God something to be grasped, but made himself nothing, taking the very nature of a servant, being made in human likeness. And being found in appearance as a man, he humble himself and became obedience to death even death on the cross! Therefore, God exalted him to the highest place and gave him the Name that is above every Name, that at the Name of Jesus every knee should bow, in heaven and on earth and under the earth, and every tongue confess that Jesus Christ is Lord to the glory of God the Father." (Philippians 2:4-11) NIV

Our Lord Jesus Christ left his incomparable glory in heaven and took the humble position of a servant, becoming obedient to death for the sake of others. Christ's humility of heart and mind should be found in us his followers, who are called to be like Jesus in this life Jesus Christ is the true Son of God, in his very nature of God and equal with the Father before, during and after his time on earth. Jesus Christ did not consider equality with God something to be grasped means he let go of his privileges and glory as deity in heaven in order that we on earth might be saved. Jesus Christ voluntarily emptied himself, laid down his heavenly glory, position, his eternal riches, and his divine attributes. He accepted all human limitations, suffering, ill-treatment, misunderstanding death on the cross.

Prayer:

Lord Jesus Christ you empty yourself and came to us to save us from our sins, what a wondrous love you have for us. In your mercy, O' Merciful and Mighty God keep us to yourself, make us your own forever, and help us to be useful for you now and forever. Amen.

JULY 6TH

THE WORD OF GOD IS A TRANSFORMATION LET THE WORD TRANSFORM YOU TODAY

Today's Scripture Reading:

"Jesus told them parable: The kingdom of heaven is like a man who sowed good seed in his field. But while everyone was sleeping, his enemy came and sowed weeds among the wheat, and went away. When the wheat sprouted and formed heads, then the weeds also appeared." (Matthew 13:24-26) NIV

Our Lord Jesus Christ gave us this parable - the parable of the wheat and weeds emphasizes that Satan will sow alongside those who the Word of God. The field represents the universe, and the good seed represent the true sons of the kingdom. The Gospel and true believers will be planted throughout the world. Satan also will plant his own people, the sons of the evil one, among God's people in order to counter act God's truth. The principal work of Satan's emissaries within the visible kingdom of heaven will be under mining the authority of God's Word. One of the basic sins of humankind in the world is unbelief in God's Word. Most people of this world like to promote unrighteousness and false doctrine. Jesus Christ spoke of a great deception among his people because of these professed Christians who are really false teachers; they will present the Gospel in a different way that will make to be in the world and in Christ. Jesus Christ teach and preached in parables and tries all ways and so many ways, methods to do good to the Souls of men. Christ preached by parable wisely and in a figurative manner which can help to get the attention of the people in a diligent way.

Prayer:

Lord Jesus Christ, bless us in a way that we will be able to understand your Word and follow your commandment. We give you thanks and adoration throughout our days on this earth. Let the sinners and the lost be converted unto you. In your Holy Name, we pray now and forever more. Amen.

JULY 7TH

THE WORD OF GOD IS A TRANSFORMATION LET THE WORD TRANSFORM YOU TODAY

Today's Scripture Reading:

"You adulterous people, don't you know that friendship with the world is hatred toward God? Anyone who chooses to be a friend of the world becomes an enemy of God. Or do you think Scripture says without reason that the spirit caused to live in us envies intensely? But he gives us more grace. That is why Scripture says: God opposes the proud but gives grace to the humble." (James 4:4-6) NIV

All the believing Christians must know that friendship with the world is a spiritual adultery for example: unfaithfulness to God and our pledge of commitment to him; it involves embracing the world's attitudes, values and sinful ways – God will not accept such friendship, for he is a jealous God. The Spirit of and unbeliever full of envies and desires the sinful pleasures of the world. When Christ dwell in the heart, he change all the worldly desires, and all the sinful nature and envies. By God's grace which comes to all who humbly accept salvation in Christ. While God opposes the proud, he increases grace to the humble. We must submit our self to God in order to obtain more and more grace. We must come near to

God with the Spirit of Humbleness, in worship, praise and thanksgiving, with prayers and fasting, and in fellowship with the Holy Spirit.

Prayer:

Lord Jesus Christ blesses all those who believe in you with the Spirit of humbleness to serve you on this earth. To be able to call the sinner and the lost unto you with perfect spirit of submission to your Lordship. Bless us with everything we need to lay our life for you from this world to heaven. Let your blessings flows like a river to us every day of our life. In your mighty, marvelous Holy Name, we pray now and forever. Amen.

JULY 8ᵀᴴ

THE WORD OF GOD IS A TRANSFORMATION LET THE WORD TRANSFORM YOU TODAY

Today's Scripture Reading:

"Set your minds on things above, not on earthly things. For you died, and your life is now hidden with Christ in God. When Christ, who is your life, appears, then you also will appear with him in glory." (Colossians 3:2-4) NIV

Believers life are in Jesus Christ who is seated in heaven at the right hand of God, we must set our minds on Jesus and let our attitudes be determined by things above. We must view and evaluate everything from an eternal and heavenly perspective. Believer's goals and purpose and pursuits should be centered in Jesus Christ - by resisting sin and being clothed with Christ's life and character. Spiritual graces, power, experiences, and blessings are all with Christ in heaven. He bestows blessings on all who sincerely and diligently pursue him with all their heart. Jesus Christ has gone before us to secure the heavenly happiness; and therefore, we should seek what he has purchased at fast an expense. The heart soars upwards upon the wings of affection – things on earth are set in opposition on things above. Heaven and earth are contrary one to the other, and the prevalence of our affection to one will proportionally weaken our affection to the other will. We are dead to the earthly and the new man is hid with Christ, this is our comfort that our life is hid with Jesus Christ, and laid up safely with him.

Prayer:

Lord Jesus we are in you, you are in us, hide us in you secret place for our security and protection. Help us to seek your face at all time in everything we do, you alone can set our minds and our hearts to you, so that we can be able to focus on our eternal blessing of living with you in heaven for ever. Amen.

JULY 9TH

THE WORD OF GOD IS A TRANSFORMATION LET THE WORD TRANSFORM YOU TODAY

Today's Scripture Reading:

"For everyone born of God overcomes the world. This is the victory that has overcome the world, even our faith. Who is it that overcomes the world? Only the one who believes that Jesus is the Son of God." (1st John 5:4-5) NI

In order to overcome the world and its sin nature we must be born of God through Jesus Christ our Savior. The faith that overcome, the world, is the faith that sees the eternal realities, experiences God's power and loves Christ to such an extent that the world's sinful pleasures, secular values, ungodly ways and selfish materialism that not only lose their attraction focus, but also are looked on with disgust, aversion and grief. He that is born of God is born for God, and consequently for another world. Faith is the cause of victory. In faith and by faith we cleave to Christ in opposition to the world. It receives and derives strength from the object of it, the Son of God, for conquering the world. It is the real believing Christians that are the true conqueror of the world. He who believes that Jesus is the Son of God, also the believers therein that Jesus came from God to be the Savior of the world. And he whoso believes must needs by this faith overcome the world.

Prayer:

Lord Jesus Christ our Lord and our Savior; hear our prayers and answer our prayers. You are the only one who overcomes the world of sin for those who loved you. Bless us with the power of the Holy Spirit that we might be saved and give our life to you faithfully and sincerely. Hear our cry when we cried to you, solve all our problems, and fulfills all our needs, you are the one who saved us, loved us, and bought us with your precious blood on the cross. In your great mighty matchless Holy Name , we pray. Amen.

JULY 10TH

THE WORD OF GOD IS A TRANSFORMATION LET THE WORD TRANSFORM YOU TODAY

Today's Scripture Reading:

"And you have been given fullness in Christ, who is the head over every power and authority. In him you were also circumcised, in the putting off sinful nature, not with a circumcision, done by the hands of men but with the circumcision done by Christ, have been buried with him in baptism and raised with him through your faith in the power of God, who raised him from the dead."(Colossians 2:10-12)NIV

In the Old Testament, circumcision was the sign that the individual Israelites stood in a covenant relationship with God. It symbolized a cutting away, or separation from sin and all that was unholy in the world. The believing Christians under the new Testament covenant has undergone a spiritual circumcision, namely, the putting off of the sinful nature – such as circumcision is a spiritual activity whereby Jesus Christ cuts away our old unregenerate nature of rebellion against God and imparts to us the spiritual, or resurrection life of Jesus Christ – It is a circumcision of the heart. In Jesus Christ we are circumcised by the power of the blessed Holy Spirit, the Spirit of God. Jesus Christ is the Lord and the head of all the new creation that all the powers in heaven and on earth are in his hands. We are both buried and rise with Jesus Christ in baptism and in his resurrection, we die to sin and we live in Christ righteousness.

Prayer:

Lord Jesus Christ we are in your presence as we are baptized and buried and raised with you in baptism. You are the Holy one who calls us from darkness into your marvelous light. Bless us with your life. Bless us with your life unchanging so that we can serve you with the newness of life throughout our life on this earth. Help us to know you better every day of our of our life. With the power of your Holy , we pray now and forever. Amen.

JULY 11TH

THE WORD OF GOD IS A TRANSFORMATION
LET THE WORD TRANSFORM YOU TODAY

Today's Scripture Reading:

"The Spirit of the Lord is on me, because he has anointed me to preach God news to the poor. He has sent me to proclaim freedom for the prisoners and recovery of sight for the blind, to release the oppressed, to proclaim the year of the Lord's favor" *(Luke 418) NIV*

Our Lord Jesus Christ revealed to them in the Synagogue during his earthly ministry that God the Father has anointed him purposely for the work of the Gospel; his spirit anointed ministry is to preach the Gospel to the poor, the destitute, the afflicted, the humble, those who were crushed in the spirit, the broken hearted and to those who tremble at God's Word. Jesus was anointed to heal those who are bruised and those who are oppressed. This activity of Jesus healing involves the whole person, both physically and spiritually. Jesus was anointed to open the spiritual eyes of those who are blind by the world; by Satan in order that they might not see the truth of God's good news. Christ was anointed in order to proclaim the time of the true freedom and salvation from Satan's domain, sin, fear, and guilt. All the believing Christians who are filled with the Spirit are called to share Jesus Christ's ministry to others in this way. All the gifts and graces of the Spirit were conferred upon Christ without measure, as upon the prophets; Christ was fully anointed in Spirit and was commissioned, to preach. Jesus Christ preached the Gospel first before anyone else in the world.

Prayer:

Lord Jesus Christ our Lord and our Savior, we prayed and call unto you to anoint us with the power of the Holy Spirit so that we can be able to preach, teach, and proclaim the Gospel to the poor the distresses and to the sinners and the lost. Empower us with your Spirit our Lord. Amen.

JULY 12ᵀᴴ

THE WORD OF GOD IS A TRANSFORMATION
LET THE WORD TRANSFORM YOU TODAY

Today's Scripture Reading:

"New there have been many of those priests, since death prevented them from continuing in office; but because Jesus lives forever, we has a permanent priesthood. Therefore, he is able to save completely those who come to God through him because he always lives to intercede for them. Such a high Priest meets our need – one who is Holy, blameless, pure, set apart from sinners, exalted above the heavens." (Hebrews 7:23-26) NIV

Jesus Christ our Lord and Savior lives in heaven at the right hand of God interceding for everyone that belongs to him faithfully and sincerely. The Gospel dispensation is more full, free, and efficacious, then that of the law. Jesus Christ has united the divine and human nature together in his own person, and there in given us the assurance of reconciliation; and he has, united God and man together in the bond of the everlasting covenant. There is a remarkable change in the number of priests: but in Jesus Christ there is but one and the same, our high Priest of a new covenant continues for ever, and his priesthood is an unchangeable one, the people of his world will always have a high priest, there will be no time or a minute that the earth will not have a high priest in heaven that represents us at the presence of the Father.

Prayer:

Lord Jesus Christ our high Priest of a new covenant in heaven, pray for us the prayer that can never be uttered. Help us, and bless us with the power of your love. Do not leave us nor forsake us, make us Holy so that we may be able to serve you better, Lord Jesus Christ, use us mightily for your great glory on this earth anointed us with the power of your Spirit. Amen.

JULY 13TH

THE WORD OF GOD IS A TRANSFORMATION LET THE WORD TRANSFORM YOU TODAY

Today's Scripture Reading:

"Do not think that I have come to abolish the law or the prophets; I have not come to abolish them but to fulfill them. I tell you the truth, until heaven and earth disappear, not the smallest letter, not the least stroke of pen, will by any means disappear from the Law until everything is accomplished"(Matthew 5:17-18)NIV

The expression the Law and the prophets sometimes are used comprehensively for the entire Old Testament. It was Jesus Christ intention to abolish any of the Old Testament revelation but rather to see it fulfilled in the lives of his followers and fellow believers. the New Testament believers' relation to the law of God involves that believers are obliged to keep consists of the ethical and moral principles of the old Testament as well as the teaching of Jesus Christ and the apostles. These Laws reveal God's moral nature and his will for the lives of his people and therefore, still apply today. Believers must not view it as a system of legal commandments by which to obtain merit for forgiveness and salvation. Faith in Jesus Christ is the point of departure for the fulfilling of the law. Through faith in Jesus Christ, God almighty becomes our Father. Therefore, our obedience as believers is done not only out of a relationship to God as a sovereign law giver, but also out of a relationship of children to their Father.

Prayer:

Lord God Almighty have mercy upon us, make us Holy and clean to be able to do your will and live a life that pleases you. You are our Father in heaven, hold us tight do not let us go far away from your sight, watch us to grow in grace and in sanctification throughout our life on this earth, in your mighty Holy Name , we pray forever. Amen.

JULY 14ᵀᴴ

THE WORD OF GOD IS A TRANSFORMATION
LET THE WORD TRANSFORM YOU TODAY

Today's Scripture Reading:

"I have told you these things, so that in me you may have peace. In this world you will have trouble. But take heart I have overcome the world" (John 16:33) NIV

There are many pressures that always arise and come to us when we are openly identified with Jesus Christ, proclaim the Gospel, and totally gave our life to him in obedient and in total surrender to his Lordship in this world. These pressures are the fact of life, but we believing Christians must take courage because Jesus Christ has triumph in his resurrection especially and we share in his triumph Jesus Christ comfort believers with the promise of peace, in him, by virtue of his victory over the world. Whatever believer's trouble might be Jesus is there to meet the need at the right time, and at the correct timing. The end and the goal of Christ is that believer might have peace in him. It is the will of Jesus Christ that his disciples should have peace within them, within whatever their troubles may be peace in Christ Jesus is the only true peace. Through him we have peace with God, and so in him we have peace in our own mind. Jesus gave believers the word of encouragement, he wants all those who believe in him to be of good cheer because he has overcome the world of sin, evil, death, violence, and war.

Prayer:

Lord Jesus Christ, compassionate gracious loving God, have mercy upon us, Most Merciful and Mighty God, bless us with your peace that we may live and worship you, honor you, and proclaim your Holy Name. Bless us with your peace that surpasses all understanding within us and outside us physically and spiritually forever; help us to be able to abide in your Word of Comfort. Now and forever. Amen.

JULY 15TH

THE WORD OF GOD IS A TRANSFORMATION LET THE WORD TRANSFORM YOU TODAY

Today's Scripture Reading:

"You, however, did not come to know Christ that way. Surely you heard of him and were taught in him in accordance with the truth that is in Jesus. You were taught, with regard to your former way of life, to put off your old self, which is being corrupted by its deceitful desires; to be made new in the attitude of your minds, and to put off falsehood and speak truthfully to his neighbor, for we are all members of one body"(Ephesians 4:21-25)NIV

Jesus Christ is the lesson; we must learn Christ; and Christ is the teacher, we are taught by him. Because the truth is in Jesus Christ – We have been taught the real truth, as held forth by Christ himself, both in his doctrine and in his life. The truth of Jesus Christ appear in its beauty, power, when it appear as in Jesus. All the believers must be sanctified, the sanctification comply of two things the old man must be put away, which is the corrupt nature it is the old Adam, from whom we inherit. The New man must be put on. It is not enough to shake off corrupt principles, but we must be actuated by gracious ones, by the new man I mean new nature, the new creature, the new man is created by God's almighty power.

Prayer:

Lord Jesus Christ you are the one who gave us new heart, new mind, and a new spirit; help us to use it for the glory of your Holy Name. fill us with the Holy Spirit baptizes us with your Holy spirit so that we can be fully complete in you, serve you with the power of the Holy Spirit, converting souls of sinners and the lost unto your Holy hands with the power of your Holy spirit help us to live for the glory of your Holy Name and forever more. Amen.

JULY 16TH

THE WORD OF GOD IS A TRANSFORMATION LET THE WORD TRANSFORM YOU TODAY

Today's Scripture Reading:

"When Jesus spoke again to the people, he said I am the light of the world, whoever follows me will never walk in darkness, but will have the light of life" (John 8:12) NIV

Jesus Christ the only Son of God is the true light; he removes darkness and deception by illuminating the right way to God almighty Father our Lord Jesus Christ and also illuminating the right way to salvation. All those who follow Jesus Christ are delivered from the darkness of sin, the world and salvation. Those who still walk in darkness do not follow Him. Christ said "whoever follows me" which means it is a present participle which picturing a following whoever keep on following Christ, whoever totally believes in him, whoever surrender to Christ Lordship, whoever persevere in trials and tribulation of this world, and continue, without waiver, or doubt, will never walk in darkness. As sin is the visible light of the world and that one Sun enlightens the whole world, same is the one Jesus Christ who enlightens the people of this world with his light and salvation. Without Jesus Christ by whom the light came into the world. It is our responsibility with love and to follow him – Jesus Christ is the true light. It is the happiness of those who follow Jesus Christ that shall not walk in darkness. Follow Jesus Christ, and we shall follow him to heaven.

Prayer:

Lord Jesus Christ, you are the true light of this world, keep us save our Lord, shine your great light upon us from heaven, and do not let us walk in the darkness of this world. Help us to rejoice in your light from this universe to heaven; help us to live in your true light forever. Amen.

JULY 17TH

THE WORD OF GOD IS A TRANSFORMATION LET THE WORD TRANSFORM YOU TODAY

Today's Scripture Reading:

"Zechariah asked the angel, how can I be sure of this? I am an old man and my wife is well along in years. The angel answered, I am Gabriel. I stand in the presence of God, and I have been sent to speak to you and to tell you this good news" (Luke 1:18-19) NIV

Zachariah asked angel Gabriel, how he can be sure of the angel's prediction to him because his wife is an old woman, and he believes that Elizabeth his wife has already passed the age of childbearing. And Zechariah was thinking about her own age, he was not sure, if he was strong enough to produce a baby. Therefore, Zechariah was looking for a sign otherwise, he will not believe; even though the message was given to him in the temple when he was praying and burning incense, and, Zechariah has a firm belief that God has an almighty power, and with him nothing is impossible was more than enough to silence all his doubt and his objections. Yet, Zachariah was considering about this old age, and the day, they believed in the power of the almighty God, in God's miracles, but they still doubted when God miraculously exercised his power in their life. We must believe that in and through Jesus Christ, who is more than able to do great things for us.

Prayer

God the Father Almighty, Father of our Lord Jesus Christ, Holy Spirit forever one God. Bless us with the Holy Spirit Power. Without the power of the Holy Spirit no one can live a Christian life according to your commandment. Empower us with the manifestation of the Holy Spirit, baptize us with Spirit power and tongues of fire to serve you faithfully and sincerely in spirit and in truth with holiness of heart from this world to heaven. Help us to live a life that is pleasing and justified in your sight. Your presence is heaven to us; draw us close to you our Lord and Savior now and forever, in your great Holy Name we pray. Amen.

Prayer:

Lord God almighty, we give you praise and thankfulness because of what you have done in our life, since you brought us to this world up to this present moment; and what you are still going to do for us during our life time on earth. You are God of miracle, we thank you for your miracle power in our lives, Holy and merciful and mighty God in your Holy Name , we pray now and forever. Amen.

JULY 18TH

THE WORD OF GOD IS A TRANSFORMATION LET THE WORD TRANSFORM YOU TODAY

Today's Scripture Reading:

"Jesus answered, I am the way and the truth and the life, no one comes to the Father except through me."(John 14:6) NIV

Jesus Christ is the way, the only way to God the Father. Christ came to this world to show us the way to the Father, to reconcile all the humanity to God the Father. Christ is the mediator of a new covenant; the nature of his mediator – is that he is the way, the truth, and the life. The first thing to be considered distinctly is Christ is the way in him God and man meet, and are brought together. Jesus Christ is another way to the tree of life which God the Father instituted after the fall of Adam and Eve in the Garden of Eden. Disciples and all the believing Christians as long as they continue following Jesus Christ is the true way to life, to a peaceful well control by the Holy Spirit, the giver of life, who proceeded from the Father and the Son. Jesus Christ is the true and living way; he is the true way to life. Jesus Christ came purposely to this world to show us the way to the Father, so that we can have life in him.

Prayer:

God the Father Almighty, our Lord and Savior, Holy Spirit, the comforter, counselor, we pray for your full presence in our lives. , we pray that you continuously showing us the way, because you are the only way to God the Father, let your full presence be known in our lives solved all our problems fulfill all our needs, comfort us in time of sorrow, and earthly trials, strengthens us in all the areas where we are weak so that we can be able to serve you better more and more every day of our life. Amen.

JULY 19ᵀᴴ

THE WORD OF GOD IS A TRANSFORMATION
LET THE WORD TRANSFORM YOU TODAY

Today's Scripture Reading:

"Therefore he is able to save completely those who come to God through him, because he always lives to intercede for them." (Hebrews 7:25) NIV

Jesus Christ is our great intercessor in heaven. Jesus Christ lives in heaven in his Father's presence, interceding for each and every one of his followers according to the Father's Will. Through our Jesus Christ's ministry of intercession, believing Christians experiences God's love and his presence, and they find mercy and grace to help us in times of need, temptation, weakness, and earthly trials. We are sinners who are in need of a high Priest that will make satisfaction and intercession for us. No Priest could be suitable or sufficient for our reconciliation to God, but one who was perfectly righteous. The Lord Jesus Christ was exactly such a high Priest as we wanted, for he has a personal holiness, absolutely perfect; he is Holy. No sin dwells in him, he is harmless and blameless never did any wrong to God and man. He is able to completely save those who come to him with sincere heart and mind.

Prayer:

Lord Jesus Christ, you are our Lord and Savior, you call us to yourself, you reconciled us to leave with you and the Father, hear our prayers and grant us with your full presence, so that our prayers will go straight to you where you seated at the right hand of God. Let those who seek you sincerely with their whole hearts finds you, and worship you in spirit and in truth because this is the worship that the father approved. Amen.

JULY 20TH

THE WORD OF GOD IS A TRANSFORMATION
LET THE WORD TRANSFORM YOU TODAY

Today's Scripture Reading:

"The son is the radiance of God's glory and the exact representation of his being, sustaining all things by his powerful word. After he had provided purification for sins, he sat down at the right hand of the Majesty in heaven" (Hebrews 1:3) NIB

Jesus Christ is the exact representation for example: it refers to the mark that an engraving stamp leaves on a wax seal or on a coin; which is the correspondence between the engraving stamp and the engraved impression is exact. Jesus Christ God's Son radiates God the Father's glory because he shares God's nature and essence. Whatever, God is in his character and nature, Jesus Christ's personhood is the exact representation. Therefore, God's revelation of himself is no longer fragmentary and incomplete as in the Old Testament times. In Jesus Christ, the Son of God, he is the revelation of the Father is full and complete. As the only begotten Son of God, he has the same nature, he is the glory of God the Father, shining forth with a truly divine splendor. Jesus Christ's personhood is that he is God manifest in the flesh. Jesus Christ is the true image and character of God the Father. When we are beholding the power, wisdom, and goodness of our Lord Jesus Christ, we are beholding the power, wisdom, and goodness of the

Father. This is the glory of the person of Christ in whom the fullness of the Godhead dwells.

Prayer:

Lord God the Father, Son, and the Holy Spirit we adored you, magnify your Holy Name, fill us with the power of the Holy Spirit so that we can proclaim the honor of your Holy Name, take the Gospel to the end of the world, and under the earth. All our thankfulness and praises belong to you in whom the glory of Godhead dwells forever. Amen.

JULY 21ST

THE WORD OF GOD IS A TRANSFORMATION
LET THE WORD TRANSFORM YOU TODAY

Today's Scripture Reading:

"Again, I tell you that if two of you on earth agree about anything you ask for, it will be done for you by my Father in heaven. For where two or three come together in my Name, there am I with them. And teaching them to obey everything I have commanded you. And surely, I am with you always, to the very end of the age."(Matthew 18:19-20, 28:20)NIV

All the believers have two great promises from our Lord and Savior Christ. He gave us the authority and the power in the prayer of agreement. Jesus' statement points to the principle of synergism in the realms of faith and prayer. The principle is that the united actions of two or more separate agents when harmoniously working together have a greater total effect than the sum of their individual efforts. Our Lord Jesus promises two positive results of the prayer of agreement (a) The Father takes action in heaven on their request. (b) The presence of Jesus Christ will be in the midst on earth, Jesus Christ promise that his presence and authority would be with all believers who go worth to make disciples among all nations. Jesus Christ is presently with us in the person of the Holy Spirit and through his Word. All the believing Christians was encouraged with the an assurance of the presence of Jesus when they gather together and pray in Jesus' Name, he promised to be in the middle of them; that means in their hearts it is spiritual presence, the presence of Jesus Christ's Spirit with believer's Spirit, Christ will be right there in their midst this is an encouragement to all who believes in Jesus. It is not the multitude of people, but the faith and sincere devotion, of the worshippers that invites the presence of Jesus Christ. What Jesus said to the apostles, was said to all those who believed in him and serve him today.

Prayer:

Lord Jesus Christ fulfills your promise in our life; be there with us when we gather together to pray in your Holy Name. Let your full presence fill us up, let the place where we gather full of your light from heaven, let us know that you are right there in midst of us, Lord Jesus Christ listen to our prayers and answer our prayers. Let our prayers reach the hearts of the sinners and the lost, so that they can be converted unto you, let your mighty Holy Name be magnify in our lives now and forever. Amen.

JULY 22ND

THE WORD OF GOD IS A TRANSFORMATION
LET THE WORD TRANSFORM YOU TODAY

Today's Scripture Reading:

"For there is one God and one mediator between God and man, the man Christ Jesus, who gave himself as a ransom for all men – the testimony given in its proper time. And for this purpose I was appointed a herald and an apostle – I am telling the truth, I am not lying and a teacher of the true faith to the Gentiles."
(1st Timothy 2:5-7) NIV

Believing Christians access to God and his throne of grace is exclusively through Christ Jesus as our mediator Priest, as we rely on his sacrificial death to cover our sins and pray in with for strength and mercy to help us in all the areas where we experience weaknesses. We must not allow any other created being to take Christ's place by praying to him or her. The one and only God of heaven will have all men to be saved and come to the knowledge of repentance and pray for forgiveness of sins which is only in Christ Jesus. Believers must make it their responsibility to get the knowledge of the truth, because that is the way to be saved. As the mercy of our Lord extends itself to all his works, that is how, or them same way the mediation of Christ extends to all the children of men, so that as a rule of life because they are under grace. We deserve to have died, but Jesus Christ died for our sin on the cross. He put himself into the office of mediator between God and man.

Prayer:

Lord Jesus Christ, you are the mediator of a new covenant, the one and only advocate of a new covenant. You are the only one that sited at the right hand of God the Father: hear our prayers, and asked the Father for all what we needed to be a good believer and purge us clean from any unrighteousness now and forever. Amen.

JULY 23RD

THE WORD OF GOD IS A TRANSFORMATION
LET THE WORD TRANSFORM YOU TODAY

Today's Scripture Reading:

"For the grace of God that brings salvation has appeared to all men. It teaches us to say 'No' to ungodliness and worldly passions, and to live self-controlled, upright and godly lives in his present age, while we wait for the blessed hope – the glorious appearing of our great God and Savior, Jesus Christ."
(Titus 2:11-13) NIV

The blessed hope of all believers means a fullness of blessing as well as God's gracious favor and the happiness of being in our new bodies that will be immortal and that will not be subjected to corruption or decay. Believer's great blessed hope relates to the glorious appearance of the Lord Jesus Christ which will clearer when he come for his people, his bride Christ is the husband of the church, believers must wait patiently for this blessed hope of Christ appearing with prayers, and in purity of heart with faith, and with fervent desire as a faithful and Christ bride. Saving grace appeared to all the people in the world. Everywhere, not just the elect or selected people, believers must reject all the things that are ungodly passions, pleasures of the present age and regard them as abominable. Believers must be empowered to live uprightly, decisively and stay away from any form of sin, and immoral lives that is going on in the world. Jesus Christ returns to judge the dead and the living is our blessed hope.

Prayer:

Lord Jesus Christ, our Lord, and our Savior through the baptism of the Holy Spirit the apostle was able to spread the Gospel to the end of the earth as well as they do great thing with your Holy Name. empower all the believing Christians on this earth; baptize them with the Holy Spirit so that they may be able to win souls into your Holy hands. Amen.

JULY 24TH

THE WORD OF GOD IS A TRANSFORMATION LET THE WORD TRANSFORM YOU TODAY

Today's Scripture Reading:

"After he had dismissed them, he went up on a mountainside by himself to pray. When evening came, he was there a lone, But Jesus immediately, said to them: Take courage! It is I Don't be afraid." (Matthew 14:23, 27) NIV

Our Lord Jesus Christ gave believers example while on earth, Jesus often sought time to be alone with God – Time alone with God is very essential to the spiritual wellbeing of every believing Christians. Lack of desire for solitary prayer to a communion with Jesus Christ and our heavenly Father is an unmistakable sign that the spiritual life within us is in a process of decline. If this is happening, we must turn from all that offends the Lord and renew our commitment to persevere in seeking the face of God and his saving grace. Believers go through a lot of negativities, there are many things to fear, fear of rules of laws and regulations of nations, fears of persecution, and fear of discrimination against believers; yet Christ Jesus wants us to look to him and not be afraid. His Words of encouragement are founded on his limitless power and his intense personal love for all who truly belongs to him. Jesus Christ encourages his people not to be afraid of any earthly troubles. Christ was alone at prayer; that was his example that he set before us we must find time out of our busy schedule to be alone, one to one with Jesus Christ our Lord.

Prayer:

Lord Jesus , we pray that during solitary with you in prayer and supplication you will come to us and let your great glory shine upon us, let your full presence fill us up. Listen to our prayers and fulfilled all our request in prayer in the glory of your Holy Name , we pray. Amen.

JULY 25ᵀᴴ

THE WORD OF GOD IS A TRANSFORMATION
LET THE WORD TRANSFORM YOU TODAY

Today's Scripture Reading:

"He, who has an ear, let him hear what the Spirit says to the churches. To him who over-comes, I will give the right to eat from the tree of life, which is in the paradise of God." (Revelation 2:7) NIV

What Jesus Christ said to the church in Ephesus, he said to all churches in every place and in all the years up till today. Jesus Christ our Lord and Savior gave a promise of great unending mercy to those who overcome all the obstacles. An overcomer is one who by God's grace received through faith in Jesus Christ; and experienced the power over sin, the world's system, and Satan. Surrounded by great opposition and rebellion, overcomer will refuse to conform to the world and to any ungodliness within the visible church and its Luke-warm culture. They will hear and respond to what the Spirit says to the churches, they will remain faithful to Jesus Christ to the very end and accept only God's standard revealed in his Holy Word. The promise to overcomers, is that they will eat of the tree of life, and they will not get hurt by the second death, they will receive hidden Manna and be given a new Name in heaven, they will also be given authority over the nations,

Christ will not have their names removed from the book of life, their Name will be honored by Jesus before his Father and the angels. They will remain with God in his temple and will bear the Name of God, Christ, and the New Jerusalem; overcomer will sit with Christ on his throne and will be forever God's children forever.

Prayer:

Lord God Almighty, Father, Son, and Holy Spirit, we pray that you help us to be worthy from this earth to heaven to live a life, that will make our Name to be in the Book of the Lamb, and in the Book of Life. Fill us up with your Spirit, and help us to be totally surrendered to your Lordship and serve you to the end. Amen.

JULY 26TH

THE WORD OF GOD IS A TRANSFORMATION
LET THE WORD TRANSFORM YOU TODAY

Today's Scripture Reading:

"Sovereign Lord, as you have promised, you now dismiss your servant in peace. For my eyes have seen your salvation, which you have prepared in the sight of all people, a light for revelation of the Gentiles and for glory to your people Israel. The child's father and mother marveled at what was said about him." (Luke 2:29-33) NIV

Simeon was in the temple when Jesus Christ was presented to God. Righteous Simeon was devoted to God and filled with the Holy Spirit, waiting in faith, with patience and great longing for the coming of the Messiah. Same with all the believers today, waiting for the blessed hope the return of Jesus to the world, while some believers loose hop, there will be some that will be able to wait in strong hope till Christ returns. Believers' greatest blessing is to see Jesus Christ face to face when he comes and to live forever in his presence, to behold his gory, the glory of only begotten Son of God full of grace and truth. This is the encouragement which was given to those who keep themselves purer and undefiled by the world or earthly desires. The reward to the persevering victorious believing Christian is very powerful ushering in an authority and dominion in Christ over worldly powers, to include power and influence over the nations. Jesus Christ is the bright and the morning star.

Prayer:

Lord Jesus Christ empower all the believers with the power of the Holy Spirit, so that we can be able to live for you forever. Help us to wait for your promise and fulfill your promises in our life. Bless us and empower us in order to be able to wait for the promise of your Second Coming. Christ, when you return, helps us to be to be useful to you forever. Amen.

JULY 27TH

THE WORD OF GOD IS A TRANSFORMATION LET THE WORD TRANSFORM YOU TODAY

Today's Scripture Reading:

"The Jesus declared, I am the bread of life. He who comes to me will never go hungry, and he who believes in me will never be thirsty. At this the Jews began to grumble about him because he said, I am the bread that came down from heaven. I am the bead of life. I am the living bread that came down from heaven. If anyone eats of this bread, he will live forever. This bread is my flesh, which I will give for the life of the world." (John 6:35, 41, 48, 51) NIV

Jesus Christ our Lord and Savior gave us his word during his earthly ministry. He said: I am the bread of life; this is the first of his I am of the seven statements recorded in the Gospel of John. It emphasizes the important aspect of the personal ministry of Christ our Lord. It means that Jesus Christ is the sustenance that nourishes spiritual life of believers. Jesus Christ is the bread of life that believing Christians must be eating so that they can be alive in him. Chris is believer's immortal food; all the believers must feed upon him. Believer who desires with earnest to live on Christ will be abundantly satisfy, that they cannot be hunger or thirst again.

Union with Jesus Christ and communion with God in Christ are everlasting life begins.

Prayer:

Lord Jesus Christ be our bread of life to all those who feed on your bread of life. Be our immortal food for all those who put their trust, faith, and hope in you. Do not let anything delay your blessings from us make us alive in you by feeding us with your bread of life from this earth to heaven. Amen.

JULY 28TH

THE WORD OF GOD IS A TRANSFORMATION
LET THE WORD TRANSFORM YOU TODAY

Today's Scripture Reading:

"For as the Father has life in himself, so He has granted the Son to have life in himself. And he has given him authority to judge because he is the Son of man." (John 5:26-27) NIV

The Father granted the Son to have life in himself Jesus Christ's own nature is a source of eternal life; it is what was inherent within him. God the Father, however, has not given believers the power to have eternal life inherent in themselves. Believers have life only as they maintain intimate fellowship with Jesus Christ. Jesus Christ living inside believers through the living faith relationship. As Christ has almighty power, so he has a sovereign jurisdiction. Jesus Christ's commission, or delegation to the office of a judge, is spoken on this Scripture- Christ was given authority over all flesh, the Father committed all things into the Son's hands – Father was pleased to govern, rule through or by Jesus Christ. God was in Jesus Christ reconciling the world, and to him he has given power to confer eternal life. He that executes judgment upon sinners; is the same that would have brought salvation for them. The Father gave Jesus the authority, and this to the comfort of all believers, who may with greatest assurance venture their all in such hands because Jesus Christ is the Son of God, and the Son of man' his Father made him the Lord of all.

Prayer:

Lord Jesus Christ, you have blessed us with your life; you anointed all believers with the authority that the Father gave you before the creation of the world. In your mercy Lord Jesus Christ, we pray that you stretched out your Holy arms of love on the wood of the cross that everyone might be able to listen to the Gospel and come within the reach of your saving embrace; in order that you might clothe us with your Spirit that we, by reaching forth our hands in love, may bring those who do not know you to the knowledge and love of you; for the honor of your great Holy Name. Look down from heaven, mold us, shape us, purify us, as silver and gold being purified and make us your own forever, reconcile us to God the Father. In Jesus Christ great Holy Name, a Name above all names , we pray. Amen.

JULY 29TH

THE WORD OF GOD IS A TRANSFORMATION LET THE WORD TRANSFORM YOU TODAY

Today's Scripture Reading:

"Jesus said, 'This voice was for your benefit, not mine. Now is the time for judgment in this world; now the prince of this world will be driven out. But I when I am lifted up from the earth, will draw all men to myself.' He said this to show the kind of death he was going to die." (John 12:30-33) NIV

When Jesus said: The prince of this world will be driven out he means that the cross the crucial defeat of Satan, and all what he stands for that has already occurred will be finally banished forever, when he is thrown into the lake of fire of burning sulfur. Satan has influence in the world and he uses the things of the world against Jesus Christ and his church – his people. This is why that friendship with the world is hatred toward God. The grace of God is not exclusive, for some people, but not for others. However, some people because of their love for sin, and sin nature, and hardness of their hearts, they resist and nullify God's grace by their decisions and actions. What the Father said in heaven, concerning Jesus He said it for the sake of believers that we may be brought to rest upon him. By the death and resurrection of Jesus Christ Satan should be conquered, Christ speaks with a divine exultation and triumph. The death of Christ is the judgment of the world. A judgment of favor and absolution. Christ upon the cross interposed between a righteous God and guilty world. A judgment of righteous God and a guilty world. The judgment of condemnation against the power of darkness. The judgment of this world belongs to Jesus and not Satan.

Prayer:

Lord Jesus Christ we thank you and praise you, you are worthy to be praise accept our praises and thankfulness now and forever. You are our conqueror, you are the only one conquered sin on the cross; you are worthy of our praises and thankfulness forever, no one before you, no one after, you gave your life for us so that those of us that we live, we will not live for ourselves but live for you and for your glory forever rejoicing in your holiness and infinite love. Amen.

JULY 30TH

THE WORD OF GOD IS A TRANSFORMATION LET THE WORD TRANSFORM YOU TODAY

Today's Scripture Reading:

"My purpose is that they may be encouraged in heart and united in love, so that they may have the full riches of complete understanding, in order that they may know the mystery of God, namely ,Christ, in whom are hidden all the treasures of wisdom and knowledge." (Colossians 2:2-3) NIV

Believing Christians must be perfect means that they must be complete in Christ – they must be a mature Christian. It does not mean that all believer or imply an ethical perfection or flawless behavior, but it printed to believers mature relationship with the Lord. Believers must love the Lord fully with their heart and mind, seeking to do his Will, what is pleasing in his sight as well as they must love other people around them. Believers must keep up a communion by faith, hope, and Holy love, even with those of whom we have no personal knowledge. Those we never saw in the flesh we may hope to meet in heaven. It was believers welfare about which he was solicitous – the prosperity, of the soul is the best prosperity believer's knowledge must grow to the understanding of the mystery of God the Father, and of Jesus Christ.   Believers with faith growing to a full assurance and bold acknowledgment of this mystery – to a full assurance of well-settled judgment – to a free acknowledgment; of not only believe with our hearts, but ready to make confession with our mouth that Jesus Christ is the Lord to the glory of God the Father.

Prayer:

Lord Jesus Christ help us to be strong in you, in faith and in our daily walk with you; and live your life through us forever, fulfilling the great commission through us so that the Gospel will reach the end of the world in everyone's language, and all the glory belongs to you forever and ever. Amen.

JULY 31ST

THE WORD OF GOD IS A TRANSFORMATION
LET THE WORD TRANSFORM YOU TODAY

Today's Scripture Reading:

"According to the Lord's own Word, we tell you that we who are still alive, who are left till the coming of the Lord, will certainly not precede those who have fallen asleep. For the Lord himself will come down from heaven, with a loud command, with the voice of the archangel and with the trumpet call of God, and the dead in Christ will rise first. After that, we who are still alive and are left will be caught up together with them in the clouds to meet the Lord in the air. And so we will be with the Lord forever. Therefore, encourage each other with these words." (1st Thessalonians 4:15-18) NIV

Apostle Paul described how the return of Christ will be – the coming of our Lord which the church called "The Rapture of the church" The catching up the church from the earth to meet the Lord in the air – it involves only the faithful believers, those who gave their life to the Lord in full submission to his Lordship. Jesus Christ will descend from heaven for is church, the Lord Jesus will come down from heaven in all his power of the upper world. The glorious appearance of this great redeemer and judge will be proclaimed and ushered in by the trumpet of God. The principal happiness of heaven is to be with the Lord, see him, and live with him, and enjoys him forever. Believing Christians should comfort each other by these words.

Prayer:

Lord Jesus Christ, Most Merciful and Mighty, compassionate, gracious loving God, our gracious master and our great redeemer King, you redeemed us from our sins and you gave us a new life in you, a new life to worship you in spirit and in truth forever. You are worthy to be praise, we give glory great glory, and you are our hope of glory. We are waiting for your return, as we do not know the hour and the time, strengthens us with the power of the indwelling of the Holy Spirit, to direct, control, and to teach us your ways throughout our staying on earth, at the end to be able to see you face to face and live with you forever in your mighty Holy Name , we pray. Amen.

DAILY REFLECTION NOTES

467

AUGUST

AUGUST 1ST

THE WORD OF GOD CLEANSE US - LET THE WORD OF GOD CLEANSES YOU TODAY

Today's Scripture Reading:

"You, however, did not come to know Christ that way. Surely you heard of him and were taught in him in accordance with the truth that is in Jesus. You were taught, with regard to your former way of life, to put off old self, which is being corrupted by its deceitful desires." (Ephesians 4:20-22) NIV

All the believing Christians must make every effort to know Christ and to know his redeeming love for them as well as what he taught us during his earthly ministry on earth. Christians must distinguish themselves from people that are not believed, or people that does not know Christ. Those who have learned from the teaching of Jesus Christ are saved from the darkness which others lie under; and as they know more, and more of Jesus Christ is they are obliged to live in a better spiritual food than others. Jesus Christ is the lesson; we must learn Christ - and Jesus Christ is the teacher. Believer must be taught by him. Jesus Christ is the truth and the truth is in him, we have been taught the real truth, as held forth by Christ himself, both in his word and in his life. The truth of Jesus Christ appears in its beauty and power when it appears as in Jesus. Believers must put off all the corrupt nature, the old self and put on Christ.

Prayer:

Lord Jesus Christ Compassionate gracious loving God, full of truth and righteousness, abounding in love and forgiveness; our one and only redeemer King, you are the way, the truth, and the life. Help us to know you more and more every day of our lives. Feed us with your word, your word is true; teach us your word and help us to grow in grace and grow in sanctification O' Merciful and Mighty, bless us with your peace that surpasses all understanding throughout our stay on this earth. Amen.

AUGUST 2ND

THE WORD OF GOD CLEANSE US – LET THE WORD OF GOD CLEANSES YOU TODAY

Today's Scripture Reading:

"For I have come down from heaven not to do my Will but to do the Will of him who sent me. And this is the Will of him who sent me, that I shall lose none of all that I shall lose none of all that he has given me, but raise them up at the last day. For my Father's Will is that everyone who looks to the Son and believes in him shall have eternal life, and I will raise him up at the last day." (John 6:38-40) NIV

Jesus Christ came down from heaven primarily to do his Father's Will. All the believing Christians should follow the same path; after we have been saved, we must make all our efforts to do the Will Christ means make every effort to tell others about him. It is very important to understand the relationship of the Father's Will to all the believers is a responsibility. It is not God's Will that any believer should fall from grace, and subsequently be separated from God; neither is it his will that any individual should perish, or fail to come to know Christ, or come to the truth of Christ's word and be saved. Jesus Christ in his infinite mercy promises to welcome all who come to him with the heart of repentance and faith. Those who come to Jesus Christ, come in response to the grace given them by God the Father.

Prayer:

Lord Jesus Christ our Lord and our Savior you came down from heaven to save us you fulfill your Father's Will; help us to live in accordance to your Will. Fulfill the Great Commission through us, teach us the Scripture, pray through us the prayer that can never be uttered – Let your Will be done in our life, let your purpose be achieve in our life, let your full presence be known in our life and in our work for you. Amen.

AUGUST 3ᴿᴰ

THE WORD OF GOD CLEANSE US – LET THE WORD OF GOD CLEANSES YOU TODAY

Today's Scripture Reading:

"Sing to the Lord a new son, for he has done marvelous things his right hand and his Holy arm have worked salvation for him. The Lord has made his salvation known and revealed his righteousness to the nations. He has remembered his love and his faithfulness to the house of Israel." (Psalm 98:1-3) NIV

This is a song of praise for the Lord's victory and for his salvation made known to the people of Israel and for all other people in all the nations in the world. Our Lord and Savior, fulfilled his promise on the day of Pentecost with the out pouring of the Holy Spirit upon all those who believes, the Spirit empowered the apostles and they proclaimed the Gospel of God boldly, clearly, people was converted into the hands of Jesus Christ and in enthusiastic, joyful worship that fills the hearts of God's glory. People of this earth sing a new song which is a song of praises and thankfulness to our Lord who with his redeeming love, humanity regain the gift of grace to salvation, free us from sin and death. The work of Jesus is a work of wander. Our redeemer has done surmounted all the difficulties that lay in the way of redemption

Christ got the victory by his own power. What Christ has brought to us, he has revealed to us, the Gospel revelation, on which the Gospel kingdom was founded. God's promises were accomplished through Christ redemptive work:

Prayer:

God the Father Almighty you are worthy of all our praises from this earth to heaven; you fulfilled your promise through your Son Jesus Christ's work of redemption. Thank you for redeeming us from all our sins and making us your children forever and ever. Amen.

AUGUST 4TH

THE WORD OF GOD CLEANSE US – LET THE WORD OF GOD CLEANSES YOU TODAY

Today's Scripture Reading:

"The Lord had said to Abram, leave your country, your people and your Father's house hold and go to the land I will show you. I will make you into a great nation and I will bless you, I will make your Name great, and you will be a blessing. I will bless those who bless you, and whoever curses you I will curse; and all people on earth will be blessed through you." (Genesis 12:1-3) NIV

God the Father Almighty, call Abram and told him to leave his country and to where God will show him under direct guidance from the Lord. God purpose is to redeem and save all the people in the world. God intended that people of this earth to know him and serve him with a devoted heart and with faith. When God called Abraham, he separated him from his country and his family. Same with us today, God's call involve separation from all the world lust and sometimes from our family in order to be what he wants us to be. When God said "All the people on earth will be blessed through Abraham, God was referring to Jesus Christ, coming of the Messiah. He was also speaking of spiritual blessing that would come through Abraham's seed which is Christ Jesus. The blessing was referring to the Gospel of Jesus offered to the people of all the nations. Believer's blessing of regeneration and salvation become a source of blessing to other people by sharing, witnessing the Gospel to them. The idea of blessed to be a blessing was revealed in the call of Abraham. Same with all the believing Christians.

Prayer:

Lord Jesus Christ our Lord and our Savior, you have called us and ordain us, and designed our lives to be conforming to the work of the Gospel, to the people of this world who sit in the shadow of darkness. You are the channels of all blessings; bless us today, abundantly, and immeasurably so that we can be a blessing to other people in this world. Amen.

AUGUST 5TH

THE WORD OF GOD CLEANSE US – LET THE WORD OF GOD CLEANSES YOU TODAY

Today's Scripture Reading:

"Then God blessed Noah and his sons, saying to them; Be fruitful and increase in number and fill the earth. The fear and dread of you will fall upon all the beast of the earth and all the birds of the air, upon every creature that moves along the ground, and upon all the fish of the Sea; they are given into your hands." *(Genesis 9:1-3) NIV*

God the Father Almighty is a great God above all Gods, nothing beyond his reach. He said to Noah that: "As long as the earth endures seed time and harvest, cold and heat, summer and winter, day and night will never cease – and never again will I destroy all living creatures, as I have done" – God is a God of infinite love, but we human being always doing what grief the Spirit of God – Thank God for Jesus Christ work of redemption. God made another covenant for Noah. God's covenant with Abraham and with Noah were monergistic means "one worker" Covenants God provides the covenant; God carries it out; it is by God's grace we are saved. The New covenant which through Christ which is also monergistic believers will not be able to go up to heaven to bring Christ down to be born and to die on the cross. We could not go into the grave to bring him up from the dead. Therefore, God the Father did it all. God blessed Noah and his sons, he assured them of his goodwill to them and his gracious intentions concerning them; Noah also blessed God by his altar by his sacrifice and thankfulness with praise.

Prayer:

Lord God Almighty Father Son and Holy Spirit it is by your grace alone, we are save through the work of redemption of our Lord Jesus Christ, the work of grace is by faith alone in your Son alone; Blesses us with the blessings you have for us before the beginning of the creation of the world. Help us to worship you and honor you with the Spirit of adoration, live a life that will be pleasing you from this earth to heaven, we give you praises for the blessing of sanctification, glorification and your gift of grace to salvation from this earth to heaven. Amen.

AUGUST 6TH

THE WORD OF GOD CLEANSE US – LET THE WORD OF GOD CLEANSES YOU TODAY

Today's Scripture Reading:

"God blesses them and said to them. Be fruitful and increase in number, fill the earth and subdue it. Rule over the fish of the Sea and the birds of the air and over every living creature that moves on the ground. Then God said, I give you every seed bearing plant on the face of the whole earth and every tree that has fruit with seed in it. They will be yours for food." (Genesis 1:28-29) NIV

God Almighty charge man and woman with being fruitful and ruling over the earth and the animal kingdom. They were created to form family relationships. This sows the purpose of God in creation indicates that he considers a godly family and the raising of the children should be their utmost priority in the world. God expect the man woman, and required from them to be consecrated all things in the earth to him and to manage it in a God – glorifying way. This will help them to fulfill the divine purpose. God blessed his creation so that it could be fruitful and multiply. All the plants represent marvelous abundance of nature abundance of seeds, vegetables, and fruits; we must be thankful and praise God, who gave us food to eat. As we were made out of the earth, so we are maintained out of it; there are food that endures to everlasting life, that the Lord gave to us; which should make us to be thankful. God the Father, Son and Holy Spirit is for the body; from whom we receive all the supports and comforts of this life.

Prayer:

Lord Jesus Christ we give thanks for all what you have done for us, what you are doing for us now and for what you are still going to do for us in the future. Bless us with your presence so that we can live for your glory forever. Amen.

AUGUST 7TH

THE WORD OF GOD CLEANSE US – LET THE WORD OF GOD CLEANSES YOU TODAY

Today's Scripture Reading:

"Do not repay evil with evil or insult with insult, but with blessings, because to this you were called so that you may inherit a blessing." (1st Peter 3:9) NIV

Our Lord Jesus Christ called us not to return evil with evil, or insult for insult. Christians must return good for evil, kindness for insults. Christian believers must be ready to help those who are in need of their help at all times. Our Lord Jesus has a blessing for his own people, but they must live their life according to his Word and his Will. Believing Christians are called to inherit a blessing, we must repay those who insult us with blessing; even if they mistreated us, we are to return their mistreatment with a blessing, we repay them with blessings as God and our Lord Jesus Christ has blessed us regardless of what evil they have done for us. Christians should endeavor to be all of one mind in the great point of faith, in real affection, and in all Christians practice. Believers must have compassion for one another and love all other believers. We must love our enemies when they give us evil words; we return it with good words. Jesus Christ taught us to bless those that curse us, and has settled a blessing on you as your everlasting inheritance.

Prayer:

Lord Jesus Christ, you are the God of blessings; help us through the power of the Holy Spirit so that we can bless those who curse us, and return good for the evils to the people of the world of all what they are doing to all the Christians. Help us to forgive those who wrong us and move on, bless us with the mind of Christ to forgive as Christ forgives on the Cross. Help us to love our enemies, pray for our enemies as you taught us. Amen.

AUGUST 8TH

THE WORD OF GOD CLEANSE US – LET THE WORD OF GOD CLEANSES YOU TODAY

Today's Scripture Reading:

"But we have this treasure in Jar of clay show that this all – surpassing power is from God and not from us. We are hard pressed on every side, but not crushed; perplexed, but not in despair; persecuted, but not abandoned; struck down, but not destroyed. We always carry around in our body the death of Jesus, so that the life of Jesus may also be revealed in our body." (2nd Corinthians 4:7-10) NIV

The believing Christians are "Jars of Clay" who at times experience sadness, tears, troubles, persecutions, perplexities, weakness and fears; but because of the heavenly treasure Christianity is not removal of weakness, nor is it merely the manifestation of divine power through the human weakness – this means that in every affliction we may be more than conquerors by God's power and love to the point that our weakness, troubles and suffering will open us up to Jesus Christ's abundant grace as well as allow his life to fill us up and to be revealed in our bodies. If believers experience Jesus Christ's presence and power in their life, they will absolutely have no earthly problems. In order to minister life to unbelievers, we must share Christ's suffering and experience the working of death in our own lives by self-denial, disappointment for Christ's sake will allow lives to minister grace to other.

Prayer:

O' Most Holy and Most Merciful and Mighty, you are our life, without you we have no life, and it is a life that begins here and never ends, because we will continue to live with you in heaven, you are our life, the eternal life, life of eternity where we will live with you and behold your glory, the glory of one and only begotten Son of God full of truth and righteousness, the life that we will forever see you and live with you forever. Bless us with your life, life in God the Father, God the Son, and God the Holy Spirit, the three Godhead, the Holy Trinity forever one God. We adore you honor you and give you praises and adoration forever. Lord Jesus Christ you are the God of life, live your life through us; so that we may be able, with your power and love, minister to other people around us in this world; with your great Holy Name, we pray. Amen.

AUGUST 9TH

THE WORD OF GOD CLEANSE US – LET THE WORD OF GOD CLEANSES YOU TODAY

Today's Scripture Reading:

"Therefore we do not lose heart. Though outwardly we are wasting away, yet inwardly we are being renewed day by day. For our light and momentary troubles are achieving for us an eternal glory that far outweighs them all. So we fix our eyes not on what is seen, but on what is unseen. For what is seen is temporary, but what is unseen is eternal." (2nd Corinthians 4:16-18) NIV

Believers' outwardly and inwardly refers to the physical body, which is subject to decay and moving towards death because of mortality and the trouble s of life. Inwardly on the other hands, refers to the human spirit that has the spiritual life of Jesus Christ. Although our bodies age and decay, we experience an ongoing renewal through the constant impartation of Christ's life and power; Christ influence enables our minds, emotions and will to be conformed to the likeness and eternal purpose. Momentary troubles are the hardships endure in the lives of those who remain faithful to Christ they are light in comparison to the abundance of glory we have through our Lord and Savior. This glory of Christ has already present in part, but will be fully experienced in the future; when we reach our heavenly inheritance, we will rejoice and say that the severest tribulations were nothing compared with the glory of the eternal state. Therefore, Christians must not lose hope, or give up our faith as we face our problems.

Prayer:

Lord God Almighty, Father, Son, and the Holy Spirit ever one God, the Holy Trinity one God for ever and forever. In your infinite Mercy make us to be strong in you, with all what we are going through, help us to be one in you as you and Father are one. Help us to worship you with the spirit of holiness throughout our lives. Solve all our problems, our troubles more and more that anyone can imagine and bring great Glory to your Holy Name in us, and through us, now and forever. Amen.

AUGUST 10TH

THE WORD OF GOD CLEANSE US – LET THE WORD OF GOD CLEANSES YOU TODAY

Today's Scripture Reading:

"And God is able to make all grace abound to you, so that in all things at all times, having all that you need, you will abound in every good work you will be made rich in every way so that you can be generous on every occasion, and through us your generosity will result in thanksgiving to God." (2nd Corinthians 9:8, 11) NIV

Believing Christians have no reason to distrust the goodness of our Lord, because he is able to make all grace abound for his glory and for his good pleasure. The honor of God's grace is everlasting and the reward of it is eternal life. Believers who give what they have to help those who are in need will find that God's grace provides a sufficiency for their own needs, and even more, that they will abound in every good work. Believers must express generosity outwardly, so that they heart must be made rich insincere love and compassion for others. Giving ourselves and our possessions, result in supplying the needs of poorer brothers and sisters; praises and thanksgiving to God reciprocal love, from those who receive our help. God Almighty loves a cheerful giver and he is able to make our charity redound to our advantage. The works of charity are so far from impoverishing us that they are the proper means that will truly enrich us, or make us truly rich.

Prayer:

Lord Jesus Christ our Lord and Savior; you are the one and only who gave us the best gift on this earth by giving us your life for our sins. Help us to give as you give, love as you love our Lord. Bless us abundantly immeasurable financially so that we will be able to help the poor and the needy, the sick and those who will need your help among us. We need financial blessing to do your work on this earth and to do good work that will bring sinners and the lost unto you. Hear our prayers and help us to help others among us because of your blessing for us, other people lives might be touched and change through the Power of your Holy Spirit.

AUGUST 11ᵀᴴ

THE WORD OF GOD CLEANSE US – LET THE WORD OF GOD CLEANSES YOU TODAY

Today's Scripture Reading:

"To keep me from becoming conceited because these surpassingly great revelations, there was given me a thorn in my flesh, a messenger of Satan to torment me. Three times I pleaded with the Lord to take it away from me. But he said to me, my grace is sufficient for you, for my power is made perfect in weakness. Therefore I will boast all the more gladly about my weakness, so that Christ's power may rest on me." (2ⁿᵈ Corinthians 12:7-9) NIV

Apostle Paul's word "thorn" communicates the idea physical of pain, trouble, suffering; also the meaning of the thorn can be applied to spiritual issues of lessons of spiritual wickedness of this world to ourselves. Thorn may be attributed to demonic activity permitted but limited by God for his glory. At the same time, Paul's thorn was given to him, to keep him from becoming arrogant or proud over the revelations he had received from the Lord. The thorn kept him to be dependent in a greater measure on divine grace. But it also happens to all believers today. Many times when God answers a sincere prayer with refusal, something better and much better is given. What apostle Paul calls a thorn in the flesh, was grievous to him that he prayed three times for the Lord to take it away, or heal it. But the crown of thorns that Christ Jesus wore for us, sanctifies, and makes easy all the thorns in the flesh we may at any time be afflicted with. The design of the thorn kept the apostle humble, in that God will hide pride from us, and keep us from being exalted above measure.

Prayer:

Lord Jesus Christ you are our great intercessor in heaven; I pray for that you intercede for our needs, let your Infinite Love and mercy with great compassion fill us up, and overflow to the sinners and the lost now and forever. Amen.

AUGUST 12TH

THE WORD OF GOD CLEANSE US –
LET THE WORD OF GOD CLEANSES YOU TODAY

Today's Scripture Reading:

"Jesus said, my kingdom is not of this world. If it were, my servants would fight to prevent my arrest by the Jews. But now my kingdom is from another place." (John 18:36) NIV

The true nature of Christ's kingdom and its redemptive purpose, three points should be noted (a) Jesus Christ kingdom is not of this world. It did not originate in this world, nor does it seek the take over the world's system. Jesus did not come to establish a political religion, Theocracy or aspire to world dominion. Jesus States that If he had come to establish a political kingdom on earth, then his servants would have fight for him. Therefore, since this is not the nature of the kingdom, they do not resort to war, or revolution to promote Christ's purpose on earth. They do not rally themselves with political parties, social pressure groups or any secular organizations in order to establish God's kingdom. Jesus Christ's kingdom, is the kingdom of God, it involves his rule, Lordship, power, and spiritual activity in the lives of all who receive him and obey his word of truth. Kingdom of Jesus Christ is the kingdom of righteousness, peace, and Joy in the Holy Spirit. It confronts the spiritual forces of Satan with spiritual weapons. And finally, Christ kingdom in future will be, Christ's kingdom and rule will be the New Heaven and the New Earth; this will occur after the Second Coming of Christ to judge the nations, destroy the antichrist, rule on earth for a thousand years and bring Satan to a final end in the lake of fire.

Prayer:

All glory and honor to you our Lord and Savior, who came to this world and gave us your life. We glorify your Holy Name for being crucified for my sin and the sins of the people of this world. No one before you and no one after you our Lord. You reconcile us to God the Father; you are our reconciler. You are worthy of all our praises from this earth to heaven. You have done a great thing in our life Holy is your Name forever. Lord you are worthy of honor, glory, and praise for everything you have done for us. Help us to be worthy to live with you in a new heaven and in a new earth where righteousness dwells. Amen.

AUGUST 13TH

THE WORD OF GOD CLEANSE US – LET THE WORD OF GOD CLEANSES YOU TODAY

Today's Scripture Reading:

"And if the Spirit of him who raise Jesus from the dead is living in you, he who raised Christ from the dead will also give life to your mortal bodies through his Spirit, who lives in you."
(Romans 8:11)NIV

Because of sin our bodies and its ravaging effects, the body in the natural state is under the process and the sentence of death, even for the believer. Our bodies ultimately will be redeemed by resurrection or transformation at Jesus Christ's Second Coming. But because Jesus Christ came to give us life here and now the Holy Spirit who raised Jesus from the dead desires to impart life even to our mortal bodies. As we embrace Christ's life within us. The Holy Spirit is the Spirit of life; he will impart life to our mortal flesh. If Jesus Christ is in us our bodies is life, in Christ. In the midst of life we are in death, our bodies ever so strong, they are as good as dead, and it is because of sin; it is the sin and sin nature that kills the body. Therefore, love to our bodies shall make us to hate sin, because it is such an enemy to our bodies. The Spirit that is life, when the body dies, the Spirit is life. The righteousness Jesus Christ imparted to believers; secure the soul from death; the righteousness of Christ inherent in the life of believer, preserves it, and at death elevates it, and makes it to partake of the inheritance of the Saints. The body shall reunite to the soul, and clothe with the glory of our Lord.

Prayer:

Lord Jesus Christ, you are our life you are the God of resurrection eternal life. Bless, us feels us up with your light from heaven, make us to be alive in you with the power of the Holy Spirit so that we can live with you in a new heaven and a new earth where only righteousness dwell, where there will be no darkness and your light will continue shine upon us forever. Amen.

AUGUST 14TH

THE WORD OF GOD CLEANSE US –
LET THE WORD OF GOD CLEANSES YOU TODAY

Today's Scripture Reading:

"And we know that in all things God works for the good of those who love him, who have been called according to his purpose." (Romans 8:28) NIV

God in his infinite mercy in all things works for our good on this earth; His full presence is being manifest every day of our life. This sentence of Scripture has greatly encouraged God's Children all over the world. When we must endure suffering in this life. God will bring good out of all affliction, trials, persecution, and suffering, the good that God works is conforming us to the likeness of Christ Jesus our Lord; and ultimately bringing about our glorification. This promise is limited to those who love God and have submitted to him through faith in Jesus Christ. All this that God works for good does not include our sins and negligence; no one can excuse sin by maintaining that God will work it out for good. God concurrence of all his providences for the good of those that are in Christ Jesus. Notwithstanding all these privileges, believers were compasses about with various manifold afflictions, but in this the spirit's intercession is always effectual, that all this is working together for our good. Those who love God make the best of all he does for us, and they take all in good part; not according to any merit of ours but, according to God's own gracious purpose.

Prayer:

We give you thanks O' Lord for working everything we are going through, affliction, persecution, troubles, problems, and our trials in life for our own good. We give you praise and adoration, and glory. Continue to help us to lead more people unto you, let your love and mercy flows through us to all the people that does not know you, let your light shine upon them and make Souls of the people of this world your own forever. Amen.

AUGUST 15ᵀᴴ

THE WORD OF GOD CLEANSES US –
LET THE WORD OF GOD CLEANSE YOU TODAY

Today's Scripture Reading:

"For those God foreknew he also predestined to be conformed to the likeness of his Son, that he might be the first born among many brother. And those he predestined, he also called; those he called, be also glorified." (Romans 8:29-30) NIV

Our Lord and Savior before the foundation of the world he was with the Father – God the Father predestinate those he foreknew, which are also, those he for loved, God choose to bestow, love on from eternity. Foreknowledge means that God purposed from eternity to love and redeem the human race through his Son Jesus Christ. The recipient of God's foreknowledge or for love is stated in the pluralism and refers to the Church. That is, God's for love is primarily for the corporate body of Jesus Christ, it includes individuals only as they identify themselves with this corporate body through abiding faith in Christ and in union with Christ. The corporate body of Christ, if they continue to abide in his word and follow his commandment will attain to glorification. While the individual believers will fall short of such glorification if they separate themselves from that for loved body and fail to maintain their faith in Jesus Christ.

Prayer:

Lord Jesus Christ, you are the immortal, the invisible, the only wise God. You have predestinated us, God the Father to be conforming to the likeness of your Son. Hear our prayers do not let any earthly troubles, affliction and trials take us away, or separate us from your foreloved. Through the Holy Spirit empowerment, empower us to follow, and do your Will, and obey your commandment Jesus Christ our Lord, have mercy upon us we need your full presence in our lives, so that we can live a life of sanctification and glorification. Amen.

AUGUST 16TH

THE WORD OF GOD CLEANSES US – LET THE WORD OF GOD CLEANSE YOU TODAY

Today's Scripture Reading:

"The Lord your God is with you, he is mighty to save. He will take great delight in you, he will quiet you with his love, he will rejoice over you with singing." (Zephaniah 3:17) NIV

This Scripture revealed the day of God's restoration and great salvation, when the Lord almighty, all powerful will take away the punishment of Israelite, God's people will sing, shout, and rejoice with all their heart. God will rescue the lame and the oppressed, God delight in his people, he shows us his way and provide for all our needs in order to follow him, worship him in spirit and in truth. God delight quietness in his people with his love and rejoice over them with singing. Same withal those who believes in Jesus Christ and follow his commandments, he delight in the man he will shower his blessing and his love upon them. God is assigning God who delights to lavish his love on all the redeemed. When the eyes of our heart are enlightened by the Holy Spirit, to fully understand how great his love is, grace, salvation for us, we as

God's people will shout for joy, sing to him a new song, and delight greatly in the Lord. Our joy will reach its pinnacle when God manifest his full glory and majesty in all the earth. The conversion of sinners and the lost and the consolation of the Saints are the joy of the angels, for they are the joy of God himself.

Prayer:

Lord God Almighty we give you praise for all what you have done in our lives, we thank you greatly for your Mercy and infinite love for us. We give you praise for your prayers for us, no, one like you, no one has ever love us as you love us our Lord. I pray that your love fills the hearts and minds of every souls of human being on this earth. Amen.

AUGUST 17ᵀᴴ

THE WORD OF GOD CLEANSES US – LET THE WORD OF GOD CLEANSE YOU TODAY

Today's Scripture Reading:

"he replied, Because you have so little faith. I tell you the truth, if you have faith as small as mustard seed, you can say, to this mountain, move from here to there and it will move. Nothing will be impossible for you." (Matthew 17:20) NIV

Our Lord and Savior Jesus Christ frequently comments on the nature of true faith. Christ speaks of a faith that can move mountains because miracles and healing, and that can accomplish great things for God. Jesus Christ was speaking of true faith which is an effective faith that produces results. It will move mountains. True faith is not a belief faith, as a force or power, but it is a faith in God. True faith is a work of God within the hearts of Christian's believers. It involves an awareness divinely imparted to our hearts that our prayers are answered. The Holy Spirit creates the true faith within us; we cannot produce it in our own minds. Since true faith is a gift imparted to us by Christ, it is important to draw near to Jesus Christ and his word and as well as deepen our commitment to him as well as have confidence in him. Believers must depend on Jesus Christ for everything; apart from him we can do nothing. Jesus Christ, in other words, want us to seek him, he is the author and perfecter of our faith. Jesus Christ's close presence and our obedience to his word are the source and the secret of faith.

Prayer:

Lord Jesus Christ , we pray to you that, that you increase your faith in us, fill us up with unchanging faith for you, strong faith for you, help us to put everything we are doing in your Holy hands, so that we will be able to follow you with strong unfailing and unchanging faith that can move mountains, heal the sick, cast out demonic forces of the world. Bless us true faith that loves you and that will serve you till the end of our life on earth. Amen.

AUGUST 18TH

THE WORD OF GOD CLEANSES US – LET THE WORD OF GOD CLEANSE YOU TODAY

Today's Scripture Reading:

"The Lord answered, 'Who then is the faithful and wise manager, whom the master puts in charge of his servants to give them their food allowance at the proper time? It will be good for that servant whom the master finds doing so when he returns. I tell you the truth, he will put him in charge of all his possessions.' " (Luke 12:42-44) NIV

Our Lord Jesus Christ uses this parable to illustrate the two possible ways of living which open to all his followers in the light of his absence and promised return. Believers must be a faithful and obedient, ever watchful, and spiritually ready for the Lord's return at any time, and they will receive their master's blessings. They can grow careless and worldly-minded, believe that the Lord will delay his coming, cease to resist sin and depart from the path of faithfulness; they will then receive God's condemnation and inherit everlasting shame and ruin at his coming. The happiness of believers, if they approved themselves as a faithful and wise, the blessing of our Lord will be upon them. The servant of the Lord – Ministers and Pastors that obtain mercy of the Lord to be faithful shall obtain further mercy to be abundantly rewarded for their faithfulness in the day of the Lord.

Prayer:

Lord God Almighty, bless us with the Spirit of patience, to be able to wait for your blessings; bless us with the Spirit of obedience without measure in order that we may be able to obey your commandments. Have mercy upon us, direct, control and live your life through all those who gave their life to you faithfully and sincerely; perform your miracle in our life exhibit your infinite love in our life now and forever more. Amen.

AUGUST 19TH

THE WORD OF GOD CLEANSES US – LET THE WORD OF GOD CLEANSE YOU TODAY

Today's Scripture Reading:

"Ha, Sovereign Lord, you have made heaven and the earth by your great power and outstretched arm. Nothing is too hard for you. You show love to thousands but bring the punishment for the fathers' sins into the laps of their children after them. O great and powerful God, whose Name is the Lord Almighty, great are your purposes and mighty are your deeds. Your eyes are open to all the ways of men; you reward everyone according to his conduct and as his deeds deserve." (Jeremiah 32:17-19) NIV

God almighty is a living God, he sees everything, he knows everything, and nothing is close from him. He knows the heart of men, and he knows their thought afar off. God the Father almighty bestowed blessings and rewards for those who love him and follow his commandment. The purpose of God is unsearchable, and he is the beginning and the end. He always achieves his purpose in the life of those who belongs to him. Prophet Jeremiah adores God almighty and gives him the glory due to his Name as the creator of the universe. When at any time we are perplexed about the particular dispensations of providence, it is good for us to satisfy ourselves with the word of God's wisdom, power, life, motion, and perfection. God Almighty made the heavens and the earth with his outstretched arms that with him nothing is impossible, and nothing is too hard for him to do.

Prayer:

Lord God Almighty, Father, Son and Holy Spirit hear our prayers; fulfill your promise in our life, nothing is impossible for you to do in heaven and on this earth. You have the power and the authority over any circumstances we might be going through we give you praise O' Lord, all honor and glory belongs to you now and forever more. Amen.

AUGUST 20ᵀᴴ

THE WORD OF GOD CLEANSES US – LET THE WORD OF GOD CLEANSE YOU TODAY

Today's Scripture Reading:

"Hear the word of the Lord, o nations; proclaim it in distant coast lands; He who scattered Israel will gather them and will watch over his flock like a shepherd. For the Lord will ransom Jacob and redeem them from the hands of those stronger than they. They will rejoice in the bounty of the Lord – the grain, the new wine, and the oil the young of the flocks and herds. They will be like a well – watered garden, and they will sorrow no more." (Jeremiah 31:10-12) NIV

The purpose of God's love concerning his people, the Lord will bring peace that will spread to all the people in the world, this peace news was referring to the coming of Messiah Jesus Christ. Those who have been dispersed shall be brought together again, from their dispersions. And those he has gathered him into one body, one fold, and one shepherd, will keep them from being scattered again. Those who are sold shall be redeeming by the blood of the Lamb – Christ pay in full for our sin with his pressures blood. He brought us back with his blood. Therefore, with their liberty they shall have plenty, and they shall have joy, and God Almighty shall be honored, when they shall return to their own land. On the mountain of Zion the Holy mountain they shall sing to the praise and glory of God.

Prayer:

Lord God almighty maker of heaven and earth we adore you, you alone are the God of mercy and great compassion; help us to sing praise to your Holy Name when you baptizes us with the Holy Spirit so that we can serve you and love you more and more every day of our life. Amen.

AUGUST 21ST

THE WORD OF GOD CLEANSES US – LET THE WORD OF GOD CLEANSE YOU TODAY

Today's Scripture Reading:

"Where can I go from your Spirit? Where can I flee from your presence? If I rise on the wings of the dawn, if I settle on the far side of the Sea, even there your hand will guide me, your right hand will hold me fast. If I say, surely the darkness will hide me and the light become night around me, even the darkness will not be to you; the night will shine like the day, for darkness is as light to you. Search me, O God, and know my heart, test me and know my anxious thoughts. See if there is any offensive way in me, and lead me in the way everlasting." (Psalm 139: 7, 9-12, 23-24) NIV

Children of God have been sanctified by the power of the Holy Spirit they can never move beyond God's care, guidance and supporting strengths. Jesus Christ our Lord and Savior are with us in all situations, in whatever the present and the future brings. Believers must perfectly know the Lord and all his ways; because he is always with us, we are under his eye. If God is omnipotent – God is all powerful, omnipresent – God is present everywhere at the same time, he must be omniscient – God is all knowing, our God have unlimited knowledge of everything in heaven and on earth; heaven and earth include the whole creation - he is the creator of both; therefore, he not only knows both and governs both, but he fills both; every part of the creation is under the influence of God. Nothing can take us out of his Holy hands and out of his presence. There are times believers need to tell God to search him, because we don't know what we can say or do wrongly unaware; therefore, we must ask God in prayer to wash, and purge us clean from any unknown sins and any unrighteousness.

Prayer:

Lord God Almighty, the Immortal, the invisible, the only wise God; you are the one and only all powerful, all knowing, ever present Lord, nothing is close from you, and nothing is impossible for you to do in heaven and in this earth. , we pray that you purge us clean from any unrighteousness, search us and see if there is any unrighteousness in us and clean us. Let your full presence always be known in our life. You are the omnipotent, omnipresent, and omniscient Lord God our Father in heaven; you made us your children through our Lord Jesus Christ. We pray that you will always present in our live, always know what is going on in our life, and most important always show your power in our life now and forever more. Amen.

AUGUST 22ND

THE WORD OF GOD CLEANSES US – LET THE WORD OF GOD CLEANSE YOU TODAY

Today's Scripture Reading:

"Let us not become weary in doing good, for at the proper time we will reap a harvest if we do not give up. Therefore, as we have opportunity, let us do good to all people, especially to those who belong to the family of believers." (Galatian 6:9-10)NIV

Believing Christians must not be tired of doing good to people around them, it is the duty and responsibility of all who are taught God's Word to help provide material support for those who instruct; those who are worthy of support including those in the fivefold ministry, faithful teachers and elders to get so weary and refuse to give support, especially if the resources are available, is to sow selfishness and reap destruction. When believers give to those who minister in the Word is a part of doing good to those who belong to the family of believers at the proper time, we will reap both reward and eternal life. There is a recompense of reward in reserve for all who sincerely employ themselves in well doing. Though our reward may be delayed, but it will surely come. All the believing Christians are given exhortation to do good in their places whenever the opportunity arrives. It is not enough that we be good to ourselves, but we must do good to others in the household of faith. The objects of this are responsibility is more generally all Christian's men and women; we are not to confine our charity and beneficence within too narrow bounds, but we should be ready to extend it all as far as we are capable.

Prayer:

Lord Jesus Christ, bless us abundantly so that we can be a blessing to others who are in need of our support wherever they may be on this earth. Do not let us live a selfish life, help us to know what you have done for us and extend that love on the cross to other people around the world especially people that have not hear about the Gospel before and all the household of faith. Amen.

AUGUST 23RD

THE WORD OF GOD CLEANSES US – LET THE WORD OF GOD CLEANSE YOU TODAY

Today's Scripture Reading:

"I am not saying this because I am in need, for I have learned to be content whatever the circumstances. I know what is to be in need, and I know what it is to have plenty. I have learned the secret of being content in any and every situation, whether well fed or hungry. I can do everything through him who gives me strength." *(Philippians 4:11-13)NIV*

All the believing Christians must learn to be content and live a life of contentment. The key and tools to contentment is by realizing that God has given you in your present circumstances everything you need to remain victorious in Jesus Christ. The ability to live triumphantly above changing circumstances comes from Jesus Christ's power that is flowing in and through you; this ability does not come naturally, however, it must be learned through believer's dependence on Jesus Christ. All the believers of Jesus Christ can do anything through him Christ's power and grace will enable them to do all that he has asked us to do. Believer's ability to do what he wills comes from his enabling power. Christians must be content with the little he had, and that satisfied him. He must also depend upon the providence of God to provide for him from day to day, and that satisfied him. This is a special activity of the grace of God, to be able to accommodate ourselves to an afflicted condition, how to be full, not to be proud, or secure. We must see everything we are going through with the eyes of the Lord and praise the Lord Jesus with great thankfulness. It is by his constant renewal strength we are enabled to act, function in everything.

Prayer:

Lord Jesus Christ continues to help us to do everything through the power of your love. Strengthens us in all our circumstances of the ups and downs of this world. Bless us strengthens us so that we may live with you in heaven forever and ever. Amen.

AUGUST 24ᵀᴴ

THE WORD OF GOD CLEANSES US – LET THE WORD OF GOD CLEANSE YOU TODAY

Today's Scripture Reading:

"Rejoice in the Lord always. I will say it again: rejoice! Let your gentleness be evident to all. The Lord is near. Do not be anxious about anything, but in everything, by prayer and petition, with thanksgiving, present your requests to God. And the peace of God, which transcends all understanding, will guard your hearts and your mind in Christ Jesus. Finally, brothers, whatever is admirable – if anything is excellent or praiseworthy – think about such things." (Philippians 4:4-8) NIV

All the believing Christians must rejoice and gain strength by recalling the Lord's grace; nearness and promises. Jesus Christ is our blessed hope of glory, he can return anytime, we must be ready, working watching praying at all times. The main and one and only essential care for worriedness is prayer – through prayer we renew our trust in the Lord's faithfulness by casting all our anxieties and problems on him, who cares for us. God's peace will arrive to guard our hearts and minds as a result of our communion with Jesus Christ. God strengthens us to do all the things he desires for us. Therefore, we receive mercy, grace, and help in time of need. We are assured that in all things God works for our good – when we call on our Lord from the deep our hearts by remain in Jesus and his words then God's peace will flood our trouble souls. This peace is an inner tranquility mediated by the Holy Spirit. To experience God's peace and freedom from anxiety, believer must fix their minds on those things that are true, noble, right, pure, then the God of peace will be with us.

Prayer:

Lord Jesus Christ let the peace of God that transcend all understanding fill our hearts and minds to live for you alone in all our day on earth. Fill our hearts with love for you and for your services, especially what you designed for us to do you and for your glory. Help us to start it and bring it to completion with your infinite power and love. Amen.

AUGUST 25ᵀᴴ

THE WORD OF GOD CLEANSES US – LET THE WORD OF GOD CLEANSE YOU TODAY

Today's Scripture Reading:

"Praise be to the God and Father of our Lord Jesus Christ, who has blessed us in the heavenly realms with every spiritual blessing in Christ." (Ephesians 1:3) NIV

Every faithful believing Christians has life in Jesus Christ. The term in Christ Jesus is the same as in the Lord, or in him. In Christ means that now every believers of Jesus Christ live and have our activities in the sphere of Jesus Christ; Union with Christ is the redeemed Christians' new environment in Christ believers have conscious communion with the Lord, and in this relationship our very lives are seen as the life of Christ is most important thing in Christian experience. Union with Christ comes as a gift of God through faith. Believers must thank God and enlarges upon the exceeding great and precious benefits which we enjoy by Jesus Christ. Spiritual blessings are the best blessings. Christ blesses us by bestowing such things upon us as make us really blessed; we must give him praises and thankfulness. Those whom God blesses with some people; he blesses them with all spiritual blessings. It is not a temporary blessing; it is permanent blessings and their spiritual blessings from above in heavenly places. The blessing that comes from heaven, and are designed to prepare man for it. Believers must learn to center spiritual and heavenly blessings as the best blessings with which we cannot be miserable, and without which we cannot but be happy and rejoice.

Prayer:

Lord Jesus Christ you are the channels of all blessing; from this earth to heaven. Bless us with all the spiritual blessings that we may need to serve you faithfully and sincerely throughout our life. Bless us with the spirit of love and compassion for the sinners and the lost, and everyone in this world that does not know you. Help us to be a good servant of the work of the Gospel and bring the unsaved sinners into your Holy hands. Amen.

AUGUST 26TH

THE WORD OF GOD CLEANSES US – LET THE WORD OF GOD CLEANSE YOU TODAY

Today's Scripture Reading:

"I have fought the good fight, I have finished the race, I have kept the faith. Now there is in store for me the crown of righteousness which the Lord, the righteous Judge, will award to me on that day – and not only to me, but also to all who have longed for his appearing." (2nd timothy 4:7-8)NIV

All the believers must fight a good fight just as Paul lay down the example. We must consider the Christian life as good fight as the only fight in this earth that is worth fighting. Believers must be ready to fight against the Satan and all the evil spirits, fight against those who are persecuting Christians all over the entire universe; fight against all the haters of God, and the haters of the cross of Jesus Christ. Believers must be ready to fight against all other religions that is not of God and especially against pagan and Idol worshipers; against antinomianism and all kinds of immoralities in the church of God; false teachers those who distorted the Gospel, and Gospel - word and antichrist, believers must always be ready to fight them to the last minute of their life, even, if we have to spend millions and billions of money in order to defeat them. The faithful believers who fight to the end will surely receive the crown of righteousness which our Lord has prepared for those who loved him and longed for his appearance. God has reserved rewards in heaven for all who remain loyal to Jesus Christ and his Gospel.

Prayer:

Lord Jesus Christ our Lord and our Savior, this earth is our temporary place; , we pray that you keep us save and bless us with the crown of righteousness that you have prepared for those who will serve you faithfully, and those who is longing for your appearance, blesses us with your eternal glory that we may live in heaven with you forever. Amen.

AUGUST 27TH

THE WORD OF GOD CLEANSES US – LET THE WORD OF GOD CLEANSE YOU TODAY

Today's Scripture Reading:

"Set your minds on this above, not on earthly things. For you died and your life is now hidden with Christ in God. When Christ who is your life ,appears, then you also will appear with him in glory." (Colossian 3:2-4) NIV

All the believers have their life in the Lord Jesus Christ where he seated at the right hand of God. We must put all things on the things above, not on any earthly things. Because our lives are in Christ Jesus' who seated in heaven; we must set our minds and hearts on the things above and let our attitudes be determined by the things above. We must view and evaluate everything from an eternal and heavenly perspective. Our goals and pursuits should be centered in Christ Jesus, resisting sin and sin nature, and being clothed with Jesus Christ's life and character spiritually graces, power, experiences, and blessings are all with Christ in heaven. He bestows those things on all who sincerely and diligently pursue him with all their hearts. Jesus Christ who is our life, who help us to live a Holy life as an essential part of redemption in Christ, fellowship with him, love him as a person that must always be kept central and we must maintain personal communion with him. WE are dead to all the immoral and systems of the world, our true life are above where Christ seated this is our great comfort that our life is then appear with him in glory. It will be Jesus' glory to have his redeemed with him, and it will be believer's glory to come with Jesus. Believers should set all their affections upon things above.

Prayer:

Lord Jesus Christ, our Lord and Savior, we long to see your appearance. You are the only one who redeemed us. You are the only one who calls us to your eternal glory. You are the only one that said, "I am going back to prepare a place for you." You are the only one that said, "In my Father's house there are many Mansions." Hear our prayer and answer our prayer and help us to live with you in heaven; bless us, and help us to be able to be worthy to live with you in heaven in your Father's house. In your mighty matchless Holy Name , we pray. Amen.

AUGUST 28ᵀᴴ

THE WORD OF GOD CLEANSES US – LET THE WORD OF GOD CLEANSE YOU TODAY

Today's Scripture Reading:

"But now you must rid yourselves of all such things as these: anger, rage, malice, slander, and filthy language from your lips. Do not lie to each other, since you have taken off your old self with its practices, and have put on the new self, which is being renewed in knowledge in the image of its creator. Here there is no Greek or Jew, circumcised or uncircumcised, barbarian, Scythian, slave or free, but Christ is all, and in all." (Colossian 3:8-11) NIV

It is very important in the life of all the believing Christians immediately after they have completely given their life to Jesus Christ; to put down the old self, with anger, wrath, malice. Anger and wrath are very bad for children of God. Malice is worse; the product of them in the tongue is blasphemy which seems that those who practice them speak no good communication – means filthy communications. To those who have put off the old self, have put off with its deeds; and those who have put on the new self must put on all its deeds, they must be renewed in knowledge because an ignorant soul cannot be a good soul. Light is the first thing in new creation, as it was in the first creation. It was the honor of man innocence that he was made after the likeness of God. In the privilege of circumcise Jesus Christ is all and in all those who believe in him.

Prayer:

Lord Jesus Christ you are the same yesterday, today and forever, you never change, and you will never change, bless us with the power of the Holy Spirit so that we will be able to live a life that will be pleasing in your sight at all times wash us clean and make us your own take away all the filthy language from our mouth, from our tongue wrath, anger, malice from our lives, so that we can be able to serve you with the spirit of holiness. Amen.

AUGUST 29TH

THE WORD OF GOD CLEANSES US – LET THE WORD OF GOD CLEANSE YOU TODAY

Today's Scripture Reading:

"If any of you lack wisdom, he should ask God, who gives generously to all without finding fault, and it will be given to him. But when he asks, he must believe and not doubt, because he who doubts is like a wave of the sea, blown and tossed by the wind. That man should not thing he will receive anything from the Lord; he is a double minded man, unstable in all he does." (James 1:5-7) NIV

We give thanks to Apostle James with his clear and précised words in this Scripture. Believers are to ask God for wisdom and understanding for coping with any earthly trials, not just for deliverance from them. Wisdom means the spiritual capability to see what we are going through clearly and evaluate our life and conduct from God's point of view. It involves making the right choices and doing the right things according to God's will which was revealed in his Word through the leading of the Holy Spirit. Believers must pray for wisdom, Godly wisdom which is very important in our life. We must pray for wisdom to deal with our tribulations, afflictions, and trials. God gave us greatest and encouragement to deal with any circumstances he gave us wisdom without measure, if we asks for a great deal of wisdom, he will give it liberally, not to be afraid or put to shame. Believers must ask God for wisdom without waving, no doubt, we must put on the sincerity of intention, and a steadiness of mind, constitute another duty required under affliction, we must not wave like wave of the sea, distrustful, and shifting unsettle person is not likely to value favor from the Lord, cannot expect to receive anything from him.

Prayer:

Our Lord and Savior, we need a great deal of wisdom to live this earth for you, your blessing of wisdom will help us to discern any form of temptation that the enemy might be planning on our way. Bless us your wisdom abundantly, immeasurable, so that we will be able to serve you faithfully and sincerely without wavering in all the areas of our lives. Lord Jesus Christ continuously pours your wisdom upon us, with the power of anointing from above that will help us to focus on your redeeming love for us. Lord Jesus Christ helps us to be steadfast immovable, bless us with great wisdom, in times of trials, strengthens us and blesses us with the knowledge and understanding of your Word. Amen.

AUGUST 30TH

THE WORD OF GOD CLEANSES US – LET THE WORD OF GOD CLEANSE YOU TODAY

Today's Scripture Reading:

"Even though we speak like this dear friends, we are confident of better things in your case – things that accompany salvation. God is not unjust, he will not forget your work and the love you have shown him as you have helped his people and continue to help them. We want each of you to show this same diligence to the very end, in order to make your hope sure. We do not want you to become lazy, but to imitate those who through faith and patience inherit what has been promised." (Hebrews 6:9-12)NIV

All Christian's believers must be assured, especially those who remain loyal to Jesus Christ faith and in love, their hope of eternal salvation is certain and is unchangeable, because God cannot lie, and his promises remain steadfast. His promises to Abraham are true; God's truthfulness and trustworthiness apply not only to his word to Abraham, but also to his Word in its entirety in all the Scripture. God can not lie. He cannot forget all our efforts and all we have done for him. He cannot forget our love for him, day, and night that we call unto him. There are things that accompany salvation, things that are never separated from salvation. Ministers must sometimes speak by the way of caution to those who have in themselves good hopes, and also shall consider seriously how fatal it would be to fall short. Therefore, they must work out their own salvation with fear and trembling. Good works and labor proceeding from love to God are commendable and what is done to any in the Name of God shall not go unrewarded. Those who expect a gracious reward for the labor of love must continue in it as long as they have the ability and the opportunity, and those who persevere in a diligent discharge of their duty shall attain to the full assurance of hope in the end.

Prayer:

Our Lord and Savior you love us before the foundation of the world, help us to persevere in everything we are doing for the work of the Gospel. Continue to pour out the blessing of your love upon us, so that we may continue to love you more and more, and so at the end we may live with you in heaven. Amen.

AUGUST 31ST

THE WORD OF GOD CLEANSES US – LET THE WORD OF GOD CLEANSE YOU TODAY

Today's Scripture Reading:

"And, if it is hard for the righteous to be save, what will become of the ungodly and sinner? So then, those who suffer according to God's will should commit themselves to their faithful creator and continue to do good." (1st Peter 4:18-19) NIV

No one could be saving unless Jesus Christ makes them spiritually alive in him. No sinner can come to Christ on their own unless someone minister to them, with the indwelling power of the Holy Spirit. The word "ungodly" means that a person with an attitude of disrespect and contempt toward God. The grievous sufferings of good people in this world are sad presages of much heavier judgments coming upon impenitent sinners. It is as much as the righteous can do to be saved. Let the absolute necessity of salvation balance the difficulty of it your difficulties are greatest at first; God offers his grace and help. Believers must commit their souls to the hands of God, God call us to suffer for the Gospel according to his will, we must take the Gospel to the end of the world no matter how hard it is to make it happens. If the righteous have to work hard in order to bring Gospel to unsaved sinners and the lost, what will happen to the unrighteous? It will be very hard, or they may never be converted. All the suffering that good people are going, through the suffering is one of the fruits of the Spirit and is according to the will of God. It is the full responsibility of all the believing Christians to look more to the keeping of their souls then to the preserving of their bodies. Righteous have great encouragement to commit their souls to God, because he created them in his likeness and God is always faithful in all his ways and in all his promises.

Prayer:

Lord God Almighty, we praise you and adore you in everything that we do, or say, you are the one and only who call us from darkness to your marvelous light, help us to rejoice in your mercy and Love, O merciful and mighty God. Help us, and build us up for your glory from this earth to heaven. Help us to grow in grace and grow in sanctification all the days of our life. Help to live a glorifying life from this earth to heaven. Amen.

DAILY REFLECTION NOTES

531

SEPTEMBER

SEPTEMBER 1ST

THE WORD OF GOD IS A TRANSFORMATION –
LET THE WORD OF GOD TRANSFORM YOU TODAY

Today's Scripture Reading:

"Surely God is my salvation; I will trust and not be afraid. The Lord, the Lord, is my strength and my song, he has become my salvation." (Isaiah 12:2) NIV

All the believing Christians must trust the Lord, for his mercy and love and for his goodness from the beginning of the creation of the world. God's people who believed in Jesus Christ; those who put their life in his hands; will praise him when the universal reign of the Messiah begins. Even right now we must pray for as well as anticipates in faith and hope of our Lord's return and the establishment of his eternal reign in righteousness. When that day comes, we will sing the songs of praise, to him who is worthy of all our praises and thankfulness. This is the song of praise when God would work great deliverances for all the believers in all the Christian churches when the kingdom of the Messiah should be set up in the universe the scattered churches all will be united into one body, body of Christ, they will therefore, praise the Lord. This promise is very sure, and the blessings contained when they are bestowed, will furnish the church with abundant matter for thanksgiving. When many sinners and the lost are brought home to Jesus Christ not only our Savior, by whom we are save, but our salvation, in whom we are save, he is our salvation, and he is the rock of our salvation.

Prayer:

Lord Jesus Christ you are our rock of our salvation, purified our spirit, soul and body so that we can be one body of Christ, doing what is pleasing in your sight guide us, keep us safe, be with us always and forever, guide us with you Holy hands. Amen.

SEPTEMBER 2ND

THE WORD OF GOD IS A TRANSFORMATION -LET THE WORD OF GOD TRANSFORM YOU TODAY

Today's Scripture Reading:

"You Samaritans worship what you do not know; we worship what we do know, for salvation is from the Jews. Yet a time is coming and has now come when the true worshipers will worship the Father in Spirit and truth, for they are the kind of worshipers the Father seeks. God is Spirit, and his worshipers must worship in Spirit and in truth." (John 4:22-24) NIV

Jesus Christ teaches several things; in spirit points to the level at which true worshiper occurs. One must come to God in complete sincerity and with a spirit that is directed by the life and activity of the Holy Spirit. Holy Spirit is the characteristic of God; he is the incarnate in Jesus Christ, Holy Spirit intrinsic to the Holy Spirit and he is at the heart of the Gospel. Therefore, worship must take place according to the truth of the Father that is revealed in the Son and received through the Spirit. Those who advocate a worship that sets aside the truth and the word of God have in reality set aside the only foundation for true worship. Jesus Christ is the truth; the live in union with Jesus Christ requires speaking the truth and honesty. To claim to have fellowship with Jesus Christ and to possess salvation, yet not to live and speak according to the truth is to deceive. Those who have not truth in them; show the real condition of their hurts, without truth we remain in deception and darkness and therefore we are outside the kingdom of heaven.

Prayer:

Lord Jesus Christ, Almighty God, our Father in heaven, help us to know you, get close to you every day of our life, you are our ever living Savior, compassionate gracious loving God; empower all the Christian believers with the Holy Spirit, so that we can be able to approach the throne of grace and worship you in Spirit and in truth because these are the people you want to worship you; hear our prayers O Merciful and mighty God. Amen.

SEPTEMBER 3RD

THE WORD OF GOD IS A TRANSFORMATION – LET THE WORD OF GOD TRANSFORM YOU TODAY

Today's Scripture Reading:

"Above all, love each other deeply, because love covers over a multitude of sins. Offer hospitality to one another without grumbling." (1st Peter 4:8-9) NIV

All believing Christians must love each other dearly and truthfully. They must not condemned each other or think that they are more spiritual than each other love will cover multitude of sins, means if you have love for one another truly, you will not have time to think evil against each other, you will maintain a clear mind with each other at all times. And you will be ready to help each other if it is possible for you to do so. Love with one another will help you to think good at all times with one another. You do not return evil for evil; you will not have a revengeful mind against each other. Believing Christians must love one another. This mutual affection must not be cold, but fervent that means, sincere, strong, and lasting. This type of earnest affection must be recommended above all things, which shows how important it is to love one another, one excellent effect of love for one another is that it will cover, or reduced multitude of sins because the believer will not plan or do bad things to one another, there will be no fight, no anger, and no wrath they will have common respect for one another. It prepares for mercy at the hand of God, who hath promise to forgive those that forgive others.

Prayer:

God the Father, our Lord Jesus Christ, Father, Son, and the Holy Spirit one God, the Holy Trinity, teach us how to love one another with fervent love, create in us the spirit to love from one person, to another person, so that we can be able to live with you, for you, in righteousness and peace that surpasses all understanding now and forever. Amen.

SEPTEMBER 4TH

THE WORD OF GOD IS A TRANSFORMATION –
LET THE WORD OF GOD TRANSFORM YOU TODAY

Today's Scripture Reading:

"Let no debt remain outstanding, except the continuing debt to love one another, for he who loves his fellowman has fulfilled the law. The commandment, Do not commit adultery, Do not murder, Do not steal, Do not covet, and whatever other commandment there may be, are summed up in this one rule: love your neighbor as yourself. Love does no harm to its neighbor. Therefore love is the fulfillment of the Law" (Romans 13:8-10) NIV

Believing Christians should have no unpaid debts if it is possible for them to pay it, they must pay their debt. This does not mean that we are prohibited from borrowing from others, or from the Bank, in case of serious need. But it speaks against both going into debt for unnecessary things and showing an attitude of indifference in repaying debts. The only debt from which there is no release is love for one another. Our Lord and Savior said we should love our neighbors; love is fulfilled not only by positive commands but also by negative command. All of the commandments mentioned here are negative in form, love is positives, yet it is also negative in that it accounts for human propensity toward sin, selfishness, and cruelty. The first evidence of believers is a turning from sin and all that brings harm and sorrow to others. Our Lord and Savior summed up all our duty in one word, and that is a short four letter word and is a sweet word "love", which is the beauty and the harmony of the world.

Prayer:

Lord Jesus Christ, our gracious master and our God, help us to love as you love, help us to love you, be the number one in our heart to love you, do not let anyone, anything replace your love from our hearts and mind help us to love our neighbor as we love ourselves, build us up for your service on this earth, that your love will over flow through us to other people around us; you are the Alpha and Omega, we give you praise and thankfulness our Lord; help us to live a life of love every day of our staying on this earth, in your Holy Name , we pray. Amen.

SEPTEMBER 5TH

THE WORD OF GOD IS A TRANSFORMATION— LET THE WORD OF GOD TRANSFORM YOU TODAY

Today's Scripture Reading:

"For I am convinced that neither death nor life, neither angels nor demons, neither the present nor the future, nor any powers, neither height nor depth, nor anything else in all creation, will be able to separate us from the love of God that is in Christ Jesus our Lord." (Romans 8:38-39) NIV

All the believing Christians must live confidently on God's unfailing love at all times. If anyone fails in his or her spiritual life, it will neither be from a lack of divine grace and love; nor from external force or over whelming adversity but from their own neglect to remain in Jesus Christ. Only in Christ Jesus is God's love revealed, and only in him do we experience the love of God. The love of God is always in Christ Jesus our Lord and nothing in creation can change it. Only as we remain in Christ Jesus as our Lord can we have the certainty that we will never be separated from God's love. And here he enumerates all those things which might separate between Christ and believers, and concludes that it will never be done, neither fear or death nor hope of life. We shall not be separated from that love either in death or in life. The good angels will not separate us, and the bad angels shall not separate us. Time shall not separate us; eternity shall not separate us from the love of Jesus Christ which comes from God the Father, and in God the Father. Nothing can do it but sin. This is the ground of the steadfastness of the love because Jesus Christ, in whom he loves us, is the same, yesterday, today, and forever.

Prayer:

Lord Jesus Christ, hold us with your Holy hands, with your unfailing love, with your great compassion; we cannot doubt your tender mercies, you have been our guide throughout every day, every minute and every second of our life, with the power of the Holy Spirit; do not allow any sin to come to us, baptizes us with the Holy Spirit and fire, keep us under your Holy arms now and forever. Amen.

SEPTEMBER 6TH

THE WORD OF GOD IS A TRANSFORMATION – LET THE WORD OF GOD TRANSFORM YOU TODAY

Today's Scripture Reading:

"What must I do to inherit eternal life? What is written in the law? He replied. How do you read it? He answered: Love the Lord your God with all your heart and with all your soul and with all your strength and with all your mind, and love your neighbor as yourself. You have answered correctly, Jesus replied. Do this and you will live." (Luke10:25-28) NIV

Jesus Christ told the man that he is not too far, if he can follow the commandment of God, he will live. The love of God is unique in relation to the width, length, height, and depth of God's love for all the believers in Jesus Christ, and which he pours into our hearts as believers by the power of the Holy Spirit. With this gift of Christ's love, we are to love God with our whole heart, mind, and Spirit and with our Soul. We are to fervently in return love our neighbor as we love ourselves, do unto them as we want people to do unto us. Children of God are required to love all people, including their enemies. There are also commanded to love all true bon again children on a special way. The love of believers for their Christian brothers and sisters, their neighbors and their enemies must be subordinated to, and controlled and directed by, their loving affection and devotion to God. Our love for God is the greatest and first commandment. Therefore, in our practice of love for all the people, we must never compromise the supremacy of our love for God and the righteous standard of his word.

Prayer:

Lord Jesus Christ , we pray that you will bless us with your Spirit of love so that we can be able to love our neighbors as we love ourselves and we can be able to love our enemies; let your love in us continue to grow more and more every day of our life, increase your love in our hearts and minds; help us to walk with you from this earth to heaven. Amen.

SEPTEMBER 7TH

THE WORD OF GOD IS A TRANSFORMATION- LET THE WORD OF GOD TRANSFORM YOU TODAY

Today's Scripture Reading:

"One this I ask of the Lord, this is what I seek: that I may dwell in the house of the Lord all the days of my life, to gaze upon the beauty of the Lord and to seek him in his temple." (Psalm 27:4) NIV

All those who believe in Jesus Christ must make this important word of the Scripture our main goal in life: to be able to be worthy to behold, and dwell in the house of the Lord, worship him with our hearts and minds throughout the days of our live. To seek his presence it is the most treasured one thing most valuable than gold and silver or diamond in this life. We must pray for it with singleness of heart and purpose which is to seek his face dwell in his house. Believers must strive to dwell in God's presence; we are given the firm assurance that no matter what trials come to our way, the Lord will never forsake us. Believers have no reason for despair; God almighty's goodness has been reserved for his children. Believers need a constant communion with our Lord and

Savior in the power of the Holy Spirit. All God's children must desire to dwell in God's house, behold the beauty, and be able to live with him after this earth. This is one thing that we need to ask the Lord desire of the Lord, behold the harmony of all his attributes, the beauty of his nature, the glory of the Lord that shines forever on his people.

Prayer:

Lord Jesus, the God Almighty, the compassionate, Father, Son and Holy Spirit, the Holy Trinity forever one God. , we pray that you will bless us with your Spirit in order to be able to seek your face and your full presence in our life. Help us and hear our prayers and our supplication. We pray that we may live in your house forever to behold the beauty of your presence and to live with you forever in your temple. In your mighty Holy Name I pray. Amen.

SEPTEMBER 8TH

THE WORD OF GOD IS A TRANSFORMATION-
LET THE WORD OF GOD TRANSFORM YOU TODAY

Today's Scripture Reading:

"An enemy did this, he replied. The servants ask him, Do you want us to go and pull them up? No, he answered, because while you are pulling the weeds, you may root up the wheat with them. Let both grow together until the harvest. At that time I will tell the harvesters: First collect the weed and tie them in bundles to be burned; then gather the wheat and bring it into my barn." (Matthew 13:28-30) NIV

This parable of our Lord was emphasizing about the mixed condition of believers with unbelievers concerning the growing together – Christ's true followers and Satan's children who masquerade as believers. There are many important points: (a) Throughout the ages of the Gospel this type issues co-existence will occur. God almighty will not command his angels to destroy the children of the evil one until the end of the age.

(b) It must be understood that this parable does not concern the church discipline or partial solution to evil individuals in the kingdom. God and his angels will make the final separation at his time. (c) A faithful believer must always be alert to the subversive elements and the individuals that Satan is pleasing within all parts of God's work. They will in many ways look like true children of God. Jesus Christ is the Lord of the field, the sower of the good seed – whatever good seed there is in the world, it all comes from the hands of Christ, and is of his sowing truths, preached, grace planted, souls sanctified, are good seed, and all owning to Christ Jesus. Ministers and Pastors are the instruments in Christ's hand to sow good seed. The field is the world; the world of humankind; a large field, capable of bringing forth good frits; the more it is to be lamented that it brings forth so much bad fruit. Tares are the children of the wicked, Satan, of the Devil.

Prayer:

Lord Jesus Christ, you the one that know who belongs to you, keep us under your wings, so that we be able to be what you wants us to be, and live for your glory forever, do not let us be Tare or Weeds our Lord. Be our immortal food, live your life through us, and in us, with us for ever so that we can be truly faithfully belongs to you from this earth to heaven. Amen.

SEPTEMBER 9TH

THE WORD OF GOD IS A TRANSFORMATION - LET THE WORD OF GOD TRANSFORM YOU TODAY

Today's Scripture Reading:

" But if I drive out demons by the Spirit of God, then the kingdom of God has come upon you:" (Matthew 12:28)NIV

The kingdom of God or heaven that Jesus Christ was emphasizing to those who are listening to his teaching carries the idea of God coming into the universe to exercises his power, glory, and rights against Satan's dominion of the present course of this world. It is more than our salvation, and the church of Jesus Christ; it is God almighty expressing himself powerfully in all his words. The kingdom of God is primarily and assertion of his power in action. God Almighty is beginning his spiritual rule in this universe in the hearts and minds among his people; he came into the earth with power. This reality of God's power spreading into the world involves: Spiritual authority over Satan's dominion and rules, the coming of the kingdom marks the beginning of the destruction of Satan rules. The Lord Jesus said that, if he cast out the devils by the Spirit of God, the kingdom of the Messiah is about to be set up among all believers, and in the world. The destruction of the Satan and the Devils' power is done by the spirit of God. Christ showed how easily and effectual he could cast the devil out of people's bodies, he encourages all believers to hope that whatever power Satan might usurp and exercise in the souls of men, Jesus Christ, by his grace, will break it.

Prayer:

Lord Jesus Christ, all power belongs to you in heaven and in this earth. Help us to quench the fiery flames of the work of Satan in this world from all those who call unto you spirit, soul, and body. Blessed and baptizes them with our Holy spirit so that they may live and can be able to serve you forever. Amen.

SEPTEMBER 10TH

THE WORD OF GOD IS A TRANSFORMATION-LET THE WORD OF GOD TRANSFORM YOU TODAY

Today's Scripture Reading:

"Hear, O Israel: The Lord our God, the Lord is one. Love the Lord your God with all your soul and with all your strength. These Commandments that I give you today are to be upon your hearts. Impress them on your children. Talk about them when you sit at home and when you walk along the road, when lie down and when you get up." (Deuteronomy 6:4-7) NIV

Believing Christians must love God with all their soul and with all their hearts and strength, moreover, they must teach their children their faith diligently to their children. These affirm that God is the one true God, not a pantheon of different gods, and is all powerful among all the gods and spirits of the world. This God is the sole object of the children of Israel's love and obedience. This aspect of oneness serves as the basis for prohibiting the worship of other gods. Therefore, do not think it contract the New Testament revelation of God as a triune being who though one in essence, and is manifested as Father, Son, and Holy Spirit God Almighty seeks fellowship with his people and gives them one indispensable command that will attached them to himself; they will come to know and enjoy him in a covenant relationship. On this, which is the first commandment, as well as with the second commandment which says to love one's neighbor as we love ourselves hangs all the law and the prophets. True obedience to God and his commands is possible only when it springs from faith in and love for God.

Prayer:

Lord God Almighty Father, Son and Holy Spirit, the Holy one of Israel and the seed of David, you are the channels of blessings, from you all the good things comes from. You are our great intercessor in heaven pray for us the prayer that can never be uttered. Be at the center of our heart and mind, through the power of the indwelling of the Holy Spirit; help us to follow your commandment, and do you will, now and forever. Amen.

SEPTEMBER 11TH

THE WORD OF GOD IS A TRANSFORMATION—
LET THE WORD OF GOD TRANSFORM YOU TODAY

Today's Scripture Reading:

"I will make those who are of the Synagogue of Satan, who claim to be Jews though they are not, but are liars. I will make them come and fall down at your feet and acknowledge that I have loved you since you have kept my command to endure patiently, I will also keep you from the hour of trial that is going to come upon the whole world to test those who live on the earth."(Revelation 3:9-10) NIV

One Lord and Savior promised that all the enemies of the Church will be subjected to the Church; those enemies, such as false teachers of the Word of God, those people in the synagogue and in the church that call themselves Christians, and believers of the Word of God, but they are really the messenger of Satan. They are the enemy of God; they will be convicted by the power of the Holy spirit of wrongdoing. The power of God will touch the hearts of his enemies, and by the discovery of God's favor in their lives and, in the churches. Jesus Christ will reveal this in such a way that his favor to his people in such a manner that their very enemies shall see it, and they shall be forced to acknowledge it. This will, by the grace of Jesus Christ, through the power of the Holy Spirit will soften the hearts of our enemies. The Gospel of Jesus Christ is the word of his patience. It is the fruit of the patience of God to a sinful world. Those who keep the Gospel in a time of peace; shall be kept in the hour of temptation. Christ Jesus will persevere.

Prayer:

Lord Jesus Christ, fulfill your promise for all those who believe in you, those who call unto you sincerely, do not let any fall in to sin, protect them in the time of temptation, keep them in your perfect peace that they may live, serve and honor your Holy Name from this earth to heaven, now and forever. Amen.

SEPTEMBER 12TH

THE WORD OF GOD IS A TRANSFORMATION—
LET THE WORD OF GOD TRANSFORM YOU TODAY

Today's Scripture Reading:

"Jesus replied, if anyone loves me, he will obey my teaching. My Father will love him, and we will come to him and make our home with him. He who does not love me will not obey my teaching. These words you hears are not my own; they belongs to the Father who sent me." (John 14:23-24) NIV

Our Lord Jesus Christ said that those who truly love him and obey his words will experience the immediate presence and love of the Father and the son through the empowerment of the Holy Spirit. The Father and the Son come to believers by the means of the Holy Spirit. Jesus Christ reveals himself to the obedient believers through the Holy Spirit who makes known the personal presence of Jesus in and with the one who loves him. The Holy Spirit makes us to be aware of the nearness of Jesus Christ and the reality of his love, his blessings, and his help in the life of the believing Christians. This is one of the Holy Spirit's primary responsibilities. The truth that Father, and Son comes to us through the empowerment of the Holy Spirit should, or move us to respond in love, worship him in spirit and in truth with a good devotion. The Father's love for us is a conditional love it based on our loving Jesus Christ, be loyal to his word. Wherever Jesus Christ is formed the image of God is stamped. God will not only love obedient believers, but he will rest his love to them, he will be with them and make their heart his home. This gives all believers a good reason to bind, glue us to observe the condition and encourage us to depend upon the promise of God.

Prayer:

Lord God Almighty Father, Son, and Holy Spirit, Most Merciful, Most Holy, we give you praises and adoration for all what you have done through our Lord Jesus Christ to us and what you will continue to be doing through our Lord, let your Holy Name be glorify, honor and praise forever. In Jesus Christ's glorious, mighty Holy Name, we pray. Amen.

SEPTEMBER 13TH

THE WORD OF GOD IS A TRANSFORMATION –
LET THE WORD OF GOD TRANSFORM YOU TODAY

Today's Scripture Reading:

"You are forgiving and good, O Lord, abounding in love to all who call to you. Hear my prayer, O lord; listen to my cry for mercy. In the day of my trouble I will call to you, for you will answer me. Among the gods there is none like you, O Lord; no deeds can compare with yours. All the nations you have made will come and worship before you, O Lord; they will bring glory to your Name. For you are great and do marvelous deeds, you alone are God. Teach me your way, O Lord, and I will walk in your truth; give an undivided heart, that I may fear your Name." (Psalm 86:5-11)NIV

This is a prayer of King David that come out his heart of humility, during the time that he was going through affliction and in great need of God's deliverance from his enemies. King David pleads to God for God's good work will be manifest in his life by which he had qualified for a token of his favor. Believers must pray without ceasing for everything and every day. We must have confident that our Lord hears and listen to our prayers. Believers must ask for forgiveness because he is the forgiving Lord, gracious merciful God – slow to anger full of truth and righteousness. Believers must give glory to the Lord among all gods, none like him, there are many false gods on earth, but none like the Holy Trinity ever one God. All nations of this world shall still worship the true God and Jesus Christ is only Son in true holiness. Jesus Christ is the center of all being and he is the fountain of all being, he is the center of all our praises and thankfulness. He made all nations of one blood; they derive all their being from him, with constant dependence on him, and therefore, the people of all nations will worship him with the spirit of holiness.

Prayer:

Lord God Almighty you have made all nations with one blood, through your precious blood, bless us, keep us in your Holy hands, help us to be with you forever, be useful for you, live for your great glory, take the Gospel to the ends of the world in everyone's language. Take care of your children, solve our problems, and fulfill all our needs according to your Will and desires. Amen.

SEPTEMBER 14TH

THE WORD OF GOD IS A TRANSFORMATION – LET THE WORD OF GOD TRANSFORM YOU TODAY

Today's Scripture Reading:

"My Son, do not despised the Lord's discipline and do not resent his rebuke, because the Lord disciplines those he loves, as Father the son he delights in. Blessed is the man who finds wisdom, the man who gains understanding, for she is more profitable than silver and yields better returns than gold." (Proverbs 3:11-13) NIV

As a believer of our Lord Jesus Christ, we have to be able to abide in him and do what is pleasing in his sight at all times. At times God allows us to pass through trials and difficulties in order to be able to mold us more perfectly to his holiness and to his Will for our lives. Believers must conduct themselves in a rightly manner under any tribulations and afflictions. We must not despise an affliction, be it ever light, short, nor to be stocks, and stones under our afflictions, by hiding ourselves under it, must we believe that God has the power over any earthly afflictions and troubles. A divine correction sometimes comes from the Lord therefore, we must not be weary of it, for the Lord knows our frame, he knows what we need, and most especially he knows what we can bear. A fatherly correction comes not from his vindictive justice as a judge, but from his wise affection as a Father. The Father corrects the Son whom he loves, and because he loves him, he desires that he may be wise and good.

Prayer:

Lord God Almighty we praise you and worship you, there is none like you, we give you glory, and we welcome all your Fatherly disciplines so that we can be one with you as you and Father are one. Forgives us if we say, or do anything wrong in your sight, forgive us, if we left what we should have done undone, and do what we are not supposed to do; correct and protect us from any form of evil that is spreading around in the world. Be at the center of our hearts forever and ever. Amen.

SEPTEMBER 15TH

THE WORD OF GOD IS A TRANSFORMATION—
LET THE WORD OF GOD TRANSFORM YOU TODAY

Today's Scripture Reading:

"We ought always to thank God for you, brothers, and rightly so, because your faith is growing more and more, and the love every one of you has for each other is increasing. Therefore, among God's churches we boast about your perseverance and faith in all the persecutions and trials you are enduring." (2nd Thessalonians 1:3-4) NIV

All the believing Christians must give thanks for what the Lord is doing in their lives. They must encourage each other for their strong faith and perseverance during persecution and trials. Believers attitude which was the evidence of God's righteous judgment meaning that God judge every believer to be worthy of his grace and his kingdom for which that were suffering. Paul thanks God for Thessalonians' Church. Same with us today we must thank God for what is doing in individual believers' life. We must give thanks for their faith, love, and patience and for the blessing of the grace of God in their lives. Because where there is the truth of grace, as we are there will be an increase of it. And where there is the increase of grace God, it must have the glory of it. Believers are as much indebted to Christ for the improvement of grace, as we are from the very beginning. If our faith grew exceedingly, the growth of our faith will appear by the work of faith; proportionally our charity will be abounded as well as our patience. Where faith grows love will abound, patience as well as faith increased in all our persecution and afflictions. And patience will then have its perfect work when it extends itself to all trials.

Prayer:

God bless us with the fruit of the Spirits: Faith, Love, patience, to serve you on this earth, and to call sinners and lost unto you; every day and every minutes. Produce all the fruits of the spirit within us without measure and help us to use each one of it for your glory, especially the fruit of the spirit self-control, and long suffering that will build us up for your service on this earth. Amen.

SEPTEMBER 16ᵀᴴ

THE WORD OF GOD IS A TRANSFORMATION— LET THE WORD OF GOD TRANSFORM YOU TODAY

Today's Scripture Reading:

"It was not by their sword that they won the land, nor did their arm bring them victory; it was your right hand, your arm, and the light of your face for you love them. I do not trust in my bow, my sword does not bring me victory; but you give us victory over our enemies, you put our adversaries to shame." (Psalm 44:3, 6-7) NIV

We give you all the glory Lord Jesus Christ because you always fight our battle you always put our enemies to shame, when we call unto you, you answered us. You are alone our deliverer, and our divine help from all our enemies. It was not by our strength but by your strength you defeat our enemies, who persecuted us because we belong to you. The Land of Canaan was given to the Israelite by your love and power it is not their sword. Because you made the land their procession before the creation of the universe. Same with all the believing Christians; you are the one who planted the Christian churches in the world, by the teaching and preaching of the Gospel, Idol worshipers, Pagans forsake their wicked ways and turn to you, same with the people of all other religions, they turn to you our Lord. It is not by any human power or policy, but by your great wisdom and the power of God – in Christ by the Spirit you conquer the enemies of the cross of Christ.

Prayer:

Lord Jesus Christ you are the wisdom of God and the power of God, you chose the weak and the foolish things of the world to conquer to great things of the world. Hear our prayers continue to use us for your great glory now and forever. Amen.

SEPTEMBER 17ᵀᴴ

THE WORD OF GOD IS A TRANSFORMATION—
LET THE WORD OF GOD TRANSFORM YOU TODAY

Today's Scripture Reading:

"For he chose us in him before the creation of the world to be Holy and blameless in his sight in love he predestined us to be adopted as his sons through, Jesus Christ, in accordance with his pleasure and Will." (Ephesians 2:4-5) NIV

God the Father's choice to those who believe in Jesus Christ is very important; he choose Jesus Christ and in him people who he predestine to be confirm to the likeness of his son, will be Holy and blameless in his sight – because God will protect them, and program them in such a way that he will make them alive in him. Those who made alive in him will listen to his word and abide in him. God almighty will show his infinite love in giving us as his finite creation every spiritual blessing through the redemptive work of his son Jesus Christ. Election of humans occurs only in union with Jesus Christ. He chose us in Christ. Jesus Christ is the foundation of our election only in union with Jesus Christ through faith in him and through his blood the election to salvation and holiness of the body of Christ always certain. God himself is the center of this great change the love of God is a great love, and his mercy is rich mercy. The grace that saves sinners is a free undeserved goodness and favor of God, and saves us through faith in Jesus Christ both faith and salvation is the gift of God.

Prayer:

Lord Jesus Christ you love us before the foundation of the world, help us, in your most merciful and mighty power to be alive in you, through Jesus Christ our Lord. Guide us and bring us close to you, that we may live and worship you with the spirit of holiness. From you all the goodness flows, rain down your blessings from above to us now and forever. Amen.

SEPTEMBER 18TH

THE WORD OF GOD IS A TRANSFORMATION— LET THE WORD OF GOD TRANSFORM YOU TODAY

Today's Scripture Reading:

"If I speak in the tongues of men and angels, but have not love, I am only a resounding gong or a clanging cymbal. If I have the gift of prophecy and fathom all mysteries and all knowledge, and if I have a faith that can move mountains, but have not love, I am nothing." (1st Corinthians 13:1) NIV

All believing Christians must seek important spiritual gifts from the Lord. Apostle emphasizes that the functioning of spiritual gifts without having love for God is unprofitable. The most excellent way is to exercise of spiritual gifts in love, the only context in which spiritual gifts can fulfill God's Will; love must be the governing principle of all spiritual manifestations. Believers must earnestly desire the things of the spirit because they sincerely want to help comfort and bless others in this life. Those who's live are filled with all the religious activities which as speaking in tongues, prophecy and they display great work faith, but have no love are lacking knowledge of true spirituality. God is not impressed with religious works, without love it all nothing in his sight. Being in Christ and filled with his love for people precedes our doing this for him; otherwise we have no real place in his kingdom. Believers must express true love to God and man. Miraculous faith that can move mountain is an achievement in the eye of men; but one act of love in God's eye is of much greater worth than all the faith in the world. We must love God because he loved us first; he is our redeemer king and our blessed Savior.

Prayer:

Lord God Almighty Father of all mercies, sustainer of all things, Jesus Christ is only begotten Son full of truth and righteousness, abounding in love and forgiveness. We pray that you teach all your children how to love you, and how to love others, bless us with the spirit of love without measure, baptize us with the spirit of love, keep us save for your services wherever we may go to preach and teach the Gospel. In your great Holy Name , we pray. Amen.

SEPTEMBER 19TH

THE WORD OF GOD IS A TRANSFORMATION— LET THE WORD OF GOD TRANSFORM YOU TODAY

Today's Scripture Reading:

"The mouth of the righteous is a fountain of life, but violence overwhelms the mouth of the wicked. Hatred stirs up dissension, but love covers over all wrongs."(Proverbs 10:11-12)NIV

Believer of and those who know the Lord and follow His way will lead others into the full life given by God. Where the Spirit is living in the believer is regarded as a source of living water. As this living water flows through the believers, it brings eternal life to other. Believing Christians should pray that the Holy Spirit will flow through them to bring life and blessings to other people in the world. The mouth of a good man communicating his goodness! It is a constant spring for edification of others. The mouth of a wicked man concealing his badness to do hurt, his mouth is full of violence. The great mischief makers of violence are malice. Even where there is no manifest of strife, with the hatred in their heart they stirs up malice. Spiteful ill-nature people who take a pleasure in setting their neighbors tale bearing, evil surmises at which with an unaccountable pleasure, they warm their hands. The great peace makers, is love, which covers all sins, that is, the offences among relations which occasion discord love, instead of proclaiming and aggravating the offence, love will excuse the offence; when we are able to say that there was no ill intended, but it was an over sight, and we love our friend notwithstanding. Love will also overlook the office that is given us, and cover it, and by this means love strife is prevented.

Prayer:

Lord Jesus Christ, you show by coming to us. You paid all our sins with your precious blood. Help us to love our neighbors as we love ourselves, and as we want them to love us. Open our hearts to do good to our neighbors and help us to abide in your love and follow your commandments all the days of our life. Amen.

SEPTEMBER 20ᵀᴴ

THE WORD OF GOD IS A TRANSFORMATION—
LET THE WORD OF GOD TRANSFORM YOU TODAY

Today's Scripture Reading:

"Be very careful, then, how you live – not as unwise but as wise, making the most of every opportunity, because the days are evil. Therefore do not be foolish, but understand what the Lord's Will is." (Ephesians 5:15-17) NIV

Believers that love the Lord dearly, sincerely, and truthfully must be able to live their life according to the will of God. Believers must discipline themselves to be wise in everything that is going on around them every day; seek the knowledge of news media, what is going on with the persecution of Christians around the world be well known to them so they can pray about it every day. Believers must make every opportunity to spread the Gospel around the world. Believers must walk in the right way, circumspect walking which comes out of true wisdom, but the contrary is the effect of folly. Christians must be good husbands, good wives, children, and friends to one another during their time on Earth. They should make the best use they can of the present seasons of grace.

Believers' time is a talent given us by God for some good end, and it is misspent and lost when it is not employed according to God's design. If we have lost our time heretofore, we must endeavor to redeem it by doubling our diligence for the future.

Prayer:

Lord God Almighty, Father , Son, and Holy Spirit , we pray that you live your life in us forever, help us to worship you, honor you and help us to adore you from this earth to heaven. Help us and have mercy upon us through the power of the Holy Spirit so that we can make every opportunity for your great good in the work of the Gospel in the teaching, preaching, witnessing the Gospel to an unbelievers, and light up their lives through the illumination light of the Holy Spirit; because the days are evil our Lord, help us to wisely doing your will and following your commandment now and forever. Amen.

SEPTEMBER 21ST

THE WORD OF GOD IS A TRANSFORMATION—
LET THE WORD OF GOD TRANSFORM YOU TODAY

Today's Scripture Reading:

"Delight yourself in the Lord and he will give you the desires of your heart." (Psalm 37:4) NIV

All believers' needs to delight themselves in the Lord, To delight yourselves in the Lord is to desire and enjoy the oneness of his presence and the truth and righteousness of his Word. Those who delight themselves in the Lord, the Lord give the desires of their hearts. God Almighty will answer the cry of our hearts if our desires are in accordance with his Will. When we delight ourselves God the Father, God the Son and God the Holy Spirit and in his Will, God himself places desire within our hearts that he then will set out to fulfill. God's grace works in his children to produce in them both the desire and power to do his will. However, God' work is not one of compulsion of irresistible grace. The work of grace of God within us always dependent on our cooperation dend our response of faith. Believers are commanded to do good, and then follow this command of delight in God, which is as much a privilege as a task. This pleasant task has a promise imparted to it; He said that He will give us the desires of our heart on one condition, if he know that the desires of our heart is in accordance to his will, and most especially that the desires of our hearts is good for us and it will bring glory to his Holy Name. The desires of a good believing Christians is to know the Lord, love him and live with him, to please him and to be pleased in him.

Prayer:

Lord Jesus Compassionate gracious loving God, Jesus Christ our blessed Savior, fulfill our hearts desires if it is good for us and it is according to your will, bringing glory to your great Holy Name. Help us to delight in you all the days of our life. Amen.

SEPTEMBER 22ND

THE WORD OF GOD IS A TRANSFORMATION—
LET THE WORD OF GOD TRANSFORM YOU TODAY

Today's Scripture Reading:

"Be still before the Lord and wait patiently for him; do not fret when men succeed in their ways, when they carry out their wicked schemes." (Psalm 37:7) NIV

This Scripture reveals how the righteous must react when the wicked prosper in spite of their evil and immoral ways. Believers must steadfastly persevere in faith while waiting for God to bring about justice and vindicate us. Patience while going through trials troubles and suffering is possible through the help of the Holy Spirit who assures us that God will reward the righteous and punish the wicked. The Lord God almighty he is the great I am, if he promise his children that call unto him sincerely every day, he will fulfill his promise. He said one jot of his Word will not pass without being fulfill, heaven and earth may pass away but his Word will not pass away. Believers must patiently wait on the promises of the Lord. Believers let us compose ourselves by strong faith and believing in the Lord; that is we must be well focus on Christ Jesus and reconciled to all he does, and be well satisfied that he will still makes all to work for good to us, though we know not how or which way. Let us not discompose ourselves at what we see in this world. The Lord is powerful and compassionate. He will make our work to abound for his own glory when we do not expect his blessings to come.

Prayer:

Lord Jesus Christ, bless us with the Spirit of patience without measure, so that we can honorably wait for your promises for us. You are the great I am. Baptize us with the Spirit of patience, so that we can wait for your blessings, now and forever. Amen.

SEPTEMBER 23RD

THE WORD OF GOD IS A TRANSFORMATION—
LET THE WORD OF GOD TRANSFORM YOU TODAY

Today's Scripture Reading:

"Whatever you do, work at it with all your heart, as working for the Lord, not for men. Since you know that you will receive an inheritance from the Lord as a reward. It is the Lord Christ you are serving. Anyone who does wrong will be repaid for his wrong, and there is no favoritism." (Colossians 3:23-25) NIV

All the believing Christians must regard all their labor as a service rendered to the Lord. Believers must work as though Christ is their employer, knowing that all works are performed for the Lord. Believing Christians must learn how to demonstrate love, justice, and fairness to one another. This Scripture should be taken seriously, as well as must be studied in the Church, congregations, and within the family, to include all other households of faith. Believers must learn that mistreatment of others by Christians is a serious matter, which will be affecting our future glory in heaven. Those who treat others in love and goodness will receive reward from the Lord; anyone who mistreats and does wrong to another believer will be repaid for his wrongdoing. It sanctifies a servant's work when it is done as unto the Lord, and merely as unto men. Believers are really doing their duty to the Lord when they are faithfully carried out their duty. A good and faithful servant is never far from heaven, serving masters according to the command of Jesus Christ. We serve Christ, and he is our paymaster. Christ will punish the unjust, as well as reward the faithful servant.

Prayer:

Jesus Christ, our Lord and Savior, have mercy upon us, and in your great mercy, help us in our service to you, help us to see you in every earthly work we are doing. We are dedicated to you because you are our gracious Master and our God. Amen.

SEPTEMBER 24TH

THE WORD OF GOD IS A TRANSFORMATION—
LET THE WORD OF GOD TRANSFORM YOU TODAY

Today's Scripture Reading:

"Since you are my rock and my fortress, for the sake of your Name lead and guide me. Free me from the trap that is set for me, for you are my refuge. Into your hands I commit my spirit; redeem me, O Lord, the God of truth." (Psalm 31:3-5) NIV

This Scripture revealed King David song to God Almighty. It is the same with us today as New Testament believers of Jesus Christ. We must be confident to hide ourselves under the shadow of his wings. This is a personal prayer which expresses distress and lament because of enemies, illness, trials, and disappointments. Our Lord and Savior quoted from this Scripture when he was on the cross. The prayer expresses the heart cry of all believers who suffer afflictions because of illness, troubles, from the world system. It reveals that in times of deep sorrow and affliction we can hide in the shelter of our Lord, and be preserved. These words were Jesus Christ's last on the cross. These words are also used often by faithful believers in their last moments on this earth. Believers express dependence on the Lord and faith in his goodness to his people. It is much appropriated to commit ourselves into the Lord's care during times of troubles and difficulties. Believers must give glory to God for all his provisions with confidence in him. The Lord is our strength. He is our rock and our fortress in whom we trust forever.

Prayer:

Lord God Almighty, Jesus Christ his only Son, Holy Spirit the giver of life, who proceeded from the Father and the Son, we pray that your full presence will always be upon us, and that you will continue to be our rock, our fortress, and our refuge throughout our days on this earth. You are a new covenant God, open our heart, abide with us by believing in your covenant, strengthen us in all the areas of our lives to make us to be useful for you, now and forever. In Jesus Christ's glorious, mighty Holy Name, we pray. Amen.

SEPTEMBER 25TH

THE WORD OF GOD IS A TRANSFORMATION—
LET THE WORD OF GOD TRANSFORM YOU TODAY

Today's Scripture Reading:

"A new command I give you love one another. As I have loved you, so you must love one another. By this all men will know that you are my disciples, if you love one another. " (John 13:34-35) NIV

All the believing Christians are commanded to love in a greater and in a special way, all true Christians believers whether or not they are members of one's own church, or from the different household, or members of the same household, State, Community, different Country, or they belongs to one's particular theological persuasion. Believers must distinguish true Christians from those whose profession is false by examining their love for and obedience to Jesus Christ and their loyalty to God's Holy Word. Any person who possesses a living faith in Jesus Christ; maintain his or her loyalty to the Holy word of God. Loving all true Christians, including those who are not of your church assembly, does not mean that we must compromise or accommodate our particular biblical beliefs. Believers must seek organizational unity in the service of the Lord.

Therefore, the relationship among all believers must be characterized by a devoted concern that sacrificially seeks to promote the highest good of our brothers and sisters in Christ. Our Lord Jesus Christ gave us a new commandment; he not only commands it, not only counsels but commends it; and he makes it one of the fundamental laws of his kingdom. Believers must have love, not only show love, but have it in the root and habit of it; have it ready; brotherly love is the badge of Christ's people and disciples.

Prayer:

Lord Jesus Christ be with all those who believe in you with your love, and bless us with love for one another, and let the people of this world see your love in us and give you glory in heaven where you sited at the right hand of God the Father. Amen.

SEPTEMBER 26TH

THE WORD OF GOD IS A TRANSFORMATION—
LET THE WORD OF GOD TRANSFORM YOU TODAY

Today's Scripture Reading:

"Make every effort to live in Peace with all men and be Holy; without holiness no one will see the Lord. See to it that no one misses the grace of God and that no bitter root grows up to cause trouble and defile many." (Hebrews 12:14-15) NIV

Believers must make every effort to be Holy, to be Holy as well as to be separated from sin and set apart for the Lord purpose; it is to be close to Jesus Christ, to be like him and to seek his full presence in righteousness and in fellowship with all our hearts. Moreover, above all thing, holiness is God's priority for God's children. Holiness was God's purpose for his children when he planned their salvation in Christ Jesus our Lord and Savior. Holiness was also Jesus Christ purpose for his people when he gave himself for us for atonement for our sin on the cross, Therefore, holiness is the purpose of God in making us a new creation and in giving us the Holy Spirit. Without holiness we cannot be able to live a Christian life. Life that God require from us. Holiness God gave us the Holy

Spirit through his Son to be our helper from this earth to heaven. Without holiness we cannot be able to get close, or have a spirit nearness in word be able to fellowship with God. Without holiness no one can be useful to God; all believers will be interpreting Scripture differently. And more over, most especially without holiness no one can be able to see the Lord. The word bitterroot refers to a deep resentment in one's heart that continues to grow and has consequences for others. It also refers to an attitude of better resentment toward God's disciple instead of humble submission to God is will for our lives.

Prayer:

Lord God Almighty Father of all mercies, compassionate gracious loving God, takes away spirit of bitterness from all your children. Help them to live a life of forgiveness, and a life that is justified in your sight. Do not let bitterness be named in all the areas of our lives. Bless us with a pure heart that is full of your love and joy in the Holy Spirit, joy of the living heart. Lord Jesus Christ helps us to purge out all the root of bitterness from all your children so that they may live a life that will be pleasing to you. Amen.

SEPTEMBER 27TH

THE WORD OF GOD IS A TRANSFORMATION—
LET THE WORD OF GOD TRANSFORM YOU TODAY

Today's Scripture Reading:

"For Chris's love compels us, because we are convinced that one died for all, and therefore all died. And he died for all, that those who live should no longer live for themselves but for him who died for them and was raise again." (2nd Corinthians 5:14-15) NIV

God almighty through Jesus Christ atoning death on the cross he has removed the barrier of sin and he has opened a way for sinner to return to God. The love of God has constraining virtue to excite ministers, pastors and all believing Christians in their responsibility. Our love to Jesus Christ will have this virtue; and Jesus Christ's love to us will have this effect upon us. What believing Christians must do is best to continue to be able to abide in Jesus Christ who died for us that we may live and worship him. Dead in sins and trespasses, a spiritual death. Believer's responsibility for Jesus Christ who loved us first and died for our sins, we should live in him forever, love him forever. We live a new life in Jesus Christ who died for us and raise to life again. Jesus

Christ must be entered in our hearts, the love of Christ is in our hearts, and the spirit of the Lord must live in us forever, his love and compassion abide with us when we live for Jesus Christ his mercy flows through us and fills us.

Prayer:

Lord Jesus Christ, Compassionate loving God; you know us, you gave your life for us, you chose us and make us a new creation; in your mercy and with your infinite love bestow your blessings upon us help us to live a life of love, loving you forever and adore you, you gave us your life help us through the power of the Holy Spirit to be able to abide in you, be one in you as you and Father are one. Create in us the spirit of love for you, be one in you as you and Father are one, help to continue to call sinners and the lost unto to you. Amen.

SEPTEMBER 28ᵀᴴ

THE WORD OF GOD IS A TRANSFORMATION— LET THE WORD OF GOD TRANSFORM YOU TODAY

Today's Scripture Reading:

"There is one body and one Spirit just as you were called one Lord, one faith, one baptism, one God and Father of all, who is over all and through all and in all." (Ephesians 4:4-6) NIV

Believers must consider that the Christian unity should be in one heart; because there is one body and one spirit. If there is only one body all that belongs to that body should be one heart. If we belong to Jesus Christ, we are all actuated by one and the same spirit, and therefore, we should all be one. There is one Jesus Christ that they all hope, and one heaven that they are all hoping for; therefore they should be of one heart. One Lord, who is our Lord Jesus Christ. One faith, that is the Gospel, or it is the same grace of faith whereby all Christians are saved. One baptism, which is what we profess our faith. One God and Father of all which is one God, who owns all the true believers of the church for his children; and this one God is above all, and through all, which by is providence upholding all believers, by the power of his Spirit. One Lord is essential to Christian's faith and unity is the confession that there is only one Lord means only Jesus Christ he is the Lord through his work of redemption which is perfect and sufficient and completes our salvation. Believers draw near to God through Christ alone. One Lord also means that to profess equal or greater allegiance to any authority other than God who is revealed in Jesus Christ. There is one lordship of Jesus or unity of spirit apart from the affirmation that the Lord Jesus is the ultimate authority for all believers and that his authority is communicated in God's written Word.

Prayer:

Lord Jesus Christ whom all things of the unity of the spirit belongs to in heaven and on earth, bless us with the authority of your word to love you as one Lord, One faith, and one God Father of all who is in all forevermore. You are the Father's glory, Son for evermore, bless us, shine your glory on all the things we are doing for you on this earth in the service of the Gospel. Guide us; keep us save everywhere we may be, and in our service for you. Amen.

SEPTEMBER 29TH

THE WORD OF GOD IS A TRANSFORMATION— LET THE WORD OF GOD TRANSFORM YOU TODAY

Today's Scripture Reading:

"Do not confirm any longer to the pattern of this world, but be transformed by the renewing of your mind. Then you will be able to test and approve what God's will is - his good, pleasing and perfect Will." (Romans 12:2) NIV

All the believing Christians must not be conforming to any worldly sins, or immorality that runs the life of unbelievers. Believers must be transformed immediately when they give their life to Jesus Christ and welcome him to take total control of their lives. The Holy Spirit begins the work of transformation in their heart and mind every day. There is a pressure from unbelievers to conform the believing Christians to the pattern of this present world system and be squeezed into its mold in many different levels. This must be completely and firmly resisted by all true believers. The kingdom of Jesus Christ is not of this world; on the one hand more over believers are called to be a light in the midst of darkness. Transformation results when Jesus Christ and his word renew our mind so that our vision, values, and plans are governed by God's revelation and his eternal truth, rather by the world temporal and deceptive pattern. The believer's body must be present to the Lord, as a clean and without blemish; as a living sacrifice and dedicated to the Lord; our persons and our performances must be tendered to God through Jesus Christ as a sacrifice of acknowledgment to the honor of God, as a free will offering.

Prayer:

Lord Jesus Christ helps us to be able to present our body to you as a living sacrifice perfect with no immorality or sins. Bless us with the power of your love for us that will constrains us to live a life that will be pleasing in your sight, life that will resists all the worldly lust , temptations, through the power of the indwelling of your Spirit. In Jesus Christ's glorious, mighty Holy Name, we pray. Amen.

SEPTEMBER 30TH

THE WORD OF GOD IS A TRANSFORMATION—LET THE WORD OF GOD TRANSFORM YOU TODAY

Today's Scripture Reading:

"Surely goodness and love will follow me all the days of my life and I will dwell in the house of the Lord forever." (Psalm 23:6) NIV

In this Scripture which is the most popular prayer of King David: This prayer is for all the Christians believers today and it will continue forever. This Scripture is referring to Jesus Christ as a good shepherd who takes good care of his sheep. The goodness of the shepherd to his sheep and to all his lost sheep will never fail. With the shepherd accompany believers through life's pilgrimage; I will receive constant grace, help, kindness, and support. No matter what happens I can trust the good shepherd to work in all things for my good. The goal of my following the shepherd and experience his goodness and love is that one day I may be with the Lord forever see his face and serve him forever in his house. The Lord has provided for me all things for my body and my soul, for now and from eternity, hope rises, and his faith is strengthened by being exercised; it shall follow me as the water out of the goodness of God shall follow all believers throughout their life, even to the last; for whom God loves to the end. Goodness and mercy of our Lord will follow all those who belong to him surely though their life, and at the end they shall dwell in the presence of the Lord and behold his beauty and his face forever. They will live with him in his Father's house above where there are many Mansions.

Prayer:

Our Lord Jesus Christ , we are in this world to behold your glory, the glory of the one and only true Son of God, full of grace and truth. You are a good shepherd, continue to take good care of your sheep here on earth and in heaven. Bless us to live with you in heaven. Correct, protect, guide, and lead us to your everlasting life. Empower us with the power of the indwelling of your Holy Spirit, solve all our problems, and fulfill all our needs. In Jesus Christ's glorious, mighty Holy Name, we pray. Amen.

DAILY REFLECTION NOTES

OCTOBER

OCTOBER 1ˢᵀ

THE WORD OF GOD TRANSFORMS LIFE –
LET THE WORD OF GOD BE YOUR TRANSFORMATION TODAY

Today's Scripture Reading:

"The Lord will rescue me from every evil attack and will bring me safely to his heavenly kingdom. To him be glory for ever and ever. Amen."(2nd Timothy 4:18) NIV

Our Lord Jesus Christ our great intercessor, intercedes for us. He stands with us in times of troubles; he will rescue us from any form of evil attack on us, or on our children, our brothers, and sisters, on our friends and relatives on our entire family. Christ Jesus has the power to keep us safe for his heavenly kingdom. Jesus helps us to be a victor in our troubles not a victim. Our Lord is always standing by those who belong to him. As he stands by us, he strengthens us, and his presence will be more than the supply of everyone's absence. Believers must remember former deliverance of our Lord, and that should encourage future hopes. Believers must always remember what our lord has done for us in the past and what he can still do for us at any time of our life on earth; his former activities in our live should encourage our future hopes. Therefore, we must give God the glory of all our past, present, and our future deliverance and give him the honor, the glory throughout our lives. Jesus Christ is always our deliverer in times of troubles, trials, afflictions, and tribulations he is worthy of all our praises and thankfulness.

Prayer:

Lord Jesus Christ, I praise your Holy Name for everything you have done in our lives past, present and future, you are always with us, you never live us, nor forsake us, we give you praises and thankfulness delivering us from all the trouble that the enemies sent to us every day. We glorified your Holy Name now and forever. Amen.

OCTOBER 2ND

THE WORD OF GOD TRANSFORMS LIFE – LET THE WORD OF GOD BE YOUR TRANSFORMATION TODAY

Today's Scripture Reading:

"For we do not have a high Priest who is unable to sympathize with our weaknesses, but have one who has been tempted in every way, just as we are yet was without sin. Let us then approach the throne of grace with confidence, so that we may receive mercy and find grace to help in time of need." (Hebrews 4:15-16) NIV

Our Lord Jesus Christ is our high Priest in heaven, he is seated at the right hand of God the Father Almighty, he is coming back to judge the dead and the living and all the eye shall see him. Christian believers must not only set out well, but they must be firm and steadfast, immovable in the Lord. As believers we should encourage ourselves to come boldly to the throne of grace. The throne of grace is set up in heaven for all the believing Christians. God has chosen to set up a throne of grace, where grace reigns, and acts with sovereign freedom, power, and bounty. It is our duty to be often found before this throne of grace. it is good for us to be there. Our service at the throne of grace should be that we may obtain mercy and grace which is very essential in the life of believers; mercy to pardon all our sins and grace to purify our souls. In all our approaches to the throne of grace for mercy, we should come with a humble spirit freedom and boldness; we should ask in faith, nothing doubting. we are indeed to come with reverence and with godly fear; not as if we are dragged before the tribunal of justice, but kindly invited to the mercy seat, where grace reigns and love to exert and exult itself towards us.

Prayer:

Lord Jesus Christ help us to increase our faith so that we can boldly, confidently approach the throne of grace for everything we may need and also for whatever we might be going through in our lives. God of Mercy and love, compassionate gracious loving God, let your mercy and your grace abound more and more in all the areas of our lives from this day forward. Amen.

OCTOBER 3RD

THE WORD OF GOD TRANSFORMS LIFE -
LET THE WORD OF GOD BE YOUR TRANSFORMATION TODAY

Today's Scripture Reading:

"If any of you lack wisdom, he should ask God, who gives generously to all without finding fault, and it will be given to him. But when he asks, he must believe and not doubt, because he who doubts is like a wave of the sea, blown and tossed by the wind." (James 1:5-6) NIV

Apostle James makes this part of the Scripture clear and helpful to all the believers. Believers need and must ask for Godly wisdom in other to be complete in Christ and live a godly life that Jesus Christ call us to live. Godly wisdom will help us to cope with our trials and tribulations, not just deliverance from troubles. Wisdom that James mentions here is the spiritual wisdom in full capacity that will help us to think clearly and to be able to evaluate life and conduct from God's pint of view. It involves making the right choices and doing right things according to God's Will revealed in his Word through the leading of the Holy Spirit. Believers can receive godly wisdom by coming to God ask for it by faith. If we approach the throne of grace and for a great deal of wisdom because small wisdom will not serve our purpose, God will give it to us liberally and abundantly. God promised to give us wisdom as much as we do, especially to do his work. There must be no wavering, no staggering at the promise of God through unbelief. One thing we need to observe in our asking the sincerity of our intention, and the steadfastness of our mind.

Prayer:

Lord Jesus you are the God who have all the godly wisdom, blesses us with your godly wisdom without measure. Help us to be able to use your blessings of godly wisdom in your service; so that we can be able to bring sinners and the lost to you and we will be able to live righteously in peace with one another, we will be full of patience without anger toward anyone, we will be able to solve problems without panic, or fear, we will be able to pray to you confidently approach the throne of grace, and receive mercy, and grace will abound more and more in all the areas of our life. Bless us with great wisdom, to raise our children, wisdom for our business, to work in peace with our fellow workers in the office, Lord Jesus Christ you are the God of wisdom, bless us with wisdom to service you faithfully, truthfully on this earth, to take the Gospel to where the Gospel has never be heard before. Great wisdom to live in peace and in good harmony with our husband, our wife, our parents, and our neighbors, wisdom to love everyone as we love ourselves, all these and more and more , we pray accept our prayer in the mighty Name of Jesus Christ who is the one and only the wisdom of God and the power of God now and forever. Amen.

OCTOBER 4ᵀᴴ

THE WORD OF GOD TRANSFORMS LIFE - LET THE WORD OF GOD BE YOUR TRANSFORMATION TODAY

Today's Scripture Reading:

"Let us not become weary in doing good, for at the proper time we will reap a harvest if we do not give up. Therefore, as we have opportunity; let us do good to all people, especially to those who belong to the family of believers." (Galatians 6:9-10) NIV

It is the responsibility of all who serve the Lord Jesus Christ, minister, and pastors, all who are taught of God's Word to help, to provide material support for those who instruct the people. Those who are worthy of support included those in the fivefold ministry. Christians should not be tired of doing good especially in the service of the Lord, because they have a reward waiting for them here on earth and in heaven. There is a recompense of reward which is in reserve for all who sincerely employ themselves in well doing. Therefore all the Christians must always be ready to help others when the time is available for them to do so. WE should be ready to extend our charity to unbelievers by doing this they will see the light of Jesus Christ in us and be converted. Believers must be good to other people around them, on their job, in the community. We are to have a special regard to the household of faith; although we must not exclude others. Yet, our Christian brothers and sisters are to be preferred.

Prayer:

Lord Jesus Christ, bless us abundantly and exceedingly so that we can be able to help those who are poor and in need around us. Help us to follow your commandment and serve you faithfully and sincerely. Help us in your infinite mercy to be able to follow the government rules and regulations and be a good citizen of our country. Provide all our needs; bless us with peace that surpasses all understanding that only comes from you now and forever. Amen.

OCTOBER 5TH

THE WORD OF GOD TRANSFORMS LIFE - LET THE WORD OF GOD BE YOUR TRANSFORMATION TODAY

Today's Scripture Reading:

"In the Name of the Lord Jesus Christ, we command you, brothers, to keep away from every brother who is idle and does not live according to the teaching you receive from us" (2nd Thessalonians 3:6) NIV

All the Christian believers must not sit idle doing nothing they must engage themselves with work, work training, seek how to go to school for more education that can get them a better job, vocational training, of all kinds, that will help them to take care of their family. This is the reason why our Lord sends the Holy Spirit during the Pentecost that will be helping believers in everything they may need. The Holy Spirit is our teacher, our helper in everything we are doing or about to do. Those who were idle were people who were loafing and unwilling to work. They were taking advantage of the church's generosity and receiving support from brother who work hard and made a living by ordinary occupations - such people must be discipline by keeping away from them and not associating with them although Jesus Christ as our advocate of a new covenant in heaven will send help to those who are really in need, he nowhere the believers will get food or money to able-bodied people who refused to work steadily for a living. The best Christian assembly may have some people who like to be idle, lazy among them, there is perfection in any church of the Lord; there is always idle persons and busy-bodies minding people's business, Idle and disorderly conduct people. It does hurt fellow believers to see their brothers idle around because it is required of all persons that they do good. Some of them might believe that Christ is coming any time, so they leave their work of their calling, and live in idleness. The same persons who were idle were busy bodies also, most commonly those persons who have no business of their own to do. or who neglect it, busy themselves in other men's matters.

Prayer:

Lord Jesus Christ you are the Head of the Church, the foundation of the Church and the cornerstone; have mercy upon those who live a life of idleness among us, or those who are busy bodies over another person's life. Turn them around, let them be busy and get a job, bless them with the spirit of love to love themselves and others, in order that the Church will be able to help those who are really in need in their own life will be better, then they are enabled to follow your commands and your Word. Wash away the spirit of idleness from them; replace it with the spirit of activeness in their lives and in your service at the end they may serve you in heaven forever. In your Holy Name , we pray. Amen.

OCTOBER 6TH

THE WORD OF GOD TRANSFORMS LIFE - LET THE WORD OF GOD BE YOUR TRANSFORMATION TODAY

Today's Scripture Reading:

"For this reason I remind you to fan into flame the gift of God which is in you through the laying on of my hands. For God did not give us a Spirit of timidity, but a Spirit of power, of love and of self-discipline." (2nd Timothy 1:6-7) NIV

Our Lord and Savior is a gift giver, when he gave a gift to his people, the gift passion from generation to generation. The gift given to Timothy is compared to a fire that he must fan into flame. The gift was probably a special anointing and power from the Holy Spirit to be able to fulfill his ministry. Same with all the believers today the gift and power bestowed on us by the Holy Spirit do not automatically remain strong and vital. The must be fueled by God's grace through reading the word of God, through our prayer, our faith, obedience, and diligence. Believers must stir up the gift that is in us as fire under the embers we must take all the opportunities to have gifts and to use the gifts, for that is the best way to increasing the gift. God Almighty has delivered us from the Spirit of fear, and he had given us the Spirit of Power, Spirit of love and Spirit of a sound mind. The Spirit of power; of courage and resolution; the Spirit of love to God which will set us above the fear of man, and the Spirit of a sound mind, quietness of mind, for we are oftentimes discouraged in our work by the creatures of our own imagination, which a sober, thinking mind would obviate. We must write about as well as witness to the unsaved among us.

Prayer:

Lord Jesus Christ bless all the believing Christians on this earth with the Spirit of witnessing, Spirit of power to glorify your Holy Name, and to magnify your Holy Name so that the Gospel will reach the unreachable in their own language. Bless our home, our children, our family and friends and most important help us; build us up to have more love for you now and forever our Lord. Amen.

OCTOBER 7ᵀᴴ

THE WORD OF GOD TRANSFORMS LIFE - LET THE WORD OF GOD BE YOUR TRANSFORMATION TODAY

Today's Scripture Reading:

"He came and preached peace to you who were far away and peace to those who were near. For through him we both have access to the Father by one Spirit."
(Ephesians 2:17-18) NIV

Our Lord and Savior came to this earth teach and preach to the sinners and the lost people in the world. Apostle Paul prayed for believers then and now and he did not stop his prayers for us in heaven because that is the service of all the body of Christ in heaven; whereby they pray for all the believing Christians on earth. We also are in need of prayer because of our heavenly inheritance; we have to thank God the Father for the blessing of the Holy Spirit through our Lord Jesus Christ. We also must pray that our Lord Jesus Christ will in his mercy and compassion that he would give greater measures of the Holy Spirit, the illumination of our understanding; and that our knowledge might increase and abound; to be of a practical and experimental knowledge. The graces and comforts of the Holy Spirit which are communicated to the souls of believers by the enlightened of the understanding. believers' knowledge of God must come through Jesus Christ who is a God of Knowledge; for the Spirit of God is the teacher of all the Christian believers. believers have the revelation of the Holy Spirit in the Word and in the knowledge of the Holy Spirit in our lives.

Prayer:

Lord Jesus Christ - empower us with the Holy Spirit the giver of life, who proceeded from the Father and the Son and being glorified - to be controlling, directing, teaching us your way, and helping us to live to live a life of peace in this world of danger and troubles. Bless us with resurrection power of the Holy Spirit that we may be able to live a life that is pleasing to you from this earth to heaven. We give you thanks and praises now and forever. Amen.

OCTOBER 8TH

THE WORD OF GOD TRANSFORMS LIFE - LET THE WORD OF GOD BE YOUR TRANSFORMATION TODAY

Today's Scripture Reading:

"And God is able to make all grace abound to you, so that in all things at all times, having all that you need, you will abound in every good work. As it is written: He has scattered abroad his gifts to the poor; his righteousness endures forever." (2nd Corinthians 9:8-9) NIV

Our Lord Jesus Christ increase our faith as we get closer and closer to him every day of our lives. Believers who give what they can to help those who are in need are sowing a good fruit that will bear, hundreds and millions of fruits. they will find out that God's grace provides a sufficiency for their own needs, and even more, that they abound in every good work. Faith is mentioned first, for that is the root. Those who abound in faith will abound in all other graces and good work. Father is mentioned first, for that is the root. Those who abound in faith will abound in all other graces and good work also; their faith was added utterance, knowledge. They abound also in all diligence. Those who have great knowledge and with ready utterance are not always the most diligent Christians. Great talker or preacher is not always the best doers of the Word. And moreover, they always exercise abundant love for their Pastors and ministers not for Christ Jesus. Believing Christians must be able to give to the poor and to the needy among us.

Prayer:

Lord Jesus Christ blesses us to continue to grow in grace and to grow in your infinite mercy and love that we may be able to abound in grace every day of our lives. Lord Jesus Christ, let your grace abound in us every day of our lives and help us to be able to grow in grace and grow in sanctification, in order that we can be able to win millions, and millions of Souls into your Holy hands. Let your kingdom come soon our Lord, and let your Will be done on this earth has it is written in heaven. In your merciful and mighty Holy Name , we prayer now and forever. Amen.

OCTOBER 9TH

THE WORD OF GOD TRANSFORMS LIFE - LET THE WORD OF GOD BE YOUR TRANSFORMATION TODAY

Today's Scripture Reading:

"Do not be afraid, little flock, for your Father has been pleased to give you the Kingdom."(Luke 12:32) NIV

All believing Christians are urged to seek above all things God's kingdom and his righteousness. Believers must continuously seek the kingdom of God - they must make their goal on this earth, his kingdom, and his righteousness, and all the blessings that our Lord knows they need will surely be supplied unto them. God Almighty has promised to provide for our daily bread, our clothing and all the necessary things we may need in order to be good Christians and good servants, to include a good follower of Jesus Christ. Believers must not worry; if we seek to let God reign in our lives, we can be sure that he will assume full responsibility for those who fully surrender to Jesus. Believers must seek a means to engage in a search for something, or make a strenuous and diligent effort to obtain something - Jesus Christ mentioned two objects of our seeking. One is his kingdom - we must have the power of God demonstrated in our lives and in our assemblies. WE must pray that God's kingdom will come in the mighty power of the Holy Spirit to saves sinners and the lost, and to deliver people from demonic bondages and strongholds. We are to be able to pray and heal the sick, and diseases that are troubling the children of God. We must be able to magnify the Name of our Lord Jesus Christ. WE must seek his righteousness through the power of the Holy Spirit. We must seek to obey the commands of Jesus Christ, and possess Christ's righteousness, while we remain separated from the world and show Christ's love toward everyone.

Prayer:

Lord Jesus Christ I pray that your kingdom come, your will be done in our lives as it is written in heaven. Bless us abundantly, immeasurably, and exceedingly in all the areas of our lives. Live in our hearts forever, and live your life through us forever. Let your purpose be achieved in our lives, let your full presence be known in our lives. Let the people of this earth see you clearly through us and be converted unto you; let those who seek you find you, and when people pray unto you sincerely, answer their prayers, stretch your Holy hands from heaven and fulfill all that they request in prayer if you know what they asked for in prayer is good for them, and at the right time and is according to your Will for their life. In Jesus Christ's glorious, mighty Holy Name, we pray. Amen.

OCTOBER 10TH

THE WORD OF GOD TRANSFORMS LIFE - LET THE WORD OF GOD BE YOUR TRANSFORMATION TODAY

Today's Scripture Reading:

"Before the mountains were born or you brought forth the earth and the world, from everlasting to everlasting you are God"(Psalm 90:2) NIV

This Scripture reveals God's eternal existence, having no beginning and no end. Everlasting means that is endless duration in time, no past, no present, and no future; God is always be and he will always be. This Scripture affirms God's eternity in continuation, not timelessness. God knows the past as past, and the present as present, and the future as future. The Scripture says that: A thousand years in his eye is like a day, and a day is like a thousand years, God has no beginning and no end. Our God is immortality we may take comfort from God's immortality. We must give God the glory for his eternity, before the creation of the world God is always be, and he will always be. God in his mercy have absolute sovereign dominion over man, and he has power to dispose of him as he pleases, but he want men to repent of their sins and live a new life. The Lord has committed himself to be the believers' faithful and constant guide throughout life, in the experience of death and beyond death to the eternal home where we will be with him forever.

Prayer

Lord God Almighty, Father, Son and Holy Spirit ever one God, we praise your Holy Name because you alone is the true God, you alone is from everlasting to everlasting before you created the universe you are our God. Bless us with long and healthy life to serve you as we ought to serve you on this earth to honor you and bless your Holy Name forever, let your Holy Spirit fell upon us, and bless us abundantly with eternal life. Help us to live for your glory, and adored you throughout our life. In Jesus Christ's glorious, mighty Holy Name, we pray. Amen.

OCTOBER 11ᵀᴴ

THE WORD OF GOD TRANSFORMS LIFE - LET THE WORD OF GOD BE YOUR TRANSFORMATION TODAY

Today's Scripture Reading:

"Do you not know? have you not heard? The Lord is the everlasting God, the creator of the ends of the earth. He will not grow tired or weary, and his understanding no one can fathom. He gives strength to the weary and increases the power of the weak, even youths grow tired and weary, and young men stumble and fall; but those who hope in the Lord will renew their strength. They will soar on wings like eagles; they will run and not grow weary, they will walk and not be faint."(Isaiah 40:28-31) NIV

All the believing Christians must have hope in the Lord, and trust him fully throughout our lives; believers must be looking at Jesus the author and the perfected of our faith. We must be looking to him as our source of help and grace in time of need. those who hope in the Lord are promised: God's strength to revive them in the midst of exhaustion and weakness, of sufferings and trials, the ability to rise above all our difficulties like an eagle that soars into the sky; and the ability to run spiritually without tiring and to walk steadily forward without fainting at, or when God delays. God Almighty promised that if those who believe in him, his own people will patiently trust him, he will provide whatever is needed to sustain them constantly throughout their life. Jesus Christ our Savior gives strength to his people, he helps them to be able to help themselves, and he revives their souls through the power of the Holy Spirit. God will help those who humbly dependence upon him, he will help them to do well, those who do their best, they will think stronger and feels stronger by faith they will trust the Lord and they will soar up towards God.

Prayer:

Lord Jesus Christ our Lord and our Savior compassionate gracious loving God, the everlasting Lord, help us, and bless us to be strong in you and soar like eagle forward towards heaven, help us to walk, run to the way of your commandments; cheerfully throughout the days of our life. Help us to triumph in any adversities, afflictions, sickness, and diseases that plague all the people in this world. Let the people of this world turn to you for all their problems, and seek your face so that you can heal them; let the nations of this earth turn to you for their problems so that you may heal their land and they can live in peace with other nations. Amen.

OCTOBER 12TH

THE WORD OF GOD TRANSFORMS LIFE - LET THE WORD OF GOD BE YOUR TRANSFORMATION TODAY

Today's Scripture Reading:

"Be at rest once more, O my Soul, for the Lord has been good to you. For you, O Lord, have delivered my Soul from death, my eyes from tears, my feet from stumbling, that I may walk before the Lord in the land of the living." (Psalm 116:7-9) NIV

All the believing Christians must give thanks to the Lord for deliverance from death, they must declare the praises of all afflicted believers who have been rescued by the Lord and have been spared to death or stick by great calamity. Our Lord and Savior said we should call unto him and he answer us, and deliver us from work of the enemies; and from the hands of our enemies. It is God's great mercy to us that we are alive; and the mercy is the more sensible if we have been at death's door and yet have been spared and raised up. The deliverance of the soul from spiritual death is especially to be acknowledging by all those who are now sanctified and shall be shortly glorified. God always deal kindly with his children and therefore, we must not worry or weary in whatever we might be going through, he will surely deliver our souls from death. believer's souls must rest in the Lord; believer must rejoice in the Lord all the days of their lives- He is able and willing to always deliver us from destruction.

Prayer:

Lord God Almighty, Jesus Christ our Lord, we pray to you for mercy and for your great compassion, touch the heart and mind of all the Christians believers to be strong in you, worship you in Sprit and in truth - continue to deliver us from any earthly afflictions that can bring destruction to us and our family. Protect us at all times, guide us and lead us to the way everlasting. In Jesus great Holy Name , we pray. Amen.

OCTOBER 13TH

THE WORD OF GOD TRANSFORMS LIFE - LET THE WORD OF GOD BE YOUR TRANSFORMATION TODAY

Today's Scripture Reading:

"Blessed is the man who fears the Lord, who finds great delight in his commands. He will have no fear of bad news; his heart is steadfast; trusting the Lord. His heart is secured, he will have no fear; in the end he will look in triumph on his foes." (Psalm 112: 1a, 7-8a) NIV

Believers must concentrate on one important thing in this life which is how to find great delight in the Word of God, and in his commandments; this is what should matter most in the life of all believers. They must also make sure that God's will is done on earth. Believers must be people who love the Lord God's laws because his commands represent his righteousness in the world. God Almighty loved righteousness and hates anything that is evil. Believers must hate anything that is evil. Jesus Christ was devoted to righteousness during his earthly ministry and he hated wickedness in his life, ministry, and in his death on the cross. Jesus Christ's faithfulness to the Father while on earth, demonstrated by his love of righteousness and hatred for wickedness. Therefore, it is the basis for God anointing of his Son. In the same way, it motivates believer's with an anointing that will come only as we identify with Jesus Christ's attitude towards righteousness and evil. Believers have reasons to praise the Lord that there are people in this world, who fear him and serve him. They are a happy people; they owed their happiness entire to the grace of God. They are the blessed people of God. The blessedness of God is upon those who are good and love the Lord.

Prayer:

Lord Jesus Christ, Father, Son and Holy Spirit, you love us before the foundation of the Universe. Bless us abundantly and exceedingly our Lord. We are calling unto you sincerely; you are our blessed hope, do not leave us nor forsake us. Hold us in the beauty of your holiness that we may be in you from this day forward and forever. Amen.

OCTOBER 14TH

THE WORD OF GOD TRANSFORMS LIFE - LET THE WORD OF GOD BE YOUR TRANSFORMATION TODAY

Today's Scripture Reading:

"Create in me a pure heart, O God, and renew a steadfast Spirit within me. Do not cast me from your presence or take your Holy Spirit from me. Restore to me the joy of your salvation and grant me a willing spirit, to sustain me. (Psalm 51:10-12)NIV

All the believers need God's Spirit to create in them a pure heart that hate sins and renewed Spirit that desires to do God's will. God Almighty is the only one that can make us a new creation and restore us to the true godliness. That is why David prays this prayer to God after he fell unto sin with Uriah's wife. David knows that if God removes the Holy Spirit's presence from his life, then all the hope of redemption is gone. David knows that the Lord is the only one that can restore the joy of salvation, but the Scripture says that we will reap life from the Spirit, if we sow to please the sinful nature we will reap to the sinful nature. A believer's great concern is to get our corrupt nature changed, and therefore, we must pray to ask God to completely remove our sinful nature.

Prayer:

Lord Jesus Christ, our Lord, and our Savior, bless us with spiritual strength, God almighty, you are the only one that can renew our Spirit, Soul and Body. We pray for continuance of your good will towards humankind, enhance the progress of your good work in us. Lord God Almighty, cast not your Spirit away from us, and we pray that you do not take your Holy Spirit away from us. Help us to constantly walk in your ways and fulfill your Will. Let your full presence be known in our lives, and help us to get closer and closer to you from this earth to heaven, create in us a new spirit. In your great Holy Name , we pray Amen.

OCTOBER 15TH

THE WORD OF GOD TRANSFORMS LIFE - LET THE WORD OF GOD BE YOUR TRANSFORMATION TODAY

Today's Scripture Reading:

"Jesus Straightened up and asked her, Woman, where are they? Has no one condemned you? No one, sir, she said. Then neither do I condemn you Jesus declared. Go now and leave your life of sin. When Jesus spoke again to the people, he said, I am the light of the world. Whoever follows me will never walk in darkness, but will have the light of life." (John 8:10-12) NIV

Our Lord Jesus Words reflect his redemptive love for the lost and is placed in contrast to the unloving attitude of the Pharisees. The response of the Pharisees to the woman was condemnation and a judgment of death. Jesus Christ response to her was kindness, forgiveness and offer of a new life if she leaves a life of sin. Same with us today, when we give our life to Christ, we leave our old life, so that we can have a new life in Jesus Christ. There is no sin that Jesus cannot forgive if the person renounces it and desire to put on the new life. Jesus Christ offers this woman a salvation and a way out of her life of sin. Jesus Christ is the light of the world; the true light that shines forever and no darkness can comprehend it. He removes darkness and deception by illuminating the right way to God and salvation. All those who gave their life to Jesus Christ in faith are delivered from darkness of sin and sin nature, the world and they receive salvation. Those who still walk in darkness do not follow him Jesus Christ said whoever follows me, must continue to follow me, keep on following till eternity. Jesus Christ does not take half, half, people that follow him must stay out of sin and sin nature and all the deceitful things of this world.

Prayer:

Lord Jesus Christ, bless us with your Holy Spirit and help us to renounced all the sins and sins that can course us to break away and stop following you, help us, strengthens us, in order that we may continue to follow you and do your will now and forever. Continues to help all the people in this world who fall into sins; especially sin of sexual immoralities that is ruining the life of men and women of this world. Create in us a new life that we will respect, and know how valuable we are to you; help us to seek you for comfort instead of running to drug or alcohol, or other abomination lifestyle. Have mercy upon us; O Merciful and mighty God. In your Holy Name , we pray now and forever. Amen.

OCTOBER 16TH

THE WORD OF GOD TRANSFORMS LIFE - LET THE WORD OF GOD BE YOUR TRANSFORMATION TODAY

Today's Scripture Reading:

"When I saw him. I fell at his feet as though dead. Then he placed his right hand on me and said: Do not be afraid. I am the living one; first and the last. I am the living one; I was dead, and behold I am alive for ever and ever! And I hold the keys of death and hades." (Revelation 1:17-18) NIV

There is no one like Jesus, he is the Alpha and the Omega, the beginning and the end, the first and the last, he is alive forever more. John was in a great surprise when he saw the representation of the church under the emblem of the seven golden candles sticks. The churches are compared to candlesticks because they hold forth the light of the Gospel to advantage. He saw the representation of our Lord Jesus Christ in the midst of the golden candle sticks. The glorious form in which Jesus Christ appeared; the impression this appearance of Christ made upon the apostle John. He was overpowered with the greatness of the luster and gory in which Christ appeared though he had been so familiar with Christ before during his earthly ministry. The condescending goodness of the Lord Jesus to his disciple. He raised him up; he put strength into him, he spoke kind words to him Word of comfort and encouragement - fear not - Christ never let us fear, of whatever situation we may find ourselves. his words of instruction are always clear "do not fear" I am - telling him who he was that appeared to him, he acquaints him with his divine presence.

Prayer:

Lord Jesus let your full presence be upon us, let your love and great compassion be upon us, let your mercies flow to us and through us to those who need your salvation and forgiveness, you are our immortal food feed us with your full presence and help us to abide in you forever. Amen.

OCTOBER 17TH

THE WORD OF GOD TRANSFORMS LIFE - LET THE WORD OF GOD BE YOUR TRANSFORMATION TODAY

Today's Scripture Reading:

"Again, I tell you that if two of you on earth agree that anything you ask for, it will be done for you by my Father in heaven. For where two or three come together in my Name, there am I with them." (Matthew 18:19-20) NIV

All the believers must take or claim the authority and the power in the prayer of agreement Jesus's statement points to the principle of synergism in the realm of faith and prayer. The principle is that the united actions of two or more separate agents when harmoniously working together have a greater total effect than sum of their individual efforts. Our Lord Jesus Christ promises of two positive results of the prayer agreement: (a) God the Father will takes action in heaven on their request and (b) The presence of Jesus Christ our Lord will be in their midst on earth. Believers must gather together in Jesus Christ Name in meeting for worship, we must have an eye for Jesus; and in communion with all that in every place that call upon him. When we come together to worship God in a dependence upon the Spirit and grace of Christ, having an actual regard to him as our way to the Father, and our advocate with the Father, then we are meet together in his Name. Believers were encouraged with an assurance of the presence of Jesus Christ. He is in the midst of them, Christ is in their hearts; It is a Spiritual presence, the presence of Christ's Spirit with their Spirits that is here intended.

Prayer:

Lord Jesus Christ you said to us that where two, or three gathers together, you will be right there with us, Lord Jesus, bless us with your full presence in our prayers and services to you. Let your full presence fill us up, and bless us with life everlasting, life that will always seek your presence in our prayer. Amen.

OCTOBER 18TH

The Word of God Transforms Life – Let
The Word of God be your Transformation Today

Today's Scripture Reading:

"The Son is the radiance of God's glory and the exact representation of his being, sustaining all things by his powerful word. After he had provided purification for sins, he sat down at the right hand of the Majesty in heaven." (Hebrews 1:3) NIV

Christ Jesus provided the forgiveness of our sins by his atoning death on the cross; he took his place of authority at God's right hand. Christ's redeeming activity in heaven involved his ministry of reconciliation, divine mediator, high Priest, intercessor, and the baptizer in the Holy Spirit. Exact representation refers to the mark that an engraving stamp leaves on a seal, or on a coin; the correspondence between the engraving stamp and the engraved impression is exact. God's Son nature and essence and whatever God is in his character and nature; Jesus is the exact representation. Therefore, God's revelation of himself is no longer fragmentary and incomplete as in the Old Testament times; in Jesus Christ, the Son, is the revelation of the Father is full and complete. Jesus Christ is the only begotten Son of God, and as such he must have the same nature. The person of the Son is the glory of the Father, shining forth with a truly divine splendor. Jesus Christ is God manifest in the flesh. Jesus Christ is the true image and character of the Father in beholding the power, wisdom, and goodness of the Lord Jesus Christ; we behold the fullness of the Godhead who dwells in him.

Prayer:

Lord Jesus Christ, the immortal, the invisible, the only wise God, make yourself visible in our life, let your full presence be known in your lives; shine your great glory upon us, let your mercies flow and bless us with your grace, especially those who does not know you. Rain down your blessings and the gift of grace to salvation upon every individual people living on this earth. Rain down the Holy spirit as in the Day of Pentecost. Let every soul of human beings be filled with your Spirit, the Holy Spirit, the Spirit of God the Father, the Son, and the Holy Spirit, the forever one God. Bless us with love for one another, which is bound in peace. Amen.

OCTOBER 19TH

THE WORD OF GOD TRANSFORMS LIFE - LET THE WORD OF GOD BE YOUR TRANSFORMATION TODAY

Today's Scripture Reading:

"He is the image of the invisible God, the first born over all creation. For by him all things were created; things in heaven, and on earth, visible and invisible, whether thrones or powers or rulers or authorities; all things were created by him and for him. He is before all things, and in him all things hold together." (Colossians 1:15-17) NIV

Jesus Christ is the first born over all the creation means - Jesus Christ was a created being, which also means to be first in position. Jesus Christ is the heir and ruler of all creation as the eternal Son. Apostle Paul affirms the creativity of Christ Jesus. All this means both material and spiritual, owe their existence to Christ's work as the active agent in creation. In Jesus all things hold together and are sustained in him. Jesus Christ is the image of God as the son is the image of his father, who has a natural likeness of him. Chris is the heir and the Lord of all; he has his dominion over all things representing eternity. Chris is the creator - all things were created by him and for him. He not only had a being before he was born of the Virgin Mary, but he had a being before all time before the Universe was made. The entire creation is kept together by the power of the Son of God, and made to consist in its proper frame. Everyone on this earth belongs to Christ they must repent of their sins and live a peaceable life. In Jesus Christ there is life and life everlasting.

Prayer:

Lord Jess Christ, we give you honor and glory, you are the one and only true Son of God, the very God, the King of kings, the Lord of lords, the God of gods, the God of light; help us to live a life that is approve of you, a life that is justify in your sight, and a life that please you, guide us to your truth, help us to call sinners and lost unto you everywhere we may be on this earth. Keep us safe, provide for all our needs, let your full presence be known in our lives, help us to worship you in Spirit and in truth throughout our lives now in this world and in eternity in heaven. Amen.

OCTOBER 20TH

THE WORD OF GOD TRANSFORMS LIFE - LET THE WORD OF GOD BE YOUR TRANSFORMATION TODAY

Today's Scripture Reading:

"Now the crowd that was with him when he called Lazarus from the tomb and raised him from the dead continued to spread the word. Many people, because they had heard that he had given this miraculous sign, went out to meet him." (John 12:17-18) NIV

Our Lord and Savior, the giver of life raised Lazarus from the dead. He pray to the Father, and called the Name of Lazarus, because if he did not mention and called the Name of Lazarus, every one that is in the tomb will comes out. And Lazarus walked out of the tomb after four days. Believers should know that the remembrance of what is written will enable us to understand what was done, and the observation what is done will help us to understand that it is written. When the people saw this miracle of Jesus, the respect him and they give glory to God. Those who considered it as a proof of Jesus Christ's mission, and a ground of their faith in him, the truth of Jesus' miracles was stand evidenced by incontestable proof, it also had an influence upon them, some of them out of curiosity, were desirous to see that he had done such a wonderful work. Others out of conscience, studied to do him honor, as the one sent by God. Those who oppose Jesus Christ will be made to perceive that they prevail nothing. God will accomplish his own purposes in spite of their opposition. Jesus Christ have the power to raise up the dead from the grave; he is still exercising his power at the right hand of God the Father where he is seated.

Prayer:

Lord Jesus Christ you are the giver of life; you're the sustainer of this world, in your infinite mercy and love, give life to those who are spiritually dead, make them alive in you as you raised Lazarus from the dead and he worshiped you. Give life to those who do not know you, so that they can worship you now and forever with the spirit of holiness. Amen.

OCTOBER 21ST

THE WORD OF GOD TRANSFORMS LIFE - LET THE WORD OF GOD BE YOUR TRANSFORMATION TODAY

Today's Scripture Reading:

"Therefore, since we are surrounded by such a great cloud of witnesses, let us throw off everything that hinders and the sin that so easily entangles, and let us run with, perseverance the race marked out for us. Let us fix our eyes on Jesus, the author and the perfecter of our faith, who for the joy set before him endured the cross, scorning its shame, and sat down at the right hand of the throne of God." (Hebrews 12:1-2) NIV

Believing Christians must run this race well, with all perseverance, with all patience, and with all endurance - pressing onto the finish line. The race must be run by throwing off the sin and sin nature that so easily entangles us, which are the most besetting sins, and, by fixing our eyes on Jesus, who persevered to the end by enduring the cross. The race must be run with an awareness that our greatest danger is the temptation to give up and yield to sin. In our race of faith, we look to Jesus as our example of trusting God of commitment to his will, of prayer, of overcoming temptation and suffering, of enduring loyalty to the Father and of seeking the joy of completing the work to which God assigned for us to do - Jesus Christ is our source of strength, love, grace, mercy and help. Jesus Christ is the author and the finisher of our faith, he is the finisher of grace, and the work of faith with power in the souls of his people and he is the judge and the rewarder of our faith. All Christians have a race to run; the race that was set before us by God, marked out for us, by the Word of God, and as an example of all the faithful servants of God, with cloud of witnesses with which we are compassed about, as he is the great leader and precedent of our faith.

Prayer:

Lord Jesus Christ in your infinite mercy and love, increase our faith, help us to have strong faith in you, grant us with faith like a mustard seed that can move a mountain. Bless us with your abundant grace, love, and compassion for the things we need. Help us to know you better in our lives, and to be useful for you throughout our lives in this world. In your Holy Name, we pray. Amen.

OCTOBER 22ND

THE WORD OF GOD TRANSFORMS LIFE - LET THE WORD OF GOD BE YOUR TRANSFORMATION TODAY

Today's Scripture Reading:

"When they saw him, the worshiped him, but some doubt. Then Jesus came to them and said; All authority in heaven and on earth has been given to me. Therefore, go and make disciples of all nations, baptizing them in the Name of the Father and of the Son and of the Holy Spirit, and teaching them to obey everything I have commanded you. And surely I am with you always, to the very end of the age." (Matthew 20:17-20) NIV

The disciples were waiting patiently for Jesus in Galilee same with us today waiting patiently for the Second Coming of our Lord. Disciples gave a divine honor to Jesus, they were all affected with the appearance of Jesus Christ, and they worship him the one who lives forever more. All the people of this earth that see our Jesus with an eye of faith are obligated to worship him Christ did not stand far away from them, he came near, right in the middle of them in order to show them a convincing proofs of his resurrection, and turned to who wave and doubt, he made them triumph over their doubts. Jesus Christ spoke to the disciples as a friend, speaks to one another - he then delivered the message of his kingdom in the world. He was sending them out as his ambassadors, gives them also their credentials. Jesus Christ said that all authority has been given to him - God's people are promised authority and power to proclaim the Gospel throughout the world. He told them to obey his command, to wait for the promised of the Father, which is the power of the Holy Spirit at Pentecost. We cannot expect the power to accompany our going to the nations without first following the pattern of the great commission to go to all the nations and preach and teach the Gospel.

Prayer:

Lord God Almighty bless us with the Holy Spirit to do your work on this earth, fulfill the great commission through us , help us by equipping us with everything we may need to proclaim the Gospel boldly and clearly to everyone in all the nations of the world. Live your life through us and let the Gospel reach the unreachable through us on this earth in their own language. With your mighty, matchless Holy Name we Pray now and forever. Amen.

OCTOBER 23RD

THE WORD OF GOD TRANSFORMS LIFE – LET THE WORD OF GOD BE YOUR TRANSFORMATION TODAY

Today's Scripture Reading:

"As he taught, Jesus said, watch out for the teachers of the law. They like to walk around in the flowing robes and be greeted in the marketplaces, and have the most important seats in the synagogues and the places of honor at banquets. They devour widows houses and for a show make lengthy prayers. Such men will be punished most severely." (Mark 12:38-40) NIV

Jesus Chris our Lord warns his disciples and his followers then and all the believers today that we should watch out for religious leaders who seek recognition and honor from others. Christ called such leaders hypocrites and describes them as frauds and deceivers in the area of observable righteousness people like that do not possess the indwelling Holy Spirit and his regenerating grace. While remaining in this condition, they cannot escape being condemned to hell. Some of religious leaders then and today advantage of unsuspecting and lonely widows. They receive offerings from the, exploiting the widows willingness to help those whom the widows believed to be men of God. By way of manipulation these leaders persuaded the widows to give more than they could afford, while they themselves lived in luxury on these misguided offerings, this same pattern continues to occurred throughout the history of the church, till today; ad has its experts in the art of religious extortion. Jesus Christ warns believers to be aware of those who did not practice what they preached.

Prayer:

Lord Jesus Christ help us to expose those who exploit people in the Church for various reasons, turn them around from evil to good, from greediness to people who are living a contemptible life. Bless us with your love and help us to follow you with a sincere heart that honor you and bring glory to your Holy Name. Amen.

OCTOBER 24TH

THE WORD OF GOD TRANSFORMS LIFE - LET THE WORD OF GOD BE YOUR TRANSFORMATION TODAY

Today's Scripture Reading:

"This is a trustworthy saying that deserve full acceptance (and for this we labor and strive), that we have put our hope in the living God, who is the Savior of all men, and especially of those who believe. Command and teach these things."
(1st Timothy 4:9-11) NIV

Jesus Christ our Lord and Savior want us who believes in him to set example for all other believers who want to hold a high position in the Church. This is the most important qualifications for a church leader. Elders in the church must set an example, if pastors, Ministers must be a model of faithfulness, purity, and perseverance in godly living. Leaders must live a godly life worth of emulation. believers must encourage each other to proceed in the ways of godliness where they profit balance the loss faithful saying which is worthy of all acceptation that our labors and losses in the service of God will be abundantly recompensed, so though we lose for Jesus Christ, we shall not lose by him. Jesus Chris is the rewarded of those who seek him and serve him. The Salvation that Christ has in store for those that believe is sufficient to recompense them for those that believe and is sufficient to recompense them for their services and sufferings. Believers were command to teach the Gospel faithfully and truthfully those who teach the Gospel must teach by their life.

Prayer:

Lord Jesus Christ teach us how to teach, preach, witnessing to the unsaved people of this world; and to proclaim the Gospel boldly and confidently to all the people in all the nations, help us to spread the true word of the Gospel with joy, fulfill the great commission through us, and let your Holy Name be exalted in all the earth and under the earth in the heart and mind, spirit, soul, and body of all the people of this earth. Touch the heart of the people so that they can be able to listen to the Gospel when witnessing to them, make them alive in things of God, not in the things of the world. Wash them clean, and use them for your great glory now and forever. Amen.

OCTOBER 25TH

THE WORD OF GOD TRANSFORMS LIFE - LET THE WORD OF GOD BE YOUR TRANSFORMATION TODAY

Today's Scripture Reading:

Do not commit adultery, do not murder, do not steal, and do not covet, and whatever other commandment there may be, are summed up in this one rule; love your neighbor as yourself." *(Romans 13:9) NIV*

All the believing Christians must be united and must be identified with Jesus Christ our Lord. We must obey all the commandment of God in our lives. Imitate the life of Jesus Christ as our pattern for good living, adopt his principles, most especially obey all his commands, and become like him. Believers must show the love of God; if the love of God is sincere, it is accepted by the fulfilling the love. We serve a good master, that has summed up all our duty in one word, and that a short word, and a sweet word love, the beauty and harmony of the universe. Loving and being loved is all the pleasure, joy, and happiness, of an intelligent being, for God is love. The last five words of the Ten Commandments, which he observes to be all summed up in this Royal law. One important Law that all the believers must watch out for is "Do not commit adultery" if husband and wife love each other they would not commit adultery against each other; this commandment is under the Name of love. It is a great violation of killing and stealing if there is love they will not do evil to each other by killing each other, or stealing from each other. Everyone will live in peace therefore, killing and stealing is under the Law of love. He that tempts other to sin, though he may pretend the most passionate love they really hate each other's; same with do not covet each other's properties. If they love each other they will not covet each other's property.

Prayer:

Lord Jesus Christ, our Lord and our Savior, compassionate gracious loving God, the true Son of God who came down from heaven to save us from all our sins. Lord Jesus Christ you are our redeemer King, listen to our prayers and answer our prayer, let the hearts of those who believe in you rejoices in you, let those who are spiritually dead be alive in you, call them to you our Lord, you are the channel of all blessings. Plant your Law in the heart and mind of sinners and the lost and people of all other religions. Bless us with the Spirit of steadfastness, so that we do not sin against you. Forgive us our past, present, and future sins, and wash us cleanse us from any unrighteousness, and clothe us with your righteousness and your endless love. Turn those who committed crimes of killing, coveting their neighbor's properties, those who are living adulterous life, forsake their ways and turn to you with repentance, and give their life to you. Bless them with a new life in you our Lord, and a new spirit, a new heart, a new mind that looks for the good of themselves and good of others around them, that loves everyone without prejudices, or hatred. Let your love grow in our hearts now and forever. Amen.

OCTOBER 26TH

THE WORD OF GOD TRANSFORMS LIFE - LET THE WORD OF GOD BE YOUR TRANSFORMATION TODAY

Today's Scripture Reading:

"Fathers, do not embitter your children, or they will become discouraged Slaves, Obey your earthly masters in everything; and do it, not only when their eye is on you and to win their favor, but with sincerity of heart and reverence for the Lord. Whatever you do, work at it with all your heart as working for the Lord, not for men, since you know that you will receive an inheritance from the Lord as a reward. It is the Lord Christ you are serving."
(Colossians 3:23-24, 21) NIV

Father and mother must make their responsibility to raise their children very well and lead them to Jesus Christ. Fathers and mothers must give their children the instruction and correction that belong to a Christian upbringing. Parents must follow the examples of Christian life and conduct. Slaves must obey their masters and people must follow the rules and regulations in their offices, either private office or government office. Everyone must practice living in a Christians way, even within their undesirable situation. Believers must regard all their labor as a service rendered to the Lord. We must work as though Christ were our employer, knowing that all work performed for the Lord will someday be rewarded. Fathers and mothers must be tender hearted toward their children, as well as children are to be obedient to their parents. They must not let their authority over their children be exercised with rigor and severity, but with kindness and gentleness, let us by holding the reins too tight might make them fly out with greater fierceness. As a believer we are really doing our duty to God when we are faithful in our duty to men.

Prayer:

Lord Jesus Christ blesses us with the spirit of gentleness and tenderness to train our children and lead them to your way, which is the way of peace. Help us to raise godly children for you our Lord, so that they will be useful for you from the beginning of their life to the end. In your great Holy Name , we pray now and forever. Amen.

OCTOBER 27ᵀᴴ

THE WORD OF GOD TRANSFORMS LIFE – LET THE WORD OF GOD BE YOUR TRANSFORMATION TODAY

Today's Scripture Reading:

"But if I drive out demons by the finger of God, then the kingdom of God has come to you. He who is not with me is against me, and he who does not gather with me, scatters." (Luke 11: 20, 23) NIV

Jesus Christ reveals the work of the devils and the success of the kingdom of God. The success of the kingdom of God on earth is in direct proportion to the destruction of the Devil's work and the deliverance of Sinners from the bondage of sin and the demonic; Satan and all his demonic the coming of Jesus Christ's kingdom on earth. Jesus demonstrates God's power and authority in driving out demons, overcoming Satan and overpowering Satan and plundering his possessions. For more on this - it means - the kingdom is primarily an assertion of God's power in action; God's kingdom will carry the idea of God coming into the worlds to assert his power, glory and right against Satan's dominion and the present course of this world. It is our God expressing himself powerfully in all his works. During Christ earthly ministry many synagogue rulers were against him It is impossible to remain neutral in the spiritual conflict between Christ's kingdom and the power of evil. Those who do not, belong with Christ, oppose Satan and evil have in reality set themselves against Jesus Christ. Every unbeliever was fighting either on the side of Christ and his righteousness, or on the side of Satan and the ungodly. Jesus Christ's Word indicts any attempt spiritual neutrality or compromise with unrighteous or any partial obedience.

Prayer:

Lord Jesus Christ let your Word abide in us. Be one with us as you are one with the Father. Bless us with the Holy Spirit power so that we can be one in you not against you. Empower us with your Spirit so that we can drive out demon just as you drove out demons during your earthly ministry. Let your kingdom come to this world and your will be done as it is written in heaven in the life of people in this world. All these, we pray now and forever. Amen.

OCTOBER 28TH

THE WORD OF GOD TRANSFORMS LIFE - LET THE WORD OF GOD BE YOUR TRANSFORMATION TODAY

Today's Scripture Reading:

"However, I consider my life with nothing to me, if I may finish the race and complete the task the Lord Jesus has given me - the task of testifying to the gospel of God's grace." (Acts 20:24)NIV

Believers must not count their life as very important; because our life is in the hands of Jesus Christ, who has the love and power to keep us safe so that we may be able to run the race that he gave us. Jesus Christ has the authority to preserve us from any evil; we believer cannot preserve our own life; what count most was that we finish the race in which God had called us. Wherever intended, even if in the sacrifice of our life, we would finish his course with joy and our prayers is that Christ Jesus will be exalted in my body, whether by life or by death. For Paul, and believers, life and the service of Jesus Christ is represented as a race that one must run with absolute faithfulness for our Lord. believers must lay in their heart Jesus Christ and heaven; Jesus is the only one and only believer's life. Our Prayer is to start the work that our Lord Jesus assigned for us to do for him on this earth and bring it to completion. Those that have their conversation in heaven can look down, not only upon the common troubles of this earth but upon the threatening rage and malice of hell itself, and say that none of these can hurt them, yet to an eye of faith life in Christ is the best life.

Prayer:

Lord Jesus Christ you are our Lord and Savior, our gracious master, and our great redeemer. be with me and do not let your Holy Spirit be taken away from you. Bless us with the Spirit of endurance so that we can be able to let go of our self and put you at the center of our heart now and forever. Amen

OCTOBER 29TH

THE WORD OF GOD TRANSFORMS LIFE - LET THE WORD OF GOD BE YOUR TRANSFORMATION TODAY

Today's Scripture Reading:

"I will give you the keys of the kingdom of heaven; whatever you bind on earth will be bound in heaven, and whatever loose on earth will be loosed in heaven." (Matthew 16:19) NIV

Our Lord Jesus Christ during his earthy ministry reveals to us the power of his kingdom in heaven that: God's kingdom's to be entered with keys, and the keys represent authority for entry. The keys are also related to the binding and loosing. Jesus, to whom the Father gave all authority in heaven and on earth, delegated his authority which, represented by the keys to Peter and the church for carrying out the great commission. This authority for proclaiming the Gospel includes his delegated authority to bind and to loose on earth. In the spirit filled proclamation of the Gospel, the church has been given the keys means the authority to bind demons and diseases and to lose the prisoners of sin, addictions and sickness from the bondage and captivity into salvation just as Christ did while he was on earth. The binding and losing an already accomplished provision because of Jesus' finished work on the cross that is now release on earth through the church to those who will believe in Christ into salvation. As the master of the house gives the keys to the steward; the keys of the store where provisions we kept. It is a power to bind and loose, to shut and open. It is a power which Jesus Christ has promised to own the due administration of; it shall be bound in heaven, and it shall be loose in heaven. The word of the Gospel, in the mouth of faithful minister; is to be looked upon, not as the word of man, but as the word of God, and is to be received accordingly. Now the keys of heaven are as follows. The key of knowledge and understanding which is the extra-ordinary power of kind which means things that were for bidden by the Law of Moses Old Testament will now to be allowed, and something allowed Old Testament now are for bidden, believers and apostles were empowered to reveals this truth to the world. Jesus Christ gave all the believing Christians the power to shut or open the Gospel book to people of the world as the case required. The key of discipline: Christ Jesus ministry have a power to admit into the church go and disciple all nations, baptizing them; those who profess faith in Christ, and obedience to him, admit them, then by baptism.

Prayer:

Lord Jesus, you call us into your eternal glory. Keep us save, and guide us with the power of your Spirit. Live your life through us that every work of the enemy we bound on earth will be bound in heaven. Bless us with your full presence all the days of our life, use us mightily for your glory, and fulfill the great commission through us and in us. Amen.

OCTOBER 30TH

THE WORD OF GOD TRANSFORMS LIFE - LET THE WORD OF GOD BE YOUR TRANSFORMATION TODAY

Today's Scripture Reading:

"He replied, blessed rather are those who hear the word of God and obey it. No one lights a lamp and puts it in a place where it will be hidden, or under a bowl. Instead he puts it on its stand, so that those who come in may see the light. Your eye is the Lamp of your body." (Luke 11:28, 33-34) NIV

The Lord Jesus Christ does want to get carried away by the flattering word of the woman; He replied that it is a blessing for those who hear his word and obey it; keep it to the heart, learn from it, study it and grow in the knowledge of God through it. This type of word of flattering is still going on today, lest make a Minister, or Pastor be proud of their position, or to make themselves feel too important and, and they do not give glory to the Holy Spirit who indwell them and who is their teacher. Jesus Christ let the woman knows that the faith full and obedient followers are more blessed. The eye is the Lamp of our body means that the eye is the body's receiving light. If the eye is healthy, then one can fully receive and use light. If the eye is defective, then darkness prevails, and one cannot see in order to walk or goes to work. Likewise, when people's spiritual eyes, their attitudes, motives, and desires are directed toward God's will, then the light of his word enters their hearts to produce blessings of fruits and salvation. But if their desires are not focused on things of God, then God's revelation and his truth will have no effect.

Prayer:

Lord God Almighty, Father, Son and the Holy Spirit, bless us with your word your word is true, make us a light to those who sit in the shadow of darkness in this world so that the Gospel will reach them and light up their life and they will be useful for you. In Jesus Christ's glorious, mighty Holy Name, we pray. Amen.

OCTOBER 31ST

THE WORD OF GOD TRANSFORMS LIFE - LET THE WORD OF GOD BE YOUR TRANSFORMATION TODAY

Today's Scripture Reading:

"My son, do not forget my teaching, but keep my commands in your heart, for they will prolong your life many years and bring you peace and prosperity." (Proverbs 3:1-2) NIV

This Scripture reveals a life of communion with God where God will be of unspeakable advantage. Believers must have a continuing regard to God's precepts, God's law, and his commandments, as our rule. Not on our heads, but on our hearts, believers must keep God's commandments; it will encourage us to submit ourselves to all the restraints and injunctions of the Divine Law. We are assured that it is a certain way to long life and prosperity is to submit ourselves to all generally speaking, obeying God, and living by his Holy principles will result in better health, a longer life, and happiness and more prosperous life. However, this is a general principle it must not be taken as an absolute guarantee to which there is no exceptions. At times, the righteous are afflicted and they do not live long lives. Conversely, sometimes it is the wicked that are healthy and prosperous, though their final judgment is the same. God's mercy in promising and his truth in performing this is the greatest honor that we are capable of this world, to have interest in the mercy and truth of God. Believers must take a pleasure to apply the Word of God to themselves assuredly and thinking about the Word of God.

Prayer:

Lord God Almighty, we glorified your Holy Name for everything you have done for us on this earth. You call us and chose us to serve you with joy unspeakable throughout our life. In your mercy bless us with joy, live your life through us forever; make what people think is not possible, possible in their lives. Help us to love you more and more every day of our lives. Amen.

DAILY REFLECTION NOTES

NOVEMBER

NOVEMBER 1ST

THE WORD OF GOD CLEANSES US –
LET THE WORD OF GOD CLEANSE YOU TODAY.

Today Scripture Reading

"Meanwhile, when a crowd of many thousands had gathered, so that they were trampling on one another, Jesus began to speak first to his disciples, saying: Be on your guard against the yeast of the Pharisees, which is hypocrisy. There is nothing concealed that will not be disclosed, or hidden that will not be made known. What you have said in the dark will be heard in the daylight, and what you have whispered in the ear in the inner rooms will be proclaimed from the roofs." (Luke 12:1-3)NIV

Jesus Christ our Lord and Savior condemns the hypocrisy of the Pharisees; he warned his disciples to be careful that this sin does not enter their own lives and ministry. Hypocrisy means acting as if you are what you are not for example, acting publicly as godly and faithful believer, when in reality you harbor an addictive habit or some other hidden sin such as lust, greed, jealousy, or bitterness. The hypocrite is a deceiver in the area of observable righteousness. Since hypocrisy involves living lives of lie, it means that the person is living under the dominion of Satan, the father of lie. Jesus Christ warns his disciples that all hypocrisy and hidden sin will be exposed, if not in this life, certainly on the Day of Judgment. What is done secretly behind closed doors will be at some point, openly revealed. Hypocrisy is a sign that one does not fear God, and does not possess the Holy Spirit with his regenerating grace.

Prayer:

Lord Jesus Christ take away any form of hypocrisy behavior from your children through the power of the Holy Spirit, wash them clean from any unrighteousness, clothe them with your righteousness and love so that we can serve you with the spirit of holiness, and full of grace and truth, serve you sincerely and truthfully throughout our life. Amen.

NOVEMBER 2ND

THE WORD OF GOD CLEANSES US – LET THE WORD OF GOD CLEANSE YOU TODAY.

TODAY SCRIPTURE READING

"He who heeds discipline shows the way to life, but whoever ignores correction leads other astray."
(Proverbs 10:7) NIV

All Christian believers must listen to instruction and face discipline so that they can live a life of peace and joy. Those who are in the right, and do not only receive instruction, but retain it, keep it for their own use, that they may govern themselves by it, and keep it for the benefit of others, that they may instruct them. Those who do not want to be instructed do not follow instruction. They were given instruction, but they did not receive, but willfully and obstinately refuse it. They will not be taught their duty or responsibility because it discovers their faults to them. They are like a traveler that has missed his way, and cannot bear to be shown the right way. Believers who makes it a practice to listen to godly instructions stay on the road of life. The one who turns his back on good advice goes astray himself and heads other astray as well.

Believing Christians must be diligent and ready to face discipleship, study to show himself, or herself a good soldier of the Lord Jesus Christ. Believers must listen to Fatherly instruction, physically, or through the instruction of the Holy Spirit.

Prayer:

Lord Jesus Christ open our heart, minds, and soul, so that we can be able to listen and follow your instruction through your Word, help us to be able to grow in your Word, obey your Word, and grow in your Word. Lord Jesus, bless us abundantly, immeasurable so that we may be able to do your will and follow your instructions in order that we may have a live in you forever. Amen.

NOVEMBER 3ᴿᴰ

THE WORD OF GOD CLEANSES US- LET THE WORD OF GOD CLEANSE YOU TODAY.

TODAY SCRIPTURE READING

"Wealth brings many friends, but a poor man's friend deserts him, He who gets wisdom loves his own soul; he who cherishes understanding prospers." (Proverbs 19:4, 8) NIV

The Scripture reveals what is going on in our society every day. There are always superficial friends that are attracted to the wealthy as flies are drawn to honey; a poor person has few friends because he or she cannot provide anyone with financial or personal gain. New Testament believing Christians were warns not to follow this type of attitude. They must love and be friends to everyone either poor or wealthy. Get wisdom, get knowledge, and grace, and be acquaintance with God, those that do so, show that they love their souls, and they will be found to have done themselves the greatest kindness imaginable. He that keeps understanding shall certainly find goodness, and all the good things in life. It is a form of enlightened and self-interest to seek wisdom and commonsense. As well as to hold on to understanding and insight is a sure road to success. The fact that wealth makes many friends is a proof of the innate self-fishiness of the human heart. The poor is separated from his friends because the latter wants only the friendship that will benefit him. Even within the local church people clip to each other because they feels that they were wealthier than the other person or they are more educated than the other person. Believers should love each other the same as Jesus Christ loves the church.

Prayer:

Lord Jesus Christ, compassionate, gracious loving God, Father of all mercies, sustainer of all things, we your people need wisdom; bless us with your great wisdom, we need godly wisdom to serve you in our lives – great wisdom will help us to follow you without changing to the left or to the right, but help us to love you more and more every day of our life on this earth. Shower all your great blessings, success upon us as well as great knowledge and understanding of the people of this world. Amen.

NOVEMBER 4TH

THE WORD OF GOD CLEANSES US—
LET THE WORD OF GOD CLEANSES YOU TODAY.

Today Scripture Reading:

"For to me, to live is Christ and to die is gain. If I am to go on living in the body, this will mean fruitful labor for me. Yet what shall I chose? I do not know." (Philippians 1:21-22) NIV

Apostle Paul said: "to die is gain" *True* believing Christians those who believe in Jesus Christ, they don't need to fear death. They know that God has a purpose for their living and that death, when it comes, is simply the end of their earthly mission and the beginning of a greater life with Jesus Christ. Believing Christians should not live for money, fame, or pleasure. The object of Paul's life was to love the Lord, worship, and serve the Lord Jesus. He wanted his life to be like the life of Christ. He wanted the Savior to live his life through him to died is to be with Christ and to be like him forever. It means to serve the Lord with truthful heart and with the feet that will never go astray. Believers must be praying to the Lord to live longer so that they will be able to serve him, and call more sinners and the lost to him. This should be the undoubted character of all the believers, and every good Christians to live in Jesus Christ. The glory of Christ should be the end of our life. All those who live in Christ to them, to die will be gain. Death is a great loss to a carnal people who are worldly; but to a good Christians it is gain.

Prayer:

Lord Jesus Christ, bless us in all the areas of our lives, reserve us so that we can be able to serve you, and be more useful to you keep us safe at all times, help us to be one in you as you and Father are one, help us to love you more and more every day of our life, bless us with a new life in you, that will honor you glorify you, adore you every day of our lives. Amen.

NOVEMBER 5TH

THE WORD OF GOD CLEANSES US–
LET THE WORD OF GOD CLEANSES YOU TODAY.

Today Scripture Reading:

"I tell you the truth, some who are standing here will not taste death before they see the Son of Man coming in his kingdom. "
(Matthew 16:28) NIV

The Son of Man coming in his kingdom refers to the event of Pentecost when Christ baptized his people with the Holy Spirit and great power, accompanied by miraculous signs is demonstrations of Christ's exaltation and kingdom's presence. It was so near, that some people attending him should be so near, that people attending or standing there, thought that it will happen in their lifetime. Jesus Christ at the end of time shall come in his Father's glory, but now, in the fullness of time, Christ was to come in his own kingdom, or his mediatorial kingdom. The Apostles and all the believing Christians were to set Christ's kingdom; the nearer the church's deliverances are, the more cheerful should we be in our suffering for Jesus Christ but by their sufferings. This shall be done and the reward of our Lord Jesus, according to their service is going to be done shortly in this present age. The reward is deferred to that day, the day of his Second Coming according to their works, and according to what they were and did, now in the fullness of time, he was to come to his own kingdom, his mediatorial kingdom.

Prayer:

Lord Jesus Christ you are our blessed hope, let your Will be done on earth as it is written in heaven, let your full presence be known in our lives; let the people of this earth give their life to you faithfully and sincerely. Let those who seek you find you, our Lord, when people of this earth call unto you sincerely look down from heaven and answer their prayers. Fill up our life with yourself Lord Jesus; we cannot live without you on this earth our Lord. Amen.

NOVEMBER 6TH

THE WORD OF GOD CLEANSES US–
LET THE WORD OF GOD CLEANSES YOU TODAY.

Today Scripture Reading:

"He chose to give us birth through the word of truth, that we might be a kind of first fruits of all he created." (James 1:18) NIV

Our Lord Jesus Christ saves us not by any merit of our own, but his own free will. Jesus Christ has unmerited love for us on this earth. The assignment that the Lord assigned to us can only be done by obedience to the word of truth. The Word of God applied to all believers by the power of the Holy Spirit. The love of Jesus Christ was entirely voluntary on his part. This will make us to worship him truthfully and spiritually. By our spiritual birth we become adopted as a child of God. God Almighty is unchangeable, and our changes and shadows are not from any mutability, or shadows, alterations in him, but from ourselves. A true believing Christian is a creature begotten anew. It is God's own will; not by our skill, or power; but purely from goodwill and the grace of God. Whereby this means which is effective, that is, by the Gospel. This Gospel is indeed the Word of truth, or else it could not have produced such real, such casting, and such great and noble effects. Jesus Christ is the one and only the first fruit among the brethren. Christians in Christ are the first fruits among all the creatures.

Prayer:

Lord Jesus Christ protect and lead us to your way everlasting. Create in us a new heart that we may be able to worship you with prayers in sanctification with supplication. Remember us in time of affliction and danger; you are our deliverer - hear our prayers O' lord and have mercy upon us. Amen.

NOVEMBER 7TH

THE WORD OF GOD CLEANSES US—
LET THE WORD OF GOD CLEANSES YOU TODAY.

Today Scripture Reading:

"The Lord upholds all those who fall and lifts up all who are bowed down. The eyes of all look to you, and you give them their food at the proper time. You open your hand and satisfy the desires of every living things." (Psalm 145:14-16) NIV

The Lord God Almighty supports all those who are sinking, and it is honor to help the weak, and the distress, even they fall God will not cast them out, or down. When those who are bowed down by oppression and afflictions are raised up, it was God that raised them. And those who are under the burden of sin, if they come to Christ by faith, he will have mercy on them, and he will raise them up. Jesus Christ is very ready to hear their prayer and answer their prayers. The goodness of God appears in what he does, for all his creatures in general; all the creatures live upon God, and, as they had their being from him at first, so on him they depend for the continuance of it. The creatures that have no knowledge of God, nor are capable of the knowledge of God, and

yet they are waiting upon God, because they seek their food according to the instinct which the God of nature has put on them. Believers in particular, Christ Jesus governs them as reasonable creatures. The Lord is just and right in all the activities of his government. He will hear our prayer and help us if we worship him and serve him with the Spirit of holiness.

Prayer:

Lord Jesus Christ, you are our Lord, there is no other God like you, you uphold us with your Holy hands, when we are falling you do not let us fall, your merciful eye watch us grow. You are God of all creations; bless us with the Spirit of holiness so that we can serve you forever. Amen.

NOVEMBER 8TH

THE WORD OF GOD CLEANSES US –
LET THE WORD OF GOD CLEANSES YOU TODAY.

Today Scripture Reading:

"Do everything without complaining or arguing, so that you may become blameless and pure, children of God without fault in a crooked and depraved generation in which you shine like stars in the universe; as you holdout the word of life – in order that I may boast on the day of Christ that I did not run or labor for nothing." (Philippians 2:14-16a) NIV

Our Lord Jesus Christ and the apostles in their teaching emphasized that the Universe we live now is an unbelieving and perverse generation. The people of the world are in deception and in darkness, and they have a different view of life in value and in religion. They follow immoral ways of life and reject the norms of God's Word. Whereby, believing Christians have a different worldview and values, and are therefore, separated from the world. Believers are to be like Christ in loyalty to the Lord Jesus Christ. We are to be blameless, pure undefiled and without fault, in order to proclaim Christ's glorious redemption to the lost world.

Believers must not quarrel, but be in a cheerful obedience to the commands of God. Believers must obey God's commands, be peaceable and love one another. We should all our work without disputing, or grumbling or complaining. The light of the truth and the life of religion are often lost in the midst of disputation. Believers must let their conversation be blameless toward all people. Believers must be different from all other people in the world.

Prayer:

Lord Jesus Christ bless us with the spirit of humbleness, gentleness, and obedience without measure. Let your light shine upon us, so that people of this world will see your light shining upon us and be converted unto you, and give their life to you faithfully and sincerely. May they worship you as they should, and show other people around them the way of salvation. Amen.

NOVEMBER 9TH

THE WORD OF GOD CLEANSES US –
LET THE WORD OF GOD CLEANSES YOU TODAY.

Today Scripture Reading:

"All Scripture is God – breathed and is useful for teaching rebuking, correcting and training, in righteousness, so that the man of God may be thoroughly equipped for every good work." (2nd Timothy 3:16-17) NIV

The Holy Scripture is God breathed means that our heavenly Father, Jesus Christ his only Son, Holy Spirit the giver of life, forever one God, breathe on all the believing Christians, the breathed of life through is Word. Jesus Christ yesterday, today, and forever still continue to breathe on us the breath of life through his Word, Minster's preaching, and teaching, witness the Gospel to the people of the world. God Almighty exalted his Holy Name above all things. God exalted his Holy Name above all things. God exalted his Holy Name, and his Word unchanging. God have authority in all things pertaining to life and godliness. Believers must use the authority of the Word of God in all the church, for teaching, rebuking when people do wrong and for correcting, for teaching, rebuking when people do wrong and for correcting and training when people lack the knowledge of the word of God. No one can submit to Jesus Christ's lordship without submitting to God's word as the most important and ultimate authority. God's inspired word is the expression of his great wisdom and character and therein, he was able to give wisdom and spiritual life through faith in Jesus Christ to those who love him, and those who receive his word, and thoroughly filled with the indwelling power of the Holy Spirit to do good work.

Prayer:

Lord Jesus Christ, let your word be our spiritual food; feed us with your word, your word is true, help us to grow in your word, help us to be able to do good work with your word growing inside us, and bring sinners and the lost unto you through all the days of our lives. Amen.

NOVEMBER 10TH

THE WORD OF GOD CLEANSES US –
LET THE WORD OF GOD CLEANSES YOU TODAY.

Today Scripture Reading:

"Therefore God exalted him to the highest place and gave him the Name that is above every Name, that at the Name of Jesus every knee should bow, in heaven and on earth and under the earth, and every tongue confess that Jesus Christ is Lord, to the glory of God the Father." (Philippians 2:9-11) NIV

God Almighty exalted our Lord Jesus Christ because he humbles himself to the cross. Jesus Christ voluntarily laid down his glory and empty himself, his heavenly glory, his position and eternity, right, especially the use of divine attributes, his deity all were suspended and he put on humanity suffering, ill-treatment, hatred and death on the cross for my sin and for the sins of the people in the world. Because Jesus Christ humbles himself, God exalted him; and highly exalted him as a person, the human nature as well as the divine. His exaltation here is made to consist in honor and power of God almighty give Christ a Name above every Name. God want the whole creation must be in subjection to Jesus Christ;

everything in heaven and everything on earth and under the earth, all the inhabitants of heaven and earth, the living, and the dead. Believers and unbelievers people of all other religion, Idol worshiper, Pagan worshipers must worship our Lord Jesus Christ all should pay a solemn homage to the Lord. The kingdom of Christ reaches to heaven and earth, and to all the creatures on earth and to the dead as well as to all the living all their tongue to confess that Jesus Christ is the Lord to the glory of God the Father.

Prayer:

Almighty God and our everlasting Father, by your Spirit the whole body of your faithful people is governed sanctified and rejoice; receive our supplications and all our prayers every time we kneel down to pray to you. Help us to truly love you and serve you throughout our lives. Lord Jesus Christ in your powerful Holy Name hear our prayer, help us to worship you in Spirit and in truth bless us with yourself so that we can love you better; you are our Lord and Savior all life dwell in you. Amen.

NOVEMBER 11ᵀᴴ

THE WORD OF GOD CLEANSES US –
LET THE WORD OF GOD CLEANSES YOU TODAY.

Today Scripture Reading:

"The God who made the world and everything in it is the Lord of heaven and earth and does not live in the temple built by hands. And he is not served by human hands, as if he needed anything, because he himself gives all men life and breath and everything else. From one man he made every nation, that they should inhabit the whole earth; and he determined the times set for them and the exact places where they should live for in him we live and move and have our being. As some of your own poets have said, we are his offspring." (Acts 17:24-28) NIV

On one occasion that Paul visits in Athens, he taught them that the true God, by his work of creation and providence, is the God who made heaven and the earth and everything in it. The same thing is still going on among us today. People should come out of idolatry and worship the true living God. Our God, according to the operations of his infinite power, and according to the contrivance of an infinite wisdom, made the world and all things therein, the origin of which was owing to an eternal mind. God is the Creator of all men. He made the first man, and he makes every man. He has made all nations of men, not only men in all nations but as nations. He made them of one blood, of one and the same nature, that they may be engaged in mutual affection and assistance. God is an infinite Spirit. He is close unto us to receive our services we render to him and to give us his mercies as we ask him, wherever we are, even if we did the asking close to the altar, or temple. We may be in a palace, cottage, in a crowd, or in a corner, in city, or in a desert, in a cave, in a village or in the depth of the sea, or far away in the mountain wilderness – God is not far from every one of us. Believers have a necessary and constant dependence upon God's providence, as the streams have upon the spring, and beams upon the sun.

Prayer:

Lord Jesus Christ, in you we move, we have our being, we give you thanks that you are not too far from those who loved you. In your mercies, forgive all our sins and make us your own forever. In honor of your glorious Holy Name, we pray. Amen.

NOVEMBER 12ᵀᴴ

THE WORD OF GOD CLEANSES US –
LET THE WORD OF GOD CLEANSES YOU TODAY.

Today Scripture Reading:

"But just as he who called you is Holy, so be Holy in all you do; for it is written: be Holy, because I am Holy." (1ˢᵗ Peter 1:15-16) NIV

God Almighty spoke through Apostle Peter in this revealed Scripture: "Be Holy", because I am Holy". Our Lord and Savior Jesus Christ want all believing Christians to be Holy, and to live a Holy life. God is Holy, and what is true of God the Father Almighty must be true of his people. Holiness carries the thought of being separated from the ungodly ways of this world and set ourselves apart for the love of our Savior Lord, for the service and for the worship of our God. Holiness is the goal and the purpose of our election in Jesus Christ; it means that believer must be like God and being dedicated all our being to him, living for him the true life living to please him in everything we do. Believing Christians are made Holy by the sanctifying work of the Holy Spirit by the power of the cross in delivering us from sin by being renewed in the likeness of Jesus

Christ, and by an infusion of grace to obey God according to his Word. God Almighty calls us through Jesus Christ his only begotten Son to be Holy and set apart for his personal use. It is a great favor, godly favor to be called effectually by divine grace of God into this possession of all the blessings of the new covenant; and great is the favor with strong obligations; believers were enabling as well as oblige to be Holy. God almighty Father So and Holy Spirit required complete holiness, he desired, and he made a task for every believing Christians to be Holy as he is Holy.

Prayer:

Lord Jesus Christ, help us to be Holy and live a Holy life from this earth to heaven with the power of your Word. Plant your Word in our heart and mind; make it fruitful, and bear more and more fruits to your kingdom. Help us by fulfilling your heart desire and plan of salvation in our life, let your will be done in our life and let your purpose be accomplished in our life. In your great mighty Holy Name , we pray. Amen.

NOVEMBER 13TH

THE WORD OF GOD CLEANSES US –
LET THE WORD OF GOD CLEANSES YOU TODAY.

Today Scripture Reading:

"For this is what the high and lofty one says – he who lives forever, whose Name is Holy: I live in a high and Holy place, but also with him who is contrite and lowly in Spirit, to revive the spirit of the lowly and to revive the heart of the contrite." (Isaiah 57:15) NIV

Our Lord Jesus Christ comfort those who are lowly and of contrite spirit. God lives in a high and Holy place promises to dwell with those who are contrite and lowly in spirit. Contrite means those who are broken hearted because of their sinfulness or because of the enemy's oppression, and who cry out to God for deliverance - David cry out to God because of his sin with Bathsheba Lowly in spirit means those who humble, or bowed down by adversity. God responds to the cry of such people in order to revive them with the light and life of his presence. People of this world who are contrite, it means those who trust God with their hearts shall be revived. God's glory will appear very high in his greatness and in his majesty. God is the high and lofty one; there is no one, no creature like him, no one to be compared with him. God is both immortal and immutable – there is an infinite rectitude in his nature. His Name is Holy and all that, people to be acquainted with him must know him as a Holy God who dwell in the high and Holy place, the people of this world must know who God is; he dwell above the heavens.

Prayer:

Lord God almighty from whom all the blessings flows, who dwells above the heavens, heaven is your throne and the earth is your foot stool, help us to call unto you in everything we are going through, revive us and make us your own, help us to live a Holy life from this earth to heaven, with the honor of your Holy Name now and forever. Amen.

NOVEMBER 14ᵀᴴ

THE WORD OF GOD CLEANSES US –
LET THE WORD OF GOD CLEANSES YOU TODAY.

Today Scripture Reading:

"Blessed are those who are persecuted because of righteousness, for there is the kingdom of heaven. You are the light of the world a City on a hill cannot be hidden. Neither do people light a lamp and put it under a bowl. Instead they put it on its stand, and it gives light to everyone in the house." (Matthew 5:10, 14) NIV

Our Lord Jesus Christ points this out during his earthly ministry that the believing Christians will face persecution. Persecution will be the lot of all who seek to live in harmony with God's Word for the sake of righteousness: Those who uphold God's standards of truth, justice and purity, and who at the same time refuse to compromise with the present evil society or the life style of lukewarm believers will undergo unpopularity, rejection and criticism. Persecution and opposition will come from the world and at the time from those within the professing church. Everyone who wants to live a godly in Jesus Christ will be persecuted. They are persecuted for righteousness sake, they are very happy this is the greatest paradox of all, and is very peculiar to all the Christians. They were persecuted, they are blessed, it is an honor to them; it is an opportunity of glorifying Jesus Christ and experiencing special comfort and tokens of his presence. They are the light of the world, but more glorious, truly the light of the first day of the way, so is the morning light of everyday, so is the Gospel, and those who spread it around the world. All those who around them admire them have an eye upon them, command, rejoice in them, some people hate them, as the light of the world they are intended to illuminate and give light to others.

Prayer:

Lord Jesus Christ compassionate gracious loving God, slow to anger full of truth and righteousness, merciful and mighty God, we give you thanks O Lord, you are the only one that listen to our prayers and answer prayers help us to be the light of this world, let your light shine through us so that we can know you, give our life to you. Help us to grow in your light; and let your light shine through us to other people around us. Let our life full of your light, that there will be no darkness, and the power of darkness cannot prevail against us. Let the people of this world, those who sit in the shadow of darkness see your light follow your light and stay in your light forever. Amen.

NOVEMBER 15ᵀᴴ

THE WORD OF GOD CLEANSES US –
LET THE WORD OF GOD CLEANSES YOU TODAY.

Today Scripture Reading:

"His brothers then came and threw themselves down before him, We are your slaves, they said. But Joseph said to them, Don't be afraid. Am I in the place of God? You intended to harm me, but God intended it for good to accomplish what is now being done, the saving of many lives. So then, don't be afraid, I will provide for you and your children. And he reassured them and spoke kindly to them." (Genesis 50: 18-21) NIV

After the death of Jacob, his older sons were afraid of Joseph, they thought Joseph will revenge and punish them for what they did to him many years ago, selling him to slavery but Joseph with a great deal of compassion with his brothers. They humble themselves before him, confessed their fault, and begged for his pardon – forgive the trespass we have done, they pleaded, and we are the servant of God by Father. Joseph with a great deal of compassion, confirm his reconciliation and affection to them, his compassion appears, Joseph wept, and tears of tenderness came out of his eyes upon their submission. Joseph replies and directed them to look up to God in their repentance, make your peace with God, and then you will find it an easy matter to make your peace with me. He told them that God brought great good wonderfully and powerfully out their evil did. Same today God always bring good out of evil, and promotes the designs of his providence even by the sons of men; not that he is the author of sin, but his infinite wisdom overrules events, that, in the issue, that ends in his praise which in its own nature had a direct tendency to his dishonor as putting of Christ death. He assures them of the continuance of his kindness to them.

Prayer:

Lord God almighty you that forgive those who put you on the cross, forgive us our sins and bless us with the spirit of forgiveness so that we can be able to forgive those who persecute us for righteousness; we give you praise for the work redemption, resurrection of the body and life everlasting. Help us to be able to forgive as you forgive our Lord. Amen.

NOVEMBER 16TH

THE WORD OF GOD CLEANSES US –
LET THE WORD OF GOD CLEANSES YOU TODAY.

Today Scripture Reading:

"Let us, then, go to him outside the camp, bearing the disgrace he bore. For here we do not have an enduring city, but we are looking for the city that is to come." (Hebrews 13:13) NIV

All the believing Christians who are followers of Jesus Christ involve in going outside the camp; the camp represented Judaism. For believers, it represents the world with all its sinful pleasures, ungodly values, and temporal goods. Believers must bear the disgrace that our Lord Jesus Christ bore in order to follow him, sympathize with him, be his friend, identify with him and bear his testimony to the world. In going outside the gate we find ourselves strangers and aliens on the earth. Yet, we are not without a city, for we seek a city that is to come, a city with foundations whose architect and builder is God. Believers must be willing to bear Christ's reproach; we must necessarily go forth in a little time by death, we should go forth by faith, and seek in Jesus Christ the rest and settlement which this world cannot afford. Let us make a right use of this altar let s bring our sacrifices to the altar – The sacrifice of praise to God, which we should offer up to God continually. Believers must include all adoration and prayer, as well as thanksgiving, which is the fruit of our lips.

Prayer:

Lord Jesus Christ, our Lord, and our Savior, gracious and full of truth and righteousness, you are the God of blessings from you all the goodness flows. Bless us with your life, in order that we may be a blessing to others who need your blessings. Create a new heart In all your children, wherever they may be on this earth to serve you and honor your Holy Name. Create in us a new spirit, so that we can be able to pray to you in spirit and in truth forever. Amen.

NOVEMBER 17TH

THE WORD OF GOD CLEANSES US –
LET THE WORD OF GOD CLEANSES YOU TODAY.

Today Scripture Reading:

"When a Samaritan woman came to draw water, Jesus said to her, will you give me a drink? His disciples had gone into town to buy food. Jesus answered her. If you knew the gift of God and who it is that asking you for a drink, you would have asked him and he would have given you a living water." (John4: 7-8, 10) NIV

Our Lord Jesus Christ was having conversation with the Samaritan woman at Jacob's well, Christ reveals his commitment to his heavenly Father's purpose and his own inner desire to bring this person to eternal life Jesus concerning passion was to save the lost, a goal infinitely more important to him than food and drink. All the believing Christians must follow Jesus's example. All around us people are ready to hear God's Word; we must find ways to speak to them about their spiritual need and about Jesus, who can meet their need. We see here in this story of a Samaritan woman and our Lord Jesus Christ, how the divine providence brings about a glorious purpose by an event which seem to us for future and accidental. Jesus did not go to the city with his disciples for food. But he sat down at the well weary and tired, thirsty, and hungry for food which is not an earthly food but a spiritual food. He had a good work to do at that time. Jesus Christ preach to multitude desire also to preach to a single person, he told us that it is a great joy in the middle of angels in heaven when one sinner save, and he is setting us an example by preaching to the Samaritan woman at the well, and woman, a poor woman a stranger, and most especially a Samaritan woman, this is to teach us who will follow his footstep that it is really a joy in the heaven when one sinner saved, Christ teach us to do likewise, as those that know what a glorious achievement it is to help to save one soul from death. Here Jesus Christ becomes a beggar in order to save soul of the same Samaritan woman "give me to drink". The Scripture says he became poor, so that he can save sinners. Christ is still begging through his members' believers today; he wants us to help those who are poor in his Name. Believers must be like Jesus, put on goodness and kindness. Jesus used this opportunity to introduce her to divine and heavenly things, and that her life is in need of a Savior. Jesus Christ is the gift of God to the world, the richest token of God's love to us.

Prayer:

Lord Jesus Christ, you are a blessed Savior, the unspeakable gift of God to the world, help us to know you more and more in our life. Help us to be full of your divine presence everyday of our life. Witness through us to the sinner and to the lost. In Jesus Christ's glorious, mighty Holy Name, we pray. Amen.

NOVEMBER 18ᵀᴴ

THE WORD OF GOD CLEANSES US –
LET THE WORD OF GOD CLEANSES YOU TODAY.

Today Scripture Reading:

"When you fast, do not look somber as the hypocrites do, for they disfigure their faces to show others they are fasting. Truly I tell you, they have received their reward in full. 17 But when you fast, put oil on your head and wash your face, 18 so that it will not be obvious to others that you are fasting, but only to your Father, who is unseen; and your Father, who sees what is done in secret, will reward you. (Matthew 6:16-18 NIV)

The Scripture refers to the discipline of abstaining from food for spiritual purpose. Fasting is also practiced as a spiritual discipline along with continuous prayer. There are three main forms of fasting in the Scriptures (1) The normal fast abstaining from food, solid or liquid but not from water; (2) The absolute fast which means abstaining from all foods and water some people call it total fasting. This type of fasting must not be observed for more than three days because of health reasons, such as kidney problems, and risk of the kidneys that may shut down and the body may dehydrate. Moses and Elijah took this type of fasting for 40-days but only under supernatural conditions; (3) The partial fast is a restriction of diet rather than complete abstention. Our Lord Jesus Christ practiced this discipline and taught that it should be part of Christian devotion and an act of preparation for His return. The New Testament church practiced fasting. Fasting with prayer has several purposes a to honor God, to humble ourselves before God Almighty, and to experience more grace and God's intimate presence. Fasting is also a way to mourn over personal sin and failure, mourn over the sins of the church, nation, and the Universe.

Prayer

Lord Jesus Christ, our Savior, and the Savior of the people in the world, merciful and mighty, compassionate, and faithful, Holy God. When we fast and pray have mercy upon us and hear our prayers and answer our prayers in your timing. Wash us clean from any unrighteousness, protect, provide, guide, and lead us to the way of Holiness and life everlasting. Strengthen us in our prayer life, and bring us closer to you, so that you can use us in a higher level with Holy Spirit Power. In Your Holy Name we pray, amen.

NOVEMBER 19TH

THE WORD OF GOD CLEANSES US–
LET THE WORD OF GOD CLEANSES YOU TODAY.

Today Scripture Reading:

"But if Christ is in you, your body is dead because of sin, yet your spirit is alive because of righteousness. And if the spirit of him who raised Jesus from the dead is living in you, he who raised Christ from the dead will also give life to your mortal bodies through his spirit, who lives in you." (Romans 8:10-11) NIV

Because our sins and its ravaging effect, the body in the natural state is under the process and sentence to death, even for the believer. Our bodies ultimately will be redeemed by the resurrection or by the transformation at Jesus Christ's Second Coming. Jesus came to give us life have now at his first coming; the Holy Spirit who raised Jesus Christ from the dead desire to impart life even tour mortal bodies as we embrace the life of Jesus Christ within us. The Holy Spirit is the life giver – is the spirit of life. The law of the spirit of life is the regulating, activating power and life of the Holy Spirit operating in the hearts and mind of all believing Christians the true believers receive Christ, if Christ now lives in our body and souls our body and soul good and dead because of sin, sin can no longer dwell in the body that Jesus Christ live in because it is the sin that kills the body, but Christ lives in our body the body is life to righteousness because the spirit is life. When the body dies the spirit is life and is fit to partake of eternal life. The righteousness of Jesus Christ imparted to us believers secures our souls from death.

Prayer:

Lord God almighty, Father of our Lord Jesus Christ, we give you great thanks for helping us to live a Holy life, and for sending your Son to us to live in us forever so that we will no longer be a slave to sin, but a slave to righteousness we thank you and glorify you, for your love for us now and forever. Amen.

NOVEMBER 20TH

THE WORD OF GOD CLEANSES US –
LET THE WORD OF GOD CLEANSES YOU TODAY.

Today Scripture Reading:

"Do not suppose that I have come to bring peace to the earth. I did not come to bring peace, but a sword. For I have come to turn a man against his father, a daughter against her mother, a daughter -in-law- against her mother-in –law a man's enemies will be the member of his own household. Whoever finds his life will lose it, and whoever loses his life for my sake will find it." (Matthew 10:34-35, 39) NIV

Jesus Christ stated during his earthly ministry that he did not come to earth to bring peace because people of this world did not like the Gospel, they did not want to change from darkness to light. The truth of the Gospel must be proclaimed in love; Christians have been going through persecution, Father killing their own family because they converted to Christianity. There is a sense in which his coming land the proclamation of the Gospel of God will bring division, and do so intentionally, because people of this earth like darkness instead of light. Faith in Jesus Christ separates the believer from the sinner and the world. The proclamation of God's word and its truth will bring division and opposition as well as various forms of persecution. A life lived according to Jesus Christ' righteous standards will bring a ridicule and scorn. The defense of the New Testament apostolic faith against heresy will surely bring a division. The teaching of Jesus about peace and unity must be faithfully held intension with the truth that he did not come to bring peace, but a sword, sword of the spirit that will separate the sinner from the righteous.

Prayer:

Lord Jesus Christ you are our life, we have no life without you, without you we are nothing. Let those who believe in you rejoice in you, let our soul and spirit magnified your Holy Name. let our spirit rejoice in God our Savior, you have done a great thing in our lives Holy is your Name forever. Amen.

NOVEMBER 21ST

THE WORD OF GOD CLEANSES US–
LET THE WORD OF GOD CLEANSES YOU TODAY.

Today Scripture Reading:

"The thief comes only to steal and kill and destroy but I have come that they may have life, and have it to the full." (John 10:10) NIV

Jesus Christ came to this world to give us life, life everlasting. This is a spiritual dynamic of the Holy Spirit in human activity in our world. Satan is the thief whose primary mission is to steal, kill and destroy people's lives, health, families, purpose in life and everything that is good. Jesus has come to counter and destroy Satan's work of evil by the power of the cross and by giving life that is redemptive and full to those who believe and receive him. No one can know and experience the fullness of life apart from Jesus Christ and the indwelling presence of his life giving Holy Spirit. By faith in Jesus Christ we come into covenant, and to communion with God; we have promises of eternal life. This is the privilege of our home; we shall be forever happy with our Lord and Savior. True believers are at home in Jesus Christ. We are not as strangers, but we have liberty to come in and go out as we should. Jesus Christ is not a thief; the thief comes to steal and kill. Deceivers of souls are murderers of the soul. The gracious design of the Shepherd is that he comes so that they may have life, and have it in full. Those who believed in Jesus Christ faithfully and sincerely will have full life in him. They will not be shut out.

Prayer:

Lord Jesus Christ you are, our Lord and Savior, you are the giver of life, bless us with your life, help us to be able to live in you and you in us forever. Lord Jesus Christ, reveal yourself to the unsaved people of this world, and let them know you and worship you in Spirit and in truth; we pray that you will bless those who do not know you, and will come to know you. You will make them spiritually alive in you, now and forever. We give you praise, our Lord, forever. Amen.

NOVEMBER 22ND

THE WORD OF GOD CLEANSES US –
LET THE WORD OF GOD CLEANSES YOU TODAY.

Today Scripture Reading:

"Then Peter, filled with the Holy Spirit, said to them: Rulers and elders of the people. Salvation is found in no one else, for there is no other Name under heaven given to men by which we must be saved." (Acts 48, 12) NIV

All the believing Christians must proclaim the Gospel to unsaved people in all the nations of earth. The disciples were convinced that the greatest need of every individual was salvation from sin and the wrath of God, and they preached that this need could be met by no one other than the person of Jesus Christ. This truth reveals the exclusive nature of the Gospel and the Church's heavy responsibility of preaching the Gospel to every person. If there were other ways of salvation, the Church could be of ease. But according to Jesus, he is their hope, for no one has salvation apart from, and through, him. This is the basis for the missionary imperative. Peter was filled with the Holy Spirit which brought a sudden inspiration, wisdom, and boldness by which to proclaim the truth of God. It is theologically significant that the filling with the Holy Spirit was not a one time experience, but a repetitive one. As there is no other Name by which a diseased body can be cured, so there is no other by which a sinful soul can be saved. Our salvation is our chief concern. Our salvation is not in ourselves. We can only save with the honor of Christ's Name. Believers must call his full Name in everything they are doing, or about to do. Jesus' Name is a powerful Name, a Name above all names.

Prayer:

Lord Jesus Christ, in your Holy Name, let those who are spiritually dead be alive in you. In your Holy Name let the dead rise up from the dead. In your Holy Name take all divers diseases such as cancer, leukemia, lupus, diabetes, and all other diverse diseases, disappear from those who are sick. Help us to visit the children in cancer hospitals and heal them my Lord. You are the great healer, the Great Physician. You know the names of all diseases, and you can call it out of the people with your healing power. Continuously help us to heal diseases in this world. In your Holy Name, we pray Amen.

NOVEMBER 23RD

THE WORD OF GOD CLEANSES US – LET THE WORD OF GOD CLEANSES YOU TODAY.

Today Scripture Reading:

"For you know that it was not with perishable things such as silver or gold that you were redeemed from the empty way of life handed down to you from your fore fathers, but with the precious blood of Christ, a Lamb without blemish, or defect." (1st Peter 1:18-19) NIV

God almighty Father freely offers us eternal life and Jesus Christ, but the life can only be available to us is sometimes difficult can only be possible through salvation, redemption, and Justification. Jesus Christ is the only way to the Father, because salvation is provided for us by God's grace. Which he gives us freely in Christ Jesus which was based on his death and resurrection. Jesus Christ continues to intercede from heaven at the right hand of God. Believers must always remember that they were redeemed by a ransom paid to the Father. We were redeemed; our redemption is a constant and powerful inducement, to holiness, and the fear of God. God expects that all Christians should live answerable to what he knows, not after the silver and gold, or any corruptible thing of the world, can redeem anyone's soul. The things of the world are corruptible things, and therefore, Jesus Christ is the only price of man's redemption. The design of Jesus Christ is shedding his most precious blood was to redeem us, not only from external misery hereafter, but from a vain conversation in this world. Christ was manifested to be that Redeemer whom God had for ordained before the foundation of the world.

Prayer:

Lord Jesus Christ, you are our blessed Savior and our Redeemer King, who redeemed us from our past, present, and future sins. Help us to fight our battle against all the powers of darkness, hindering spirits that tortured the children of God, rebuke them, and let them be far away from your children. Wash your children clean from any unrighteousness, now and forever. In Jesus Christ's glorious, mighty Holy Name, we pray. Amen.

NOVEMBER 24ᵀᴴ

THE WORD OF GOD CLEANSES US –
LET THE WORD OF GOD CLEANSES YOU TODAY.

Today Scripture Reading:

"The Lord is not slow in keeping his promise, as some understand slowness. He is patient with you, not wanting anyone to perish, but everyone to come to repentance." (2ⁿᵈ Peter 3:9) NIV

God almighty has promised all believers the end of the godly on this earth; with judgment, if there seems to be a delay, it is because is patient, he did not want anyone to perish; he wants them to come to the knowledge of repentance and pray for forgiveness which is only in him. The delay of Christ's return is related to the preaching of the Gospel of the kingdom to the entire people in the world. God wants everyone to hear the Gospel word he did not want anyone to perish, eternally. This truth does not mean that all the people will be save, all those who reject God's grace and salvation will sadly be lost eternally. The Lord is not slow in keeping his promise, he does not delay beyond the appointed time; he will keep to the time appointed in coming to judge the world. Good man are thinking that God stays beyond the appointed time that is, the true which they have set, but they set onetime and God set another time. What the people count as slowness is truly long suffering, and that to us –ward; it is giving more time to his own people that they may bring glory to God, and improve in a meeting for heaven; for God is not will to let anyone is this world should missed the opportunity of going to heaven. God has no delight in the death of sinners. His goodness and forbearance doing their own nature call to repentance, God gave them more time to repent.

Prayer:

Lord God almighty compassionate gracious loving God slow to anger full of truth and righteousness we give you glory and praise for giving the people of this earth more time for them to repent of their sins and come to you, in order that they may receive the gift of eternal life which is only from you. Lord Jesus Christ continuously sending the laborer into the harvest field because you did not want anyone to be perished. In your mighty Holy Name, we pray. Amen.

NOVEMBER 25TH

THE WORD OF GOD CLEANSES US –
LET THE WORD OF GOD CLEANSES YOU TODAY.

Today Scripture Reading:

"For this is what the Lord has commanded us: I have made you a light for the gentiles, that you may bring salvation to the ends of the earth. When the Gentiles heard this, they were glad and honored the word of the Lord; and all who were appointed for eternal life believed." (Acts 13:47-48) NIV

The Apostles brought the Gospel to the Gentiles; they glorified the Lord for the glorious announcement to them of the "Good News" of the Gospel. The Jews rejected the Gospel; the Apostles took the Gospel to the Gentiles. The Gentiles gave their life to God and they received eternal life. The Lord Jesus Christ commanded the Apostles to take the Gospel to the Gentiles. This is according to what was foretold in the Old Testament. "When the Messiah, shall come, they will not accept him. For I have set thee to be a light of the Gentiles, that they should be for salvation to the end of the earth." Christ is set up to be a light; he enlightens the understanding to save souls. He is to be light and salvation to the

Gentiles to the ends of the earth. All nations shall at length become his kingdom. This prophecy was accomplished in part in the setting up of the Kingdom of Jesus Christ in this earth. Gentiles were very happy at the good news spoken to them. They gave God the praise and they confided in his Holy Name: Oh what a light, what a power, what a treasure, does this Gospel bring along with it. Many were sincerely obedient to the faith.

Prayer:

Lord Jesus Christ you are the God of love and mercy, compassionate gracious God. We give you praise and thankfulness for your mercy for all the sinners and the lost, in your infinite love continuously calling the Gentiles in so many ways to you our Lord, bless us financial so that we can be able to reach all the Gentles unto you for the work of the gospel, and make them your own forever, in you all the souls of the people of the earth can be save. Amen.

NOVEMBER 26TH

THE WORD OF GOD CLEANSES US –
LET THE WORD OF GOD CLEANSES YOU TODAY.

Today Scripture Reading:

"Do you not know that the wicked will not inherit the kingdom of God? Do not be deceived; neither the sexually immoral no idolaters nor adulterer nor male prostitutes nor drunkards nor slanderers nor swindler will inherit the kingdom of God." (1st Corinthians 6:9-10) NIV

Some people in Corinth during the early Christianity were directed into believer that even if they broke fellowship with Christ, disowned him, and lived in immorality and injustice, their salvation and inheritance in God's kingdom were still secure. Apostle Paul made it clear to them that if they continue sinning, they will face spiritual death for the consequence. No one can live for immoral gratification and still inherit the kingdom of God. People who lives are characteristically unrighteous will not inherit the kingdom of God. We must not also be deceived, for all who are wicked will not inherit the kingdom of God. Salvation without the regenerating and sanctifying work of the Holy Spirit has no place in the New

Testament apostle Paul warns the believers in Corinth, he put the plain truth to them that such sinners will not inherit the kingdom of God, he secures several sorts of sin which also against second commandments idolaters, covetous and drunkards, heaven will not be intended for this people; he warns them against deceiving themselves; men are very much inclined to flatter themselves that they may live in sin and yet die in Christ, that they may lead the life of the Devil's children and yet go to heaven with the children of God. We cannot hope to sow to the flesh and yet reap everlasting life.

Prayer:

Lord Jesus Christ, strengthens those who are falling away revive them unto you, make them strong in their daily walk with you, heal them from all forms of sins and sin nature, heal them from all form of temptation now and forever. Amen.

NOVEMBER 27TH

THE WORD OF GOD CLEANSES US –
LET THE WORD OF GOD CLEANSES YOU TODAY.

Today Scripture Reading:

"If any of you has a dispute with another, dare he take it before the ungodly for judgment instead of before the saints'? Do you not know that the saints will judge the world? And if you are to judge the world, are you not competent to judge trivial cases." (1st Corinthians 6:1-2) NIV

When trivial disputes between Christians occur, they should be settled within the Church and not in courts of law. The Church must judge the right or wrong involved and render a verdict, possibly exercise discipline, if needed. This teaching does not mean that a believer may not use the court system in serious cases with unbelievers. And it does not mean also that the Church must allow its numbers to unlawful abuse or mistreat the innocent, such as widows, children, or the weak. Paul was speaking of the issue where there was no clear right or wrong sinful action must not be tolerated, but handed according to Christ's instruction, whereby cases that involve divorce, child abuse, child support from the mother or father may go to judicial courts. Paul was talking about minor disputes where the wrong could be accepted and tolerated. Christians should not contend with one another, for they are brethren, going to the law before on a hearing for little matters reproach Christianity; they are brothers and believers. They should have a forgiving temper, they must not harbor anger, wrath, or malice toward one another.

Prayer:

Lord God Almighty Father of all mercies helps us to quench the fiery flame of violence in all your churches; let everyone worship in peace and honor your Holy Name. Wash them clean from any unrighteousness, clothe them with your righteousness and holiness and let them worship in peace together. In your mighty Holy Name, we praise you. Amen.

NOVEMBER 28ᵀᴴ

THE WORD OF GOD CLEANSES US –
LET THE WORD OF GOD CLEANSES YOU TODAY.

Today Scripture Reading:

"For the grace of God that brings salvation has appeared to all men. It teaches us to say no to ungodliness and worldly passions, and to live self-controlled, upright and godly lives in this present age." (Titus 2:11-12) NIV

This Scripture reveals the character and the purpose of God's saving grace. Saving grace has appeared to all the people everywhere in the world, not just to a selected few favorite who supposedly are the elect from eternity. Believing Christians must decisively reject the ungodly passions, pleasure, and the value of the present age, and regard them as abominable, as well as empower believers, commanding them to live upright and godly lives, while waiting expectantly for the blessed hope and the appearing of Jesus Christ. A believer who obtained the grace of God to salvation must believe in the Gospel, trusting Christ, loving him, and living in his presence. They must not add anything to the

Gospel of Jesus Christ, and they must not take anything away from the Gospel, or promote made in humanistic wisdom, or some worldly philosophy. The Gospel of grace is open to all, and all are invited to come and partake of the benefit of it. The nature and the design of the Gospel is instructional and teaches all people to a right standard and conduct of living righteously; grace is obliging and constraining to goodness. The Gospel of grace brings salvation; it is called the word of life that brings faith and life. The old dispensation was comparatively dead and only a shadow, while grace is clear and a shining light. The Gospel is to teach; it is not for speculation, but for practice and right ordering of life.

Prayer:

Lord God Almighty, Father, Son and Holy Spirit bless those believers who live soberly with respect to themselves, and righteously toward all people. Fill us up with your mercy and love now and forever; hear our prayers, and bless us with your abundance of grace. Visit us and make yourself visible in our lives, you are the immortal, invisible, and the only wise God. Listen to our prayer and bless us so that we can receive blessings in all the areas of our lives. Amen.

NOVEMBER 29TH

THE WORD OF GOD CLEANSES US –
LET THE WORD OF GOD CLEANSES YOU TODAY.

Today Scripture Reading:

"Jesus looks at them and said, with man this is impossible but with God, all things are possible with God." (Mark 10:27) NIV

Believers must learn how to put their trust, their faith without waver in God. God is the most powerful, most merciful, and most compassionate, loving God. There is nothing he cannot do for those who love him. Nothing is impossible for him to do, in heaven and on this earth. God is the all-knowing, all powerful, he sees and knows all things; nothing is impossible for him to do – he heals all our diseases, makes a way where there is no way, brings water out of the rock, he parted the sea for the children of Israel. All the believing Christians need to hope in the Lord Jesus Christ, reconciling them, by referring to the almighty power of God, to help even rich people over the difficulties that he is the way of their salvation. What Christ means is that there is nothing the grace of God cannot do, for with Christians all things are possible. There is a great reward for those who gave all they have for the sake of salvation and the Gospel of Christ. They will be abundantly recompensed, and not only they shall be recompensed, who have left a little, but also for those that have left so much of the Gospel work.

Prayer:

Lord God Almighty, Jesus Christ, his only son, Holy spirit, ever one God, perform your miracle in our life, exhibit your infinite love, help us to do what it is impossible for men on this earth, make it possible for us. Straighten out our lives. Live your life through us, feed the poor, and the needy through us. Preach and teach, feed the poor and the needy through us with the word of the Gospel, that they may live and worship you. Preach, teach the Gospel through us, make what it is impossible, possible through us. Amen.

NOVEMBER 30TH

THE WORD OF GOD CLEANSES US –
LET THE WORD OF GOD CLEANSES YOU TODAY.

Today Scripture Reading:

"Enter through the narrow gate. For wide is the gate and broad is the road that heads to destruction, and many enter through it. But small is the gate and narrow the road that leads to life, and only a few find it." (Matthew 7:13-14) NIV

Jesus Christ, the true Son of God, full of truth and righteousness taught the people during his earthly ministry that the majority of the multitudes would not follow him on the road that leads to life. Because (1) Comparatively speaking those who enter the humble gate of true repentance and deny themselves to follow Jesus, sincerely endeavor to obey Christ commands. They earnestly seek his kingdom and his righteousness, and persevere until the end in true faith, purity, and love are not many, but few. Jesus Christ, during his teaching of his Sermon on the Mount, describes the great blessings that accompany disciples in his kingdom. It is the same with all those who have believed in him through them. Christ made it clear that following him involves heavy obligations concerning righteousness, acceptance of persecution, love for enemies and self-denial. Jesus Christ deals with us faithfully, and tells us sincerely that the gate is narrow, and that this means conversion and regeneration are the gate by which we enter into this way. Out of a state of sin into a state of grace we must pass, by the new birth, this gate is hard to find, and hard to get through like a passage between two rocks; there must be a new heart and a new spirit, old things must pass away, all this must be new, the soul must be changed. Therefore, if few are going to heaven, there shall be more room for me.

Prayer:

O' Merciful and mighty Father, let all the people of this world follow the right path, which is the narrow gate that leads to eternal life. Magnify your life in us, help us to praise you every day of our life and forever. Lord God Almighty lead us to the narrow gate which leads to life, with the power of your Holy Spirit. Revive our soul to love you, and follow you forever. Amen.

DAILY REFLECTION NOTES

DECEMBER

DECEMBER 1ST

THE WORD OF GOD IS A TRANSFORMATION –
LET THE WORD OF GOD TRANSFORM YOU TODAY.

Today's Scripture Reading:

"For if, when we were God's enemies, we were reconciled to him through the death of his Son, how much more, having been reconciled, shall we be saved through his life!" (Romans 5:10) NIV

All the believing Christians salvation is in Jesus Christ's blood and his resurrection life, whereby the believer is forgiven and reconciled to God. This experience is the initial salvation. Believers must continue to be saved by a living faith, and by union with the living Savior. If God loved us so much, and enough to send his Son to die for us while we were his enemies, how much more, now that we are his children, he will make every provision to save us from the wrath to come through our present faith in his Son. Justification and reconciliation are the fruit of the death of Jesus Christ. Believers were justified by his blood, sin is pardoned, the enmity slain, and end made of iniquity and an everlasting righteousness was brought in. Immediately upon our believing, we are actually put into a state of justification and reconciliation justified by his blood. Our justification is ascribed to the blood of Jesus Christ because without blood there will be no remission of sin. All the propitiatory sacrifices, the sprinkling of the blood was of the essence of the sacrifice. If God justified us and reconciled us when we were enemies, how much more will he save us when we are justified and reconciled.

Prayer:

Lord Jesus Christ, you have done great things for us when we were enemies. You make us friends; we pray that you use us now that we are your friend, and be kind to us. Bless us with everything we need that will help us to serve you, make your way in us and fill us up with your life, so that we may be more useful for you forever. Bless us with your power of love, so that we will be able to love you forever in true holiness. Amen.

DECEMBER 2ND

THE WORD OF GOD IS A TRANSFORMATION – LET THE WORD OF GOD TRANSFORM YOU TODAY.

Today's Scripture Reading:

"I am not ashamed of the gospel, because it is the power of God for the salvation of everyone who believes: first for the Jew, then for the Gentile." (Romans 1:16) NIV

Jesus Christ came to this world to bring us salvation which means deliverance – bringing someone safe, keeping him or her from danger. God revealed himself in the Old Testament as the one who saves his people. God revealed himself in the New Testament as the way or road that leads through to external union with God in heaven. The road to salvation must be walked to the very end. Salvation is a gift of God by grace; therefore, salvation is provided for us by God's grace, which he gives us freely in Jesus Christ based on his death and resurrection, and continued intercession for all believers. Jesus Christ lives in heaven in his Father's presence interceding for each and every one of us who follows him according to his Father's will. Believers experience God's love and presence and find mercy and grace to help us in times of need. The salvation of believers, as it revealed in the Scripture, is the believers' final end. It is the wisdom of God and the power of God unto salvation. No one should be ashamed of the Gospel of God, in salvation, because that is where the righteousness of God is being revealed and renewed, from faith-to-faith, as the just shall live by faith.

Prayer:

Our Lord and Savior you are the one who loved us; we pray to you and give you thanks O' Lord. No one has ever cared like you and no one has ever loved like you. We Praise you O' Lord, for all what you have done for us. Help us never to be ashamed of the Gospel; help us to preach and teach the Gospel in all the four corners of this earth in so many ways by the power of the Holy Spirit. Amen.

DECEMBER 3RD

THE WORD OF GOD IS A TRANSFORMATION –LET WORD OF GOD TRANSFORM YOU TODAY.

Today's Scripture Reading:

"Though the fig tree does not bud and there are no grapes on the vines, though the olive crop fails and the fields produced no food, though there are no sheep in the pen and no cattle in the stalls, Yet I will rejoice in the Lord, I will be joyful in God my Savior. The Sovereign Lord is my strength; he makes my feet like the feet of a deer, he enables me to go on the heights." (Habakkuk 3:17-19) NIV

The Scripture reveals that God almighty, the same God who came with salvation in the past in Egypt, will come again in all his glory. All who were waiting for his coming will live and see his triumph over all the nations. Habakkuk testified that he love the Lord and serve the Lord not for what he gave him but because he was God. Habakkuk chose to rejoice in the Lord; who is his Savior and who is the source of his unfailing source of strength. Habakkuk new beyond a doubt that a righteous remnant would survive, and he proclaimed with confidence the ultimate victory of all who live by faith in the Lord. Habakkuk delight and triumph in God; same with all believers today we must follow the example of Habakkuk when all what we have is gone, but we have our God who is always with us, who said he will never leave us nor forsake us, those who are emptied can enjoy all in God, and they can sit down upon heap of ruins and sing to the praise and glory of God. This is the principal ground of our joy in the Lord, he is the God of our eternal salvation, the salvation of our soul; and, if he be so, we may rejoice in him in our greatest distresses.

Prayer:

Lord God Almighty you are our life, the life that never end and will never ends, help us to rejoice in you no matter what happens in our lives. You have the power and authority to take total control of our lives. In your mighty Holy Name , we pray. Amen.

DECEMBER 4TH

THE WORD OF GOD IS A TRANSFORMATION –
LET THE WORD OF GOD TRANSFORM YOU TODAY.

Today's Scripture Reading:

"And hope does not disappoint us, because God has poured out his love into our hearts by the Holy Spirit, whom he has given us. Very rarely will anyone die for a righteous man, though for a good man someone might possibly dare to die. But God demonstrates his own love for us in this: While we were still sinners Christ died for us." (Romans 5:7-8) NIV

Believers have hope in God, hope that something good is going to happen now or in the future, hope of confidence from God concerning his promises, is sure because it is based on the integrity of God's word. All believers will experience the reality of hope because God is the God of hope and he is the object and assurance of our hope. Believing Christians experience the love of God, God's love for believers in their hearts through the power of the Holy Spirit, especially in times of trouble. This hope will not disappoint us, because it is sealed with the Holy Spirit as a Spirit of love. The love of God, that is, the sense of God's love to us, draws out love in us to him again. The ground of all our comfort and holiness, and perseverance is laid in the shedding abroad of the love of God in our hearts. Jesus Christ died for ungodly not all the helpless creature, but the guilty sinners. Jesus Christ did for sinners neither righteous nor good, not only such as were useless, but such as were guilty. God almighty commanded his love, not only proved but magnified it and made it illustrious, not only put it past dispute, but rendered it the object of the greatest wonder and administration.

Prayer:

Lord Jesus Christ, our Lord and our Savior, our great redeemer, we give you praise and honor. In the time of trouble, protect and guide your people from all dangers of this world. We praise and thank you for your love for us by shedding your pressure precious blood on the cross for our sins. In your mercy hear our prayers and answer all our prayers, let the sinners come to you. In your Holy Name , we pray. Amen.

DECEMBER 5TH

THE WORD OF GOD IS A TRANSFORMATION –
LET THE WORD OF GOD TRANSFORM YOU TODAY.

Today's Scripture Reading:

Then they came to Jericho. As Jesus and his disciples, together with a large crowd were leaving the city, a blind man, Bartimaeus that is, the son of Timaeus, was sitting by the roadside begging when he heard that it was Jesus of Nazareth, he began to shout, Jesus Son of David, have mercy on me. Many rebuked him and told him to be quiet, but he shouted all the more, Son of David, have mercy on me. Jesus Stopped and said, call him they called to the blind man, cheer up! On your feet! He's calling you. Throwing his cloak aside, he jumped to his feet and came to Jesus. What do you want me to do for you? Jesus asked him. The blind man said, Rabbi I want to see Go, said Jesus, your faith has healed you. Immediately he received his sight and followed Jesus along the road." (Mark 10:46-52) NIV

The blind man knows the Scripture, even though he was unable to see, but he followed the Word of God as they read in the Synagogues, that the Messiah is the Son of David. When they rebuked him to stop shouting, he shout more and more because he is in need of a Savior same with all of us till today, we need the Savior, Jesus Christ the Son of God, the Son of David. Believers should take that example of the blind Bartimaeus and call on Jesus Christ whatever we might be going through, to cry, shout, or scream until, he show his great compassion upon us. Christ Jesus show his loving power, and compassion on us well as he demonstrate his mission, that he came to save the sinners and the lost, Christ Jesus stood still he did not move, until they brought the blind man to him. Christ exercises his power of healing and told him that his faith has healed him. Jesus wants believers to have strong faith in him, he want us to know that he is the all-powerful.

Prayer:

Lord God Almighty, you have made all the inhabitant of this universe for your glory, to serve in freedom and in peace, strengthens us the we may use our liberty according to your will, run and cry to you in time of needs in sickness and in health, so that we can follow you as the blind man got healed and follow you our Lord. Lord Jesus Christ hears our prayers and fulfills all our needs; solve all our problems in Jesus great Holy Name. Amen.

DECEMBER 6TH

THE WORD OF GOD IS A TRANSFORMATION – LET THE WORD OF GOD TRANSFORM YOU TODAY.

Today's Scripture Reading:

"For the Son of Man came to seek and to save what was lost." (Luke 19:10) NIV

Our Lord Jesus Christ came to the world to seek the sinners and the lost. This is the points to the heart of Jesus Christ earthly ministry, this is his mission, and his mission became believer's mission, when he ascended to heaven. Believers are called to fulfill the Father, Son, and the Holy Spirit's mission on earth. Believers must do their auto best to reach the sinners and the lost to Christ's hand before is Second Coming. The Lord said that this Gospel of the kingdom will come to the end only after the Gospel of the Kingdom has been adequately preached in in the whole world the Gospel must be preached in the power and righteousness of the Holy Spirit which must also be accompanied by the major signs of the Gospel. Only God the Father will know when this task is going to be accomplished according to his purpose. Believer's responsibility and task is to faithfully and continuously press onto spread the Gospel to all the nations, till the Lord returns to take his church to heaven. Christ came to call sinners to repent of their sin and turn to God. The people of the entire world were lost, just like a traveler is lost when he has missed his way in the wilderness, the gracious design of the Son of God is that he came from heaven to earth to seek that which was lost.

Prayer:

Lord Jesus Christ help us to seek the lost and the sinners, call them to you every minute every second, made them spiritually alive in you, and help us to call them, to come to you so that they can be saved and live for you forever. Bless them with your peace and love that surpasses all understanding in their lives now and forever. Amen.

DECEMBER 7TH

THE WORD OF GOD IS A TRANSFORMATION – LET THE WORD OF GOD TRANSFORM YOU TODAY.

Today's Scripture Reading:

"and free those who all their lives were held in slavery by their fear of death. For surely it is not angels he helps, but Abraham's descendants. For this reason he had to be made like his brothers, in every way, in order that he might become a merciful and faithful high Priest in service to God, and that he might make atonement for the sins of the people." (Hebrews 2:15-17) NIV

Jesus Christ is the Son of God; the son's mission in his incarnation was to help Abraham's descendants in every way. The Son became like Abraham's descendants for three purposes (a) To be their merciful and faithful high Priest   (b) to make atonement for the sins of the people. (c) The Son to intercede for and give help to those who are being tempted – Jesus Christ fulfills these threefold ministries on behalf of all believers, both Jews and the Gentiles. The High Priest is applied to Christ Jesus and his ministry of mediation only in Hebrews among all the New Testament books Jesus represents us as believers before God, just as the Old

Testament high priest represented Israel on the day of atonement. In Jesus' ministry of High Priest, Jesus' death makes atonement by removing God's wrath against believers because of their sins. As a result, believers can now approach God with confidence. As our high priest he also mercifully sympathizes with us when we are tempted and comes to our aid because he, as a human, has experienced suffering, trials, and temptation, yet he did not sin.

Prayer:

Lord Jesus Christ, you are the way, the truth, and the life we adored you, honor you and lift up your Holy Name higher and higher, because of your love for us. Jesus Christ, you came to this world; let your full presence in heaven fill us up on this earth forever. Amen.

DECEMBER 8TH

THE WORD OF GOD IS A TRANSFORMATION – LET THE WORD OF GOD TRANSFORM YOU TODAY.

Today's Scripture Reading:

"You give me your shield of victory, and your right hand sustains me; you stoop down to make me great. You broaden the path beneath me, so that my ankles do not turn." (Psalm 18:35-36) NIV

Lord Jesus Christ has given us the shield of salvation. And he has compassed us on every side. He is our protector, his providence never fails, and his mercy endures forever. You have compassed on every side. I have been delivered from the strivings of the people who aimed at our destruction - particularly from the violent man, that is means God had prospered him in his designs; he was made his way perfect and it was his right hand that holds him up. Those whom God has abandoned are easily vanquished. The Lord Jesus Christ is the sustainer of his people; he sustained them in any form of earthly dangers. The Lord Jesus Christ rose up who are oppressed and afflicted. God raise believers to the throne, and not only delivered him and kept him alive but dignified him and made him great. When our Lord delivered us from any trouble, he got all the victory and honor, he is worthy of all our praises. Believers need to honor our Savior with humbleness, reverent, adorations of divine glory and perfection. Believers must magnify, endeavors, with praises and thanks, magnify God almighty to bless him and exalt him.

Prayer:

Lord God almighty we magnified adored your Holy Name, do not leave us nor forsake us, keep us save at all times and deliver us from any unrighteousness, Lord Jesus create in us a new heart, that will focus on you that you will get all the glory, let your will be done in our lives, let your mercies flows, and your full presence be known in our life now and forever. Amen.

DECEMBER 9TH

THE WORD OF GOD IS A TRANSFORMATION – LET THE WORD OF GOD TRANSFORM YOU TODAY.

Today's Scripture Reading:

"Therefore come out from them and be separate, says the Lord. Touch not unclean thing, and I will receive you. I will be a father to you, and you will be my sons and daughters, says the Lord Almighty." (2nd Corinthians 6:17-18) NIV

The concept of separation from evil is a fundamental to God's relationship with his people according to the Scripture, separation involves two dimensions one negative and two, second one is positive. Believers must separate themselves morally and spiritually from sin and sin nature and from everything that is contrary to Jesus Christ, righteousness, and God's word; drawing near to God every day in a close and intimate fellowship through prayer, supplications, worship, the Word and through loving service. The second fold of separation is results in a relationship where God is our heavenly Father who lives with us and is our God, and we in turn are his sons and daughters. God people are called to be Holy in the Old Testament and in the New Testament different and separated from all other people in the world in order to belong to God as his very own. God call all believers to be separate from all the corrupt of the world system and from unholy compromise. There are many people in the churches all over the world who sins and refused to repent such false teachers, churches or cults who teach error and deny Biblical truth.

Prayer:

Lord Jesus Christ, you're the one who saved us, separate us from the world of sin, so that we may live our life for you faithfully, sincerely in righteousness and in holiness according to your will. Use all those who belongs to you highly and protect them with the power of the Holy Spirit. Amen.

DECEMBER 10TH

THE WORD OF GOD IS A TRANSFORMATION –
LET THE WORD OF GOD TRANSFORM YOU TODAY.

Today's Scripture Reading:

"As far as the east is from the west, so far has he removed our transgressions from us. As a father has compassion on his children, so the Lord has compassion on those who fear him; for he knows how we are formed, he remembers that we are dust." (Psalm 103:12-14) NIV

God the Father, Son and the Holy Spirit shows mercy to those who truly fear him. The fear of God is a redeeming fear that motivates us to turn away from evil, to keep God's precepts, and to seek the Lord's nearness and grace, and to turn away from evil. The blessings that God gave to those who fear him are: his mercy, his love and forgiveness, his fatherly love and compassion, his faithfulness and goodness to his children. God has compassion on his children because he knows their weaknesses and infirmities. Even the best of his followers stand in need of his compassion. As a father has deep compassion for his children when they fail, suffer, or are mistreated, so also our heavenly father hurts when his own children are hurting. In the midst of trouble, failure, and struggle, we must not think that our Father is uncaring, or ignore us rather; we must remember that his eyes look on us with compassion, and he will help us according to our need. All the believing Christians must live confidently on God's unfailing love. God's mercy s much above the merits of those that fear him most so much above and beyond them that there is no proportion at all between them. The fullness of his pardons is an evidence of the riches of his mercy.

Prayer:

Lord God Almighty Father of all mercies sustainer of all things in heaven and in earth, in your infinite mercy and love, help us to serve you with a loving heart and sing praises to your Holy Name now and forever. Amen.

DECEMBER 11ᵀᴴ

THE WORD OF GOD IS A TRANSFORMATION – LET THE WORD OF GOD TRANSFORM YOU TODAY.

Today's Scripture Reading:

"For God so loved the world that he gave his one and only Son, that whoever believes in him shall not perish but have eternal life. For God did not send his Son into the world to condemn the world, but to save to save the world through him." (John 3:16-17) NIV

The Scripture said: "For God the Father so loved the world" it is one of the most important scriptures that reveal the heart and the purpose of God to the people of this world. God's love is wide enough to embrace all the people in the world. God gave his Son as an offering for sin on the cross. The atonement proceeds from the loving heart of God. Jesus Christ voluntarily gave himself up for the offering on the cross; he offered himself for the sin of the whole world. We must believe that Jesus Christ is the Son of God and the only Savior for all of the lost humanity. With a self-surrendering fellowship with the Lord and obedience to Jesus Christ, believers must be full-assured of the trust in Jesus Christ, and that he is able and willing to bring you to final salvation and to fellowship with God in heaven. God did not want anyone to perish, which is a spiritual death not physical death. Eternal life is the gift God bestowed on all believing Christians when they are born again. Eternal life is a different quality, divine type of life; a life that frees us from what is merely earthly in order to know God. Believers must look up to Jesus Christ, the offer of Jesus is to all, that they shall have eternal life.

Prayer:

God almighty Father, Son, and the Holy Spirit, you love us so much and you gave us your one and only begotten Son to us. Helps us, guide us, bless us with your power of the Holy spirit, so that we may be able to serve you with all our hearts and minds, as well as be able to serve you with all our hearts and minds and honor your Holy Name through our lives. Amen.

DECEMBER 12ᵀᴴ

THE WORD OF GOD IS A TRANSFORMATION –
LET THE WORD OF GOD TRANSFORM YOU TODAY.

Today's Scripture Reading:

"Like new born babies, crave pure spiritual milk, so that by it you may grow up in your salvation, now that you have tasted that the Lord is good." (1ˢᵗ Peter 2:2)NIV

All the new believing Christians as well as older ones should long for the pure nourishment of God's Word. The Word of God stands forever as the earth itself, human life, human glory, and human achievements such as a Culture, Science and Philosophy are temporary, and it will pass away. But the word of God remains and stands forever. All the human endeavors and the prevailing spirit of the world must constantly be measured by the Scripture rather than the Scripture being judge by them. A sure sign of good spiritual health is a deep desire to feed on the living and enduring word of God. The best spiritual hunger and thirst for God and his word diminish or has been destroyed entirely by wrong attitudes, or by being choked by life's worries, riches, and pleasure. Our best service towards God will neither please him nor profit us if we are not conscientious in our duties to men. A new life requires suitable food, intents desire common milk, and their desires towards it are fervent and frequent. Such must be Christian's believers who desire before the word of God they may grow thereby strong desires and affections to the word of God we are sure evidence of a person's being born again. Growth and improvement in wisdom and grace are the desire to every Christians. The Word of God does not leave a man as it finds him.

Prayer:

Lord Jesus Christ, you are the Word of God made flesh and dwell among us, we behold your glory, the glory of one and only Son of the Father full of truth and grace, we give you praise for the work of redemption, and we give you praise for the forgiveness of our sins, resurrection of the body and live everlasting. Amen.

DECEMBER 13TH

THE WORD OF GOD IS A TRANSFORMATION –
LET THE WORD OF GOD TRANSFORM YOU TODAY.

Today's Scripture Reading:

"For in the gospel a righteousness from God is revealed, a righteousness that is by faith from first to last, just as it is written; the righteous will live by faith." (Romans 1:17)NIV

The righteous person continues to live by faith, and in so doing grows from one level of maturity to another. In this way, the believer progresses along the path of righteousness to live a rich and full spiritual life. Justification of the believer is the way that the righteousness of God was revealed it is what shows us the way to salvation as well as the way of justification. The Gospel make known righteousness, there is righteousness revealed in the Gospel. This righteousness is called the righteousness of God; it is God's appointing righteousness, which was cut off all pretensions to a righteousness resulting from merit of your own works. It is the righteousness of Jesus Christ; which is from faith to faith. From the first faith, by which we put into a justified state: to after faith, by which we live; from faith engrafting us into Christ, to faith deriving virtue from him as our root; where both implied in the next words, the righteous shall live by faith, therefore, there is faith maintaining us. Faith is all in all; but in the beginning and progress of a Christian life. It is an increasing, continuing persevering faith. Being justified by faith he shall live by it both the life of grace and of glory. Therefore, the evangelical righteousness from faith to faith found Old Testament faith in Jesus Christ to come to New Testament faith in all Christ that already come.

Prayer:

Lord Jesus Let your life shine upon us, help us to walk by faith, not by sight, to have strong faith in you, and to love you more and more every day of our life. Plant your faith in our heart, and let it grow, more and more. Destroy the work of wicked people in our lives; destroy the power of darkness in our lives. Amen.

DECEMBER 14TH

THE WORD OF GOD IS A TRANSFORMATION – LET THE WORD OF GOD TRANSFORM YOU TODAY.

Today's Scripture Reading:

"But our citizenship is in heaven. And we eagerly await a Savior from there, the Lord Jesus Christ." (Philippians 3:20) NIV

Our Lord Jesus Christ is our Savior; he is at the right hand of God in heaven. Therefore, first and for most our citizenship as a believing Christians is in heaven, not in this world, we have become strangers and aliens on this earth. In regard to our life's walk, values and directions, heaven is now our fatherland. We have been born from above. Our names are written in heaven's register our lives are guided by heavenly standards; and our rights and inheritance are reserved in heaven. It is to heaven that our prayers ascend, and our hope is directed. Many of our friends and families members are already there, and we will be there soon. Jesus Christ is there also, preparing place for us, and he has promised to return and take us to himself. For these reasons we long for a better country a heavenly one. Therefore, God is not ashamed to be called our God, and he has prepared for us an eternal city. The life of a Christians is in heaven, where Christ's home is, and where Christ hopes to be shortly. It is good having fellowship with those who have fellowship with Jesus Christ. We are expecting his Second Coming and expect to be happy and glorified there with the glory reserve for all the believing Saints.

Prayer:

Lord Jesus Christ our Lord and our Savior, we praise you, glorified you, adore you now and forever, for your unending love for us, and your everlasting mercy upon us, heal all our diseases, solve all our problems, let those who seek you find you, when people of this world call on to you sincerely look down from heaven and answer their prayers; make us your very own forever. Amen.

DECEMBER 15TH

THE WORD OF GOD IS A TRANSFORMATION –
LET THE WORD OF GOD TRANSFORM YOU TODAY.

Today's Scripture Reading:

"So then, let us not be like others, who are asleep, but let us be alert and self-controlled." (1st Thessalonians 5:6) NIV

Believers must stay awake and keep watch. Believers of Jesus Christ must be physically and spiritually prepared in order to escape the wrath of that day. If we want to escape God's wrath, we must remain spiritually awake and mutually, morally alert, and continue in faith, love, and the hope of salvation since the faithful will be protected from God's wrath. They need not fear the day of the Lord, but expectantly wait for his Son from heaven Jesus Christ who rescues us from the coming of wrath. Believers must be self-controlled means - a state of abstinence from wine, not to drink wine, to be completely unaffected by wine, and be sober it carries a figurative meaning of alertness, self-control, self-restrain or self-control. Believers must be watchful and sober minded, not sloth and idleness. God is love there is no unrighteousness in him he will clothe us with his righteousness. Believers must be ready being alert to proclaim the Gospel to the unsaved at all time. Believers must stay away from drunkenness, and sexually immoral lives that can defile the soul and the spirit.

Prayer:

Lord Jesus Christ you call us from darkness into your marvelous light, do not let anything in this world move, or take us back into darkness. Strengthens us with the power of the Holy Spirit, so that we do not go into the world's way of life and fall into sin. Cleanses us with your precious blood and make us your own forever. Increase your faith in us, have mercy upon us, O merciful and might God now and forever Amen.

DECEMBER 16ᵀᴴ

THE WORD OF GOD IS A TRANSFORMATION – LET THE WORD OF GOD TRANSFORM YOU TODAY.

Today's Scripture Reading:

"For the message of the cross is foolishness to those who are perishing, but to us who are being saved it is the power of God." (1ˢᵗ Corinthians 1:18) NIV

Jesus Christ has done a great thing in our lives Holy his is Name. The message of the cross not only involves the wisdom and the truth of; but the active power of God coming down to save, heal, drive out demons, and redeem people from sins power. Jesus Christ crucified is a stumbling block to the Jews, they did not believe in him, they rejected him, they despised him, and looked upon him as execrable, because he did not gravity them with a sign to their mind, though Christ divine power shows out and done, in memorable miracles. The Jewish people still require a sing; they laughed at the story of a crucified Savior; they were sorting for wisdom. Jesus Christ' teaching and preaching is foolishness to them. It is not the method of preaching that is foolishness to the Jews, but the message of the Lordship of the crucified and the resurrection of Christ. God almighty shows the foolishness and weakness in Jesus Christ to provide a solution to the sin's problem in the world.

Prayer:

Lord Jesus Christ you are the only one and only the wisdom of God and the power of God to the people of this world. Come to us Lord Jesus and help us to live for your glory forever, help us to know you, to worship you, help us to honor you and proclaim the Gospel of God to the unsaved people of this world. Help us to have you at the center of our hearts and minds throughout our life. Amen.

DECEMBER 17TH

THE WORD OF GOD IS A TRANSFORMATION –
LET THE WORD OF GOD TRANSFORM YOU TODAY.

Today's Scripture Reading:

"By this gospel you are saved, if you hold firmly to the word preached to you. Otherwise, you have believed in vain. For what I received I passed onto you as of first importance that Christ died for our sins according to the Scripture." (1st Corinthians 15:2-3) NIV

Believer must hold firmly the Gospel that was preached to them. They are not those who merely have faith in Jesus Christ. Jesus Christ is revealed in the full Gospel message. Believer's faith in Jesus Christ is always bound to God's Word and commands. For this reason believers can be described as the people who submit to the Christ of the Scripture as Lord and Savior and who live under the Word of God. The Gospel must be continually preached to all the people on earth constantly. It was the first Gospel in which they stand, and must continue to stand. The message of Jesus's death and resurrection is at the foundation of Christianity. If we remove this foundation, and the entire messages will fill, it was this foundation alone by which they could hope for salvation. There is no salvation in any other Name but upon supposition of his death and resurrection. These are the saving truths of our Holy religion. Believers must retain this truth in their mind, and they must hold on to it fast.

Prayer:

Lord Jesus Christ our gracious master and our great redeemer. You gave your life to us so that we may live, and worship you and honor you. Help us in our undertakings; do not let us work in vain or labor in vain, Bless us abundantly, immeasurable, so that we may be able to do your work, take the Gospel to the end of the world and under the world. In your great Holy Name , we pray. Amen.

DECEMBER 18TH

THE WORD OF GOD IS A TRANSFORMATION –
LET THE WORD OF GOD TRANSFORM YOU TODAY.

Today's Scripture Reading:

"I am sending him – who is my very heart back to you I would have liked to keep him with me so that he could take your place in helping me while I am in chains for the Gospel. No longer as a slave, but better than a slave, as a dear brother. He is very dear to me but even dearer to you. Both as a man and as a brother in the Lord. The grace of the Lord Jesus Christ be with your spirit." (Philemon 1:12-13, 16, 25) NIV

All the believing Christians must learn from our Lord the forgiveness whatever someone did to us; we must forgive them as Jesus Christ forgive us our sins. On this Scripture Paul the apostle wrote Philemon to take back his slave Onesimus, who took one of his master's good, but when he got to Rome, he was converted by Paul. Paul now sends Onesimus back to Philemon with this letter. As Jesus is our advocate of a new covenant in heaven Paul advocate for Onesimus so that Philemon can take him back. Onesimus could have been set free, if he desires; the love demanded in the Gospel of Christ all point, but Paul did not state it directly. He wants Philemon and all other masters to do it voluntarily on their own. Instead of direct confrontation, guidelines were laid down for both the Christians slaves and their master that undermine slavery from within and eventually bring about its abolition. Slavery cannot exist among believers who have seen the truth of Christian brotherhood. Onesimus must no longer be treated as a slave, but as a fellow believer and dear brother, one who God's sight as equal with Paul and Philemon. Same today some Christians believers still treated their housekeeper, cleaner, companion differently which is against the law of Christ. In Christ there is no slave, no black, no white, no Greek, no Jews, no man, no woman we are all one in Jesus Christ.

Prayer:

Lord Jesus Christ we give you thanks for making us one in you as you and Father are one. Help us to keep the unity of faith in the bound of peace from this earth to heaven. Amen.

DECEMBER 19TH

THE WORD OF GOD IS A TRANSFORMATION –
LET THE WORD OF GOD TRANSFORM YOU TODAY.

Today's Scripture Reading:

"Jesus wept." (John 11:35) NIV

Jesus Christ our Lord and Savior wept for our sins, sin of unbelief, and His spirit was grieved because of our unbelief. Christ wept for the whole human race, because of sin and death. These two words revealed the deep sympathy God feels for the sorrow of his people. Jesus wept – means that our Lord Jesus Christ burst into tears, then wept silently. Let this be a comfort to all who experience sorrow Jesus Christ feels the same sympathy for you that he felt for the relatives of Lazarus. He loves you that he always sorrows when you're sorrow. Jesus Christ the Son of God, and the Son of man, he have deep, emotional, and sympathetic love for all believers. Jesus wept is the shortest verse in the Scripture, it carry many useful instructions – Jesus Christ really and truly man, susceptible of the impressions of joy, and grief. Jesus Christ gave this proof of his humanity in both senses of the word; that as a man, he could weep, and, as a merciful man, he weep, before he gave this proof of his divinity. Jesus Christ was a man of sorrows and he acquainted with our grief as it was foretold in the book of Isaiah. We have never read in the Scripture that Jesus Christ laugh, we only read that rejoice in the spirit, but more than once we have him no tears – which is tears of compassion which becomes Christian and makes them most to resemble their Lord.

Prayer:

Lord Jesus Christ, we give you great thanks for all what you have done for us, you show us your love by constantly sympathizing with us in the time of sorrow and grieve, and we give you praises and honor our Lord. Amen.

DECEMBER 20TH

THE WORD OF GOD IS A TRANSFORMATION –
LET THE WORD OF GOD TRANSFORM YOU TODAY.

Today's Scripture Reading:

"Then Jesus said. Did I not tell you that if you believed, you would see the glory of God? When he had said this, Jesus called in a loud voice Lazarus, come out! The dead man came out, his hands and feet wrapped with strips of linen, and a cloth around his face. Jesus said to them, take off the grave clothes and let him go." (John 11:40, 43-44) NIV

Jesus Christ told Mary and Martha to believe in him so that they can see the glory of God. Same way Jesus Christ is telling us today, to believe in him and in the power of his resurrection so that we can see the power, love, and the glory of God. Jesus Christ in us the hope of glory – there is nothing Jesus Christ that is living inside us cannot do, he is all powerful all compassionate gracious loving God. The miracle of Lazarus's resurrection was a sign pointing to Jesus as the God of resurrection and the life. Christ demonstration of what God will do for all believers who have died, for they too will be raised from the dead because of this astounding miracle, many Jewish put their faith in Christ. This miracle of raising Lazarus from the dead was the final issue that caused the Jewish leaders to decide to put Jesus Christ to death. Power went out with the word of Jesus Christ to reunite the soul and the body of Lazarus, and then he came forth from the grave. The miracle is described, not by its invisible sings to satisfy our curiosity, but by its visible effects, to confirm our faith. Lazarus was so thoroughly revived that he gets us out of his grace as strongly as ever he got up out of his bed, and returned not only to life, but to good health.

Prayer:

Merciful and Mighty God, Father of our Lord Jesus Christ, you sent your messengers, prophets to preach repentance of sin, show us the way of salvation; give us the heart to believe, always help our unbelieves, in order to be saved from our sins. Blesses us with a life in you, so that we can bless others around us. Make the people of this world spiritually alive in you, so that they can worship the true God and live in a new Heaven and a new earth. Amen.

DECEMBER 21ST

THE WORD OF GOD IS A TRANSFORMATION – LET THE WORD OF GOD TRANSFORM YOU TODAY.

Today's Scripture Reading:

"When the day of Pentecost came, they were all together in one place; suddenly a sound like the blowing of a violent wind came from heaven and filled the whole house where they were sitting. They saw what seemed to be tongues of fire that separated and came to rest on each of them. All of them were filled with the Holy Spirit and began to speak in other tongues as the spirit enable them." (Act 2:1-4) NIV

Our Lord Jesus Christ fulfilled his promise for the apostles on the day of Pentecost. Pentecost was the second great festival of Jewish year. It was a harvest when the first fruits of the grain harvest presented to God. In the same manner Pentecost symbolized for the church the beginning of God's harvest for human's souls in the universe. At Pentecost there were three observable manifestations that the Holy Spirit was descending upon 120-followers of Jesus Christ including the disciples in the fulfillment of Jesus Christ promise: (a) There was an audible manifestation – sounding like a violent blowing wind. Holy Spirit comes with power wind is one of the signs of the Holy Spirit. (b) visual manifestation – appeared visibly – seemed to be like tongues of fire by the Holy Spirit that empowered them to be fiery witnesses for Jesus.(c) Speech manifestation followers were filled with the Holy Spirit, they began to speak in other tongues as the Spirit enabled them. Which, with all other languages of people in the world, they understood the language of other nations with the power of the Holy Spirit. It is the same today when missionaries travel to other nations, the Spirit empowers them to understand and speak the language of that nation quickly.

Prayer:

Lord Jesus Christ bring us the day of Pentecost ,empower us, and baptizes all the believing Christians with the Holy Spirit, so that they can serve you with the power of speaking other languages in the Gospel words. Amen.

DECEMBER 22ND

THE WORD OF GOD IS A TRANSFORMATION –
LET THE WORD OF GOD TRANSFORM YOU TODAY.

Today's Scripture Reading:

"Surely he took up our infirmities and carried our sorrows yet we considered him stricken by God, smitten by him, and afflicted. But he was pierced for our transgressions, he was crushed for our iniquities; the punishment that brought us peace was upon him, and by his wound we are healed." (Isaiah 53:4-5) NIV

This Scripture was in reference to Jesus' ministry of healing the sick, both physically and spiritually. The Messiah would endure punishment in order that we may be delivered from our sins, diseases, and sicknesses, as well as from our sins. It is, therefore, right, and good for us to pray for our physical healing, as Jesus Christ bore our sins. He also took upon himself the infirmities and diseases that belong to us, and carried them, so that we can be freed and healed. Jesus Christ was crucified because we have sinned and are guilty before God. Jesus as our substitute, he took the punishment due to us, and paid the penalty for our sins. The penalty of death on the cross. Therefore, we can be forgiven and have peace with God. Believers were healed by Jesus Christ wounds means that our healing refers to salvation with all its benefits; spiritual and physical sickness and diseases which resulted from Satan's activities in the world. Jesus Christ appeared in the world to destroy the work of the devil. Our Lord and Savior gave the gift of healing to the church and commanded believers to heal diseases, as part of their proclamation.

Prayer:

God the Father Almighty, we pray that you bless us with the power of healing to heal the sick and diseases, to be able to cast out demons, and all the work of darkness from the people. Bless us with power from above to serve you better and take the Gospel to the end of the earth and under the earth. Fill us with your power of indwelling of the Holy spirit. Amen.

DECEMBER 23ᴿᴰ

THE WORD OF GOD IS A TRANSFORMATION –
LET THE WORD OF GOD TRANSFORM YOU TODAY.

Today's Scripture Reading:

"And he said: I tell you the truth, unless you change and become like little children, you will never enter the kingdom of heaven." (Matthew 18:3) NIV

Jesus Christ was teaching and preaching during his earthly ministry. He was telling them to change; the change that Christ required is in conversion that begins with becoming like a little child means being a humble person, a gentle person, an unpretentious, dependent on the Father and mother for everything: weak, teachable, and willing to trust the Heavenly Father. Scripturally, after the initial childlike step of humility, the conversion, or change required by Christ consists of two components and/or parts: (a) Conversion that will bring about repentance and embracing an attitude of a new life. This is very important and necessary because by nature we follow a way of life that leads away from God and leads toward eternal death – conversion is the human response to God's gift of salvation, accomplished by the grace of God and the power of the Holy Spirit received through faith. Because of our new relationship with God, conversion involves changes in the areas of relationships, habits, commitments, pleasures, and our whole view of life. Conversion is a part of genuine saving faith and is a basic part of salvation and sanctification. Jesus Christ our Lord required, and he insisted upon it, that humility is the important and necessary tool for conversion – because converting grace makes us like little children. As children we must be very careful of nothing but leave to the hands of our Heavenly Father who cared for us.

Prayer:

Lord Jesus Christ, we are your children, you have the power and authority in heaven and earth to take care of all our problems, in your mercy hear our prayers and answer all our prayers. Amen.

DECEMBER 24TH

THE WORD OF GOD IS A TRANSFORMATION – LET THE WORD OF GOD TRANSFORM YOU TODAY.

Today's Scripture Reading:

"While they were there, the time came for the baby to be born, and she gave birth to her first born, a son. She wrapped him in cloth and placed him in a manger, because there was no room for them in the inn. But the angel said to them. Do not be afraid. I bring you good news of great joy that will be for all the people. Today in the town of David a Savior has been born to you, he is Christ the Lord." (Luke 2:6, 10-11) NIV

Jesus Christ was conceived by the Holy Spirit born of Virgin Mary. Christ was born in manger – in a stable, a place where animals were kept. The stable was probably a cave and the manger a feeding trough for animals. The birth of the Savior, the greatest man that ever lived, the greatest event in the history of the earth that he was created. Jesus Christ's birth occurred in the humblest circumstances, Jesus Christ was the King of kings, but he was neither born as a king nor lived like a king in this life. It is the same with all the believers. All God's people are kings and priests, but in this life, we must be as he was humble and simple. Jesus Christ was called a Savior at his birth. As a Savior, he has come to deliver us from our sins and from Satan's domain, to include the ungodly world, fear, death and from the condemnation of our transgressions. The Savior is also Christ the Lord. He has been anointed as the Messiah of God and the Lord who rules over his people in the Name of Christ. No person can have Jesus as Savior without submitting to his lordship.

Prayer:

Almighty God, you have poured upon your people the new light of your incarnate Word; bless us that this light, enkindled in our hearts and shine in our lives through Jesus Christ, who lives and reigns with you with the power of the Holy Spirit. One God, Lord Jesus Christ, our Savior, the Holy child of Bethlehem, you came to the world with our flesh, you showed us your love, helped us to be born in you, and you are born in us every day of our life. We give you praise O' lord; you are worthy to be praised. Amen.

DECEMBER 25TH

THE WORD OF GOD IS A TRANSFORMATION –
LET THE WORD OF GOD TRANSFORM YOU TODAY.

Today's Scripture Reading:

"I give them eternal life, and they shall never perish, no one can snatch them out of my hand. My Father, who has given them to me, is greater than all, no one can snatch them out of my Father's hand. I and my Father we are one." (John 10:28-30) NIV

This promise was given to all the believing Christians. This precious promise was given to all who are Christ's sheep. They will never be banished from God's love, or from his presence, nor will any power, or circumstances on earth take them from the Shepherd. They will always be in safety and in security, even the weakest sheep who follows and listens to the Good Shepherd will rejoice in him. Our Lord Jesus Christ has provided happiness for all the believers; he gave us eternal life. Man has a living soul; therefore, the happiness that Christ provided is life. Man as an immortal soul; therefore, the happiness provided is eternal life. Life eternal is the felicity and the chief goal of an immortal soul. It is given by the free grace of Jesus Christ. Christ gives the assurance of it, heaven in the seed, in the bud, in the embryo. Jesus Christ undertakes believer's security and preservation to their happiness. As we have eternal life, we also have eternal destruction. Believers shall not come into condemnation by the power of the Holy Spirit. Jesus Christ has promised and assured none of his sheep shall perish, none, not one. Believers cannot and they can never be kept from their everlasting happiness.

Prayer:

Lord Jesus Christ, our Lord and Savior compassionate gracious loving God, you are the Great Shepherd, the chief shepherd, the Good Shepherd of the sheep. You will keep all your sheep secure and save till the end. Have mercy and love on us; you will not let anyone perish, because you are always with us in Spirit and in truth, through the power of your indwelling of the Holy Spirit. We give you praise and thankfulness forever. Amen.

DECEMBER 26TH

THE WORD OF GOD IS A TRANSFORMATION – LET THE WORD OF GOD TRANSFORM YOU TODAY.

Today's Scripture Reading:

"Anyone who receives a prophet because he is a prophet will receive a prophet's reward, and anyone who receive a righteous man will receive a righteous man's reward." (Matthew 10:41) NIV

Jesus Christ's teaching that a prophet must be received in the name of a prophet is kindness shown to all who serve the Lord, either elders, ministers, or pastors have shown Jesus Christ kindness as shown to pastors, missionaries, are valued in the book of our Lord; it has been recorded. Because the righteous were righteous bearing Christ likeness, they must receive as a righteous kindness to Jesus Christ, as people and all believers, shall not only be accepted, but it will be richly and suitably rewarded. We cannot merit anything as wages from the hand of God, but they shall receive a reward from the free gift of God. They shall never lose their reward. The reward that God gave to a prophet and righteous men: are the blessings conferred upon them shall even distill upon their friends, children, and relatives according to an answer to their prayer. A Prophets' reward is spiritual blessings in heavenly things, and if we know how to value them, we shall take things on them as good payment. Our Lord speaks about receiving a prophet and righteous man, those who are most frequently rejected and persecuted because of their stand for godliness and the proclamation of the truth. For this reason those who accept prophets or a righteous man and receive their messages will receive God's special rewards. If believers commit to truth and righteousness, it shows that they devote their life providing a cooperating with encouragement of God's ministers who are righteous, then your reward will be the same.

Prayer:

Lord Jesus Christ, help us to know you more and more every day of our lives. Help us to be useful for the work of your kingdom, to behold your glory, the glory of the only begotten Son of God full of truth and righteousness. In your Holy Name , we pray accept our prayers. Amen.

DECEMBER 27ᵀᴴ

THE WORD OF GOD IS A TRANSFORMATION – LET THE WORD OF GOD TRANSFORM YOU TODAY.

Today's Scripture Reading:

Jesus knew that the Father had put all things under his power and that he had come from God and was returning to God; so he got up from the meal, took off his outer clothing; and wrapped a towel around his waist, after that, he poured water into a basin and began to wash his disciple's feet, drying them with towel that was wrapped around him." (John 13:3-5) NIV

Jesus Christ put down his position, to wash the disciples' feet, just as he put down his glory and became flesh and dwell among us. The foot washing occurred on the last night of Jesus life on earth. Jesus Christ demonstrated to his disciples how much he loved them, and we well as it was a foreshadow his self-sacrifice on the cross and to convey the truth that he was calling his disciples to serve one another in humility. Christ wants his disciples and us today all the believing Christians to follow his example instead a passion to be great, which continually plagued them. Jesus Christ wants them to see that the desire to be first, to be superior, and honored above all other Christians is contrary to the spirit of their Lord. Jesus Christ has a cordial love for his own that is in the world; he was now going to his own in heaven; but he seems very concerned for his own on earth, because they needed his care; Those whom Christ love he loved them to the end nothing, can separate a believer from the love of Jesus Christ; he loves his own Jesus Christ manifested his love this disciples by washing their feet, same with all the believers today Jesus Christ always wash our feet so that we do not go astray, or get lost .

Prayer:

Lord Jesus, we give you thanks for your love for us and for all your provisions in our lives. We give you glory, for washing our feet from destruction and temptation. All glory and honor belongs to you forever. Amen.

DECEMBER 28TH

THE WORD OF GOD IS A TRANSFORMATION –
LET THE WORD OF GOD TRANSFORM YOU TODAY.

Today's Scripture Reading:

"Now there was a man in Jerusalem called Simeon, who was righteous and devout. He was waiting for the consolation of Israel, and the Holy Spirit was upon him. It had been revealed to him by the Holy Spirit that he would not die before he had seen the Lord's Christ. He was moved by the Spirit; he went into the Temple court. When the parents brought the child Jesus to do for him what the custom of the law required, Simeon took him in his arms, and praised God saying, "Sovereign Lord, as you have promised, you now dismiss your servant thine peace. For my eyes have seen your salvation." The righteous Simeon was a devoted to God and filled with the Holy Spirit, and waiting with faith, patience, and great longing for the coming of the Messiah. It is the same today, as people, believers, are waiting for the blessed hope of Christ's Second Coming. There will always be the faithful, like Simeon; the faithful will keep on watching for the return of our Lord. Our greatest blessing is to see face-to-face the Lord Christ, and for us to be ready when he comes; and to live with him forever in his presence. Simeon lived in Jerusalem, and was eminent for his pity and his communion with God. Simeon was waiting for Messiah, the Christ, not the author of his people's comfort, but the Master and the foundation of comfort. Those who are waiting are continuing to wait, even up until today, some Jews are still waiting for their Messiah to come. The Holy Spirit moved mightily in the life of Simeon and directed him to the Temple where he saw the Messiah. He prayed that the Lord should release him from this world of sin, that the Messiah came to change.

Prayer:

Lord God Almighty compassionate gracious loving Savior, baptize us with your Holy Spirit, so that we will be able to know your ways and do our will, as well as follow your commandment in our lives. Amen.

DECEMBER 29TH

THE WORD OF GOD IS A TRANSFORMATION –
LET THE WORD OF GOD TRANSFORM YOU TODAY.

Today's Scripture Reading:

"Master, said John, we saw a man driving out demons in your Name and we tried to stop him, because he is not one of us. Do not stop him, Jesus said, for whoever is not against you is for you." (Luke 9:49-50) NIV

Jesus Christ told the apostles that they should not stop those who are driving out demons in his Name. Today we have many pastors and they used the Name of Jesus Christ to heal diseases and cast out demons and evil spirits from people; we must follow the commandment of our Lord to stop them, or be violent with them because the Scripture says only God knows who belongs to him. Jesus Christ did not want any believing Christians to discourage one that honored him and served him, but was not of their communion, but, upon occasional hearing of Christ, believed in him, and made use of his Name in faith and prayed in a serious manner, that the devils were cast out. This man, they wanted to rebuke and restrain. They would not let him pray and preach, even though it was to the honor of Jesus Christ. Jesus Christ said they should leave such a minister alone, so far, he is not against Christ. But rather encourage him for he is carrying on the same design that the believers are carrying. He will meet you in the same end, though he does not accompany you in the same way. We need not lose any of our friends while we have so few friends, and may enquires of those who do not follow Christ, but use his Name may be found, faithful followers of Christ, and such may be accepted of him, though they do not follow with us.

Prayer:

Eternal Father, Father of our Lord Jesus Christ, you gave your incarnate Son the Holy Name of Jesus to be the sign of our salvation. Plant in every heart, the love of him who is the Savior of the world. Christ, you are the friend of the sinners and the lost; bless us with everything that we may need to serve you faithfully and sincerely on this earth. Let your glory shine in our hearts and minds. Call those you are using your Name falsely unto you and use them in the right way. Amen.

DECEMBER 30TH

THE WORD OF GOD IS A TRANSFORMATION – LET THE WORD OF GOD TRANSFORM YOU TODAY.

Today's Scripture Reading:

"There was also a prophetess, Anna, the daughter of Phanuel, of the tribe of Asher. She was very old; she has lived with her husband seven years after her marriage, and then was a widow until she was eighty-four. She never left the temple but worshiped night and day fasting and praying coming up to them at that very moment, she gave thanks to God and spoke about the child to all who were looking forward to the redemption of Jerusalem."(Luke 2:36-38) NIV

Anna just like Simeon has been revealed to her through the Holy Spirit. Anna was a prophetess who earnestly hoped for the coming of Jesus Christ she remained a widow for many years, never remarried, but devoted her life to the Lord with fasting and praying, night and day. The Scripture revealed that the unmarried state can be a greater blessing than the married. It is the same with Paul who states that the unmarried have greater opportunity to be concerned about the things of the Lord – how to please him and give him undistracted devotion – but our Lord and Savior, knows how he want us to serve him when the Holy Spirit empowers you. There is no assignment you cannot do for the Lord because you are not the one doing the assignment, the indwelling Holy spirit of the Lord is going the work through you. Therefore, believers must not be discouraged, Christ in you is the hope of glory. He gave everyone in the Church different roles, some apostle, some prophets, some pastors, teachers, writers, may God receive the glory great, this he has done.

Prayer:

Lord Jesus Christ the moment we surrendered our life to you, bless those who have been born again and made your children by adoption and grace. May daily we be renewed by your Holy Spirit. Use us in so many ways that will bring great glory to your Holy Name, and bring sinners and the lost, people of other religions to you. Help us to live with you forever. Amen.

DECEMBER 31ST

THE WORD OF GOD IS A TRANSFORMATION –
LET THE WORD OF GOD TRANSFORM YOU TODAY.

Today's Scripture Reading:

"And if anyone takes words away from this book of prophecy, God will take away from him his share in the tree of life and in the Holy city, which are described in this book. He who testifies to these things says yes, I am coming soon amen, come, Lord Jesus." (Revelation 22:19-20) NIV

Apostle John ends the book of Revelation from Jesus Christ to all people in the world. He warns about the terrible possibility of losing one's share in the tree of life and the Holy City. If believers, or nonbelievers, have a careless attitude toward the book of God, the Holy Scripture, such attitude is manifested if we choose to believe only certain parts of God's revelation and rejects other parts of God's revelation as unworthy or untrue. The same warning applies to those who add their own word as if they were part of God's revelation. From the beginning of human history, failure to take God's Word with absolute seriousness is a matter of life and death. The Scripture ends with the promise of Jesus Christ, "Yes I am coming soon," to which all believers always say, "Come Lord Jesus." All the believers shared this longing and waiting patiently for Christ's return. This word of prayer is a confession that until Christ comes, our redemption remains incomplete, evil is not yet over and this world is not yet renewed, but we believe that the day is approaching when who is called the Word of God, will come from heaven to take his faithful bride away from this earth to his Father's house where there are many mansions. We will triumphantly return in glory to reign forever with him.

Prayer:

We pray, come quickly Lord Jesus, you are our only and one and only blessed hope. We are waiting for your return, to judge the dead and the living, and all eyes shall see you. Purify our hearts and minds with your full presence everyday of our lives. We love you and give you great glory forever, and ever. Amen.

DAILY REFLECTION NOTES

SONG OF REJOICING

*So send I you-- by grace made strong triumph o'er
hosts of
Hell, o'er darkness, death, and sin, my Name to
bear and in that Name to
Conquer-- so send I you, my victory to win.
So send I you-- to take to souls in bondage the
Word of
truth that sets the captive free, to break the bonds
of sin, to loosen death's
fetters – so send I you, to bring the lost to me.
Son send I you— my strength to know in weakness,
my joy in
Grief, my perfect peace in Pain, to prove my power,
my grace, my promised
Presence – so send I you, eternal fruit to gain.
So send I you— to bear my cross with patience, and
then one
day with joy to lay it down, to hear my voice, well
done, my faithful
servant— come, share my throne, my kingdom, and
my crown
As the Father has sent me, so send I you.*
Words: Margaret Clarkson, 1962 Music: .John W. Peterson,
1954

NEW YEAR PRAYER
FOR ALL THE PEOPLE IN ALL THE NATIONS OF THE WORLD

Prayer:

God the Father Almighty, Jesus Christ his only begotten Son, Holy Spirit one God. You are the maker of heaven and earth, the sea and everything that dwells in it. We give you glory Jesus Christ the Son of God, full of truth and righteousness, we give you praise our Lord and Savior. You are worthy to be praised. Lord Jesus Christ, you are the way, the truth, and the life, the Alpha and Omega, the beginning and the end, the first and the last. You're the Great Shepherd of the sheep, the chief shepherd, and the Good Shepherd. All life dwells in you.

We pray for your mercy and protection every day of our life, keep us safe from violence, hatred, wars and rumors of wars, and bless us with your unending protection every day of our lives from all the violence, persecutions that is going on in all the nations of the earth. Protect your people, especially the police, the firemen, running around the city to save life, save their own life our Lord. Also, the news media men, who are trying to get the news to us. Protect the Army who are protecting our country, the children, the senior citizens, including men and women of all ages. Protect us from Islamic terrorists, the Taliban, Al Qaeda, ISIS, Boko-Aram and Hezbollah and all other terrorists in the world, in Sudan, in Kenya, Somalia: turn them from evil to good, from hatred to love, from violent to peace, from wickedness to good. They turned the Holy

Koran and the Muslim religion into violence. Deliver us our Lord, let them know the truth and let the truth set them free. They are killing people in the Mosques and in the churches all over the earth, destroying all the historical things of God. Turn them around from enemies of God to the children of the ever-living and ever-loving God. Deliver you people, the innocent people who are going through all forms of oppression, violence, murder and from sudden death. Open Abu-Bakr's heart, mind, spirit and soul, the head of the ISIS to know that he is killing his own brothers and sisters and children every day.

We glorify God, the Holy Spirit the giver of life, who proceeded from the Father and the Son. We are on earth today because you breathed on us the breath of life; you blessed us with your spirit and as a sustainer of life, you sustain us, keep us safe. You provide for our needs and you fulfilled all our needs. Lord Jesus Christ you are the God of all nations; the government is upon your shoulder. You ordained the government of all the nations of this world. They are chosen by you, and they are your servants. Let them know that they are serving you in all the areas of governmental positions.

Thank you, our Lord and Savior. All power dwells in you; you are the channel of blessings, from you all the goodness flows. You are the Prince of Peace, the wonderful counselor, our Prophet and our High Priest in heaven, the ascended God and seated at the right hand of God, interceding for us at the right hand of God the Father. You are worthy of all our praises and thankfulness our God from the beginning of this year to the end; you are the Prince of Peace. Help us to start this New Year with your love, mercy, and great compassion. O' God, most merciful Father, we give you praise for sending your only Son Jesus Christ, who took on himself the form of a servant, and humbled himself, becoming obedient even to death on the cross. We give you praise and exalt your Holy Name. You made Jesus the Lord of All, and through him, we know that whoever wants to be great must first be a servant. We give you praise for the ministry of all your churches in the all the nations of this world. Open the gates of heaven and let people of this world see your light unending. In your great, matchless and Holy Name , we pray amen, amen, amen.

CONCLUSION

Prayer is a petition between the Divine and humanity; God created us in his own image. All Christian believers must make prayer the number one commitment to God. Prayer is communication with our Lord and Savior, the Head of the Church, the foundation of the Church, and the chief cornerstone. In prayer we are totally surrender in our spirit, soul, and body to the Lordship of Jesus Christ, our great intercessor in heaven. In prayer we communicate with the Lord, as children communicate with the father. In prayer we put our heart desires in his Holy Hands. In prayer the Holy Spirit illuminates our heart with fire, and the power of darkness, the work of evil and the plan of evil is destroyed. Prayer is the sword of the Holy Spirit that dwells in us. We cannot live a Christian life when we do not daily communicate in prayer with our Lord and Savior; or live a life that God the Father, Son, and the Holy Spirit required for us to live for him; which is a glorifying life. Prayer helps us to live a peaceful life and helps us not to follow a worldly life. Prayer takes us from any form of temptation; prayer deliver us from all forms of known and unknown evil. In prayer the gates of heaven opens and our Lord Jesus Christ rains down his blessings upon us abundantly, exceedingly, immeasurably without ceasing. Let us make prayer part of our lives. The Scripture revealed: "Around the throne are twenty-four thrones, and seated on the thrones are twenty-four elders, dressed in white robes, with golden crowns on their heads. The twenty-four elders fall down before him who sits on the throne, and worship him who lives forever and ever, They cast their crowns before the throne singing." *(Rev.4: 4,10) NIV*

SCRIPTURE INDEXES FROM NIV

JANUARY
John 3:45;4:23-24, Romans 11:37;Luke23:34,43; John19:26-27;Mark 15:34;John19:38,30; Luke 2:3-46;Matthew 6:9-13; Genesis 1:1-2;Psalm 136:1 Genesis 2:24, 2:20,2:21-22, 2:23, 1:26, 2:25, 24:66-67; Exodus 20:17, Leviticus 19:18; Psalm 143:8; Proverbs 3_3, 3:3-4, 1st John 4:16; Ephesians 5:21, 5:18, 5:20;Romans 14:19-20, 15:3-4, 14:21-22; Ephesians 1:7-8 Proverbs 31:10-11, Psalm 68:3-5;Act 6:1 1st Corinthian 7:8-11, 1st Timothy 5:3-4, James 1:21-22 Exodus22:22-23, Deuteronomy 10:17-18; Psalm 146:7-10.

FEBRUARY
John 17:17, Ephesians 1:13-14, Isaiah 1:17-18, Luke 21:1-4; Act2:42-45, Hosea 1:1-3;Malachi 2:14-15;Matthew 1:20-21, Luke 1:35;Mathew 19:3-6; Luke 17:32,18:29-30;1st Corinthian 7:2-3,32-34; Ephesians 5:23-24; 1st Timothy 2:3-4; Revelation 21:9-10; 1st Corinthian 13:4-7; Psalm 143:8-10; 1st Corinthian13:2-6; Romans 12:9-14; Ephesians 3:16-17; Proverbs 3:3-4; 1st John 4:16-17; 1st Corinthian 2:9-10; 1st John 3:1. 5:4-5; 1st Peter 4:8-10; 1st John 5:14-15.

MARCH
2nd Timothy 3:12=15; John15:13-15 Isaiah 49:15-16;2nd Thessalonian3:5; 1st John 4:19; Ephesians 5:25-26; Isaiah 43:4-5; Exodus 33:14-17; Romans 5:1-2;Deuteronomy 31:8; Psalm16:8-11, 27:1, 3-4, 34:17-20, 32:3-7,42:5, 8, 61:1-4,62:1-2, 91:1-2, 91:14-16, 103:2-5,112:1,7-8, 127:1-2, 139:7,9-10, 23-24, 145:17-20; Proverbs 3:5-6; Isaiah 12:2-4, 26:3-4,30:15, 40:28-31, 41:10, 43:16.

APRIL
Jeremiah 16:19-21, 29:13-14;Isaiah 55:11-14;1st Corinthian 15:35-39 Jeremiah 32:17-19; Matthew 6:31-34; Jeremiah 32:27; Matthew 11:28-30; Luke 12:6-7, 12:35-37;Romans 12:1-2;John14:25-27,15:4-5,7,10; Romans *:28, 8:35, 37-39; 2nd Corinthian 12:9-10; Philippians 4:4-7;2nd Timothy 1:6-7; Hebrews 4:16,13:5-6; James 1:5-6; 1st Peter 5:7-11; Exodus 14:13-14; 2nd King 4:14-15; Joshua 1:8-9; Psalm 9:9-11; Ephesians 3:16-17; 1st Corinthian 13:9-13; Romans 8:16-17 1st Peter 2:4-6.

MAY
Psalm 27:4, 13-14; Jeremiah 1:4-5;Romans3:23-25;John 3:16; Ephesians 4:3-4 James 1:21; Psalm 3:3-6, 24:2-10,33:18-19,86:11-13;

John 4:3-4, 1:1-5,1:6-9; 1st Peter 1:8-9, 6:35-38; Ephesians 5:15-16, 5:18; John7:26; 1st Corinthian 6:1-3; Galatians 5:6; John5:10; Psalm 121:7-8; Colossian 3:23-25; Proverbs 13:3; John 3:3, 5-8; 1st Peter 3:9-11; James 3:13-14; Act 20:24-26; Proverbs 10:21-22; psalm 91:14-16; 2nd Corinthian 5:1-3.

JUNE

Philippian 2:13-16; Matthew 16:26-28,6:25-27; Isaiah 57:15-16; Philippians 1:23-26; 2nd Corinthians 5:1-4, 10:3-6; Romans 8:6-10; Act 17:28-30; Hebrew 12:1-3, 12:7-10; Galatians 5:4-7,2:20-21; Romans 6:1-5, 4:8-10, 8:11, 17-21; 2nd Corinthians 6:9-10; 1st Peter 1:8-9; 2nd Timothy 1:9-10; Act 4:12; Isaiah 44:35; Romans 1;16-17; Matthew 7:13-14; Habakkuk 3:10-18; Mark 10:27, 52; Psalm 18:1-3; Hebrews 9:28, 7:25-26; Isaiah 52:7.

JULY

Proverbs 21:2-23;Psalm 103:1-5; John16:2-4;Psalm91:9-12;Philippians 2:14-4; Matthew 13:24-26; James 4:4-6; Colossians 3:2-4;1st John5:4-5; Colossian 2:10-12;Luke4:18;Hebrews 7:23-26;Matthew 5:17-18;John 16:33; Ephesians 4:21; John8:12; Luke 1:18, 14:6;Hebrews 7:25, 1:3; Matthew 18:14-20,28:20; 1st Timothy 2:5-7;titus 2:11-13; Matthew 14:23, 27; Revelation2:7; Luke2:29-33;John 6:35, 41,48,51,5:26-27, 12:30-33; Colossian2:2-3; 1st Thessalonians 4:15-18.

AUGUST

Ephesians 4:20-22; John6:38-40; Psalm 98:1-3;Genesis 12:1-3,9:13, 1:28-29;1st Peter 3:9;2nd Corinthians 4:7-10, 4:16-18, 9:8, 11, 12:7-9; John 18:36;Romans 8:11, 8:28, 8:29-30; Zephaniah 3;17; Matthew 17:20;luke 12:42-44; Jeremiah 32:17-19, 31:10-12;Psalm 139:7, 9-12, 23-24;Galatians 6:9-10;Philippians 4:11-13, 4:4-8; Ephesians 1:3; 2nd Timothy 4:7-8;Colossians 3:2-4, 3:8-11; James 1:5-7;Hebrew 6:2-12; 1st Peter 4:18-19.

SEPTEMBER

Isaiah:12:2;John4:22-24;1ST Peter 4:8-9; Roman13:8-10, 8:38-39; Luke10:25-28; Psalm 27:4; Matthew 13:28-30,12:28; Deuteronomy 6:4-7; Revelation 3:9-10;John14:23-24;Psalm 86: 5-11;Proverbs 3:11-13; 2nd Thessalonians 1:34;Psalm 44:3,6-7; Ephesians 2:4-5; 1st Corinthians 13:1;Proverbs 10:11-12;Ephesians 5:15-17;psalm 37:3,37:7;Colossian 3:23-25;Psalm 31:3-5; John 13:34-35; Hebrew 12:14-15;2nd Corinthians 5:14-15; Ephesians 4:4-6;Romans 12:2; Psalm 23:6.

OCTOBER

2nd Timothy 4:18; Hebrew4:15-16;James 1:5-6;Galatians 6:9-10; 2nd Thessalonians 3:6; 2nd Timothy 1:6-7;Ephesians 2:17-18;

2nd Corinthians 9:8-9; Luke 12:32' Psalm 90:2; Isaiah 40: 28-31;Psalm 116:7-9;,112:1,7-8, 51,10:12;John 8:10-12; Revelation 1:17-18; Matthew 18:19-20; Hebrew 1:3; Colossians 1:15-17; John 12:17-18; Hebrew 12:1-2; Matthew 20:17-20;Mark 12:38-40; 1st Timothy 4:9-4; romans 13:9; Colossians 3:23-24, 21; Luke 11:20-23; Acts 20:24; Matthews 16:19; Luke 11:28, 33-34; Proverbs 3:1-2.

NOVEMBER

Luke 12:1-3; Proverbs 10:7;, 19:4, 8; Philippians 1:21-22; Matthew 16:28; James 1:18; Psalm 145:14-16; Philippians 2:14-16; 2nd Timothy 3:16-17; Philippian 2:9-11; Act 17: 24-28; 1st Peter 1:15-16; Isaiah 57:15;Matthew 5:10-14; Genesis 50:18-21; Hebrew 13:13; John 4:7-8,10; Romans 8:10-11; Matthew 10:34-35,39; John10:10; Act4:8,12; 1st Peter 1:18-19; 2nd Peter 3:9; Act 13:47-48; 1st Corinthians 6:9-10,6:1-2;Titus 2:11-12;Mark 10:27; Matthew 7:13-14.

DECEMBER

Romans 5:10,1:16; Habakkuk 3:17-19; Romans 5:7-8; Mark 10:46-52;Luke 19:10;Hebrew 2:15-17; Psalm18:35-36; 2nd Corinthians 6: 17-18; Psalm 103:12-14;John3:16-17;1st Peter 12:2;Romans 1:17; Philippians 3:20; 1st Thessalonians 5:6; 1st Corinthians 1:18,15:2-3;Philemon 1:12-13, 16, 25; John 11:35,11:40, 43-44; Act 2:1-4; Isaiah 53:4-5; Matthew 18:3; Luke2:6, 10-11; John 10:28-30; Matthew 10:41; John 13:35; Luke 2:25-30, 9:49-50, 2:36-38; Revelation 22:19-20.

ABOUT THE AUTHOR

Grace Dola Balogun graduated from Fordham University Graduate School of Religion and Religious Education with an M. A. in Religion and Religious Education. She has been a prayer mentor and advisor for many Christians of all denominations. Grace is also the author of Prayer the Source of Strength for Life, published in English and Spanish; and Spirit Power, Volumes One and Two, as well as the Cross and the Crucifixion, The Three Simple Solutions for World Peace, and Justification by Faith Alone in Christ Alone.

Visit Grace online at: graceligiliousbookspublishers.com

OTHER BOOKS OF GRACE DOLA BALOGUN PUBLISHED BY

GRACE RELIGIOUS PUBLISHING BOOKS & DISTRIBUTORS, INC.
NEW YORK:

JESUS CHRIST THE ONLY WAY THE ONLY WAY TO HEAVEN

JESUS CHRIST THE ONLY TRUTH

JESUS CHRIST THE ONLY LIFE

CHRIST THE CONSUMMATION OF PEACE FOREVER

BE HOLY FOR I AM HOLY

GOD'S PREDESTINATION

GOD'S ELECTION

SHE MUST BE SILENT

JESUS CHRIST THE JOY OF CHRISTMAS

FORGIVE OUR DEBTS AS WE FORGIVE OUR DEBTORS

ALL CHURCHES BE ONE

CHRIST'S LIFE IN THE LIFE OF CHRISTIANS

I AM THE ETERNAL LIFE

THE CHURCH THE BODY OF CHRIST

ME AND MY FATHER ARE ONE.................. ETC.

ORDER FORM

TO ORDER YOUR COPY OF ANY BOOK:

NAME: ___________________________________

ADDRESS: _________________________________

TELEPHONE: _______________________________

FAX#:_____________________________________

MAIL: ____________________________________

QUANTITY: ________________________________

MAIL TO:

Grace Religious Books Publishing & Distributors, Inc.
New York
248 Lombard Street 2nd Fl.
New Haven, CT 06513

ORDER ONLINE FROM: GRACE RELIGIOUS PUBLISHERS.COM

AMAZON, GOOGLE, SMARSHWORDS, BARNS & NOBLE, BOOKS A MILLION

INGRAMSPARK/LIGHTENING SOURCE ETC.

www.ingramcontent.com/pod-product-compliance
Lightning Source LLC
Chambersburg PA
CBHW070331170726
48291CB00001B/11